Steal the Light

Also from Lexi Blake

ROMANTIC SUSPENSE

Masters And Mercenaries
The Dom Who Loved Me
The Men With The Golden Cuffs
A Dom is Forever
On Her Master's Secret Service
Sanctum: A Masters and Mercenaries Novella
Love and Let Die
Unconditional: A Masters and Mercenaries Novella
Dungeon Royale
Dungeon Games: A Masters and Mercenaries Novella
A View to a Thrill
Cherished: A Masters and Mercenaries Novella
You Only Love Twice
Luscious: Masters and Mercenaries~Topped
Adored: A Masters and Mercenaries Novella
Master No
Just One Taste: Masters and Mercenaries~Topped 2
From Sanctum with Love
Devoted: A Masters and Mercenaries Novella
Dominance Never Dies
Submission is Not Enough
Master Bits and Mercenary Bites~The Secret Recipes of Topped
Perfectly Paired: Masters and Mercenaries~Topped 3
For His Eyes Only
Arranged: A Masters and Mercenaries Novella
Love Another Day
At Your Service: Masters and Mercenaries~Topped 4
Master Bits and Mercenary Bites~Girls Night
Nobody Does It Better
Close Cover
Protected, Coming July 31, 2018

Masters and Mercenaries: The Forgotten
Memento Mori, Coming August 28, 2018

Lawless
Ruthless
Satisfaction
Revenge

Courting Justice
Order of Protection
Evidence of Desire, Coming January 8, 2019

Masters Of Ménage (by Shayla Black and Lexi Blake)
Their Virgin Captive
Their Virgin's Secret
Their Virgin Concubine
Their Virgin Princess
Their Virgin Hostage
Their Virgin Secretary
Their Virgin Mistress

The Perfect Gentlemen (by Shayla Black and Lexi Blake)
Scandal Never Sleeps
Seduction in Session
Big Easy Temptation
Smoke and Sin
At the Pleasure of the President, Coming Fall 2018

URBAN FANTASY

Thieves
Steal the Light
Steal the Day
Steal the Moon
Steal the Sun
Steal the Night
Ripper
Addict
Sleeper
Outcast, Coming 2018

LEXI BLAKE WRITING AS SOPHIE OAK

Small Town Siren
Siren in the City
Away From Me
Three to Ride
Siren Enslaved
Two to Love
Siren Beloved
One to Keep, Coming August 7, 2018

Steal the Light

Thieves, Book 1

Lexi Blake

Steal the Light
Thieves, Book 1
Lexi Blake

Published by DLZ Entertainment, LLC
Copyright 2013 DLZ Entertainment, LLC
Edited by Chloe Vale and Kasi Alexander
ISBN: 978-1-937608-17-0

This is a work of fiction. Names, places, characters and incidents are the product of the author's imagination and are fictitious. Any resemblance to actual persons, living or dead, events or establishments is solely coincidental.

Sign up for Lexi Blake's newsletter
and be entered to win a $25 gift certificate
to the bookseller of your choice.

Join us for news, fun, and exclusive content
including the free short stories

You Will Call Me Master (Daniel's Story)
and
She Will Be My Goddess (Dev's Story)

There's a new contest every month!

Go to www.LexiBlake.net to subscribe.

Author Foreword

In my career, this book will be denoted as my thirty-first book published (between Lexi and Sophie Oak), but I feel compelled to explain that in so many ways, Steal the Light was really the beginning. I need to tell the story of its existence because in so many ways, this book explains why Lexi and Sophie exist at all.

In 2007 my husband completed his MBA. He was working and going to school at the same time, so I spent two and a half years keeping everything at home running. At the end, he hugged me and told me I could have anything I wanted. I think he expected me to ask for a trip or to go back to school. What I asked for was a baby.

Flash forward to 2008. I was thirty-seven years old and healthy and never once thought that I would have a problem. The pregnancy itself was perfect. The delivery was not. My two older babies had been delivered via C-section, so this one was scheduled. I won't bore you with medical details, but it went poorly. I was on the table for hours and nearly bled out. I remember listening to the doctor as he valiantly worked to save me. Once my daughter was delivered, the race was on to stitch me up. My husband witnessed this. He was forced to leave the room and to wait to discover my fate.

We had two very different reactions to this moment in time. I call it "a moment" because it has defined every breath I have taken since. I came off that table a different human being than the one who had walked the earth for thirty-seven years before. For the first time I truly felt alive. I knew there was no time to waste. There is only the now. I discovered that love and hope live in the now. My husband had a different reaction. He drifted away from me, terrified not at the thought of death in general, but that he'd nearly witnessed mine. He went to a place where I couldn't touch him.

We are years past this now. My baby girl is a shining light of life. She's as crazy and wild as the character I named after her. My husband and I just celebrated our twenty-year anniversary.

But these are the books I wrote while I waited for him to come back to me. These five books are the books I wrote when I decided not to wait for life to find its way to me.

These books are for my husband and my daughter. My husband who gave me a safe place to become myself. My daughter, whose birth spurred me to figure out just who I am.

And these books are for you readers who choose to join me on this journey. You are more than welcome to come with me.

Lexi Blake

Acknowledgments

Thanks to Chloe Vale. This has been a five year journey and I wouldn't want to go through it with anyone else. Thanks to the original readers of this series, especially Britta Graham, Mindy Romero, and Jennifer Kubenka. It's finally here! Thanks to my brilliant betas and editors, Riane Holt, Stormy Pate, and Kasi Alexander. As always thanks to my street team- the Doms and Dolls.

And to Merrilee Heifetz at Writers House, thank you for believing in me. I'm so glad we're on this journey together.

I have a deep and never-ending gratitude to Liz Berry, who has been a champion of this series from the beginning. I love you, my friend.

Prologue

Grief is a selfish beast.

I stood in the lobby of the Denton County morgue, my father's hand resting on my back. It didn't bring me comfort, and I didn't want it to. I didn't want to receive comfort, and I sure as hell didn't mean to give any. His eyes filled with tears. My father never cried, but it didn't move me because Dad might have loved Daniel, but Daniel had been my whole world.

My stomach turned at the thought. I said it in my head. Not Daniel is my world. Daniel *was* my world. Had been. Wasn't now. Wouldn't be again. Had I accepted Daniel's death without even seeing his body?

"Zoey Wharton?"

I brought my head up. A bland-looking man in scrubs stood in the doorway, a clipboard in his hand. That clipboard held all the notations and numbers that made up the end of Daniel's life. Height, weight, core body temperature. Time of death.

I should have known his time of death. Shouldn't I? I should have felt the moment his soul departed the Earth. He'd been my first lover, the first friend I could remember having. He'd been my partner in crime, and we'd made our escape together. If he'd died, shouldn't the ground under my feet have moved?

"Zoey Wharton?" He looked straight at me the second time, his eyebrows rising expectantly. There wasn't anyone else around but me and my father, but this bureaucrat obviously required acknowledgement.

"I'm Zoey." Daniel's Zoey. That was who I was. I was Daniel's friend and then his girl and then his fiancée. I was still wearing the craptastic, barely-there diamond he'd put on my finger not three months before. We'd spent a whole six hundred dollars on that ring. Everything we had.

God, don't let this be happening. Wake up. Wake the fuck up, Zoey. I tried so hard to convince myself this wasn't reality.

"I'm sorry, but we need an ID. We couldn't find his wallet." The man in the scrubs pointed toward a door. It was an ordinary door, stainless steel, swinging both directions. But I knew the truth. Those doors might open both ways, but they only took a person to one place. Once I went through them, I would never come back. I would never be the Zoey Wharton I'd been before.

And still my feet moved. I shuffled toward it.

"Darlin', please." My father looked down at me. He'd aged ten years in the hour we'd been there. The lines around his face were already deeper, as though grief had tunneled into his body in record time. "You don't have to do this."

I pulled away. I knew I could take a seat in the waiting room and my father would do this for me. He'd been the one to identify Daniel's father's body all those long years ago in a city far away while Daniel and I sat together, our feet not quite touching the ground. I remembered how blank Daniel's face had been and how he'd reached for my hand.

"I have to see him." My mouth felt numb, like someone had shot me up with Novocain and now I had to try to speak. I needed to see him or it wouldn't be real.

"Daniel wouldn't want this." My father's Irish accent was so much worse when he was emotional. Sometimes I could barely understand him, but this time I could.

"What Daniel wants doesn't matter now." I walked into the room, unable to stand there a second longer.

It's a bit like ripping off a bandage, I think. After many years of considering it, I think we all fall into one of two categories. We either pull it off, slowly, trying to process each moment, terrified of the agony but drawing it out in the process. Or we rip it off because we can no longer stand the idea of the pain and think the sooner we get through it, the better.

But in the end, the pain is all the same. Aching. Never-ending.

"Are you ready?" The coroner—or his lackey, or whoever held the sheet at two in the morning around there—asked. His gloved hands clasped the edge of the sheet. There was no question what was under that rectangle of off-white cotton. A body was there.

I wasn't ready. I would never be ready. I would be stuck in this place for the rest of my life. I could stand there and be content because until he pulled the sheet back, Daniel could still be alive.

Please wake up.

He didn't wait for me to be ready. A good thing, really, because we both might have grown old there. He pulled the sheet back revealing a body that looked nothing like my Daniel.

Oh, it was him. I knew that right away. Daniel lay there, unmoving. He wouldn't smile at me again, his face crinkling and his dimples making me sigh. His blue eyes wouldn't widen in laughter or roll when I did something stupid. He wouldn't do anything again.

I nodded. I wasn't struck by a need to hold him. He wasn't there. What was left behind was just stupid flesh and bones, and they meant nothing now without his soul to animate him.

And I was nothing without his soul to lift mine up.

I walked out of the morgue, a different human being.

I thought death was the worst thing that could happen to me and Daniel. I was very young then.

Chapter One

Dallas, TX
Five years later

"I have to say I'm surprised," the gentleman across the table from me said. "I honestly expected someone of your reputation to be, well, a bit older."

I looked up from the menu I was pretending to study. There was no actual need to read it. I had it memorized, but it gave me time to make assessments concerning my potential client.

Lucas Halfer made a memorable first impression. By all appearances, he was a man in his prime, perhaps forty or forty-five. The world I dealt in was rife with secrets and things that were not what they seemed to be, so I took nothing for granted. If he'd come to see me, he likely had something to hide.

Lucas Halfer glowed with the suave inner confidence of a man who knew he looked good in his tailored Armani suit and what had to be thousand dollar Italian shoes. He was well groomed, but there was nothing metro about him. If I had to guess, I would say he had not always been so wealthy. He'd probably fought his way to any power he accumulated. There was a certain roughness to his features that no amount of polishing could eliminate. It was his obvious wealth that put my guard up the minute he'd walked into Canelli's for our meeting.

Why would a man who always bought the best be looking to hire me?

"Looks can be deceiving, Mr. Halfer," I replied with what I like to think of as my sassy smile. Perhaps I could make up for my lack of designer labels with youthful flirting.

He studied me for a moment, assessing me with a singular purpose. Those dark eyes pinned me. Black as night, they seemed to have a power all their own.

And then the moment was gone. He smiled, a smooth expression that spoke of social ease. "A truer thing has never been said, Ms. Wharton. There is a reason we should never judge a book by its cover. Even when the cover is so very lovely. Now, what's good here?"

I breathed a sigh of relief, the odd moment behind us. It was easier to talk about the menu. But suspicion was playing at the back of my mind.

I was twenty-five years old and liked to consider myself quite the up-and-comer in the world of procurement. That's a fancy way of saying I was a thief. I was a good thief, on her way to being a great thief, but as Mr. Halfer pointed out, I was young. There were more experienced thieves out there with more ferocious reputations. Since striking out on my own, I'd run a solid ten jobs with an excellent rate of return and a low mortality rate.

Still, the jobs had been smallish up until now, and there was that incident in San Francisco. I didn't blame myself for that screw up. Normal people use alarms and high tech lasers to protect their valuables. Civilized people don't set bear traps. It was a rookie mistake I didn't plan on making again, God rest Morty O'Brien's poor soul.

Given my youth and relative inexperience, I wondered what had sent Mr. Halfer to my part of the world. I could think of half a dozen other crews I would pick if I needed an object procured and possessed sufficient funds. So what did Mr. Moneybags want with me? The waiter chose that moment to take our order. I was gratified to see that he pretended not to know me. Discretion was why I usually held my client meetings at Canelli's. It was dumpy and trapped in the fifties, with its retro booths and tables with red and white checkered linens. The walls were covered in wood paneling that had seen better days, and the bar had a solid, well-used feel to it. It was the kind of bar where you ordered a martini—not some fruity apple or peartini, but a solid gin martini, like Dino liked 'em. Canelli's had no windows, so there was a perpetual gloom to the dining area. Because there were no windows, there were also no prying eyes to look inside from the safety of the street. If you wanted to know what went on in Canelli's, you had to take a chance and enter the den. It looked like the set of a Martin Scorsese crime drama, and with good reason. It really was run by the mob, and they trained their staff well. They also made a kickass chicken piccata.

Orders taken and waiter dispersed, Mr. Halfer studied me over his expensive glass of Chianti. "Usually I prefer to handle these situations over the phone. I'm afraid I rarely get to leave the office these days, but I wanted to meet you in person. I never would have thought the daughter of Harry Wharton would turn out so lovely."

It took everything I had not to grimace at the mere mention of my father's name. It's not that I didn't love my dad. I did and I do. But liking him can be a much more difficult thing to accomplish.

"Mr. Halfer, if you're trying to get to my father through me, I can assure you it won't work," I said through a tight-lipped smile. It wasn't the first time some client tried to use me to get the great Harry Wharton to take their call. Dad was a legend in the business and rarely took on new clients. "He books his own jobs and doesn't listen to my counsel. You should call his assistant. I can give you her number, though the last time I talked to Christine, she was pushing twenty-three. He's probably traded her in for a younger model, but he always makes sure the phone number doesn't change."

Mr. Halfer laughed, a deep, rich sound that I found somewhat unsettling. "Let me set your mind at ease, Miss Wharton. I'm only interested in hiring you. This is important to me. You're the one for the job. I like the makeup of your crew. It's solid. I think your father works with too many contractors."

I wasn't buying the flattery, but smiled anyway. There was no reason to play the tough girl, not yet anyway. "I'm glad to hear that. I assure you, Mr. Halfer, my work is impeccable, and my crew is discreet. You'll find us more than capable of handling the job. What exactly is the job?"

With an elegant aplomb, he reached for the bottle of wine and filled my empty glass halfway. "Now, now, Miss Wharton, there's no need to rush things. I like to take my time and sample the pleasures this world has to offer. Please enjoy the wine. It's truly a joy to taste. There is nothing quite like it where I come from."

Now my radar was beeping. "And where do you come from Mr. Halfer?" I asked, not sure I wanted to know the answer.

In the low light of the restaurant, his eyes were like dark mirrors and his smile a slightly sinister thing. "All in good time, Miss Wharton. But if you want to get down to business, I suggest you invite your vampire to join us."

I kept my smile in place, but he'd thrown me for a loop. "What are you talking about?"

"I assume he's yours," Mr. Halfer continued, not skipping a beat. "I'm talking about the sandy-haired lad who's trying hard to look like he's enjoying a martini he can't actually drink. Or is it mere coincidence?"

Yep, that was my vampire. I sighed and gestured for Daniel to come over. His cover was blown. He slid off the barstool with a preternatural grace that set my heart racing. The ease of his movement was only one of the blessings death had brought Daniel.

"He's not human," Daniel accused flatly as he eased into an empty chair.

I somehow managed not to retort with a childish "duh," but the look in Daniel's blue eyes told me he knew exactly what I was thinking.

A human would most likely have ignored Daniel completely. Their unknowing eyes tended to slide off of his form until he wanted a person to see him. By that time, it was usually far too late to avoid becoming a late-night snack. There were humans who knew about vampires and the other members of the underworld, myself included, but I thought it unlikely that Lucas Halfer was anything so mundane as a human.

"Please don't blame yourself, Mr. Donovan." Halfer's lips curled up in a smug smile. He turned to me. "Like I said, I have done my due diligence. I knew you worked with a vampire before I contacted you. He's one of the reasons I believe you're perfect for this job. His skills will come in handy, as will those of your witch and werewolf."

His information was surprisingly up to date. Neil and Sarah were fairly recent additions to the crew. Daniel and I worked with a lot of contractors before settling on those two.

"As we don't know what the job is yet, I can't say I'll be using my skills at all." There was no lack of arrogance in Daniel's voice. His handsome features were set in a sullen pout. He didn't like having his cover blown and knowing less about the client than he knew about us. I didn't need a crystal ball to see a hearty lecture on our vetting process in my future. Daniel was staring down our potential client like a lion waiting to pounce.

This was why I handled the clients and Daniel sat his perfect ass on a barstool ten yards away and listened in. Daniel wasn't what I would call a "people person." He'd been somewhat of a misanthrope before he died. Getting hit by a drunk driver and waking up on the autopsy table had done nothing to fix his view of humanity.

The arrival of the aforementioned kick-ass piccata eased the awkwardness of the moment. The sight of Daniel's mouth tightening dimmed my enthusiasm. I knew he missed food. He'd been an enthusiastic eater before his turn. We spent our college years finding the absolute best spots on campus for burgers and pizza and the occasional splurge on high-end Italian. I counted it as the best time of my life. Those years between leaving my father's house and Daniel's untimely death were precious memories. I set my fork down. Daniel touched my arm. He smiled that slight smile of his I rarely ever saw since his return. It was his way of giving me permission to enjoy that which he could not. I glanced at the client. The satisfaction in his dark eyes told me we'd given valuable information away. Daniel pulled back and straightened into a rigid posture that proved he regretted the intimacy.

"Can I get you anything, sir?" the waiter asked Daniel politely.

"Perhaps a specialty drink from the bar?"

Daniel nodded. "That will do. I like my drink at the proper temperature."

The waiter assured Daniel he could provide the service and went to fetch the drink. The specialty drink was O positive. The proper temperature was 98.7 degrees. Once again, the mob knew how to treat a customer. I tried not to think about how they procured this specific vintage.

Halfer inhaled the scent of the marinara sauce before digging in with the gusto of a man who truly enjoyed the decadent pleasures of life. "This is excellent. I'll have to remember this place the next time I'm in Dallas."

"We were getting to the job," Daniel said, letting impatience settle into his tone.

Halfer looked amused and all but ignored Daniel. Instead he turned his unsettling eyes to me. I wondered exactly how not human he was. "I need you to steal the Light of Alhorra for me."

"I'm sorry, I've never heard of it." Honesty was usually the best policy at this stage. There were too many ways to screw up and look foolish by embellishing the truth. There would be time enough for lying later on in the relationship.

"I'm not surprised," my client replied, nonplussed. "It's an obscure artifact. It's very old and not of great consequence."

"Dark magic?" Daniel asked as the waiter placed a brass goblet on the table. The rest of the restaurant's barware was glass, but blood looked like blood even in the gloom of low light.

Halfer waved off Daniel's question. "Not at all. Please feel free to vet the artifact. It is of the purest white magic, I assure you. It brings good fortune to the one who possesses it. You'll suffer no ill effects by your brief guardianship."

"Did this artifact belong to you?" I didn't actually care about the answer. Usually people stole things that didn't belong to them. That's why they call it stealing. Sometimes I get the rare client who is seeking to get back what's rightfully theirs. They're usually the ones who try to pay the least and almost always balk when the bill comes due.

"It belonged to a colleague," he replied. "I'm merely

representing her interests. As I said, in the arcane world the object is of little consequence, but my client has a fondness for it. The artifact is a medium-sized ornate box weighing approximately twenty pounds. It was stolen two weeks ago. My intelligence places it in St. Louis. It's scheduled to be moved here in two weeks' time. It's all here in a report I prepared for you. That is, if you take the case."

I took a short swallow of the excellent Chianti. "I never take a case until I've discussed payment."

"Of course." He picked up the briefcase he'd carried in and handed it to me. The weight of the case surprised me. "It's five hundred thousand up front, with another five hundred on delivery of the object."

"There's five hundred thousand in this case?" I asked, not managing to keep the "holy crap, that's a lot of money" out of my voice.

"Yes."

"Dollars?"

Halfer smiled, obviously amused at my shock. "Yes, Miss Wharton. There is five hundred thousand cash in this case. It should cover any expenses. I take it you find the rate acceptable?"

I took a deep breath and tried to find my dignity. I forced my hand back in my lap. I was almost overwhelmed with the sudden, profound need to stroke the case and maybe give it a little kiss. Suspicion creeped along my spine. "That's an awful lot of cash."

Halfer shrugged lightly. "I'm asking you to do this job in a very short amount of time. This is important to me. I'm willing to pay top dollar to make sure it gets done right."

Top dollar was right. The lure of all that money had my head spinning, and I responded before I could really think about it. "Yes, Mr. Halfer, I believe I can get the job done for this."

I looked at Daniel, expecting to see his disapproval, but he hadn't taken his eyes off the briefcase. His fangs were slightly out.

"Yep," was all he managed to say.

"Then I will take my leave of you." Halfer pushed his chair back and slid a manila folder across the table. "Here's all the information you'll need, including my contact numbers. I'll be waiting to hear from you." He turned to walk away but looked back at me one last time. "I expect great things of you, Zoey Wharton."

My stomach turned over slightly as I wondered what this man would do if those "great things" he expected failed to materialize. I thought it best not to find out.

As the door closed behind Halfer, I was left with more money than I'd ever made on a job before and the promise of much more to come. I stared at the door he'd disappeared through. I'd never before accepted a client on the first meeting. It was one of the things my father taught me about the business. The first meeting was about learning the job and getting information on the client. My instincts failed, thrown over by the glitter of cash and the promise of glory. If I pulled this off, I would move into an entirely different playing field. I would be competing with the best and my reputation would be made. The little girl in me whispered that my father would have to acknowledge me. If I pulled this off, he would have to be proud of me. He would have to treat me as an equal.

When I looked over at Daniel, there was a panicked look in his eyes. He was staring at the chair recently vacated by Lucas Halfer.

"What is it?" I asked, not really worried. I was still thinking about the money and the potential glory. I would be the talk of my professional world. I could start being choosy about my clientele. I might even get an office and an assistant.

"Z, I am so sorry." If possible, his face was even paler than usual.

My pulse sped up, and I started paying attention. Daniel didn't usually apologize, so I knew this was something he considered a big mistake.

"I didn't feed before I came here. It's my only excuse. I was running late," he stammered. "It's so subtle. He's damn good, but I should have caught it."

"Caught what?"

"That smell." He breathed in again, his nose turning up in distaste.

"What smell?"

"Brimstone. He's a demon, Zoey."

I pushed the briefcase away as though my rejection of it would solve my problem. What seemed for a moment to be my glittering future now looked like a potential tomb with a one-way ticket to a vacation spot I didn't want to visit. I sealed the deal by taking the money. There was not a lot I could do. The damage was done.

The waiter slipped the check onto the table. I absently took note of the shockingly large amount.

I had made a deal with the devil, and the bastard stuck me with the bill.

Chapter Two

The briefcase sat in the middle of my kitchen table, the overhead light shining down like the money was about to sing a solo in a Broadway show. My entire crew sat in still silence watching the money with equal parts awe and fear.

"Dollars?" Neil pointed to the briefcase.

"Yes," I replied testily, though I'd asked the same thing myself not an hour ago. "Yes, I meant dollars. I meant five hundred thousand dollars from a demon."

"And we get another five hundred thousand dollars after we get this light thingy?" Neil never took his eyes off the briefcase.

"Another five hundred thousand from a demon," I reiterated, hoping he would get the point.

"And it's not actually light, right? I'm assuming that's a metaphor. Is it like the time we got paid to steal the Essence of Tor and it turned out to be goblin dung? Because I don't see how we steal light. Did he give you something to catch it in?" Neil gave me his best confused cute-boy look.

I was not in the mood. My one-way ticket to Hell was staring me straight in the face, and Neil was playing dumb. "According to the demon, it's a box. But as I said, this is according to the demon, who is by nature evil and probably lies a lot."

Sarah, dressed in her ever-present skinny jeans and a concert T-shirt, held herself away from the table as though it was diseased. She looked like she'd stepped straight out of a Deep Ellum club to come to this meeting, and she probably had. "This is a bad idea."

"You think?" My panic was on the verge of taking over. I reached out and brought my now lukewarm beer to my lips, swallowing gratefully. It was cheap beer I bought in a convenience store, nothing like the ultra-expensive vintage Halfer had ordered. I put the whole bill on a credit card because I didn't carry that kind of cash and I sure as hell wasn't about to open up the case and start flinging money around. The beer was cheap, but it tasted safe and normal.

"If it's such a bad idea, then give it back." Neil crossed his arms over his chest and frowned. "But I can't see that two hundred fifty grand apiece is such a bad idea. I could finally buy a car and go to Mexico, and OMG, makeover!"

Neil clapped his hands together looking nothing like the werewolf I knew him to be. It was times like this that Neil's true value came out. In his human form, there was absolutely nothing to hint at his ferocious other nature. Of course, this was also the reason he was a virtual outcast in the dual-natured world. Werewolves tended to look like bikers or roughnecks. There was nothing butch about Neil. He gravitated toward eclectic pieces he found in thrift stores and used far too much product to ever be accepted in a biker bar. In a tight-knit world, Neil was in the minority. It was one of the reasons he had come to me looking for work. After the rather terrible death of my last werewolf, I found myself *persona non grata* among that set. But I also had no problem working with and being friends with that rarest of species—the gay wolf.

Sarah smiled indulgently at her friend. "You don't need a makeover, gorgeous. You also don't understand the nature of a demon contract."

Neil ran a hand through his curly blond hair and sighed. "I understand that the last job we pulled, I got silver shot up my ass and we barely cleared ten grand a piece. I'm sick of mass transit. Do you know what a packed bus smells like to a werewolf? Have you ever had super smell on a 105 degree day? August is intolerable for me."

"Hell is hotter, buddy," Sarah said.

Neil rolled his eyes. "It's not like we sold our souls. At least I didn't sell my soul. I sure didn't give Zoey permission to sell it, and I don't think Daniel has a soul to sell."

Daniel, who had been silently brooding up until now, turned his seriously blue eyes on the werewolf. "Laugh all you like, Chewbacca, this is serious. By accepting that money, Zoey signed a contract. She might not have actually put pen to paper, but trust me, there is a record of the deal in some accounting office on the Hell plane, and it is binding. It doesn't matter that Halfer didn't properly represent himself. This is the way they play it in Hell. It's a classic demon trick. He offered far too much money for the job and Zoey took the bait."

"Don't blame it all on me, Danny." I turned on him, slamming my beer down. "You were there. You looked at that briefcase like it was an open-all-night blood bank."

"Well, I could use a new bed." Daniel ignored my outburst. "The one I have right now is crappy, and I have to spend twelve hours a day in a dead stupor in it. Do you know what kind of a crick that can put in your neck? I was thinking of getting a Tempur-Pedic. The other vampires say they are extremely undead friendly."

Vampires are very concerned with comfort. I suppose it's because they live so long in a single body that they become somewhat preoccupied with pampering it. The myth of the vampire hunting in the shadows is just that—a myth. Most vampires wouldn't be caught dead in a dark alley. They prefer the comforts of hotels and beautifully decorated homes.

The sunlight thing is true. Something about the disease makes the flesh susceptible to ultraviolet light. Despite what Hollywood will tell you, Daniel's heart beats fine as long as he keeps his blood volume up. I vividly remember laying my head against his chest and hearing the sound of his heart beating the night he rose. His skin is only a bit cooler than a human, though it gets icy if he doesn't feed properly. Garlic doesn't bother Daniel at all, and he can certainly see himself in a mirror and have his photograph taken, though he's not too big on the latter. The Council advises against photography as the picture can be found years later and questions would almost certainly come up.

I turned to Sarah, who seemed to always have a perpetually amused look on her face. Sarah was barely twenty-three, but she always seemed so much older despite her fashion sense and ever-changing hair. This month it was cut into a pixie-like bob and dyed hot pink.

"Would you like to complain about your supernatural powers to the mere mortal?" I asked, bitterness creeping into my voice. It wasn't easy being the only human in the group.

"Nope. No complaints here," Sarah said with a hint of a smile. "Although, since we're stuck, I think the best thing to do is donate the money to charity. Let's get some good karma out of this. Given the way half this crew lives, might I suggest PETA?"

The boys managed to groan in unison.

I shook my head, adamant in the belief that I could find a way to fix this. There had to be a way out. I hadn't spent any of the money. As long as we didn't spend a dime, maybe we could finesse our way out. "We're not touching this money. There's no way I'm taking this job."

"You already took the job." Sarah shook her pink head in a sympathetic fashion.

"There's no way out, Z." Daniel pondered the money quietly for a moment, and the rest of us waited as he thought.

After a brief silence, he stood and closed the briefcase. "We do the job. There's nothing else to do, so we do the job professionally and with absolutely no emotion. Emotion is where the demon will try to trip us up. I have no doubt that Halfer wants the object, but he won't turn down the opportunity to screw with us in the meantime."

It wasn't what I had hoped for, but I knew deep down that Daniel was right. Demon contracts were not something one got out of by saying "I want a mulligan." We would need to tread carefully, but if we played our cards right, we might survive intact and be richer for it. Demons liked to play the "win either way" scenario. If we succeeded, he got his object. If we failed, he got our souls to munch on for all eternity. We were trapped, and the only way to get out was to plow our way through.

"Fine." I resigned myself to the task at hand. I pulled out a thick manila folder and slapped it on the table. "Then we should get down to business. I'll read through the material the client gave us. Sarah, find out whatever you can about this Light of Alhorra. Daniel, see if you can find out anything about Halfer. This object is apparently going to be housed at a downtown hotel, so we need to see if we have any contacts who can get us inside. We'll need security information and possibly one or two of us should take a job there."

"How about me, boss?" Neil was the only one of the four of us pleased with the outcome of this meeting. I could see license plates dancing in his eyes, and I was betting they weren't attached to an economy car.

"Tomorrow night's a full moon. Try not to eat anyone," I said sarcastically. Neil was pure muscle. I had no use for him in the planning stage.

He smiled brightly as he stood and slipped into a preppy jacket that matched his shoes perfectly. There was no small amount of mischief in his eyes. "No promises. I know every other wolf in the world will be running through the woods, but I have a date tomorrow night. They can run. I get horny at the full moon. I intend to howl. His name is Trevor, he's a telekinetic, and a Libra. I can't wait to see how that works. I finally got matched at my dating site."

"Congrats, sweetie." Sarah stood, preparing to leave as well. "I wish I had thought of a gay, supernatural matchmaking Internet site. They have to be making money."

Sarah and Neil chatted happily as they walked out the door, making plans to go to a local club and dance the rest of the night away like the young, unattached people they were. As the door swung closed, I couldn't help but notice the contrast between the friends who had just gone and the two of us left in the room.

Daniel and I were young and unattached, but we weren't the dancing type. At least we weren't anymore. And the unattached part was not my choice.

Daniel strode to the window and watched Neil and Sarah walk down the street.

"What are you thinking?" I asked.

He didn't turn to look at me but kept his quiet watch. "I'm thinking that it will be a miracle if those two survive this."

I sighed. Daniel was not the most positive of thinkers. He tended to be a worst-case-scenario type. "Well, at least you don't underestimate my survival skills."

Daniel turned to me with a dismissive look in his eyes. "I would never let you die. I'm worried about Neil and Sarah because I think I will be spending all of my time and energy keeping you alive."

I folded my hands across my chest in a defensive posture. "You know I managed to run this crew for several years before you came back. I survived. We survived. Well, most of us did."

"You took on little jobs with little clients. There wasn't any serious risk in the beginning. Believe me; I had no worries about you during my time with the Council. If I had, I would have returned sooner or had someone handle it."

Shortly after his rising, Daniel had been whisked away to Paris, where the Vampire Council was located. It wasn't a voluntary thing for the newly risen vampire. The night they had come for him was branded on my brain, never to be forgotten. I had held on to him with all my might, but my human strength had been nothing for the vampires. It had been three years before I saw him again, and he was a different being altogether. This was one of the first times he'd mentioned our time apart.

"I couldn't stay on my dad's crew forever. You had to expect that I would want to work on my own." I kept my tone even. I didn't want to scare him off. Normally Daniel would already be out the door, and there was a part of me that would do anything to keep him here, even for a few extra moments. At times like this, Daniel seemed like a gorgeous beast that could run at the merest provocation. "How do you know about those years? I thought they kept you isolated from the outside world."

His eyes were suddenly wary, as if looking for traps in my every question. "They make accommodations on occasion. I promised to be a good boy if they gave me the information I wanted. I discovered I had some pull due to my youth. Our numbers are dangerously low, and someone my age is unusual. I was allowed some outside contact, though obviously not with you. You were…too close to my past life."

I struggled to shove down my rage. There was a bitterness that overwhelmed me every time I thought about those years. I had been left with nothing—no Daniel, no information, no hope. I had gone from the deepest grief at his death to an overwhelming joy at his unexpected rising. We had one night of the most complete ecstasy I had ever felt, and then he was gone. "Well, it's good they kept you up to date. As far as I knew, you were dead. If my father hadn't understood the process, I would have been grieving for you a second time. I guess the Council was pissed when your time there was up and you came right back here."

"Not at all. It was the plan all along. I was encouraged to reconnect with you after my training was complete. The Council thought you would make an excellent…" Daniel let the sentence die, but I knew exactly what he was going to say. My rage welled once more.

"Well, you sure showed them, didn't you, Danny?" I spat, unable to control myself anymore. "This is what kept you from me? You have to do the opposite of what the Council wants? You haven't touched me in years. You reject me because they're willing to accept me? That's ridiculous and you know it."

Daniel turned away, dismissing me. It was obvious this conversation was over for him, and I knew it would be a long while before the subject would come up again. "You should stay out of all Council matters, Zoey. It's really best that we not even discuss this. Simply know that what the Council approves or disapproves doesn't matter. This is about what is right for you. Now I need to go. It's only a few hours until dawn, and I haven't fed properly. We know how badly that can go. If I hurry, I can make it to my club."

That pitiful part of me wanted to beg and plead. It wanted me to throw myself at him and ask him not to leave me for some whore at his club who would feed his hunger but not touch his soul. Unlike Neil, I knew Daniel's soul was still intact, but it was infinitely harder than it had been before. I kept my mouth shut because no amount of pleading would keep him from leaving, and I would only look like a fool again.

As he opened the door to leave, I managed one last question. I wasn't sure he would bother to answer, but I needed to know.

"Why did you come back?"

It was the first time I had gotten the courage up to ask that simple question. Up until now, I wasn't sure I wanted to know, but this distance was getting impossible to take. My heart ached every time he walked out the door.

Daniel paused but didn't bother to look back. "I came back to make sure you didn't kill yourself with this business."

"Well, you should feel free to go." I had been right. I didn't want to know the answer. "I can handle myself."

"The case on the table tells me differently, Z."

The door closed behind him, and I was alone again.

Chapter Three

*C*ompanion.

The word played through my brain as I drove toward what was hopefully my final destination. Hours had passed since Daniel had gone, but my mind was still wrapped around that one word. The one Daniel hadn't said.

My craptastic car coughed and sputtered as I turned onto the lonely road that led to the third bridge I'd decided to search. Neil wasn't the only one who needed a car. The trouble was I needed way more than a car. Money couldn't buy what I needed. I needed a totally new life, but I was stuck holding fast to the old one.

At one time, I had been planning a life as Daniel's wife. Actually, when I thought about it, I had spent most of my existence planning to be Daniel's wife. Ever since we met at the age of eight, it had been in my mind. Needless to say, I was a kid who moved around a lot and struggled to maintain friendships. Daniel was a constant in my life.

My father had been the one to take in thirteen-year-old Daniel after George Donovan died on the job. He'd been a thief like my father, but not as careful. We'd been together after that and nothing could separate us.

Well, nothing except the Vampire Council.

I pulled off the road and parked my car behind a group of overgrown bushes. I looked out at the bridge. It crossed the Trinity River in a relatively unpopulated section of the city. An out of the way place, the bridge was home to a number of creatures. The bridge was one of those in-between places, not big, not tiny, not enormously popular, but by no means vacant. This was a mediocre place, a quiet place that the police didn't routinely check and the homeless didn't think to seek shelter in. It was perfect, and I knew I had found the spot when I smelled soup.

I grabbed the cache of items I'd tossed into the car when I'd given up on researching the object. I hadn't found much.

The Light of Alhorra was supposedly a mythical object of faery origin. It had been missing so long from the human world that it had passed into legend. I had found an artist's rendering on a web site, but who actually knew if it was real? It was hard to see the carvings on such a flat medium as paper, but there was a beauty to the piece. The artist believed that the carvings represented a story of faery kind, perhaps even a creation myth. The box was supposedly locked with a golden seal, and it was said that only one with pure intentions could open the box and receive the blessings inside.

It had been stupid to waste time on the Internet when I had a font of information waiting under a bridge. And all it would cost me was a couple of bottles of cheap wine and some chocolate.

When wanting to learn about a Fae object, it was best to seek out a Fae creature.

I closed the car door quietly, and as I climbed down the embankment, I was grateful I had thought to trade my strappy sandals in for a pair of sneakers. As a semi-forgotten place, the grass hadn't seen a city crew in a long time.

"Hello?" I sent out into the darkness, not wanting to frighten anything that might be waiting. Some of them had extremely sharp teeth.

"Stop." The voice was loud but held a tremble that told me he was as afraid of me as I was of him. Actually, he was probably more afraid of me since I didn't find him particularly threatening.

"It's Zoey Wharton bringing greetings to Halle the Loyal," I said in my most formal voice.

"Only greetings, Zoey Wharton?" There was no way to miss the disappointment in the question.

I smiled. "I bring greetings and a few gifts."

"Please come in and be welcome."

Trolls get a bad rap. Sure the mountain trolls one might find in the wilds of Norway or close to the Arctic Circle might be gigantic and completely terrifying, but your everyday, ordinary, under-the-bridge troll is no big deal. As long as you treat the troll with respect, they treat you with an enormous amount of old world hospitality. When most people think of faeries, they think of tiny creatures with gossamer wings, but the truth is there are many different creatures who make up the Fae world. Trolls are one of them.

Halle the Loyal was one of the Huldrefolk, a branch of the Fae that originally was native to Scandinavia. Faery kind can be found on almost every continent, but the Northern Europeans were particularly populous at one time. Sometime in the distant past, when humans began to take over the planet, the majority of Fae had chosen to find another plane of existence. It was a historical time the Fae referred to as Passing Beyond the Veil. Some had stayed and adjusted to life with humankind. Halle and his wife, Ingrid, had immigrated to the New World sometime in the 1800s. My father had befriended the pair before I was born. I had been visiting them for as long as I could remember and was well versed in greeting protocol.

"Greetings to Zoey Wharton, you are a welcome guest," Halle said as I ducked under the bridge. "It has been far too long."

I smiled. Halle was sweet and always had kind words for me. Of course, he also liked to eat small house pets, but I wasn't a poodle, so I felt fairly safe. His wife was infinitely more complex, but I didn't see her at the moment. I held out the wine and chocolate. "I come bearing gifts for a friend."

Halle's dark eyes widened as he took the gifts. He took a deep whiff of the bag containing the chocolate. "Your gifts are always much appreciated, Zoey. Are you alone tonight, or is your vampire with you? He is welcome. I promise there will be no further incidents."

The last time I'd brought Daniel with me, Halle had had some friends visiting. Needless to say, they had not appreciated a vampire surprising them. It was rather like inviting a lion to a party thrown by twelve antelope, though these antelope had weapons and weren't afraid to use them. "No, Daniel had other things to take care of tonight. And you have to stop referring to him as 'my vampire.' He isn't mine. I only work with him."

Halle shook his head as he sat by the fire. "I will never understand human relations. One minute you have a mate, the next they die and the relationship is over. We never let a thing like death keep us from our mates. And Daniel made it easy by rising. It should have been simple, but you humans make things difficult. I know. I have watched many of your reality shows."

"It wasn't my choice, Halle," I said, wanting to get off this subject as soon as possible. Trolls like gossip almost as much as they like a nice roast dachshund.

Of course, trolls could be as tenacious as any hound dog. "Have you tried to talk to Daniel? I've heard the transition can be difficult. He did not know he was a vampire. Perhaps he simply needs time to adjust."

There was good reason Daniel hadn't known he was a vampire. Vampire lore has been carefully cultivated by the Council in a successful propaganda campaign. The Council has made the public believe that vampires are a myth like the Greek gods or a fifty cent cup of coffee. They have hidden the fact that anyone alive today can be a vampire. There's no way for a person to tell until after death has occurred. Vampirism is a genetic disease carried by the parents as a recessive gene. The child lives a perfectly normal life until death, and then the vampire gene reanimates the dead tissue after a few hours. The new vampire rises after the disease takes over, and then as long as the vampire has a good supply of blood, he can go on indefinitely.

Yes, I could certainly see where it had been a shock to Daniel's system, but it hadn't done me any good either.

"He's had years, Halle. He was with the Council for three and he's been home for two." I took a deep breath and found I simply couldn't stop. I wouldn't be able to talk about this with my father. He was too close to Daniel. It didn't seem fair to talk about him to

Neil and Sarah. So Halle, who had watched over us both many times, seemed my best bet. "He told me tonight that the Council approved of me as his companion."

Halle clucked a bit and shook his head. "Dearling, you don't know what that would mean."

But I did. I'd talked to a few people and patched together what I could. In the vampire world, there are two types of women. There are blood dolls and there are companions. It's the vampire equivalent of a one-night stand versus a long-term, happy marriage. A companion is a woman who serves as wife, and more importantly, dinner. The blood a vampire needs on a day-to-day basis is small. One person can feed a vampire and never suffer ill effects if said vampire isn't a greedy bastard. Due to the passionate nature of the vampire, most select a companion and mate for the life of the human companion. The vampire sharing small portions of his blood elongates the companion's life. It keeps the companion young, but in the end, the human body breaks down no matter what you feed it. Vampires without a companion, or who find themselves apart from their companions, use blood dolls. These are women who work at the clubs and make themselves available to vampires for a late-night snack. I like to think of them as convenient, Council-approved whores.

"I understand what it means to be a companion, Halle. And I understand that Daniel is being stubborn."

Halle took a long breath, an odd weariness stealing over his features. "There is so much you don't know. Vampires are secret creatures. Even I don't understand everything about them. Ingrid and I have steered clear. To know vampire secrets is to court the Council's wrath, but I know that a companion is something a vampire guards zealously. And I've heard rumors about true companions. I don't like these rumors. Daniel is right to keep you off the Council's radar."

I didn't know what he meant by true companion. True or false, I would have taken any title just to be close to Daniel again. But three years of waiting for him followed by two years of a Daniel I barely knew had worn me down. And I hadn't come here to talk about Daniel.

"Is Ingrid around? I have a couple of questions about an object I'm hoping she's heard of."

Halle ran his fingers through his thick hair in an attempt to smooth it down. "She should be back any moment. She went walking. She will be pleased to see you."

Halle was wearing a large T-shirt and sweatpants, and he attempted to smooth the wrinkles out of his clothes as well. Trolls were very aware of their mates and always attempted to look their best. It was hard, though. Trolls like Halle looked mostly human, but there was always one piece of hair that no matter what they did to it or how much product they tried on it, always stuck straight up. Then there was the tail...

There was a pop as the cork in the wine came out, and I found myself seated comfortably by the fire with a glass of wine and a bowl of soup which looked completely housepet free. After some pleasant conversation about the weather and television shows we both liked, I got down to why I had come.

"This sounds like bad business." Halle sagely shook his head as I told him the story of my encounter with the demon. "I have not heard of this demon, Halfer, but that doesn't mean I don't know him. He would use many names and many guises when on this plane. Was there anything unusual about him? Anything that stood out?"

I thought for a moment. "I don't know. I think he was good at masking. You know how when a demon is around, people get uneasy? I never felt that with him. Daniel didn't even pick up on the brimstone until he was gone."

"Then he is either extremely old and powerful, or works for someone who is," Halle explained. "Demons sometimes share powers with their lesser servants when they need to. The powerful can share strength with lesser demons and even earthbound witches."

I took a long drink of the wine. It was starting to take the edge off my panic. Not only did I get to deal with a demon, but apparently an old, powerful demon, or a group of them led by an old, powerful demon. The day got better and better.

Halle turned his large, dark eyes on me in a sympathetic

fashion. "I'm sure it will turn out all right. You have to be careful and follow the letter of the agreement. Just remember that when dealing with demons, the devil is in the details."

"Who is dealing with demons?" a feminine voice asked from the darkness.

Halle stood and smiled as his wife emerged from the shadows. I wasn't sure what Ingrid really looked like. She was old and adept at glamour. Halle was younger than his wife and had no use for glamour. The female who emerged from the darkness appeared to be in her mid-twenties and could have been a poster child for a Swedish modeling agency. Her blonde hair was perfect and meshed with her icy blue eyes. She made an odd sight walking out of the trees in a couture gown and heels.

When I was young, I would make a game of finding the one flaw in the glamour. When using this magic, there is always one flaw, and if you can find it, the glamour no longer works on you and you can see the person as they truly are. I never could find that fatal flaw, and as I got older, I stopped trying. I realized that this was Ingrid as she wanted to be seen and to try to pull down her glamour was a rudeness I didn't wish to participate in.

"Oh, greetings to Zoey Wharton," she said with a smile.

As I stood to greet her, she lightly touched my hair in a familiar token of affection. After the formalities were taken care of, she joined us beside the fire. "You have gotten in a bit of trouble, I assume. Your father, he does not know?"

"Just a bit." I always felt like a kid around this couple. They had often served as surrogate parents when I was young. I had spent many summers with them and felt a need to make them proud of me. "It's a minor hiccup, and my father doesn't know. I'd like to keep it that way."

"I'm sure you would," Ingrid said with that tone that made me feel like I was fifteen years old all over again. "So, what is this thing the demon wants you to steal? I assume this trouble involves some form of thievery."

I winced. Halle was easy to talk to, but Ingrid didn't think procurement was a proper profession for a young lady. She had agreed with my father that college, a career, and marriage to Daniel was the only way to go. Ingrid had expressed her disappointment when I dropped out. Trolls really know how to relate feelings of disappointment. Still, she was the only person in town who might know something about this object. "The demon called it the Light of Alhorra."

Ingrid was silent for a moment, and I knew what she was doing. She was deciding if withholding the information would do any good. Luckily, she had known me for a long time. My stubbornness was legendary. "Yes, I have heard of this, but it is only a legend. It is a box supposedly filled with the blessings of the Fae. The way my mother told the story, a powerful faery tribe placed a piece of their magic in a box for safekeeping. The magic in the box grew into blessings that were then passed from tribe to tribe as a sort of ambassador of peace after the great wars. Each tribe became guardian of the ancient magic and it bound the tribes together."

"What does a demon want with faery blessings?" I was still a bit confused. "Faery blessings are things like good crops and fair weather. Unless he's starting an organic Hell co-op, it doesn't make sense."

Ingrid shrugged, a single motion of her shoulder. "This I cannot know."

My mind raced, trying to make sense of the deal I'd made. There was a pure intentions clause that went along with the Light of Alhorra. If there is one thing demons don't possess on any level, it's pure intentions. I didn't understand what Halfer wanted with a box he couldn't open and blessings he couldn't use, unless he was telling the truth and he's getting the object back for someone else. "Is it possible that the tribes on this plane are still caring for the object?"

Ingrid shook her head. "No, the time of the great tribes was done long before my mother birthed me. The tribes left here are weak. Some of the young Fae have left the traditional homes and live among the humans. There are a few tribes left, but they are only truly strong in their *sitheins*. On this plane, there are few full-blooded Fae. Such magic would never be safe here. No, the Light was taken beyond the veil when our forefathers left. Whatever this demon is looking for, it cannot be the true light. I think you're safe turning over whatever you find."

Ingrid was quiet for a moment, and I asked her a question I had always wondered about. "Ingrid, why don't you join them? Is it not possible?"

She smiled. "This is my home. This is my family."

Halle took her hand. "She is not telling the complete truth. She stays because I would never be accepted. I am only a halfling. My father was human. In the great tribes of the past, she would have been a queen. I would, at best, have been a tolerated servant."

Ingrid tenderly touched his face. I knew in that moment, I didn't exist for them. It had always been this way with the two of them. Thinking back now, it was the only solid relationship I had to look up to when I was a child. It was just the two of them in the whole world and had been since the day they met hundreds of years before.

"You are my king. As I said, this is my home and you are my family. I have no need for any other." She leaned in and kissed him before breaking the moment and turning back to me. "Now, as for you, what does Daniel say?"

I groaned. I should have known she wouldn't let this subject get away. "He says we do the job by the letter and try not to piss off the demon."

"He is a wise man, your Daniel," she said.

"Ingrid, he isn't mine. He left me." I didn't even try to keep the bitterness out of my voice. Ingrid knew how I felt. She had let me cry on her shoulder for days after they took him from me. I had spent a month traveling from bridge to bridge with them as I had when I was a child.

"Bah, he is acting like an idiot," she said dismissively. "It is— what do they call it in children? I believe the term is temper tantrum."

"It's a long temper tantrum since it's been years," I pointed out.

"It's your fault, child."

I sat straight up at that. Now I was offended. "My fault? How in all the holy planes of existence is it my fault?"

"He acts as you allow him to act. You must take the reins," she proclaimed as though it were the simplest thing in the world. She turned to Halle, who was nodding in agreement. "What do the young folk call it now, my love?"

"Scene control," Halle said. "I have heard this on MTV."

"Yes, you must get this scene control."

I threw up my hands in surrender. How could one argue with MTV? "Fine, it's my fault, but the truth is, I'm not sure what else I can do. I've tried everything. I've told him nothing has changed for me. I don't care that he's gone all fangalicious. I pledged my love. I've made a fool of myself on more than one occasion. I've tried being patient. Nothing works. He tells me this is all for my own good."

"Have you tried leaving him?" Ingrid asked.

"I don't have to. He left me."

A smile played on Ingrid's lips. "He didn't get very far, did he? I wonder how far he would go if there was…someone else? If he has moved on, you should move on as well, preferably with someone lovely who will anger Daniel in every way possible."

The thought of dating sent a chill up my spine. It had been so long since I had been on an actual date, much less…

I stopped when I realized what I had been about to think. Much less a first date. I had been on exactly one first date. I went with Daniel to the movies on what we had decided was our first official date. We were fifteen years old, and I don't think it counted as a true first date because we had known each other for so long.

What would it be like to go on a date with someone I hadn't been around for most of my life? Daniel and I had known each other since we were children, so there was never that "getting to know you" period. There wasn't an exchange of childhood stories since we knew them all. It had been an easy, laidback slide from friendship to romantic love. Up to this moment, my entire romantic life had been about one man. It had been about dating Daniel, loving Daniel, planning a future with Daniel, mourning Daniel, and trying to get Daniel back. How much of myself had I given up for Daniel? Was I willing to wait for the rest of my life for him to come back to me?

"I do not wish to see this life pass you by because Daniel cannot see the truth or because he is too afraid to take what has been offered to him." Ingrid took my hand in hers and stroked it gently as she had when I was a child and she'd comforted me. "There is too much to enjoy. If Daniel is your soul's mate, then things will work out. If he is not, then you are wasting time, child."

I shook my head as if I could clear it from those disturbing thoughts. It seemed too complicated. It was definitely too scary. "I don't know. I wouldn't even know how to find a date. I haven't dated anyone but Daniel."

"Like I said, you need someone who understands the world you live in," Ingrid explained. "You need a gentleman who is looking for love as well. And it would not hurt if this gentleman was, as they say, totally hot."

They let me sit in silence for a moment while I wondered which part of myself was going to win this particular war. The adventurous side of me, the one I had quelled for a long time, was excited at the prospect of trying something, anything to get me out of the rut I'd been in for the last several years. Then there was the part of me that was terrified at having to meet someone new and trying to fit in. Then there was the thought of sex with someone other than Daniel. That almost broke my heart, but I had to ask myself if I was willing to never have sex again. When I got down to the heart of the problem, I realized one thing. I was lonely. "And you might know this person?"

Ingrid's blue eyes practically glowed with excitement. "Oh, yes. I know just the person, love."

That's how I woke up under a bridge with a monster hangover and a date with an earthbound faery prince.

Chapter Four

"By god, girl, this is the end of the line. If you think for one minute I'm going to allow you to pull a job for a demon, then you don't know me at all!" My father had already been red in the face even before I opened the door, so I knew I was in for it. His Irish temper didn't take much to set off, but when he was this close to exploding, I knew I was in for a fight.

"You should lock your door," Sarah said quietly from behind me.

"Wouldn't make a difference." I walked into my tiny living room, despite my instincts to flee.

I'd woken up under the bridge sometime in the early afternoon with a massive headache and a slightly altered outlook on life. Halle had taken care of the headache with a mug of something herbal. I didn't ask about the contents. It worked and that was all that mattered. I bid the pair good-bye and promised not to let as much time pass between visits.

The first call I made when I got back to my car was to wake up Sarah. My blind date was picking me up at eight, and I knew I was in trouble when it came to the fashion department. Old jeans and faded black T-shirts were not going to make the first-date cut. I needed something nice, and there was no way I trusted my own instincts for something this important. It wasn't important because I thought I was going to immediately fall in love. It was important because it was the first step away from the cycle I had been in since Daniel died. It deserved new clothes and a haircut. Sarah had massive experience in both.

The last thing I needed was a visit from my father.

"What the hell are ya thinking, girl? Do you know the kind of trouble you're getting yourself into?"

I looked at my father and realized this was a turning point as well. I could cry and beg his forgiveness and ask him to help me out of the situation. He would hug me and tell me everything would be all right, and then he would completely take over. Or I could grow up and take charge. It was far past time for me to take a stand with my overbearing father.

"What do you mean 'getting myself into,' pops? According to everyone I've talked to, I'm in and there's no way out, so rest easy. The worst has happened. It's all downhill from here." I threw my bags on the kitchen table. I carefully hung up the black cocktail dress Sarah had found at a vintage store.

"Yes, downhill leads straight to Hell," he continued. "This ain't something to joke about, Zoey. Demon kind is serious about their contracts."

"I can laugh or I can cry, Dad. I can't fix this problem tonight, so I don't see the value in worrying myself to death over it. Now, who ratted me out?" I turned and immediately had my question answered. Daniel was standing in the shadows looking broody. His arms were crossed, but he let them drop as he took a close look at me. "I should have known. Did you even wait until today or did you immediately go straight from here last night to tattle?"

"Your dad called me. He has the right to know what we're going into. And why the hell did you cut your hair?" Daniel completely ignored my question.

"Well, you should be glad he told me. He's the only one with any sense," my father continued, unabated. "You're going to get yourself killed."

"You colored it, too." Daniel made his observation a veritable

45

accusation.

"I had Anton pump up the color." Sarah had been thrilled when I called her. She had dropped everything in favor of helping me with a mini-makeover. She had been trying to force me into a girls day out for a long time. If I had known how good a deluxe mani-pedi could make a person feel, I would have done it a long time before. Spending the day with Sarah had made me realize how I had been keeping everyone at a distance. It had been nice to share a day with someone as open and happy as Sarah.

My father continued his tirade. "And do you know what will happen when ya do manage to get yourself horribly murdered by whatever is waiting out there? Don't think there's not something waiting. When it gets ya, you'll find yerself on some Hell plane being some demon's bitch, and let me tell ya that's worse than any 'girls in prison' movie you've seen…"

"A couple of highlights and the red in her hair really pops," Sarah was explaining. "I also had him texturize the hell out of it. It's thick but now it lies so nicely."

"I liked it the other way," Daniel said sourly.

"Do ya know what a demon can do to ya?" My father pulled me back into the primary conversation.

"Yes, Pop. I remember the bedtime stories," I said. "It's something no three-year-old should have to listen to. I had nightmares for years. Do you remember when I accused my kindergarten teacher of having ties to Beelzebub? Do you remember the trip I had to take to the school psychologist?"

"I told ya those stories for a reason," he said seriously. "I was trying to teach ya something that should be evident to anyone with half a brain. Demons are bad. Ya shouldn't go into business with them."

Sarah was ignoring our conversation, preferring to have it out with Daniel. "I think she looks awesome."

"She's wearing too much makeup," Daniel countered.

"I didn't realize he was a demon," I defended myself. "I'm sorry my puny human senses couldn't get past his magic. It's kind of why I bring Daniel to these meetings. It's not my fault that supervamp got tricked."

"Her makeup is extremely subtle," Sarah huffed. "Do you know how hard it is to keep a transvestite makeup artist to the bare essentials?"

"You never take on a client until you've looked into his background." Dad shook his finger at me to emphasize his point.

"Oh yeah, like you would turn down a million because you hadn't done a skip trace," I scoffed.

My father's face went white. "Did you say a million?"

"She didn't need a makeover," Daniel said firmly.

"Did Daniel not mention the amount?" I asked as my dad lowered himself shakily to a chair at the kitchen table. "What a surprise since he practically drooled all over the money. It's half now and half when we turn over the object."

"This is even worse than I thought," Dad said to himself.

Sarah was shaking her pixie bob at Daniel. "That's because you don't understand the nature of women. We need makeovers. It's about renewal and feminine power."

"There's nothing powerful about mascara and new shoes." Daniel faced off with her.

My father let his head sink into his hands in what I thought was a complete over-dramatization of the situation. "How could this happen? Where did I go so wrong that my precious baby girl could get herself into a situation where she could go to Hell like this? If I could only switch places…"

Sarah had pulled out one of my brand new, altogether-too-expensive candy red stiletto heels. She pointed it at Daniel. "Let me tell you, buddy, it's gonna feel powerful when I stake you with it."

"Yer mother, God rest her beautiful soul, is crying her heart out somewhere in Heaven." My father managed to squeeze out a single tear meant to induce maximum guilt.

"My mother is in Cleveland. I talked to her Saturday. She and Leonard, the accountant, are doing fine," I pointed out. "She didn't die, Pop. She left when that pissed off client set a poltergeist on your ass."

Dad set his jaw stubbornly. "Well, she's dead to me. I prefer my version of the story." He paused for a moment and another thought came to him. "Are ya telling me ya have half a million dollars in cash sitting out in the open in this hellhole of an apartment?"

Daniel was smartly backing up as Sarah moved toward him. "I'm just saying I liked the way she looked before."

"Of course not," I replied to my father. "I totally hid it under the bed."

At least that brought the color back to his face. "Under the bed!"

Sarah continued to back Daniel into a corner with the threatening shoe. "Well, it's not up to you. Her date is going to think she looks fabulous."

"Date?" Daniel and my father said in unison, the two arguments finally coming together.

I didn't like the complete shock that both of the men had written all over their faces. "It's not like I'm some kind of a monster. I can get a date."

I didn't mention that I hadn't actually gotten this particular date, Ingrid had. They didn't need to know that.

"You have a date," Daniel said as though he needed a moment to let it sink in.

"Yes, I have a date, with an actual male," I replied sarcastically. "Someone in the world who doesn't mind being seen with me in public."

"You have a date." A smile crossed my father's face. "That's wonderful, darling. I mean, it would be wonderful if ya didn't have all of demon kind trying to eviscerate ya."

"I like the positive attitude, Dad. Now I would like to get this one date in before my inevitable death."

I picked up my dress and walked into my bedroom, glancing at the clock on the wall. I didn't have much time before my date was supposed to pick me up. I looked at myself in the mirror and smiled. Sarah had done a damn good job. I looked polished. I looked like a woman about to go on a date and not make an idiot of herself.

The door opened behind me, and Daniel let himself in. He stared at me for a moment. "I think it's wonderful. The date, I mean. It's far past time for you to start seeing someone."

It took everything I had to keep my face neutral when his words cut so deeply. I was glad I had decided to do this for myself and not to make Daniel jealous. It was so obvious that wasn't going to work. Ingrid was wrong. There was nothing left between us except his need to see me safe. When he was sure I was secure, he would leave, and I wouldn't see him again.

"Yes." I agreed, not looking at him. "I should have done this a long time ago."

He paced, walking from the door to the window and back again. "It's what I want for you. It's what I've always wanted for you."

"That's not true. Once you wanted something else."

"Things change." Daniel stopped at the window, staring out. "Now I want you to find a nice man and settle down. I want you to find someone who can give you a good life."

"You mean a normal life."

"Yes, a normal life where you don't have to worry about demons or the police or any of this. I want you to be far away from this world."

"And if I don't want that?"

"Of course you do," Daniel replied stubbornly. "You'll see. You'll find someone, and this will all seem like a bad dream."

I'd had enough. "It's good to know you have it all planned out, Danny. Now leave. I need to get dressed because the white knight who is going to sweep me off my feet and take me away to tract housing in suburbia should be here any moment. God forbid he finds me in jeans and a T-shirt."

Daniel crossed the room and opened the door but couldn't resist one parting shot. "It's for the best. You'll see."

I sank onto my bed and told myself he wasn't worth crying over. I'd done all the crying over Daniel Donovan I was going to do in this lifetime. My pride asserted itself suddenly. There was no way I was walking out there and letting him know I was hurt.

I slipped on my dress and found it to be an excellent form of armor. The jersey hugged my body in all the right places. The *V* of the bodice was deep and showed more of my ample cleavage than I normally would, but I had to admit the girls looked damn good. The bra Sarah had forced me to buy pushed them to the perfect place.

I slipped into the stilettos and admired the way they made my legs look. It had been forever since I dressed up and now I realized I

49

needed this. No matter what Daniel said, there was power in transformation. I was determined to enjoy myself. If Daniel no longer wanted me, then it was far past time to get my butt out there and discover someone who did.

"You look beautiful, girl." My father was waiting as I closed the bedroom door behind me. "You're going to make such a lovely corpse when the demon murders ya."

"Thanks, Pop." It was likely the most optimism I would get out of him.

"OMG." Sarah clapped her hands together. "You look so freaking hot. He's not going to know what hit him. I told you that dress was perfect."

Daniel walked up to me, and there was something in his eyes. He smiled almost sadly. "You don't look beautiful, Zoey. You are beautiful. He's a lucky man, your date."

"Thank you," I managed.

A knock at the door saved me from further emotional turmoil.

I hadn't meant for everyone I knew to greet my blind date. He was going to take one look at this group and run for the hills no matter how great my boobs looked. I was about to yell at everyone to hide in the bedroom when Sarah swung the door open wide.

There was no further discussion as the entire room went silent and stared at the man who stood in the doorway. He managed a smile that told me he was used to such a reception. The whole room was quiet for a moment until Daniel chose to break the silence.

"Oh, hell, no."

Chapter Five

He was gorgeous. I mean past gorgeous, and moving on to god-like, fall-to-my-knees beauty. And he was shining. He was tall and dark and everything good in the world and my heart opened to him.

I'm pretty sure I actually drooled.

There was nothing in the world except him. He was everything I could ever have wanted, and he was standing right there. All I'd had to do was reach out and take him. I was about to do that when Daniel stopped me in my tracks.

"Oh, hell, no." It was the most human thing to come out of his mouth in years, and I managed to turn away from the gorgeous, shining man in the doorway long enough to look to him. I was shocked out of my madness by the sight of Daniel. His normally dispassionate face was suddenly full of indignation.

"If you think there is any way in hell I'm letting you walk out that door with him, you are so wrong," Daniel said, sarcasm dripping from his mouth.

"Hello," the shining man said, his voice as sexy as his glorious, lean body. "I'm looking for Zoey."

"I'm Zoey!" I actually held my hand up so there could be no way he could mistake who I was.

Sarah frowned. "I'm Sarah. You don't want her."

I was about to argue with that statement, but Daniel took me by the shoulders, forcing me to look only at him. "He's not human. Can I ask you a serious question, Zoey? Do you know any humans? You should try it sometime. We live on a planet with like three billion of them. They're everywhere. But when you decide to jump back into the dating pool, can you be troubled to find one? No, you have to pick some idiot Fae who can't handle his magic."

"You don't know he can't handle his magic." I knew there was no way the lovely, shining man meant to be so very lovely and shining, but I was determined not to let Daniel win this one.

"He's glowing like a firefly, Z," Daniel pointed out.

I would have started in on Daniel if Sarah hadn't chosen that moment to take the term "jump his bones" literally.

"See." Daniel pointed to the doorway. "This is what happens when people don't respect magic. I'm surprised he managed to make it here without being torn apart by rabid females."

I turned to see my sweet friend mauling the hell out of our guest. She was trying to pull his shirt over his head, and I caught a glimpse of what looked to be a spectacular six-pack. And all that hotness was supposed to be mine. Mine, damn it.

My first thought was to tear her pretty pink hair straight out of her head, throw her to the ground, and take her place. She was messing with my man, and I had to put a stop to that.

"You get off him, Sarah!" An unholy rage took root in my gut.

Sarah turned to look briefly at me. Her eyes were darker than usual. She tightened her hold on her prey. "Stay away from him. He's mine. Can't you see how much he loves me?"

"He loves me!" I screamed. I believed it. The magic he was using surrounded me with the deep belief that the shining man and I were meant to be together.

The man was trying to walk backward as though he could get away, but he found himself against a wall. "Uhm, you should get down now."

No one was listening to him.

"If you take a step toward him, I swear I will turn you into a toad, Zoey," Sarah promised.

"Bring it on, bitch." I snarled and started toward her. I found my path blocked by Daniel's strong arms.

"Listen, Xena, as much as I'd love to watch some girl-on-girl action, I'm going to have to pass." Daniel forced me to turn toward him again. "Snap out of it, Zoey. You can fight this. Let me help you."

By "let me help you" Daniel meant to trade one magic for another. He put his hand behind my neck and gently pulled me into his arms. I fought him, struggling against his strength, but it was no use. The pull of the Fae's glamour was strong, but Daniel was stronger.

"Zoey, look at me." There was no sarcasm left in his voice. The sound coming out of his mouth was smooth and so seductive. I remembered the way it felt to be taken over by Daniel, and that feeling was far stronger than any glamour. I looked willingly into his blue eyes as his irises grew until the whole of his eyes seemed to bleed to that deep sapphire color. I felt a calm take over and knew the glamour had lost its hold. The last time Daniel had performed this magic on me was right before he'd folded me in his arms and let his fangs find the vein in my neck on the night he rose.

"Are you all right, now?" Daniel's question broke the spell.

I took a deep breath, banishing my need to beg him to continue. "I think so. Give me your jacket."

"What?" Daniel asked, distracted again by the drama playing out in my living room. "Oh, look, he wasn't smart enough to limit it to females. I think your dad is about to cry."

I turned to find my father on his knees.

"I always knew the shining ones would return." My father looked at the man with a worshipful fever in his eyes. "Prince of Ireland, I offer myself to your service. I am a man of small talents, but they are yours to command."

This had to stop. Making certain not to look at the glorious, shining man, I forced myself to focus on Daniel. "Look, you might be immune to magic, but I'm not. Give me your jacket."

There are certain tricks to dealing with faery magic. They don't work all of the time, but there are a few things a person can try. I don't know why they work only that they have been passed down through the years. With simple magic, like the glamour the shining man was using, turning a piece of one's clothes inside out will usually do the trick. His magic, while strong, wasn't cohesive. I would never have been able to break Ingrid's spell with such simplicity.

As for Daniel's magic, well, when Daniel got me locked in, I was his until he decided to let me go.

He shrugged out of his jacket, and I turned it inside out. The minute I had it on, I could breathe, and my need to murder Sarah faded. I turned to the man and was able to see past the magic. Devinshea Quinn was roughly six feet five inches tall with stark black hair and emerald green eyes. I only knew his name and the fact that he was Ingrid's friend. Well, and I knew he couldn't handle his magic.

Even being able to see through the spell, he was still hot.

"You need to turn down the glamour, buddy."

The faery was struggling with Sarah, but managed to look my way. "Is it too much?"

Daniel snorted loudly.

I ignored him. "That depends. Do you normally get strange females rubbing themselves all over you when you walk into a room?"

He shook his head as he tried to put a hand over Sarah's seemingly curious mouth. "Not normally. It sounds more fun than it is. It's actually quite disturbing. Could someone give me a hand with her?"

"Oh, I'll give you a hand," Daniel offered. "I know how to turn that sad-sack porno magic off for you. Let me go find a nice piece of wrought iron. After I shove it in your belly, you won't have that problem again."

"Daniel!" Despite the terrible way the evening had begun, I didn't want to waste all that makeover time. And the last thing I needed was to spend the rest of the evening listening to Daniel say "I told you so."

"Fine." Daniel pulled Sarah off. She sobbed in his arms. "I'm taking her to your bedroom until you get him out of here and then we'll talk, Z."

My father was prostrated on the floor singing some Irish song.

"I'm so sorry." The faery closed his eyes and seemed to concentrate for a moment. The glow dimmed to nothing.

Yep, still wretchedly way-too-out-of-my-league hot.

"We should hurry." I grabbed my purse.

A smile crossed his face. That smile didn't need magic to make my heart pound. "You're still interested?"

"Well, I'm definitely interested in avoiding a lecture." I took his hand and made my escape.

* * * *

Two hours later, I walked beside Dev out of the upscale restaurant he'd taken me to and took a deep breath of the night air.

"I know I've said it a couple million times already, but I really am sorry about what happened back at your place." Dev gave me an apologetic smile that actually made my heart skip a beat. He attempted to smooth down his white dress shirt. The shirt had been immaculate at the beginning of the night, but I found it endearing now. The slight messiness made him somehow more approachable.

"It's all right." I stared up at him and prayed I didn't have a dippy look on my face. "I mean, it's not like anyone died."

"That's looking on the positive side of things." The grin he gave me showed perfect white teeth and an incredibly sensual mouth. "I like an optimistic view."

It was easier to be optimistic after a fabulous dinner and a couple of drinks. I could laugh about the event now, though at the time it had seemed like a scene out of a black comedy, if said black comedy had the potential in ending with a juicy bloodbath.

"I can't believe Sarah actually jumped you like that." I didn't mention that only Daniel's quick thinking had saved me from a similar fate. "She's going to be so embarrassed in the morning."

He winced. "Yeah, well, that was completely my fault. I was trying to make a good first impression."

"Oh, you made a first impression, all right. Even my dad was impressed."

"Don't remind me. He's never going to forgive me."

It felt good to tease him. Dev Quinn wasn't a man who took himself too seriously. "You're kidding, right? You're like a prince of Ireland. I never would have thought my dad was stuck in feudalism. Are you really Tuatha Dé Danann?"

The Tuatha Dé Danann was a mighty group of Fae who led the second settling of Ireland. They were legendary, and there were still groups in Ireland who worshipped them. Apparently there was at least one man in America who did as well.

"If you believe my mother, then yes, but who knows? Most of the Fae I know claim kinship with the great tribes of the past. Well, I'm glad you were smart enough to combat my mistake. I don't think your father would enjoy serfdom." Dev's face flushed slightly.

I stopped teasing and reached for his hand. "It was a little mistake. Everyone does their own version of it. I was trying to do the same thing with the dress and makeup and the…presentation of certain key body parts."

Dev laughed, a throaty sound that reminded me I had female parts that still functioned. "I very much appreciate your presentation."

"I enjoyed yours as well," I agreed. "Especially once you toned it down slightly."

The valet pulled up in Dev's black Audi A8. I walked to the passenger side, but Dev raced in front of me.

"Please, let me," he said as he opened the door. "I'm going to take you to one of my favorite places in the world. You're going to love it."

I got into the car as gracefully as my dress would allow, and Dev shut the door with care. In a moment, we were driving into the night.

"I'm glad you knew the trick with the clothes," he said, returning to our previous discussion. "I don't know what would have happened if you hadn't."

"I can guess what might have happened." Daniel might have found his piece of iron and shoved it in a couple of creative places. Faeries are sensitive to iron, and given Daniel's own "sensitivities," I thought he might have been a bit more diplomatic. Daniel forced me to sell a lovely set of silverware because the sight of it disturbed him. Now I wished I'd at least kept the steak knives.

Dev turned, and his eyes were wide with questions. "Yeah, what was up with the big scary vampire? Is he your brother or something?"

"I work with him," I muttered, not wanting to go into it. "Don't worry about him. He's not very friendly. I'm so sorry I had to hit you with all those people. I didn't mean to have a greeting committee with me. They just sort of showed up."

"It's all right. I think it's great you have a bunch of people who care about you. Trust me. It's better than the alternative."

"The alternative being?" I asked out of curiosity.

"The alternative being completely cut off from your family and friends because they don't approve of your lifestyle choices." His mouth was set in a firm line as he made a right turn.

"Did that happen to you?" I was surprised. The Fae tended to bond strongly. Their relationships were passionate and family units were close.

The lights of downtown danced all around us. Though there were hundreds of people on the road and walking around the city streets, I felt like Dev and I were the only ones who mattered. There was a sweet intimacy to being next to him and talking about his past.

His hands tightened on the steering wheel. "I'm the black sheep of my family. My mother no longer speaks to me. My father died a long time ago. My brother does what Mother tells him to. I am formally an outcast, so if you're interested in Fae life, there's not a lot I can do for you. The only ones of my kind who still speak with me are Ingrid and her husband."

"Wow, did you burn a forest down or something?" I asked, thinking of the worst crime a faery could commit.

"No, it's much worse. I chose to leave the *sithein* and move to the city."

"You live here permanently?" Faeries usually can't stand to be surrounded by concrete and steel. It bothers them on a fundamental level. They can visit if they need to, but they never stay for long.

"I have a great condo." He glanced my way, a sad smile on his face. "My father was human. I always seemed to be more attuned to my human half than my brother. I was more...fragile. You should have seen my mother's face when she realized she had given birth to a mortal. My brother takes after her, you see."

"That must have been hard." Most halflings took after their Fae relations from what I understood. Dev should have been looking at a long life, but those pesky human genes had screwed him.

Dev pulled the car into a downtown parking garage. "I left five years ago, and I haven't looked back. I rarely rely on magic. I prefer to use my human talents. Especially since my human talents don't get me into the kind of trouble I got into earlier."

"So why did you use them tonight? I mean, not to inflate your ego, but you don't need glamour."

He pulled the car into a slot next to the elevator. He shut off the engine and turned to me. "Dating is hard for me. I've tried dating humans, but I have to hide so much of myself it seems pointless. I've heard stories about you for years, Zoey Wharton. Ingrid talks about you all the time. It seemed like a perfect solution. You live in the same world I do. You don't know this, but I saw you once. You were leaving as I came to visit Ingrid. I begged for your number, but she kept saying you weren't ready. I guess you had recently broken up or something. Last night she finally relented, so you'll have to forgive me if I felt the need to look my best."

I smiled as widely as I could. I wasn't about to explain why I hadn't been ready, but there wasn't anything he could have said that would have made me feel better. After years of ramming my head against the stone wall Daniel had become, it was a balm to my ego to hear someone had actively pursued me. "You're forgiven."

Dev flashed a devastating grin. "Come on, I want to show you something."

I hesitated for the briefest second. This man could be dangerous. I could be tempted to tread into some deep water, and I didn't know if I was ready for that. I was still in love with Daniel and might be for the rest of my life. But there was something in Dev's green eyes that compelled me to get into the elevator with him. I let him take my hand, never realizing that something far more dangerous was closing in on us.

* * * *

The first sign that something was unusual was the way Dev pushed seven buttons, his hands flying across the keypad in a practiced manner.

"Are we going to all those floors?"

"No, just the one, but you have to know the sequence to get where we're going," he assured me. "Don't worry, you'll like it. It's one of my favorite places in the world."

I was surprised when the elevator, which I thought was on the ground floor, started going down. It jerked slightly, and I had to step back to balance myself. Dev's arm shot out to keep me from falling and I found myself against his firm chest. I was glad for the heels Sarah had insisted I wear. They brought my head almost to his shoulders. Otherwise I would have maybe reached the middle of his chest.

I looked up, and he was smiling down at me. I knew in that instant that he was going to kiss me, and I wanted him to. I wanted those sensual lips on mine. I wanted to want someone who wanted me.

Unfortunately, the doors to the elevator opened, and the loud, insistent thud of music distracted me.

"Here we are." Dev held his elbow out in a courtly fashion. I threaded my arm through his and let him lead me into the hall. When we turned toward that music, I saw a throng of people held in line by a velvet red rope. It took me a moment, but I realized where we were.

"This is Ether." I looked around, taking it all in. "This is the nightclub, isn't it? Sarah keeps trying to get in here, but it's always packed."

It was obviously packed again this evening. The line looked to go on forever.

"It is indeed the hottest club of its kind," Dev said with what appeared to be pride.

Like humans, supernatural species are social creatures and most have gathering places. Weres have their biker bars, witches sponsor some great raves, and demons seem to prefer Starbucks for some reason. For the most part, they stick to their own species.

Ether was different because it welcomed all supernatural species. It was a place where witches danced with goblins, and trolls shared a meal with visiting brownies. Officially known as a place of peace, everyone was welcome at Ether as long as they followed the rules. Everyone was welcome with one exception.

I stopped in my tracks and knew the expression on my face was one of sheer panic. "There's no reason to wait in this line, Dev. They don't let humans in. They'll turn us away at the door."

He simply pulled me alongside him. "Who said we were waiting in line?"

I let myself be led mostly because I didn't want to cause a huge scene in front of so many people. I was dreading the confrontation that would certainly occur when we managed to make it to the front of the line and the man guarding it. I caught a glimpse of him standing in front of the door, and he was impressive. The bouncer was enormous, and from the rumors, he was a half demon with a bad temper and impressive strength. Now that I saw him up close, I didn't doubt the gossip. His skin had an inhuman red hue to it, and he was at least seven feet tall. I doubted Dev was going to be able to charm his way past that one.

The enormously scary half demon looked down at me, his eyes flaring briefly. "Good evening, sir. Good evening, Miss Wharton. Welcome to Ether."

The halfling's genteel speech was only marred by the slightest lisp made as his tongue maneuvered its way around his enormous fangs. I was speechless for a moment, and it takes a lot to render me speechless.

"If there's anything I can do to make your evening more enjoyable, please do not hesitate to ask," the demon said. "We pride ourselves on service."

"Thank you, Albert," Dev said as he led me through the door.

I stopped, forcing Dev to stop with me. "You own the club."

He laughed. "I own this club and two more. I have one in New York and one in Vegas. We're working on finding a suitable place in Miami."

So he was gorgeous and wealthy, putting him even further out of my league. "You let me think that bouncer was going to toss me out on my keester."

Dev took my hand again, leading me on. "Albert is far too civilized to ever throw a lady out on her rear. He would have politely had you escorted back to your car. He's filling in tonight. Most of my security team are werewolves, and it's a full moon. I tend to get a little thin during the full moon."

"What does Albert normally do?"

"He's my butler," Dev said seriously. "And he does my taxes."

We walked through the impressive foyer. I noticed a large sign stating the club's rules.

Welcome to Ether
No weapons allowed
This includes holy objects, silver, iron, guns, stakes, swords or the like
No humans or hunters
Please, no exorcisms on the dance floor
The bringing about of the apocalypse on the premises is strictly discouraged
Thank you and have a nice day!

I was pondering the rules when I heard a sound that made me turn. There was a shriek that managed to resound over the thumping techno beat. "OMG! I can't believe you're here!"

I turned to see Neil pushing his way off the dance floor toward me. He was dressed to impress in form-fitting black slacks and a tight white T-shirt that showed off his well-muscled chest. "Hey, I thought you had a date."

"Girl, you look good enough to eat! Witchie worked some magic on you." Neil took my hand in his and twirled me around to get a 360 degree view. "You should wear that every day from now on. Sorry to say my date turned out to be a bust. I'm so gonna call that dating agency. They are supposed to match you based on compatibility, but telekinetic boy turned out to be a vegan. You can guess how that worked out." Neil turned his attention to Dev. When I thought about it later, I realized it was a testament to our friendship that Neil had talked to me first. There was nothing he liked more than a ridiculously hot guy, and Dev fit the bill. Neil's eyes went wide as he looked Dev up and down. "Oh, honey, is this your date? Please say no. Please tell me he's your new homo friend."

Dev took it all in stride, and I liked him all the more for it. He smiled and leaned forward, offering his hand. "The name's Dev. And sorry, I'm a hundred percent hetero."

Neil shook Dev's hand and sighed. "Well, it looks like Z has cornered the market on hot guys tonight. What's a boy to do? Between this one and...oh crap. The two of you are on a date, right?"

"Yes." Did anyone think I could get a date?

"*Quelle* drama!" Neil sighed. He seemed to come to some inner decision, and he took my hand again. "Listen, I was thinking about heading out. This place is kinda dead. How about we three go somewhere else and have a drink? The bar here sucks."

Dev huffed and seemed ready to defend his club when we both saw the reason Neil was attempting to get us to leave. Sitting at the bar, dressed in an immaculate suit, was Daniel. He had his arm around a chesty blonde. He was staring straight at me, and as he realized I was looking, he curled his hand around her shoulder. I could see even from here that her IQ probably matched her bra size.

"So you work with him, huh?" Dev asked, frowning.

"There might be more to the story," I admitted with a sigh.

It was going to be a long night.

Chapter Six

"Coffee, black, please," I ordered when the bartender finally got around to me. He gave me a puzzled look but was professional enough not to ask questions. Unfortunately, he was the only one who didn't ask questions or make way too perceptive comments.

"You'll have to forgive my employer." I turned in time to see Albert settle his hulking body onto the barstool next to me. It looked like the butler/accountant/part-time bouncer was taking a break to play counselor.

"Oh, I disagree. I don't see myself forgiving anyone involved in this particular evening." I brought the coffee cup to my lips and glanced over at the scene playing out mere yards away.

Dev, Neil, Daniel, and the girl I had come to affectionately refer to as "Skank Ho" were sitting in the VIP section of the club. It was like a lushly decorated living room. There was a decadent-looking sectional sofa and a large coffee table. The room came with its own bar and bartender, and a server stood off to the side waiting to fulfill any request. The room was open on two sides, allowing a view of both the impressive dance floor and the regular bar area. Large screen plasma TVs covered the other two walls. The screens had been set to music videos when we entered the room but Dev had quickly switched to both a baseball game and a basketball playoff game.

"Thanks, Tom." Albert touched the cup placed in front of him. He seemed to be eschewing alcohol, too. He turned back to me. "He doesn't have a lot of friends, you see."

"I don't know." I glanced around the club. "He seems to be extremely social. He gave me some sob story about being an outcast, but there are a good number of faery creatures here tonight."

"Oh, they come to his clubs," Albert acknowledged. "They use the facilities and come to him for protection when they need it, but have you seen a single one of the creatures greet him tonight? Have you seen him have a pleasant conversation with one of his own kind?"

I hadn't, and I had to admit my heart softened slightly. In the last hour, only his staff and my friends had actually spoken to Dev. When we'd first seen Daniel, I had worried that he had come to force me to go home with him. Several scenarios had played out in my head, each brutal and ending in an increasingly violent death for my date. What had happened had been much worse. Daniel had been pleasant and acted completely surprised that we were here. He had been friendly, not a term I used often when referring to Daniel, and offered to buy us a drink. He had introduced Skank Ho as someone named Chardonnay or Chablis. She giggled a lot and generally made my brain hurt.

"Well, he seems to be having fun now." I wasn't sure which hurt worse, the fact that Dev had dumped me to watch sports with Daniel or that Daniel would purposefully ruin my date.

Dev and Daniel sat in the VIP room pointing and shouting at the screens. Well, Dev was shouting and Daniel was showing his displeasure in more restrained, supercool vampire ways.

"Perhaps he's simply trying to fit in with your friends. I'm a little surprised you're not with the vampire." Albert blinked as he looked at me. "You're quite vibrant."

I didn't feel vibrant. I felt dull and useless. Even Neil deserted me after half an hour of trying to pull me out of my sullenness. For some reason, Neil had decided I wasn't being friendly enough to Skank and had betrayed me by befriending the enemy. I can't think of why he did this, but he started referring to me as "Bitchy Smurf" and had ignored my bitter comments. Neil and Skank Ho had been in a deep discussion about who was screwing whom in Hollywood, and I had excused myself to go to the restroom.

"Somehow I doubt it," I replied. "I think he found something more interesting than me. Look, this whole evening was a mistake."

I should have taken Daniel's advice and tried dating a nice, quiet IT guy. The truth was Dev was so far out of my league, we weren't even playing the same game. I liked nerds. I always had, and I probably always would. I preferred going to the movies or staying in and watching bad sci-fi TV to the fast lane. I had never been one of the cool kids, and if I was honest, I hadn't liked them in the first place.

Daniel had been quite the nerd before his turn. He was a hot nerd, but a nerd all the same. Sometimes girls in school would decide to hit on him, but after ten minutes of Daniel discussing *World of Warcraft*, they would decide his hotness wasn't worth the trouble.

The truth was, Dev would be horrified if he knew who I really was. He thought I was this cool chick who happened to be a master thief. The reality was I was a complete geek who just happens to be a master thief.

Dev had an entire world I couldn't ever fit into. I lived in a cheap apartment in a crappy part of town and shopped for clothes at discount stores. This club was something out of Hollywood. The crowd was fast and the music was cutting edge. I could enjoy it for a night, but I couldn't see myself as a fixture.

"I don't believe it was a mistake. At first I was a bit worried you were a companion who had run away from her vampire master. But you haven't, have you?"

Master? Yeah, I wasn't going to ever call Daniel that. "No. Daniel and I used to be friends. Now we're business partners."

Albert nodded as though my answer had pleased him. "Then this was not a mistake. You must forgive my employer. He grew up with a brother. They were very close. I believe he misses male companionship greatly."

"Well, he's getting plenty of it tonight." The coffee was doing its job, helping to banish the slight buzz I had gotten from the cosmopolitans I had downed at dinner. I'd quickly realized on Daniel's arrival that further alcohol would probably result in me crying in a bathroom somewhere.

"It shouldn't reflect on his interest in you," Albert said. "He was excited about his date with you. He doesn't date often. He's become selective in the past few years."

I turned to the halfling. Despite the demonic nature of his body, his eyes were blue and strangely human. It was disconcerting, and I had to wonder how much of him was human. Did appearances deceive? He looked like he could rip me in half and greatly enjoy feasting on my intestines, yet he was staring at me with understanding in his soft eyes. How hard would it be to have a gentle soul trapped in a monstrous body?

"I appreciate the talk, Albert, but I think it's time I called it a night." I tried not to think further on Albert's situation. I had plenty of my own problems to worry about. "Could you have someone call me a cab?"

"I wish you wouldn't. He will be devastated when he realizes how he has treated you," Albert said quietly.

"It was a mistake to go out in the first place." I would have to call my own cab. I pulled out my phone and hoped I could get a decent signal. "I'm in too much hot water to be playing around like this. I need to focus on the job at hand, not my sad love life."

"Mr. Quinn mentioned your somewhat unusual career." I sensed a slight disapproval in Albert's voice. I didn't take it personally. "Thief" doesn't exactly look good on a resume.

"Well, I have a job right now, and a rather demanding client who quite frankly scares the crap out of me." I gave Albert a quick rundown of the story thus far. I didn't usually open up to strangers, but I found Albert easy to talk to. It was also nice to tell the story and not get screamed at for my stupidity.

"Did you get the demon's name?" Albert asked, leaning toward me.

"Only the one he chose to give me. He called himself Lucas Halfer."

Albert nodded. "Typical. It would be helpful for you to know his true name. It would give you some measure of control. It would allow you to summon him, and it might give you some insight into his true motivations."

"Yeah, that would be great. But unfortunately, he declined to be listed in the demon Yellow Pages, so I'm shit out of luck as far as I can see." I sighed. No bars on my phone. I would have to ask the bartender.

Albert looked at me for a moment, and I sensed he was coming to a decision. "I have deep connections with that world. My mother is well placed. I could attempt to find out his name for you."

"You would do that?" I was surprised. I had assumed he didn't spend much time with demon kind.

"I would, but I need you to do me a small favor." For the first time I saw a hint of calculation in his eyes.

I should have seen this coming. My search for a cab would have to wait. If there was any possibility that Albert could give me information about Lucas Halfer, I had to do whatever I could to make that happen. If that meant suffering through playoff hell, then so be it. "Fine, I'll give Dev another chance, but I can't promise you anything."

"I'm not asking for anything but understanding."

"All right. The first part of the date was great, so I guess I can stay a while. It will give me time to talk to you about how crappy your security is."

Albert's eyes widened and a frown turned his mouth down, his fangs peeking out. "It isn't bad. It can't be. We paid top dollar to a security firm."

I made note of the slapdash way the security cameras were installed. There were far too many blind spots. A nasty thought struck me. "How long has this club been open, Albert?"

"It will be six months next week."

Nightclubs aren't the richest hit in the human world. Most humans had given up carrying huge wads of cash, but our world was different, and human law didn't govern this club. I was betting there were a few differences between Ether and other more mundane clubs.

"Do you have a poker room?"

Albert nodded a bit sheepishly, if a seven-foot demon can ever resemble a sheep. "Yes, Master Dev insisted it would be a good draw. There is a room for poker and several other games. It is very popular."

"And the house takes a cut, cash only, I assume."

"Most of our business is cash."

"Oh, Albert, you're such a lucky demon," I said with a smile. "I'm about to save your boss a ton of money."

* * * *

If you want to rob an establishment, the best, easiest way to do it is to install the security system yourself. No muss, no fuss, you can walk in, get what you came for, and make it look like anything you want on the way out. Break a few locks, mess up a few cameras, and the cops never think it's an inside job. You would be surprised at how much trust people place in security professionals. Get a good ad in the Yellow Pages, establish a few legitimate clients, and let the suckers walk right through the door. I didn't know the whole story behind Dev's security firm, but I would bet they had been in business for less than five years, had good but not amazing recommendations, and placed the lowest bid.

I could feel Albert's eyes on me as I walked back to the VIP room. I knew he was hoping I would fail in our bet, but I had a feeling he was out of luck. I pulled the gold hoop out of my right ear and slipped it into my bag before smoothing down my dress. I walked up to the sofa and smiled my brightest smile. Dev looked up and smiled back.

I wasn't privy to the same insider knowledge the security company would have, so I had to use whatever assets I had at my disposal. I was going to do this the old-fashioned way. My first and most important asset was Dev himself. The safe would be located in his office on the second floor. I noted that the place seemed to be using keycards on all their private doors. Keycards are better than everyday keys but not by much. I prefer systems that require something personal from the user, whether it be a retinal scan or thumb print. Nothing is foolproof, but at least that requires some planning. All one needs to break into a room guarded by a keycard is sticky fingers.

"Hey, Zoey." Dev looked slightly chagrined, and I knew he was about to apologize, but I didn't have time for that.

I sat down on the couch next to Dev and draped my arm around him. I did this for two reasons. I needed to put him at ease. I needed him happy and thinking about how nice it was to be close to female body parts. It also put me in the perfect position for what I was about to do.

I looked up at the basketball game with what I hoped was interested eagerness on my face. "Who's up?"

Daniel was immediately on his guard, but luckily Dev didn't know me as well. He immediately started discussing the game. I feigned interest, occasionally patting his chest flirtatiously. Dev obviously enjoyed the attention. He scooted closer to me, his hand moving dangerously close to my thigh. I found what I was looking for on the second try. There it was. A thin piece of plastic in his right jacket pocket. It was the simplest thing to slip it out and into my purse while he was pointing at the screen and complaining about the Mavericks' lack of defense.

I safely tucked the package away, flipped my hair back and "discovered" I'd lost something.

"Oh, my gosh," I said in a panicked tone. "I lost my earring. Does anyone see it? It's a gold hoop."

Everyone gamely looked around the room. After a moment, I sighed. "Duh, I'm so stupid. I know where it is. I probably dropped it in the bathroom."

"Do you want me to have my staff find it?" Dev asked.

"Oh no, please, don't go to any trouble. I think I know where it is. You keep track of the game for me."

Dev gave me a huge smile and squeezed my hand before he let go. "Okay, but hurry back."

I promised I would and headed off toward the bathroom. I stood by the door for a moment, watching the movement of the security cameras as they swung back and forth. To a layperson, it would simply look like a bunch of cameras moving carefully to try to catch as much of the building as possible. To a thief, it was a path to success. The person who installed the cameras timed them perfectly to create a path from the back door of the club to the stairs that led to the second floor, all the way to Dev's office where the safe was kept. It was just a matter of timing. It took me a few minutes, but I got the sequence down and then I was off.

I realized I was smiling as I managed to make it to the stairs. I was sure the cameras had caught nothing of my journey across the club. It had been a long time since I ran a job on my own, much less one where there was no pressure, and I enjoyed it.

A large bouncer guarded the base of the stairs. I wasn't sure exactly which species could lay claim to him, but I was betting he was one of the weres who hadn't called in sick. Carefully keeping my back to the camera, I approached him.

"Sorry, miss, the second floor is off limits," the big guy said.

I smiled brightly. "Oh, Dev said it was all right."

"The boss sent you?"

This was the part where I blushed and stumbled over my words in an entirely charming manner. "Um, I kind of left something in his office this morning."

"No problem, I'll have someone run up and get it for you." He pulled a walkie-talkie out of his pocket.

"Oh, god, no!" I practically shouted. "Please, you can't do that. Look, it's kind of personal, and by that I mean it's entirely personal, and I would be horrified if anyone else had to find it. It's just Dev and I were…this is so embarrassing. I left my panties in your boss's office…there I said it. I'm so sorry. I could die now."

The big guy tried to contain his laughter, and I knew I was going to make it in. There was no way the big bad werewolf saw me as anything other than some bimbo his boss had banged, and a human bimbo at that.

I smiled my best "humans are harmless" smile and pulled out my trump card. "He gave me the key, you see. I think he realized how embarrassed I am."

"Well, don't let me keep you then." He gestured me on.

Then I was home free. I slipped the keycard into the door and sighed with pleasure as I heard that loveliest of sounds—the click of a forbidden door opening for me.

I waltzed into Dev's office. Normally I would leave the lights off, but Dev obviously wasn't concerned with conserving energy as the lights were already on. I looked around the office and realized this was much more of a window to his soul than the club. The club was a marvel of hard-edged decadence, but this office was softer. It was comfortable, with none of the pretense of the floor below. The desk was large and looked good, but it was obviously old and had a sturdy feel to it. There was a comfy-looking chair in one corner with a bookcase beside it. I let my fingers glide over the spines as I read the titles. He seemed to like thrillers as books by Steve Berry, James Rollins, and Preston and Child populated the shelf. I could see Dev sitting in that chair, reading escapist fiction like I did late at night when I couldn't sleep.

A framed picture caught my eye. I picked it up and saw a smiling man in clothes that looked like they were from sometime in the seventies. It must be his human father. His mother and the Fae side of his family would never allow themselves to be photographed. Dev said his father died, and his Fae family no longer spoke to him. This might be the only piece of family he had left. I suddenly felt like I'd seen something he might not be happy sharing with me. I felt the weight of my intrusion and decided it was time to finish the job and get out of here.

I was about to find the safe and leave the note Albert and I agreed on when something pushed me roughly against the wall. I felt the breath knocked out of my lungs and the pressure of a hard body against my back. I hadn't heard a thing and knew that whatever was behind me was dangerous. I knew in that moment what it felt like to be a rabbit right before the rattlesnake struck.

"Thief." There was a harsh whisper against my ear. "I was hoping it wouldn't come to this."

Chapter Seven

"**J**erk!" I muttered as I shoved an elbow into Daniel's chest. I used every bit of force I could muster from the position I was in, but my hearty attempt at violence didn't even elicit a groan.

Though I couldn't actually hurt him, Daniel took the hint and backed off. I turned around to face him. He stared at me with grim intensity.

"I started the night thinking I needed to save you from Dev, but it turns out Dev is the one who needs protecting." I could hear the disappointment dripping from his quiet condemnation. "I didn't realize we'd started stealing from our friends."

"I'm not stealing from Dev." It hurt that he would even think that about me. Whatever we'd become, I thought he knew me better than that.

"That's not what it looks like from my perspective, Zoey. You stole his keycard, lied about your earring, and made damn sure the cameras didn't catch you. I watched you the whole time. Did you think you could fool me? You haven't been interested in basketball once in your life."

"Not once," I admitted. "I did lie about losing my earring, and I did steal the keycard, but let me tell you it wasn't hard to make sure the cameras didn't catch me. That was the easy part."

Daniel stopped his lecture for a moment, and I could see the gears working in that brain of his as he searched for a logical reason for me to be up here rather than my need to commit a felony. "They're about to get hit…"

"…by their security company," I finished for him. I was satisfied by the slightly guilty look on his face. "I figured it out while I was talking to Albert, who knows I'm up here, by the way. Albert is Dev's right-hand…man, so to speak. Speaking of which, how did you get up here? I had the keycard, so I was able to talk my way in. I seriously doubt the bouncer let you come on up."

Daniel waved off the thought. "The bouncer was easy. He was susceptible to certain mind tricks. He gave me his key card and now he's taking a nap in the alley."

"Oh, Jedi mind tricks," I said with sarcastic fervor. I wasn't impressed by Daniel's vampiric talents. I thought they were cheating, but they did come in handy every once and a while.

Daniel smiled faintly. "Something like that. So can we go back down now?"

I folded my arms over my chest. "I can't. Albert doesn't believe I can crack the safe. You should feel free to leave whenever you want to. I didn't invite you up here. Come to think of it, I didn't invite you to crash my date."

"Would you believe it was a coincidence?"

"Not if God came down from the Heaven plane and told me himself." I glanced around the room and noticed the lovely pastoral painting on the wall. A quick pull revealed the safe I was looking for. At least Dev had it bolted to the wall. That wouldn't help him when it came to the security company, but it might deter the casual thief.

Daniel shrugged. He sank down into the chair behind the desk. It was obvious he wasn't going anywhere until I went with him. "Fine. I went out and talked to Ingrid, and she mentioned Dev owned this club. It wasn't hard to figure out he would take you here. And Ingrid told me to tell you she told you so, but I don't know what that means."

I put my hands on the safe, the metal cool under my fingers. I genuinely loved doing this. Safe cracking is an art form I became acquainted with at a young age. While other kids were learning about history and writing poems about frogs, I was studying the teachings of Harry C. Miller and his scientific approach to lock manipulation. My father spent hours teaching me to listen for the delicate sound of the notch on the drive cam sliding into place. It took time and infinite patience to expertly manipulate a lock, so I did it more for recreation than any professional purposes. During an actual job, it's much simpler to have Neil pull the door off and take what's inside. I sighed. I didn't have time today, either. As much as I loved the fine art of manipulation, it was always easiest to know the combination. I let my hands drop and turned to the desk. I was pretty sure I would find what I needed there.

"What I'm trying to figure out is why you bothered to come here in the first place. I thought you wanted me to get out and date." I shuffled through the papers on Dev's desk.

"Not him," Daniel said with a certainty that I found annoying.

I also found it annoying when he turned over the calendar on the desk. There it was. 36-12-2. Why bother having the safe if you leave the combination lying around? I always ask myself this question and people constantly surprise me with their level of stupidity when it comes to security.

Daniel echoed my frustrations. "Is that safe a Wentworth 2500? I'm betting it is because that's a try-out combination. He didn't even change the combination from the manufacturer setting. He deserves to get hit."

"You don't get to pick." I wasn't about to let him change the subject. I had spent the past years so lost in sadness and grief that the anger I felt was liberating. "You don't get to choose who I date. I didn't leave you. You left me. I don't owe you anything. You don't get to have a say in what I do with my life from here on out."

"I didn't leave you," Daniel said quietly. "I died. I didn't have a say in that either."

I clenched my fists in tight balls at my sides. "I'm so sick of that excuse, Danny. You died. Get over it. It's been five years. It's not like you're the first person who ever died or even the first to come back."

"I came back different."

He hadn't seemed different that first night. He'd been scared and worried and so grateful to be alive, but he'd been Daniel. "No, you didn't. You came back to me. You loved me. You wanted me. You didn't come back from death different. You came back from the Council different. They changed you, not death."

"They showed me that things couldn't be the same. They showed me the logic of my situation, and I am grateful to them." Despite the heated air between us, Daniel was perfectly calm. It was the crux of my frustration with him. I couldn't fight him because he never got emotional. He was always in control. "Now, could we please finish up here and get back downstairs? You need to let Dev know you can't see him again."

"I'm not going to tell him that. If he asks me out again, I'll go."

"No, you won't, Zoey," Daniel returned sharply.

I noticed his right leg was bouncing. It was a nervous habit left over from his human days that I hadn't seen in years. Perhaps he wasn't so calm. I smiled and slid onto the desk and slowly crossed my legs. I leaned forward, giving him a good view of the girls. For the first time in a while, I saw a look of trepidation pass across his face.

"I like him, Danny." I let my voice get deep and low. That leg kept bouncing. "I like him a lot. He's the first man in many a year to catch my interest, and I have no intention of letting that go. I have plans for him."

Daniel finally noticed his leg moving and forced it to still. There was only a little strain to his voice as he got to the point. "I won't have you faery struck. I won't allow him to control you like that."

I laughed long and hard at that one because it was the most ridiculous excuse I'd heard in a long time. There's a myth about faeries and their sexual prowess. I think it was probably perpetuated by faery males themselves. The legend goes that once a human had sex with a faery, they became "faery struck" and would follow the faery anywhere. The victim of the faery would become the faery's slave in exchange for the possibility of getting back into the faery's bed. As faeries had been groping humans for centuries and we weren't a population of drooling sex slaves, I seriously doubted the myth.

"I think I'm willing to take a chance on that one, Danny, but I will get back to you and let you know if it's true. I managed to survive sex with you, and that was pretty mind blowing. I haven't wasted away because you won't sleep with me anymore."

Daniel's eyes darkened, and I knew he was remembering that night. He chose to change the subject. "He'll get you into trouble, Zoey. He's surrounded by all manner of creatures with these clubs. You need to get out of this life, not deeper into it."

"That's my choice, Danny." Weariness threatened to overtake me. "The sooner you realize it, the sooner we can both get on with our lives. We can't go on like this, you know."

He looked away. "I know."

This conversation was like so much of our lives since that terrible night. It was a stalemate. "All right. Let's crack this beauty open and call it a night."

I dialed the lock and pulled the handle. I felt Daniel come up behind me. He put his hands on my shoulders and every nerve in my body went on full alert. Despite what I said earlier, I would do almost anything to get back into his arms. I was in far more danger of becoming Daniel's slave than Dev's, and I think Daniel knew it.

"I only want what's best for you." He barely touched me, but heat flared on my skin. His fingers were cool, but no amount of chill could make me forget how hot it had been between us. That single night was burned onto my soul.

"I don't suppose pointing out that being with you is best for me will change your mind?" I asked quietly.

"I'm not good for you, baby." I could feel him against me, his body making a liar of his words. His erection pressed against my hip. How many times had he worked over me, a smile on his face as he connected our bodies? He touched my hair so softly that I wondered if he meant to do it. "I was once but not anymore."

"What do we have here?" Dev asked from the door.

Daniel practically jumped back, and I turned to see Dev and Neil standing in the doorway. Dev was standing with his arms crossed, his sensual mouth set in a straight line. Neil's hand was on his hip, and I could tell from his expression exactly what he was thinking. *Damn, girlfriend, you got caught with your hands in both the cookie jars.* It was pretty much what I was thinking, too.

My heart fell. I needed to explain, and I wasn't quite sure where to start. I hadn't been caught safe cracking in…well, ever. It was a completely new experience, and one I found I didn't relish. I liked this guy, and while I might have been out of the dating scene for a while, I doubted that getting caught with my hands in his safe was the way to get a second date. To top it off, from Dev's point of view, I was stealing from him with my "ex-boyfriend." I blamed Daniel. If he hadn't followed me up here and lugged all of our baggage along, I would already be downstairs discussing the situation with Albert.

"I was just…" I started, not sure where I would go from there.

"Damn it!" Dev cursed under his breath when the safe came open. He punched a fist in the air to show his frustration. "Seriously? This is seriously happening? I can't believe it. That freaking company came highly recommended. I wanted to go American, but no, I end up off-shoring my security to a bunch of Nagas because they give me this Buddhist 'save-the-earth green security' crap. Then they turn out to be scamming me? Do you have any idea how much I laid out for that system? I have them working on my new clubs. Now I have to change everything. Crap, this is gonna cost me a fortune. Next time I'm gonna say 'fuck the whales' and hire some firm that doesn't recycle."

I let out a sigh of relief. "Albert talked to you."

Dev finally took a breath and seemed to calm down a bit. "Yeah, I didn't believe him. Then I watched the cameras from the security room. They didn't pick you up at all. They picked up the big, scary vampire though. What the hell did you do to my bouncer? He's asleep in the alley mumbling something about beef jerky and bunny rabbits."

"I wasn't trying to go unseen," Daniel said in his defense.

Neil stepped forward. "Um, Daniel, Charlene said your time was up, and she left with a hot shape shifter. She also mentioned you were a cheap date and there was some talk about your parents not being married, but I don't think that's a big deal anymore."

"I don't see how she can call me cheap with what she charges."

Daniel sounded offended. "I could only afford to pay her until two am."

"I knew she was a hooker." She had that look about her.

"Did they think I wouldn't figure this out?" Dev was asking no one in particular.

"Yes." I would have thought it was obvious, but Dev seemed to struggle with the idea.

"You didn't figure it out," Daniel seconded. "Zoey did."

"Ooo, pretty guns." Neil's eyes widened as he looked into the safe.

There were three shiny handguns in the safe along with what looked like a big hunk of cash. That security firm was losing a rich score. I decided to ask Dev to maybe not mention my name when he confronted the Nagas. Nagas were Indian river creatures who were usually peaceful, but they could turn into giant ravenous snakes, and I didn't particularly need anyone else pissed off at me. And their heist methods were actually quite earth friendly. They hadn't planned on killing anyone, and I'd heard that they gave ten percent of all their profits to Greenpeace.

"Yeah, well I'm going to be using those on one slick salesman when I can catch him," Dev swore.

Neil's head came up, his whole body on alert. "Do you normally let people come up the stairs?"

Dev frowned. "No one should be here. I'll go look."

He started for the door, but Daniel stopped him. "Neil, pass out those guns. I don't like the sound of this."

"Take it." Neil pressed a gun into my hand. He was the closest one to the safe. He tossed one to Dev, and then placed the third in Daniel's hand before anyone could speak.

"Are you sure this isn't overkill?" Dev asked. "It's probably a guest who thinks this is a snack bar or something. All of this could have been avoided if you hadn't put my bouncer to sleep."

I eased the safety off because the back of my neck was tingling. Something was wrong, but I couldn't explain that to Dev.

Neil didn't arm himself. Neil preferred the old ways. He would never use a gun when he could rip and claw an enemy. Of the four of us, Neil was the only one smiling. Despite his sweet-looking face, he genuinely enjoyed a bit of violence.

"If it's a drunk guest, we'll quietly escort them back down," Daniel explained, his voice tight.

The door to Dev's office exploded inward, silencing any further discussions.

The sound cracked the air around me, and I acted on pure instinct as pieces of wood flew everywhere. I threw myself in front of Daniel.

Pain, pure and visceral, bloomed from my shoulder. I winced as I looked down. The door had splintered into stake-like pieces and one lodged itself right under my clavicle. It wasn't deep, but there was enough blood to worry me.

"What the hell were you thinking?" Daniel twisted me around so he covered my body with his.

I decided no answer I could give would satisfy him, so I pulled the stake out of my shoulder. It easily could have been Daniel's heart had I not stepped in. The pain raced across my skin. I moved to get a glimpse of whatever had managed to make that lovely, heavy oak door explode.

Three large men walked through the door.

"Wolves?" Dev's voice showed not a hint of the panic a normal person would have. I had to believe it wasn't his first time at this particular amusement park. It was a good thing because I didn't want to be the one to babysit the civilian.

Neil breathed the air deeply. "Oh, no. Those are shifters, my friends. Don't worry. We'll be all right as long as they don't turn into bears. I'm sure they'll turn into something less frightening."

The three shifters filled the front of the office. Even without Neil's super smell, I could tell they were more than human. They moved differently, holding themselves with an odd grace that came from spending much of their time in other forms. There were two large men and a slightly smaller one whose head moved back and forth in an almost hypnotic pattern. His eyes were pitch black, seemingly endless pools of darkness. While the other men were bigger, he was the one who scared me. He was the one who seemed the most far from human.

Dev's workspace was large, but it was beginning to get the

tiniest bit cramped. Adrenaline started to pump through my system. This wasn't a friendly meeting.

The largest of the three men had scruffy gold hair and the beard to match. He stepped forward, his dark eyes on me. "Give us the human and no one has to get hurt."

And by "no one," I assumed he meant no one except me. Who the hell had I pissed off this time?

Daniel tensed beside me and leveled his gun at the biggest shifter. "Dev, please tell me these rounds are silver."

Dev took another target, aiming for the one with the beady eyes and the moving head. "Absolutely. Nothing but the best."

"Excellent." Daniel took a step forward, that gorgeous face set in arrogant lines. "Now, you tell me who hired you, and I might not fill your ass with silver. Though to be honest, I probably will anyway."

Beady Eyes hissed as he looked at the guns. "I thought you said there were no weapons allowed."

The boss smiled, a cold thing that held no humor. "We don't need weapons to take down a Fae and a human. Only the vampire and the werewolf will be the slightest bit troublesome. And if they wish to live, they'll give the human to me."

I was pretty sure I didn't want to go with them. And that whatever hot water I was in, it was beginning to boil.

I slipped off my heels. There was no way this didn't end in bloodshed.

The thing you have to remember about fighting is comfort is everything. Hollywood movies might show women in martial arts battles while wearing four-inch heels and never mussing their lip gloss, but the truth is heels hurt you and not the enemy. You can't run in them, and they break more often than you would think. They might be great as a projectile weapon, but they were not staying on my feet. They also weren't cheap, and I couldn't afford to replace them. Before my heels even hit the floor, the shifters started changing.

The air around me felt charged with power as they shifted before my eyes. Limbs moved and cracked and reformed. The largest made a loud chuffing sound as he dropped to all fours, golden fur spreading to cover his previously human flesh.

Daniel didn't wait for them to finish. He took the high ground, leaping on to Dev's desk and firing. I winced at the sound, so much louder since it was contained in a closed space.

"Look, Zoey," Neil said as he pulled off his shirt. "That one is shifting into a bear. Idiot, I'm not really afraid of bears. I just love the way they taste."

With that Neil changed so fast I could barely register it. One minute he was my debonair friend, and the next he was a hungry werewolf hot on the trail of some bear meat. The big bear roared, the heat and weight of the sound heavy on my skin. Neil went for his throat, leaping across the room.

I leveled my gun at the third shifter. Daniel was taking on the big guy who was now the largest lion I'd ever seen. The lion roared, and I was sure I could feel the office shake.

That left me and Dev with the smallest of the three, the one who seemed more animal than man. And he was. The third shifter came straight for me, and naturally he turned into a snake. I hate snakes. They're gross and tend to eat their prey alive and feet first for maximum horror. I looked too good tonight to end up in a snake's belly. I took aim and fired, but snakes are shifty fellas even when they measure at least nine feet in length and weigh a good one hundred and fifty pounds.

It looked at me with its dead eyes, and I managed to turn away before he caught me. Snake shifters have the insidious power to catch and hold their prey with those big, dead, black eyes. The very darkness is hypnotic, and you suddenly find yourself powerless to move. I shot every bullet I had into the snake's body.

Unfortunately, he kept coming. I found myself backed into a corner, trying to get a decent shot. Hitting the body hadn't slowed it down and the snake's head moved so fast, whipping back and forth until it was damn near impossible to hit. I could hear the hiss and see those white curved fangs flashing as he neared. My heart pounded, the need to flee riding me strong, but there was nowhere to go.

Dev jumped on the snake's back and started firing straight into his body, proving close contact had some effect. Blood soaked the carpet. The snake jerked, causing Dev to fall backward, his tall body crumpling.

The snake was slower now but infinitely more pissed off. He gave up his pursuit of me and turned on Dev.

I threw down my utterly useless gun and looked around for another weapon.

When fighting with supernatural creatures, I have discovered that guns, while almost always the first line of defense, don't always finish the job. Unlike my poor human body, shifters can handle a lot of bullets. Though I try to keep fighting to a minimum, I have done it enough to know that creativity can shift the balance of power.

I found what I was looking for hanging on the coat rack. I jumped over the chair and managed to avoid Neil, who was wrestling with his opponent. The bear was howling and trying to fight back, but Neil had the advantage. His enemy was on its back, writhing under the power of Neil's bite.

I grabbed the umbrella hanging on the rack and turned back to the snake. My hand accidentally hit a button on the handle, but to my surprise, the umbrella didn't open. Instead, a long, thin blade popped out of the end. I silently thanked Dev for turning his cozy office into a weapons cache, and then it was my turn to jump into the snake's den.

I planted my feet on either side of the snake's body as he was rearing back to strike Dev and positioned myself as close to the head as I could get.

I lifted the sword high and brought it down with all my might. The sword did most of the work, the silver cutting through thick skin and tissue and planting itself in the floor beneath. I threw every bit of my weight into sinking the sword in deep, pinning the snake to the floor, his natural predatory grace caught and useless now.

No one has ever properly explained to me why silver has the effect it does on weres, shifters, and vampires, but right then all that mattered was the fact that it worked. Whether for biblical reasons or because it was an allergic reaction, the snake writhed in obvious pain, and my warm heart was not moved a bit. The snake hissed and twitched the tail end of his body, using it like a whip, trying to strike at me.

Dev scrambled up and pulled yet another sword from under his comfy chair. For a man who claimed to love peace, he was awfully well armed. His hair was a bloody mess, and his clothes were torn, showing off bits and pieces of a nice-looking chest. Dev turned the sword in his hands a few times, obviously relishing the feel of it. He walked straight to the snake and lifted the silver sword with both hands.

"This is a place of peace, asshole." He swung the sword in a perfect arc. The snake's head hit the floor with a satisfying thud. He let the sword relax at his side and gave me a ridiculously sexy smile. "Is it wrong that I find you incredibly hot right now?"

I'd wanted to break out of my rut. The rut was utterly ruined and replaced by sheer panic and an oddly elated feeling. I was definitely alive.

I was about to tell him I didn't mind at all when I noticed that Daniel and the werelion had taken their fight to the balcony. The door leading out to the club was totally ruined. Daniel and the lion hadn't nicely moved their argument outside. They had decimated the structure, putting a massive hole in the wall.

Daniel was in full bloodlust mode. His fangs were long as he pulled his fist back and used his preternatural strength to shove the lion over the metal banister and down to the floor below. The lion flew through the air, but even before he could hit the ground, Daniel leapt after him. I could hear the screams from the crowd below, and then Dev was cursing as he followed Daniel over the balcony, clutching his sword.

I, not being able to physically survive a fall of that magnitude, chose to use the stairs.

The dance floor was in complete chaos by the time I got there. The blood from the werelion's fall managed to arouse some of the more bloodthirsty of the dancers, and all around me shifters were shifting, witches were chanting, and demons were licking their chops. Albert was already on the floor with the rest of the staff trying to control the crowd with water cannons that blasted the clients back and cooled some of the bloodlust. Dev's staff, it seemed, was well trained in the art of riot control.

I ran, pushing my way through the crowd.

The lion lay in the middle of the previously packed dance floor, the glitter of the surroundings marred by blood and death. Blood coated Daniel's hand. His fight with the lion seemed to have ended with him punching his way through the lion's chest cavity.

"Are you okay?" I asked the question as quietly as I could, putting as much calm into my voice as possible.

He grabbed a napkin off one of the tables close to the dance floor and wiped down his hand with precise, controlled movements, his jaw a rigid line. When he was done, he closed his eyes and took a long breath before tucking his formerly perfect white dress shirt back into his slacks. The lion's corpse was a couple of feet away, and I tried not to look at it. Daniel could do plenty of damage without a gun.

Daniel declined to answer me. When he opened his eyes again, he simply picked me up and tossed me over his shoulder in a fireman's hold. My world upended. It was obvious he was through talking to me.

Before I could protest, he turned to Dev. "I'm going to get her out of here until we can figure out who's trying to kill her. Thank you for a lovely evening. Sorry about the destruction."

Dev shouted to Albert, trying to be heard over the anarchy around him. "Get some body bags, and we're gonna need the flame thrower. And there's a werewolf having a late-night snack up in my office. Don't kill him. He's a friendly."

I managed to catch his eye as Daniel hauled me off the dance floor toward the door. He was standing there in the middle of the mayhem, with his shirt ripped and his formerly perfect hair a glorious mess. A cut bled slightly on his bicep, and his lip was a little swollen. He looked delicious, and I was the girl who destroyed his club on our first date. I should have at least had the courtesy to wait until the third or fourth date before unleashing destruction on him. He would surely regret pursuing me.

My neck was killing me, but I tried to get one last look at the man who was almost certainly going to run the next time he saw me. Then he looked up and Dev gave me a slow, sexy smile and winked. I yelled the only thing I could think of.

"Call me!"

Chapter Eight

"I'll drive."

Daniel tossed me in the back seat of his Council-owned Mercedes. A vampire needed to keep up appearances apparently. Daniel was given a yearly allowance from the Council that included an undead friendly apartment, the shiny Benz, and a clothing budget that he was supposed to use for top-of-the-line designer wear. Anything else Daniel had to scratch for like the rest of us. He was a well-dressed bum in a nice car.

I pushed myself off the fine leather and managed to straighten my now ruined dress before Daniel hopped in the front seat and decided to see if the car could go zero to sixty in ten seconds flat. It seemed the commercials didn't lie about that feature. I heard cars honking as Daniel blew through a red light.

"Hey!" I yelled as I hit the leather upholstery a second time. "You don't have to drive like a bat out of hell."

"I have to get you out of here. They just tried to kill you, Zoey." His words were tight. I could see through the rearview mirror that his whole face was locked in an angry expression.

"Does it surprise you? You've been saying you want to kill me for years." For some reason it all seemed funny at that moment. It was completely ridiculous. I laughed at the silliness of the situation. I was a second tier thief at best, but it looked like I had hit the big time. People don't hire assassins unless you're doing something right. I suppose it was the adrenaline rush hitting me, but I couldn't help the laughter that bubbled up.

"Don't you joke about this." Daniel's order cracked through the car. I stopped laughing because Danny hadn't yelled at me like that in years. Since his return, he was exquisitely controlled. He never raised his voice, preferring to use a quiet, condescending tone to show his anger. "Those three tried to kill you, and if Neil and I hadn't been there, they probably would have succeeded."

I noticed the conspicuous absence of credit for Dev's help but chose not to argue. He was right. This was serious, and we needed to talk about it. "We don't know they wanted to kill me. They wanted you to hand me over."

"They weren't inviting you to a tea party, Z," Daniel spat back as he roughly turned the car toward downtown. My apartment was the other way. I was surprised we were going to his place. He had to be really worried to take me to his apartment. "You're bleeding. You're injured. This is out of control, and tomorrow night we're going to fix it."

"It's a scratch, and it's stopped bleeding. I'm fine. Shouldn't we figure out why they wanted me in the first place?" I decided not to point out that we might have been able to answer that question had Daniel not been so quick to kill the lion.

"I know why they wanted you. The only difference between tonight and yesterday when no one was trying to hurt you is that contract with Halfer. It all goes back to that box the demon wants us to steal. Halfer didn't bother to mention there were other interested parties. There's something wrong here. He's keeping something from us, and it will only get worse. You can bet that those assholes were the first wave. Whoever is behind it will use something worse next time. You're leaving town in the morning."

"No, I'm not!" Now I was yelling. "Unless you intend to drug me and force me onto a plane, I don't see what you can do about it."

Daniel didn't answer, and I knew that he wasn't above doing just that. I was going to have to do some serious work during the day to get him off my back because I was done letting Daniel force his will on me. I hadn't let him push me around when we were together, and I was done letting him do it now.

We drove the rest of the way to Daniel's apartment in perfect silence. There was no point in telling him I wanted to go home. He was right, and I wasn't stubborn enough to argue. His complex had actual security since it housed three vampires and had room for visitors. The Council supplied a security team, and the place was warded against unwanted supernatural creatures. Daniel pulled the car into the parking garage and slid it into his space.

I got out and followed him silently into the elevator. He was just trying to protect me, but his interference in my life was starting to chafe. Meeting Dev was a turning point. Dev was someone I could really like.

In a perfect world, there would be no need for a Dev. Daniel and I would be happy, and Dev would be another hot guy, nothing special. But Daniel had changed, and he didn't want that life anymore, at least not with me. The more I thought about it, the angrier I got. And I wasn't sure who I was most angry at—Daniel or myself.

The elevator doors closed, and Daniel punched the number of the floor he wanted. The vampires all lived in below ground apartments for obvious reasons. It was too easy to accidentally open a window and let a stray beam of light burn the hell out of a sleeping vampire. I knew all of this in theory only as I'd never been invited past the lobby of the building before. I didn't know this private garage existed, and it made me feel the weight of the distance between us more than ever. His life was a secret to me, and he wanted to keep it that way. I could feel his anger at having to bring me here. I resented it with all my heart.

"Look, I don't want to taint your precious bat cave with my presence," I bit out. "I'll go up to the lobby and call my father. He'll be thrilled that I was almost killed by assassins. It plays into his every paranoid fantasy. His house is secure."

"Shut up, Zoey." Daniel's back was to me, and I snapped. The least he owed me was to look my way when he insulted me. Maybe I was stubborn enough to argue.

"I don't have to take this crap from you anymore, Daniel. I'm not your girlfriend. I'm not your daughter. Hell, as far as I can tell, I'm not even your friend. I'm not your responsibility and I don't take orders from you, so I'm going to Dad's. You can go to hell."

"I'd like to see you try, sweetheart," Daniel said.

"Try what?"

Daniel turned around, and I took a step back. His fangs were fully out, and his eyes had turned from ordinary blue to a deep, rich sapphire color. The irises bled out, coating his whole eye in that unnatural color. He looked like a gorgeous predator, and he was completely alien to me. "I'd like to see you try to get away from me."

The door opened, breaking our tension. A man stood in the hallway, waiting on the elevator. He wore a stylish blazer over a silk dress shirt and tailored slacks. His wardrobe was almost identical to Daniel's, though he didn't have bloodstains on his white dress shirt. It even looked like he shopped at the same shoe store. I knew instinctively this was a vampire and they followed a dress code. The man started to greet Daniel, but he took one look at me and suddenly Daniel wasn't the only one with fangs.

I felt like the last cupcake in a room full of hungry kids.

Daniel didn't hesitate. He walked straight out of the elevator, took the man by the throat, and shoved him high against the wall. He held the man a good three feet off the floor. His feet twitched as Daniel squeezed.

"Don't you even look at her, Michael." His hand tightened around Michael's throat. "If you so much as think about her, I will rip your head off with my bare hands. Do you understand?"

"Damn it, Dan," the vampire named Michael managed to squeak out. "I was only going upstairs for a newspaper. I'm not trying to hit on anyone, but look at her. I can't help it…she's…she's…"

"Mine," Daniel said, squeezing so tight I thought for a minute I was going to get to see the aforementioned beheading. "She's mine." Daniel released his hold on Michael who clutched his throat, checking for damage. "Get out of here."

Michael obliged, and Daniel practically tossed me through the door of his apartment. I stumbled across the threshold. He threw the door closed, and I heard a series of locks being bolted. He turned back to me, and I could see none of his rage had been spent on Michael. I complained that he was an emotionless robot, but he didn't look like one now. I admit I wasn't the foremost authority on vampires. They tend to be secretive. However, if I knew one thing about them, it is that you shouldn't piss them off.

"You want to know why I don't bring you here? That's why, Zoey." He motioned to the hall outside. "I don't want you walking around here like an open-all-night diner. That was Michael. He was born in 1892 and died during World War I. He's quite the player. Do you know how many women he's gone through? Do you know how many ended up in the hospital because he 'loved' them? Don't even get me started on Alexander. I've thought about staking him myself just so I can sleep all day. I think he might have been Jack the Ripper. Do you have any idea what he would do with you?"

"I think I can guess." Given what I knew about Jack the Ripper, it probably wouldn't be pleasant.

Daniel brought his fist down on his kitchen table. It cracked in two. "This isn't a joke! This is your life. Goddamn it, what is it going to take for you to be serious? What has to happen to get you to take me seriously?"

It was easy to fall back into old habits. Daniel rarely lost his temper before, but when he did, he could be volcanic. I'd found that staying calm was my best bet. I didn't want to add fuel to his fire, so I kept my voice even and patient. "I take you seriously, Daniel. I've spent years waiting for you because I love you. I haven't wasted my youth because I thought you were a laugh."

"That's not what I meant and you know it. When are you going to see the threat I pose, Zoey?" His voice was slightly calmer now.

This was the same excuse he gave me when he returned from France. He was too big a threat to be trusted. He was a killer by nature, and I should keep my distance, watch my back…blah, blah, blah. "Daniel, I don't care what the stupid Council told you. I trust you. I will always trust you."

"You wouldn't if you knew what I want to do to you." He groaned as he reached out and pulled me close. I slammed against him, and he was hard everywhere. It felt so good. I sighed and let my arms slide around his waist. I breathed in his scent, and though I knew it was a trick of my memory, he smelled like the old Daniel. Everything about him seemed like home. The tension of the day melted away as I let myself feel him.

Daniel ran a hand through my hair and pulled my head back, forcing me to look into his eyes. It was a part of the new Daniel he couldn't hide. He wanted me to understand that he wasn't human anymore. "Do you have any idea what you look like to me now? You're so fucking bright. I want your light. I want it so bad. I want to take you, and I want to feed, Zoey. I want to drink until I have my fill, and then I want to fuck you, sweetheart. I want to fuck you so long and so hard you'll forget that there was a time I wasn't inside you. I want to possess you. I want to bend you to my will until you'll do anything I ask. Until you'll die for me."

I was sure in Daniel's mind that this speech of his was supposed to send me screaming from the room and into the arms of someone less obsessive and fangy. I was supposed to see that he had changed. That he was a danger to my life. I was supposed to finally accept that there was a part of Daniel that could do all those things to me, and there was a part that even *wanted* to do those things to me. The problem was I'd accepted that a long time ago and loved him anyway.

The crux of our problem wasn't me accepting Daniel. Daniel had never accepted himself.

I reached up and touched his face, not worried when I grazed those sharp fangs. "Baby, you always wanted that, even when you were human. Not the feeding part, but certainly the rest of it. You might have forgotten, but I remember who you were. Who you still are. You were a manipulative bastard with a secret desire for world domination and a bit of a god complex. You controlled it then, you control it now, and I love you for it. This part of your personality has nothing to do with being a vampire and everything to do with being Daniel Donovan. Don't think you can scare me with the big bad wolf routine. If you want me out of your life, you only have to ask, but don't think you can get me to tell you I'm afraid of you."

Daniel pushed me away and slammed his hands into the wall.

The wall obligingly gave way with a thud. He was going to have to redecorate if he kept it up. "Go take a shower, Zoey. You're covered in blood, and it's making me crazy. Go get cleaned up and I'll get some bandages."

In a desire to save the rest of his furniture, I made a hasty retreat. The apartment wasn't large, and I quickly found the bedroom.

I gasped when I looked at myself in the mirror. I was covered in blood. It wasn't so surprising given the way I'd spent the evening. I opened the bathroom door and turned on the shower.

It didn't make sense that Daniel couldn't trust himself. He'd spent almost an hour with me covered in blood, and I was more than willing to give him a taste, but he sent me away. He possessed remarkable self-control. That couldn't be the reason he rejected me. Something happened to him in France, and it looked like I would never be let in on that secret.

I stepped into the shower, letting the hot water slide across my body. I closed my eyes and let myself remember that night.

* * * *

"Darlin' is there anything I can do for you?" my father asked as I forced my legs to move across the room. If I could make it to the couch, I could sit and not have to worry about things like walking.

I'd been numb all night, but since that moment when I'd looked at that dead body and been forced to confront the fact that Daniel was gone, I hadn't really felt a thing. I was in motion, but there was no meaning to it.

"No." Even to my own ears, my voice sounded flat and foreign.

I didn't need anything. I didn't want anything. I wasn't anything at all.

My father sat down beside me. He put his arms around me, but I couldn't feel them. "I know you won't believe me, but you will get through this, Zoey. Daniel was a great boy, and you'll miss him every day of your life, but the sun is going to come up tomorrow and the day after that. One day it'll be beautiful again. Daniel wouldn't want you wasting away."

I forced myself to hug my father back. My mouth moved mechanically, speaking words I knew would get my dad out of my apartment. "I know, Dad. I'm so grateful you're here for me, but I need some time to myself."

It took a few more gentle proddings, but finally, reluctantly, my father left, and I was alone at last.

The apartment was silent, and I knew it would always feel that way for me now. It wouldn't be filled with music and Daniel yelling at me to come look at some stupid thing he'd found on the Internet. God, I'd resented having to get up and leave what I was doing to watch YouTube with him, but now I would give anything to hear him calling to me one more time.

I didn't give a fuck if the sun came up tomorrow. He was gone, and I didn't know where he was. I always knew where he was. He always told me or called me to let me know, but he hadn't called me to let me know where he was now. He had left the apartment to pick up some food and…then he was gone.

It ate me alive that I didn't know where he was.

I sat there with no thought to the time passing. I didn't think about Daniel and all that he had lost. I didn't think about his lost potential or all his dreams that wouldn't come to fruition. I thought about myself. I thought about having to live fifty or more years without him holding me and telling me he loved me. I would miss loving him, but even more, I would miss the way he loved me. He was full throttle, unlike any other man I'd ever met. When he loved me, there hadn't been anyone else in the world except the two of us. He hadn't looked at other girls, though he'd had opportunities. He'd always said I was enough. He'd made me better, and I didn't know how to continue without that. I would spend the rest of my life waiting to see him again, waiting to go wherever he'd gone.

But the rest of my life didn't have to be so long. Did it? Just as the dark thought started to fill me, I heard a voice.

"God, you're so fucking beautiful."

I could hear him. He'd always told me I was beautiful.

"I need you not to freak on me, Z." Daniel's voice. It wasn't a weak whisper. For a moment, I wondered if I'd gone crazy. It wouldn't surprise me, and the truth was, if I could be with Daniel again, I wouldn't care if it was real or not.

"Why would I freak?" It was a dream. I had fallen asleep on the couch and naturally I dreamed that Daniel had come back to me. Somewhere in the back of my mind, I realized I would have to wake up and deal with his death all over again, so I was going to enjoy my dream while it lasted. "Come here and hold me."

Daniel kept to the shadows. "I thought you would be more upset. Did they not tell you, baby? Wow. I thought for sure they would call you. This is going to be difficult to explain. First off, the car is totaled, and I know this sounds bad, but that's actually the not so bad part."

"Why would I be upset to see you?" I asked, though I was actually getting antsy. Shouldn't Daniel obey me in my dreams? It was my fantasy, and I wanted everything to be perfect. I stood up to get closer to him, but I saw him retreat from me. "Damn it, Danny, I don't know how much time we have. I could wake up any minute, so please get over here. Don't make me chase you. I don't think I could handle that right now."

"Zoey, this isn't a dream. I know you've had a shock, but I need you to come out of it now. I need you to help me figure this out. Everything is weird now. You glow, baby. I don't know why you glow."

"There's nothing to figure out," I said soothingly. "You're back, and I'm happy. That's all I want to feel now. This is my dream."

Daniel stepped out of the darkness, and it was my turn to retreat. "If this were a dream, baby, would you bring me back like this?"

I was startled out of my fog. He was standing in our living room. He was alive. He totally had fangs. Long and white, they emerged from his mouth, caressing his bottom lip.

"Holy shit, Danny, you're a vampire." I walked toward him. My initial shock fled, replaced with an amazing sense of wonder. I felt a smile spreading across my face as I reached up to feel his skin against my palm. His eyes were strange and there were those fangs, but it was my Daniel, and he was alive...well, he was here. I wouldn't argue with it. I knew a bit about vampires. I knew how they could rise, and I had just won the fucking lottery. "I saw you at the morgue. Were you pretending? You seemed dead to me."

He pulled me to him, and I felt his sigh of relief as our bodies fit together. This was where I belonged, wrapped up in him, his scent filling my brain. His hands moved on my back, pulling us closer together. His dance with death hadn't slowed him down. His hips moved a bit, rubbing his erection against me. This was a deep intimacy I no longer took for granted.

Daniel's lips pressed against my forehead. "I woke up about an hour ago. I was on a table, turned out to be an autopsy table. Let me tell you, *CSI* makes that shit look glamorous. It was horrible. They cut my chest open. I had to...push it all back together. Luckily, they hadn't actually started taking stuff out yet. Surprised the autopsy guy, though."

I only got about half of what he was saying. I was too busy letting the truth of his return wash over me. I understood the process of becoming a vampire. I also knew how rare it was, and it was even more surprising it had happened while Daniel was so young. I let my head nuzzle into his chest and heard...

"Your heart is beating." It was the most glorious sound I'd ever heard.

He gave me an embarrassed smile and didn't even try to hide his fangs. "I kinda ate the autopsy guy. He's not dead or anything. Maybe a little anemic and god, he tasted horrible. I'm only feeding on chicks from now on. They have to taste better."

I hadn't exactly liked that guy. He'd been a bit of an ass, but the enormity of it all hit me in that moment. Daniel had been dead. Dead. Gone from this Earth. I'd begun the process of mourning him. Hell, I'd thought about joining him.

The tears I'd feared would never come burst forth in a tidal wave.

Daniel stopped cracking wise and swept me up, hauling me against his chest. He carried me to our bed and held me while I cried. He talked, but there was nothing like sarcasm in his words now.

First, he told me how the car seemed to come out of nowhere, and he'd only had enough time to think about me and how much he would miss me and us, and to wonder in that final moment who was going to take care of me. He told me how confused and scared he'd been when he'd first stirred. He told me how the hunger had coursed through him and the horror of realizing what he needed to do. He told me the only thing that got him through it all was the need to get back to me, to our home, to our life.

And I cried. I sobbed because I had lost him and I had no idea how to live without him. He was my world, the steady hand that held mine. I'd known him since I was a child, drawn to him even before I understood what it meant to like a boy. He'd been my friend, my boyfriend, my only lover, my everything, and then he'd been gone.

After the longest time, my tears subsided. We were lying together on our bed, the piece of crap bed we'd bought at a garage sale, our legs tangled together.

"Z, please forgive me."

There was nothing to forgive. "I don't care, Danny. You're here. It's all that matters. I don't care about the vampire thing, but we need to talk about the Council."

I wasn't totally stupid. I knew the Council trained vampires.

"I don't know, Z. I don't know exactly how it works. I can only promise that if they take me away, I'll come back for you. If they make me move, we'll go somewhere new. We're going to be okay." He nuzzled against my hair. "This doesn't change a damn thing. I want you more than ever. Baby, you have to tell me. Am I a monster?"

He couldn't think that. He was Daniel. My love. "If you're a monster, then you're my monster."

"God, Zoey, the hunger. You can't imagine it," he whispered. I could feel the tension in his body. "Just being near you makes me crazy. You're really beautiful, Z."

I sat up and looked down at him. He was the beautiful one. Death had taken all the tiny imperfections humans possessed and turned him into the ideal version of himself. His eyes were dark, and I could feel the need coming off his body. His pupils were slightly dilated and so blue I thought I could get lost in them. Desire flooded me. Every girl part I had went soft and wet. I wasn't sure what he was doing, but the air around me felt soft. My nipples peaked, straining against my shirt.

It was all coming from him. Desire poured off him, like a wave rolling over me.

He wanted. He was hungry and I could feed him. I wanted to feed him.

I shrugged out of the shirt I was wearing, and his hands began to shake. I didn't think about the implications. I only knew he needed blood and I had plenty.

"Do you think it hurts?" I wasn't scared of the prospect. I simply wanted to know what to expect.

Daniel pulled away. "No, this isn't a good idea, baby."

"Don't you want me?" If he didn't, I wasn't sure what I would do.

"I don't want to hurt you."

"You won't." If there was one thing I knew in the world, it was that Daniel Donovan wouldn't hurt me. "I trust you. I love you, Danny."

Daniel pulled me to him, and I could feel my heart racing. I should have been afraid, but all I could think of was how excited I was. I thought I'd lost him forever, but I was going to make love with him. I was seventeen again, and Daniel and I were discovering the world together. We'd had no one but each other. The world had changed and we would figure it out all over again.

I got to my knees, getting rid of my bra in the process. With anyone else, I was insecure, but Daniel was my home. Daniel was love and safety and all the good things of the world in one package. I could be naked and exposed and perfectly happy because he never looked at me with anything but desire.

"Zoey." My name was a benediction on his lips. A promise of a future I thought I'd lost. "Be sure."

"I'm always sure of you." I reached out and touched his shoulders, smooth skin covered by muscles. His flesh was cool, but his touch ignited my senses. I could feel the blood flowing through my veins.

I understood why he found that first feeding so distasteful. There was a sexual element about it that would bother Daniel. The room was heavy with anticipation, and Daniel's fangs were full and large. They weren't the only part of him that wanted to play. His erection tented his pants, his cock pointing my way.

"God, baby, you smell so good." He groaned as he nuzzled my neck, the sound skimming across my flesh. He ran his tongue across the smooth skin, and I shivered in anticipation. I let my hands roam. It was like his whole body had tightened, reforming into a perfect version of Daniel.

I could feel his cock against my belly. He moved against me as though he couldn't quite help himself. I couldn't either. It felt right to be near him. Perhaps his death simply focused my consciousness to him, but there was a deep, physical connection that hadn't been there before. I loved Daniel, but this closeness felt like something more.

It was right and good to feed him.

He leaned over and kissed me, his mouth covering my own. I was deeply aware of how much bigger he was than me. I was small in his embrace, but that was all right. He would never hurt me. I was his. I was precious. Our tongues tangled, the feeling heightened beyond anything I'd known before. Daniel seemed to inhale me, his every cell focused on my body, my soul.

I was aware of my own heart. I could hear it beating in my chest, making a rhythm we could move to. My heart was visceral, real in a way it hadn't been before. It pumped blood through my body. Blood that kept me alive. Blood that would feed my Daniel. My heart was the center of our universe.

Daniel's eyes glowed in the dim light as he rubbed our foreheads together. "I love you. I've always loved you. I don't remember a time when I wasn't full of you, baby. I think I loved you before I knew you."

I let my head fall to the side to give him better access. A delicious wave of desire pulsated across my skin. His magic. Vampires had ways to persuade their blood partners, to make the feeding process a pleasurable one. He was seducing me with his newfound skill, and I let it wash over my whole being. His arms wrapped around me. Our legs tangled together. I wasn't sure where he ended and I began. We were so close.

He growled, the sound low from the back of his throat. The

moment lengthened, blood pulsing, heart pounding, body aching.

And then he struck, fangs sinking in, finding the vein. Pleasure, pure and undiluted, coursed through me. My womb fluttered, orgasm blooming from the center of my body. I was with Daniel in that moment, feeling the glory of blood and trust and the promise implicit in the exchange.

We were more than we'd been before. I'd changed as surely as Daniel had. I was more than the woman who had wept and thought about joining her lover. Larger. The moment Daniel fed, I'd grown larger somehow.

He pulled at my neck, and another wave crested and darkness took me.

Warmth and heat surrounded me when I came back to consciousness.

"Welcome back, princess," he said, smiling down at me.

My back sank into the mattress, Daniel's weight pressing me down. My whole body was languid, utterly submissive to his. And I'd lost my pants. And underwear. And everything. He'd stripped me down and lost his own clothes and our bodies slid against each other, skin to skin.

"Wrap your legs around me." Daniel rubbed his chest against mine, the hard length of his erection nestled at my core. "Fuck, Z, you're so wet. That smells good, too. It's like I'm surrounded by your light."

I liked the sound of that. The whole world seemed like an erotic dream. I did as he asked, drawing my legs together with him in the center. It didn't take much for him to twist his hips and join us together.

This was where I belonged, with Daniel inside me. I let my hands run down to his ass to cup those muscular cheeks. He was my playground. And I was inside him, too. My blood flowed through his body, keeping him alive.

"You feel so good, Z." He sounded a bit drunk, but then I felt that way, too.

I twisted my hips, trying to take him deeper. He felt so good, rocking his cock back and forth, playing in my pussy.

He stared straight down at me, our eyes locking as he thrust in. We were so connected. I could practically feel his pleasure, and I wanted to give him mine.

And then he was Daniel again, his lips curling up and those dimples creasing his face. "I think we're going to like this life, Z."

I thrust up, impaling myself on him, fire flashing through me. Yes. This was going to be an adventure.

He leaned down, and his perfect lips found mine. I could taste the faintest hint of metal and realized it was blood. I licked at his lips, and he went a little crazy. His hips set a punishing rhythm that made me moan and beg. He pressed into me, bringing me to the edge over and over. I wrapped myself around him because he was the only real thing in the world now.

Daniel groaned and ground down, hitting my clitoris and sparking heat through my body.

Sex had been good, but this was something beyond any orgasm I'd had before. This was flying on a jet, when I'd only ever been on a bus. He finally found that perfect spot and let his cock glide over it, and I took off.

I held him so close as he released his own control and let himself fall. It was all right. We were safe there together.

He held me the rest of the night, telling me over and over how much he loved me. About an hour before dawn, they came and took him away from me.

I fought and screamed and, in the end, I begged.

It didn't matter. He was gone again, and I was left with nothing but questions.

* * * *

I turned off the shower and tried to shake the memories. I shivered since the shower had gone cold a while back, but I hadn't noticed until now. I'd been lost in the memory of the last time Daniel and I were happy. Years had passed since that moment when they hauled him from my arms, but I was still stuck there.

The thought of Dev crossed my mind. Dev was a different road, one that might not have closed yet. Was I brave enough to give it a real try?

I pushed open the door to the shower and wrapped myself in a towel. There was a clean T-shirt sitting on the countertop along with a first aid kit, and I wondered if Daniel had heard me crying. The wound in my shoulder had bled profusely but it wasn't deep. It didn't need more than antibiotic cream and a square bandage. I pulled the T-shirt over my head and went about the business of drying my hair. The night weighed on me, and my earlier adrenaline rush fled a long time ago. It was only now that I wondered exactly where Daniel was planning on putting me. I knew there was only one bedroom, and if he thought I was taking the couch, he had another think coming.

I opened the door to the bedroom and indeed there was a man on the bed, but it wasn't Daniel.

"I have chocolate chip or peanut butter." Neil held up two bags of cookies. He was dressed in pajamas that Dick Van Dyke might have worn. They were a pale blue and I would have sworn he'd had them pressed. "Daniel called me and told me to get my ass over here. Rude, much? Anyway, he's sleeping in a body bag in the den and I'm supposed to be making sure you don't do anything stupid tomorrow like leave the apartment."

So Daniel had brought in reinforcements. "You're supposed to babysit me? I should warn you, unless you plan on tying me up, I'm leaving in the morning."

His eyes lit up. "Cool, what are we going to do?"

I laughed as I sat on the bed. "You're a crappy babysitter."

"I know. It's like letting the fox watch the chickens. I have no idea what he was thinking." Neil's eyes were wide with incredulity. "The whole time he was talking I was thinking about all the things we could do after we stole his credit cards."

I found it difficult to remain morose around Neil. "We're not stealing his credit cards. We're going to find out who tried to kill me and deal with them. You don't have to go with me. I don't need a babysitter."

Neil thought about that for a minute, his eyes turning serious. He reached out and covered my hand with his. He'd only worked with me for a little over a year, but we'd become close. "I know I come off as superficial, and I am on most levels. Don't try to deny it. I'm all right with it. I like pretty things and pretty people, and I like to look at myself. But there's more to me than that. I would never let you go off like that all by yourself. I don't have family anymore, not the blood kind. They tossed me out a long time ago. The way I see it, you and Sarah and Daniel are all I have. I like to think of you as a sister, Zoey. Anyway, what I'm trying to say is I've got your back. I won't let you down, or if I do it'll be because I died trying. Of course, I'll look damn good while I do it."

For the second time that night, I teared up, but this time Neil was there with cookies and a shoulder to cry on.

Chapter Nine

The next morning, I sat across from Neil at a diner near my apartment. Daniel had seriously underestimated the not so delicate balance between a werewolf's loyalty and a werewolf's seemingly endless gut. Neil had been the one to lead the charge out the door the minute we discovered that Daniel's kitchen was beautiful and elegant and utterly devoid of food.

Neil did not do well without food.

Neil ordered pancakes, bacon, sausage, a Denver omelet, biscuits and gravy, and a cheeseburger. I requested a half a grapefruit and an English muffin, but then I didn't have that good old werewolf hyper-metabolism. Daniel couldn't have been thinking straight when he ordered Neil to keep me in all day. Neil couldn't go more than a couple of hours without a side of beef or he dissolved into a whiny ball of Ralph Lauren sportswear.

I was glad for the sportswear, though. Without Neil's blazer covering my sadly worn dress, I'm afraid I would have attracted a lot of attention. I'd gotten most of the blood out, but there was still a nice hole where the flying stake had gotten through.

"So what's the plan?" Neil asked as he dug into his über breakfast.

I didn't have to ask which plan he was talking about. It was the plan that kept me up most of the night and well into morning.

"I have a few hours until Daniel wakes up. Halfer isn't answering his phone."

Neil shook his head. "But aren't you supposed to be able to contact him?"

That was the million dollar question. "Maybe he knows I want to give him the money back. Maybe if I give back every penny, I can get out of this contract. I'll even hand over all the plans we've made to the next crew he finds."

"But Daniel already got the uniforms and everything," Neil whined slightly around an enormous mouthful of pancakes.

"And I'm sure the new crew will be thrilled with his hard work. I intend to be as helpful as possible to whoever comes after." I took a slow sip of my coffee. "But I have to find the fucker first. I talked to Albert first thing this morning. He thinks he can have a name by this afternoon."

"So you get Halfer's real name, you call him to your hand, you give back the cash, and then Daniel won't shove you into a bomb shelter somewhere." Neil neatly summed up my plan.

"Yep." It was a good plan. It was a plan that would probably fail, and I would still end up in said bomb shelter or wherever vampires shoved their troublesome ex-lovers. But I was determined to try.

"I thought I would find you here." Sarah walked up to our booth. She smiled and sat beside me, pulling me into a slightly awkward half hug. "I tried your apartment, but no one was there."

"We spent the night at Daniel's," Neil said between bites.

Sarah's eyes went wide. "Seriously? He's been back for two years, and he's never invited anyone back to his place. What's it like?"

"Very clean," I said.

"Boring," Neil said at the same time.

Nothing at all like my Daniel. But then he wasn't mine anymore. "I bet the rest of the apartments in the building look exactly alike. Vamps don't seem big on individuality."

Neil's eyes lit up as he looked at Sarah. "Daniel's apartment is bland, but our night wasn't."

He launched into a recounting of the events from the night before, but my mind was still on Daniel.

I spent a lot of time the night before thinking about that apartment. It was cold and impersonal. It was aesthetically pleasing in an *Architectural Digest* way, but there was nothing of the owner reflected in the home. The neatness of it bothered me, too. Daniel had been many things, but neat was not one of them. I had no rosy reflections of living with Daniel. He'd been a slob. The corner of the apartment where he had his desk had always been an intricate disaster area.

It was a miracle he'd been able to get out the door with books in hand most mornings. It annoyed me at times. Daniel's brain was wired differently. He could take a subject he knew nothing about and become a near expert in a short time. College had been like Disney World for Daniel.

There hadn't been a single book in his apartment. I guess that bugged me most of all.

"Tell me you didn't eat the bear." Sarah, the vegan, shivered at the thought.

Neil simply grinned. "Well, he was trying to kill me at the time."

Sarah's voice came out on a huffy breath. "Do you know how close some bears are to going on the endangered species list?"

Neil snorted, a sound he made elegant. "Sarah, he wasn't some polar bear. He was a schmo from Jersey from the sound of his accent."

"Well, I don't think that gives you the right to eat him," Sarah said primly. Today she was wearing a vintage Clash T-shirt over a micro-mini and brilliant purple tights. A sassy beret covered her shock of pink hair. She turned her attention to me, and her expression changed. Her dark eyes glittered. "Speaking of horribly murdering people, how was your date with the man I'm going to kill? I hope you enjoyed it because I have a few things to say to him the next time we meet."

"He was so sorry, Sarah." With everything that happened last night, I managed to forget how humiliated Sarah had been. "His name is Dev, and he feels awful about the whole thing. He's actually a nice guy. He's just not that great at magic."

"I looked like an idiot. I actually drooled, Z," she complained. "He made my mouth water. Daniel had to stop me from chasing after him. I also wanted to kill you for taking my man. I thought of him as 'my man' like I was stuck in a Tammy Wynette song. Do you know how humiliating that is for a feminist?"

"Again with the sorry." I wasn't sure what else to say. I would have been angry, too. But I wanted to see Dev again, and I didn't want to worry about Sarah murdering him.

Sarah's brown eyes narrowed as she thought about her problem. "You know, the most brilliant witches are almost always female. There's something about the female psyche that lends itself to witchcraft. Can you imagine the hexes they created and what those hexes can do to a penis? Have you ever seen one twist into a pretzel?"

"Ouch!" Neil waggled a finger her way. "You don't want to do that to him. He's really cool and super rich. He also happens to own Ether."

"The club you were at was Ether? OMFG!" Sarah was squealing now, and I felt old. Though I was only a few years older than the pair across from me, sometimes their ability to switch gears emotionally shocked me.

"Good, so you leave his penis in the proper shape, and I'll make sure you get into Ether. That is if it's still standing after the number we did on it last night." Albert had only told me that Dev was alive and still asleep. It made sense. He ran a nightclub. I was lucky Albert was an early riser.

"I've been trying to get into that place since it first opened. Everyone says it's awesome. If you can get me on the list, I will take that as a favor." She smiled, and I could see she was already thinking about what she would wear and what color she should dye her hair. "By the way, I did you a favor, silly girl. You totally forgot to lock your door. It was wide open when I got there this morning. I was surprised since you're usually so careful. It's okay, though. I locked it on my way out. It didn't look like anything was missing, not that you have much anyone would want. Have you seen that TVs don't need rabbit ears anymore?"

Sarah kept talking, but I shoved my way out of the booth, my brain hanging on one thought. Someone opened my apartment door. Daniel wouldn't have left it unlocked. No way. No how. He was careful, ruthlessly so.

I slammed out of the diner and crossed the street at a dead run, desperate to get to my apartment.

A thief can never be too careful. Given our internal knowledge of how many crappy things can come between a person and said person's prized possessions, one might think a thief would be particularly careful about security. One would normally be right.

On any regular night, I have what I like to call my security ritual. It consists of securing several doors with a variety of locks. There are three deadbolts, two keyless, and another two security chains. The chains aren't truly meant to keep anyone out as even a human could simply kick through them, but the actual chains themselves are made of silver and built to burst on impact, hopefully hitting whoever decided it was a good idea to kick in my door. There are several wards in my apartment meant to keep out various and sundry undesirables. Sarah even set up one on my front door that made humans wary about knocking. It made it hard to get pizza delivered, but on the plus side the Jehovah's Witnesses stopped pestering me.

There was a separate ward on my bedroom, and I knew for a fact that I didn't take it off or knock it down before I left the night before. I placed the ward on my bedroom door because when I had something important, I kept it under my bed. My father made fun of my hiding place, but it was more complex than simply shoving something in between the mattress and floor and hoping no one glanced there looking for dust bunnies. My heavy antique four-poster sat on a thick rug. If someone managed to push aside the bed and roll up the rug, they would have to look for the seams in the wood to find the door that leads to my safe.

That safe was my baby. I spent everything I had on it. It was custom made, with three-inch thick steel walls and nylon wheels to make the noise of the serrated tumbler wheels almost soundless. I eschewed electronic devices in favor of solid structure. I picked this apartment because of its placement on the first floor.

When I moved here, Daniel helped me rip up the flooring and tear up the foundation to install the safe. Sarah and Neil knew the safe existed, but only Danny, my father, and I knew the combo.

There was five hundred thousand dollars in that safe right now. My hands shook as I opened the door to my apartment. There was no way anyone could find the safe, much less open it and take the contents. I said this over and over like a silent prayer.

I stepped into the living room and breathed a sigh of relief. There wasn't anything out of order. It was exactly as I had left it. Surely if someone had broken in they would have left a horrible path of destruction.

"Is everything okay?" Sarah asked, breathing heavily. It was obvious she'd been running to try to keep up. "I'm so sorry. I thought you forgot to lock it." She ran her hands across the walls. "The wards are still strong. Even without the locks, they should be enough to keep people out."

"It isn't people she's worried about, dearie." Neil walked in, inhaling deeply through his nose. For someone like Neil, scent was a multilayered object and needed to be analyzed. "There's no brimstone. I smell vampire, witch, your dear self, that delicious faery of yours and...hmm...Irish whiskey."

"Dad was here." My dad liked his whiskey.

"That explains it then," Neil said, seemingly satisfied with his analysis. "No one else."

I let my shoulders sag in relief. My whole plan depended on being able to return the money to Lucas Halfer. I still wasn't sure it would even work, but I needed that money to be able to hope there was a way out. Without it, the job became difficult. There was still equipment to buy and people to bribe. Thievery, when done properly, was not cheap.

"Good, then we can relax." Sarah flopped down on the sofa. "We should probably get started on the prelims for the job. I have an in at the hotel. Bruce, that guy I dated about six months ago, is one of the assistant managers. I gave him this great sob story about a loan shark and getting tossed out of my apartment, so he's giving me and my roommate some cleaning shifts starting this week. Hope you look good in gray, Zoey."

"We're not doing the job," I said sharply. Something still felt off. I couldn't put my finger on it, but there was something wrong.

Sarah looked at me like I'd gone insane. "We can't back out. That's tantamount to breaking the contract."

"I haven't signed the contract, not really." I absently looked around, trying to figure out what was wrong. "The way I look at it, until I actually spend the money, I should be able to return it all. There's been no real exchange if I give every cent of the money back."

She twirled a piece of pink hair, winding it around her finger. "I don't know if that will work."

"Don't even try," Neil advised her with a sigh. "I spent most of last night trying to convince her, and she isn't listening. Something about our immortal souls or something. Immortal souls won't buy baby wolf a new car."

I took Neil by the arm and started to pull him into the bedroom. I wouldn't be satisfied until I saw it was there with my own eyes.

"Move that bed for me." I could do it myself, but why bother when Neil wouldn't even break a sweat?

"I can make a bed move, honey. I can make the earth move when I put my mind to it, but you're not my type," Neil said with a snap of his fingers.

"Now." I growled, not interested in wasting time with Neil's humor.

"Yes, ma'am." He effortlessly shoved the heavy bed halfway across the room. Before I could bark out my next order, he rolled the rug up. "See, Zoey, everything is fine."

I knelt down and pushed at the floor. The hidden door popped up, and there was my lovely safe. It was secure. And yet I still found my fingers spinning the wheel.

"Is everything all right?" Sarah asked from the door.

"It's fine," Neil replied as I heard the final notch click into place. "Zoey is just being careful."

But Zoey hadn't been careful. No, Zoey had been the opposite of careful I discovered as I pulled the door open and looked into my lovely safe. At least the bastard, whoever it was, had left my guns.

They were gleaming in the dim light like a lonely beacon.

"Shit." Neil looked down into the safe that no longer contained any money in it.

I could feel myself start to shake and then the tears started. I hated the way I always cried when I got really angry, but there was nothing I could do about it. Everything I'd worked for was gone. My soul was in question. I could spend the rest of eternity on the Hell plane with my father saying, "I told you so."

"Zoey," Neil pulled me out of my nightmare momentarily. He was breathing in, looking for a scent. He shook his head in confusion. "Was your father in here last night?"

"No, I don't think he's been in my bedroom in months." My father rarely came to my place. The night before had been one of three times he'd ever been in my apartment. I usually went to his house.

Sarah shook her head. "He left with me, and neither one of us went into her room. After you left with the hot faery, we were here for maybe ten minutes."

Neil frowned. "If your father wasn't here, then why does the whole room smell like whiskey?"

I let the door slam with a satisfying thud, but not until I pulled out my faithful Ruger. I made sure to grab an extra mag. I needed to be ready, after all.

I had a date with dear old Dad.

Chapter Ten

I drove through the manicured lawns of North Dallas, anger rising steadily with every mile. Driving up Mockingbird Lane, the traffic was always rough, even in the middle of the day, but it bothered me more than usual. I took a hard left the first chance I got and sped through the expensive neighborhood my father had called home for the last thirteen years.

Sometime around the time Daniel's father died, my own father decided to get serious about putting down roots. In our world, that meant being a big enough predator that he didn't need to be on the run. When the rest of the world fears your talents enough, they tend to leave you alone. My father carefully cultivated his reputation. Some of it was true, and a whole lot of it was the product of his devious, inventive mind, but the important thing was the world's perception of Harry Wharton. He was a bastard with a cold heart who got the job done and got rid of anyone who was in the way. Those beneath him on the food chain feared him and those above him respected him enough to leave him alone. There were some powerful people out there who owed Harry Wharton, and to Dad's credit, he knew how to hold those vouchers to his best advantage. To the supernatural underworld, Harry Wharton was a powerful man.

I, however, knew he was just a horny old bastard who loved his whiskey a little too much, and twenty-year-old girls way too much.

There was one thing in Harry Wharton's life that held his heart, and that was me. Sometimes this was a blessing, as every Christmas he showered me with gifts, but at that moment, it felt like a curse. He'd been meddling in my life for the last several years, and I was ready for it to stop.

It had all started, as most of the crappy things in my life, with Daniel's death. Up until then, Dad was willing to cede protection of me to Danny. He trusted Danny and loved him like a son and knew that Danny would never let anything happen to me. Since his turn, Dad had decided to be overprotective once again. He'd interceded on my behalf during jobs when I first started working. I suppose that in a way it helped to build my reputation, but having Daddy bail me out when I could have handled it on my own rankled.

But this was the last time, I thought as my rage threatened to turn volcanic. He'd meddled in my life for the last time. This wasn't only my fate he was messing with now. It was Daniel's and Neil's and Sarah's fates as well. I led this crew, and I made the decisions. No wonder the demon had chosen me as his bitch when my own father thought he could manipulate me so easily.

"Sweetie…" Neil said, worry evident in his voice. "Maybe we should stop and get a glass of wine—or maybe three—and talk about this. You seem tense. You know you shouldn't go see your dad when you're this pissed off."

"Neil is right." Sarah chimed in from the back seat. "You need to calm down. I'm sure your dad was taking it someplace he thought was safer. He's trying to protect you."

"Well, he needs to stop thinking about protecting me and start wondering about who can protect him," I said between clenched teeth as I pulled into the circular driveway. My heart raced, but I chalked it up to adrenaline. So I was mad—madder than I'd ever been—but I had the right to be mad. I didn't look back as I slammed the car door. The crepe myrtles that lined the drive usually held my attention at this time of year, but today I blew by their glorious blooms without so much as a glance. I used my key and threw the heavy front door open.

"Dad!" I yelled up the stairs. "Get your drunk Irish ass down here this minute and give me my money!"

I passed through the foyer. Somewhere along the way, one of my father's assistants had decorated it in what passed for post-modern, but I ignored the art and tasteful accents as my impatience grew by the moment. I hit the stairs, taking them two at a time, which wasn't easy given my short stature. I heard Neil and Sarah behind me but paid them no mind. I just wanted that money back in my possession. I realized my hands were shaking and the briefest of thoughts flitted through my brain.

Something wasn't right and I knew it, but the overwhelming emotion I felt shoved aside that bit of logic.

I needed to get that money. That was all that mattered.

My father's office was the first room at the top of the stairs. This was his private office. Dad kept two. The downstairs office was where he took clients and held meetings, and the second was a private office upstairs where he went about his business. The second floor office contained all the good stuff. This was where he kept his books on arcane treasures and magic, and all the files he compiled on various people of import. It was where the weapons were hidden and where the skeletons were kept. Well, there was only one actual skeleton, but he tried to keep a careful eye on it because if it ever woke up…

"Zoey, what are you doing here?" Christine came out of the private office dressed in a too short, too tight skirt that she undoubtedly thought looked professional. Christine was one of those girls who was actually quite intelligent but seemed so unsure of herself, it took a while to realize she had a brain.

"Where is he?" I didn't want to deal with Christine. Christine hadn't taken my money.

She shrank back a bit at my tone. "He's still in bed. He's been sick all morning."

I turned and dismissed her as I walked down the hallway straight to his bedroom. Christine would know he'd been sick since she shared that bedroom with him. The minute I moved out to go to college, the first in a long line of twenty-something assistants had moved in with my dad. Christine was the latest. Most of them knew very little about my father's actual business. He billed himself as a private detective and security specialist. He tried to keep his "girls" out of the darker aspects of the work.

"I actually think something might be wrong with him." Christine hurried to catch up with me. "I was about to call you to see if you could help."

Though it was starting to get difficult to think, I stopped. "Call a doctor. I can't help him."

"I was going to call you because a doctor isn't going to know what to do with this. I found this in your dad's pocket. If this is what I think it is, it could explain why he's acting so weird." She held up a small bag, about the size of a human hand. It was made of canvas, and I could guess what was inside. It was what anyone in the know would call a hex bag, or a gris-gris bag, depending on what part of the magical world you happened to be in. A hex bag accompanied a spell a witch was serious about. It kept the spell active as long as it remained close to the object of the spell. It was filled with lots of gross stuff like bloody bones and hair and herbs you probably wouldn't want on your Sunday dinner.

I took it from Christine and tossed it to Sarah. A disturbing sensation tingled against my palm for the single moment it was in my hand. Sarah caught it and immediately took inventory. While Sarah was studying the contents of the bag, I looked Christine over with renewed respect. She must have something if Dad trusted her enough to start to educate her in the arcane ways.

"He won't come out of his room." Christine looked toward his bedroom door. "He wouldn't let me in. He said he was sick, but he won't let me call a doctor or even unlock the door so I can take his temperature. The truth is, he sounds a little crazy. He keeps talking about demon kind and protecting his own. His own what?"

Sarah poked through the contents of the bag with her finger. "It's standard stuff. I'm betting this is either his hair or more likely yours. Nope. It looks like both."

"Mine?"

Spells tend to work best if you have something of the person you are working the spell on. The absolute best "possession" a witch can work with is DNA. There is nothing more personal than DNA, and we drop pieces of ourselves all the time. I would love to think that I would remember if someone had come up and yanked a chunk of hair out, but more than likely all the witch would need to do is follow me for a few hours to get what she needed. I'd gotten a haircut the day before.

Sarah held it up to the light. "Well, this one is your color, and the length is right. I really think it's yours. There's also some gray hairs in here. Those would be your dad's."

The twitch in my hands was getting worse, and I felt tears starting to prick behind my eyes. I was close to losing control, and I didn't like the feeling one bit. If I could make sure the money was all right, then all of this would be over. I had to find it. I had to protect it and make sure it was never stolen from me again.

"Are you all right?" Neil stood behind Sarah. He'd been quiet the whole time, as though he wasn't sure exactly what to do.

"No, I'm not fine. He has my money," I screamed, and I was surprised at that since I hadn't meant to say that, much less scream at Neil. The closer I got to my father, the worse I started to feel.

I needed to see the money, to feel it in my hands and then everything would be fine. A little voice was whispering my head. It was saying *get the money or die*. If I didn't get that money, the people I loved would be in grave danger.

I turned from Neil and Sarah and Christine and headed straight for my father's bedroom door. On my way, I managed to retrieve the gleaming Ruger from my shoulder holster. The weight of it in my hand felt like the caress of a security blanket.

Once my father understood that I was serious, he would give me the money and everything would be fine. If he chose to be unreasonable, I would simply kill my father and then I would have the money. It was as simple as that. I didn't stop and worry that I'd decided to kill my father. It made sense in my increasingly chaotic mind.

I picked up speed halfway down the hall. Unlike many of the other doors in the house, I happened to know that my father's bedroom door wasn't reinforced with metal. It was a simple wooden door that had come with the house and he'd never quite gotten around to replacing it. In other words, it was vulnerable. The thing about doors that not many people realize is that a door is the equivalent of a board balanced on two cinderblocks. If you hit any wooden door in the right place with the right amount of force, then locks don't mean a damn thing. You can have deadbolts, chains, whatever piece of metal makes you feel better, and it won't matter because the person who really wants to get in has physics on their side.

And it was on my side this time because I wanted to get through that door. I hit the door at a sprint, my shoulder leading the way, and threw my body at the dead center of that three-inch block of wood. I didn't even think about the pain as the door cracked inward. Unfortunately, it isn't like in the movies. The door doesn't explode unless someone puts supernatural strength behind it. It kind of cracks on the first go. It usually requires a couple of blows to make a hole the size of the human body. Unfortunately, I didn't have the time for a second go because a bullet doesn't need a hole. It tends to make one quite nicely without any help.

Dad had a gun of his own.

I felt the bullet whiz by my head at almost the same time I heard the gun go off. I suppose it was good fortune that I'd been thrown off by the force of hitting the door or the bullet might have landed squarely in my head. I didn't have a lot of time to think since my impulse was to get my ass back up off the ground and get through that damn door and get my money. In spite of the crazy voices in my head, I had the good sense to at least provide myself with some cover fire. I managed to get one shot through the broken door as a warning before I was tackled by 150 pounds of stronger-than-he-looked werewolf.

Neil pounced, throwing me to the ground and disarming me with startling ease. The Ruger shot across the floor and away from me. Before I could breathe, he wrapped his arms around me and was rolling away from the door. He held me tight and tried to cover my body with his.

I kicked, screamed, and to my eventual shame, pulled hair. I wasn't thinking. I merely reacted. He stood between me and my money, and it didn't matter that he was my friend. I needed to get to my money and then punish the man who had taken it from me. Anyone in my way was nothing more than collateral damage.

"Zoey, stop it." Neil tried to maneuver me away. "Something's wrong. He's trying to shoot you."

I didn't listen. I simply thrashed harder.

There was another blast from the bedroom, and Neil pinned me down with a snarl. His eyes were distinctly wolf-like, but I wasn't fazed. I continued to struggle to absolutely no avail. He was too strong. I hated him. A wealth of rage threatened to spill over from someplace deep inside me. If I could have killed Neil in that moment, I would surely have done it, and I would have reveled in it. I wanted his blood on my hands. The scream that came from my throat was barely human.

"Blasted demon, trying to kill me girl!" I heard my father shouting, his accent stronger than I'd ever heard it. There was another crack, and then the door started splintering outward as he kicked his way out.

"I'll kill ya first, I swear!" Dad struggled to get through what was left of the door.

Neil turned slightly. I think he was trying to see which demon my father was talking about, and I took advantage. I needed to get away. I did the only thing I could. It was a feminine instinct that nature bred in every one of us—to hurt the male where it would do the most damage. I brought my knee up as hard as I could as I pressed my hands into Neil's shoulders.

Neil stiffened above me, and it was as if all the air left his lungs as he slid to one side. I scooted out from under him and went straight for my gun, glistening like a beacon just out of reach.

"There ya are, black-souled demon." My father looked directly at me. It barely registered through my own shouting inner voices that something was wrong. He pointed his gun straight at me, and I felt a fierce satisfaction as I swung around and pointed the Ruger at his chest. I was starting to pull the trigger when Neil hit me again. He managed to roll us away again as the bullets flew.

"This time, you stay down." He growled as he pulled back a fist and everything turned a blissful black.

* * * *

"How do you know she's not going to try to kill me again when she wakes up?"

I heard Neil's voice from a distance as I started to come out of the warm, dark place I'd been in. I wasn't sure I wanted to leave that place but consciousness seemed to be inevitable at this point.

"She's fine now," Sarah was saying in her most placating voice.

"Well, I should be glad I didn't want to have kids because I think that option is gone now." Neil sounded bitter at the prospect. "I have great genes, you know. It's a shame."

Reality hit with the force of a sledgehammer. Everything that happened rushed back in, and I couldn't stop the moan that came with the realization that I tried to kill my father. I held a gun in my hand and pulled the trigger and prayed that the bullet found his heart. I fought Neil like a wildcat, not caring when I hurt him. I put us all at risk for that money, and now I couldn't think of why I would do such a thing. I moaned again, though this time not because of the guilt. I also had a massive headache.

"Here." Christine pressed a mug into my hand. "It's chamomile, wintergreen, and peppermint mixed with arrowroot powder."

I took a deep drink and nearly choked. "That's vodka."

Christine smiled and held out her palm. "Yes, it is. But this isn't."

She blew a thick powder in my face. It hit me everywhere. I coughed and cried as it hit my lungs and eyes. It burned. "Damn it! What the hell was that for?"

Christine slapped her hands together, brushing the rest of the dust off. "It clears the hex. The herbs and the arrowroot purify the space. We burned the hex bags once we figured out there were two of them controlling both you and Harry. Then I started making the arrowroot spell in case the hex was hanging around. I'm studying to be a witch."

"Yes, she is. Christine has been so helpful." There was a fine tone of irritation that let me know Sarah wasn't happy to share with another witch.

I brushed what I could of the powder off my face. "So what's

117

the vodka for?"

"Oh, that's for the guilt," Christine explained. "I find every time I try to kill someone, I feel crappy about it, but after a couple of vodkas, I'm okay with it. You have to learn to accept and love yourself. We're all just human, after all."

I thrust the mug out. "Yeah, I think I need more."

Christine happily trotted off in search of another bottle of Ciroc.

Sarah put a cold rag on my forehead. "She's insane, you know. She's a decent witch, but she's bonkers. I have no idea what your dad is thinking."

The cold felt wonderful against my throbbing forehead. The enormity of the situation was finally hitting me. I grabbed Sarah's hand. "Is my dad all right? I didn't manage to hit him, did I?"

"He's perfectly well. There's not a scratch on him. He's sleeping off the spell," Sarah said. "He was under it a lot longer than you were, so the effects were a bit more profound."

I looked at Neil, who was frowning at me. My dad wasn't the only one who had been endangered by my brief lapse into psychosis. "Hey, buddy, are you all right? I'm sorry about the whole maiming you thing. If you think about it, it's one of those stories we'll be laughing about years from now, won't we?"

"I am never laughing about that." Neil frowned and crossed his legs pointedly. "The only reason I'm still speaking to you is because you were under some crazy hex, and I have been informed that you were not yourself. If I have a proper apology, I might be able to forgive the loss of my manhood. Well, there's also this blazer at the vintage store that might make me feel better. I've been told it brings out the Justin Timberlake in my eyes."

Sarah stopped and looked at him, her mouth slightly agape. "Seriously? Dude, that hex bag was in your jacket. You were the target. She took the poison for you. It was supposed to be you going all postal on us."

That made me sit up. The importance of the witchcraft eluded me until this moment. This wasn't some random thing. There was a purpose behind the plan, and I only had one thing worth stealing. "Oh, god, the money is gone, isn't it?"

"Yes," Sarah affirmed quietly.

"Why use witchcraft? Why not break in and rip the door off the safe and take the cash? This seems a convoluted route to take." I tried to process the enormity of what had happened. I looked out the window. The sun was low. The afternoon was turning into evening. Daniel would be looking for me soon. My stomach knotted at the thought of having to explain this to him.

Sarah held a hand up as though taking blame on herself. "Remember when I put the wards on your bedroom? One of the wards on the bedroom is to keep out anyone with ill intent. It keeps out bad guys and also guys who want to...you know...some guy who's going to treat you like crap. I've found it keeps out the ones who want to use you for sex."

"Tell me you did not do that to my apartment." Neil gasped, horrified at the thought.

"Of course not, sweetie. You wouldn't be able to enter your own bedroom." She turned back to me. "I thought it would help when you started dating again. If you ever started dating again, which you have. So you see, the person or thing that would have stolen the money wouldn't be able to get past the ward. So they put a hex on Harry to make him believe he needed to take the money to a safer place in order to protect you. His intentions, while magically brought about, were pure, and therefore he could enter. It would be easy to take the money from him. All you would have to do is use a glamor to convince Harry he still had the money. Under the spell, he would have killed or died to protect it."

"Which he almost did." I'd come so close to killing him. "So Dad was holed up in his room protecting the money that wasn't the money?"

"It was a bag of bird seed," Neil said.

"Why put another hex on Neil?" If Neil had been cursed instead of me, the results would have been dramatically different. Neil could easily handle both me and Dad without having to hurt either one of us. If Sarah and I had been left to deal with a rampaging werewolf and a crazy Irishman with an arsenal, someone would have died.

Sarah shrugged. "I guess it was a failsafe. If it didn't work on Harry, then Neil would have done it. Or the witch was afraid Harry might be able to identify her and she...or I guess it could be a he…was worried about reprisal."

"He or she should be." If I ever found the person who had done this, I would have a bone to pick. "I don't suppose he remembers anything, does he?"

Sarah shook her head. "Not a thing. Whoever it was, she was good at her job. It was mere chance, really, that saved us."

I took a deep, steadying breath and wondered where my other vodka had gotten to. I was still a bit shaky from the effects of the hex. I could still feel faint echoes of the insanity that had threatened to overtake me. Too often we discount the power of the witch in our world. When you're surrounded by werewolves and vampires, a witch growing her herbs and casting her spells seems harmless. It's easy to forget that a spell can make you turn on those you love, and even yourself. A werewolf can tear you apart, but a spell can make you tear yourself apart and smile while you do it.

I sat back in the chair. The money was gone and with it any thought of pulling out of the job. I couldn't give the money back, so to renege on the contract was to break it, and then Halfer owned at the very least me and Daniel. Daniel's life might be unnaturally long, but I suspected he could meet with an untimely accident if the demon wanted him to. I suddenly felt like a rat in a maze, and someone had set it on fire behind me. The only way out was through, and to get through, I needed some information.

"I need my cell." I needed to do something about the situation, and there was only one person who could help. I had to hope he'd found that name. "I need to call Albert."

Neil smiled finally. "No need. Dev's already here. He called earlier and said something about some information. He wouldn't give it to me, though. He said he was coming by to deliver it in person." He looked back at the study door. "She's awake. You can come in now."

The door to the study swung open, and Dev walked in. He looked perfect in his dark suit and sunglasses. He pulled the aviators off his face and looked straight into me with his unnaturally green eyes. They seemed to glow with some inner fire, and for a moment, I was lost in them. If I'd thought that last night was just the aftereffects of his spell, I was wrong because I felt his pull and knew it had nothing to do with magic and everything to do with him.

He strode to the center of the room and stood before me. I was acutely aware of the state of my person. I was still wearing the dress I wore the night before, stained and ripped and wrinkled. I'd washed off my makeup, but had failed to apply more. And then there was the arrowroot concoction I could still feel clinging to me. I looked ridiculous, and he was a god. I wanted to hide, but there was nowhere to go.

"I need you to tell me the truth, Zoey." His voice was raw. He looked through me like the answer I gave him would determine our relationship. "Let me warn you, I will know if you're lying. Are you planning to steal a faery object?"

My heart started to beat quickly. I wanted to lie. I didn't want him to look at me with contempt and anger. I wanted him to like me, maybe love me. I felt tears pooling, but they had nothing to do with anger and everything to do with regret as I answered. "Yes."

"Good," he said, his voice hard and bitter. "I want in."

Chapter Eleven

Two hours later, Dev entered the kitchen with a hesitancy that told me he wasn't certain of his welcome.

He stopped a few feet away, his hand on the counter. "You won't regret letting me in, Zoey."

He was right to be concerned. I wasn't particularly happy to see him. I also wasn't particularly surprised. He'd let me know that he wasn't going anywhere until I acquiesced to his demands. I have to admit I had a couple of fantasies the night before where he tied me up until I gave him what he wanted, but not once had what he wanted been a career in crime. I tried to explain the problem to him, but he wouldn't listen. No amount of tough talk would get through to him. It appeared this situation rubbed some raw wound in Dev, and he wouldn't listen to reason.

And he wouldn't give me that name without my agreement.

"Oh, I already regret it." I turned my attention back to the herbs I was cutting. Sarah had left with an exuberant Christine to pick up some things we were going to need, and she'd stuck me with busy work. Now that we knew the name, we could call the demon. Apparently herbs were involved. "It's not like you left me much of a choice."

He hadn't left me any choice at all. With the money gone, my one and only option was to push through and do the job.

In order to do the job, I needed to talk to Halfer. I could have tried calling the number he'd left again, but if he picked up this time, he would have a decisive upper hand. I needed his true name, and I needed to call him to me. It wouldn't make him any less dangerous, and it was likely to make him royally pissed, but it was the only way I would have any real idea of what I was dealing with.

To know a demon's true name is a powerful and dangerous thing. It's powerful because the person who knows the demon's name has a certain, though limited, amount of power over the demon. With a demon's true name, a person can call the demon and the demon is forced to take that meeting. The demon can't claim prior engagements or call in sick. He or she simply gets pulled into the spell if it's cast properly. Upon finding himself suddenly in a protective circle not of his choosing, the demon promptly discovers he's become some human's bitch. That's the powerful part. The dangerous part is when the demon breaks the circle, and the demon always, always, always breaks the circle. It might take a while, but the longer it takes, the more the demon wants to punish whoever called him.

The key to calling a demon is to not get carried away with the powerful part. My quest was to get information out of him, not to make him my attack dog. He was a businessman, and as long as I treated him with a proper amount of respect, I believed I was going to come out of this with my body parts still attached. I was thinking of it as an impromptu business meeting.

But I couldn't get this meeting on the schedule without the proper name. Albert had come through, but he had chosen to give his boss a powerful bargaining chip, and I caved. It didn't make me happy, though. Dev could force his way on to my crew, but he couldn't make me like it.

He smiled a slow, sexy smile that spread across his face like a blanket of charm. I tried to not let my insides go all warm and gushy at the sight of that smile. "I know you have your doubts, but I promise to follow orders. You'll find me a good soldier."

I set the knife down and turned to him. "Which simply points out what you don't know. There is nothing at all military about my crew. I picked them because they can think for themselves. In the field, you have to be able to think and change the plan. There's a great deal of creativity that goes into an enterprise of this nature. This isn't war, Dev. It's an art form that takes years to perfect."

"See, I'm already learning." He leaned against the counter and looked at me seriously. "I'm not without my talents, you know. I've been on my own for a long time. I know how to survive. I think you'll find me a quick learner. I can be valuable to you, Zoey."

There was something in the way he said "I can be valuable" that made me think I wasn't the one he was trying to convince. I thought about what I'd learned about Dev. It must have been hard to be an outsider in such an insular world. In the human world, if a kid didn't fit in with his family, he usually found some group of kids he did fit with. There was always some outcast who understood his pain. It hadn't been like that for Dev. He was a mortal in a world of the eternal. His mortality was anathema to his peers. He would have no value to his family. He would have no way to prove that he was worthy.

I turned back to my work because I thought the last thing he would want to see in my face was pity. Men have a thing about that particular emotion that women don't. Women know that there's something comfortable in the eliciting of sympathy. We complain to our girlfriends about everything from a boyfriend's flaws to uncomfortable shoes, and when they pity us, they share our burdens. Men don't see it that way. They see the weakness, so I turned away.

"We'll see." I applied the knife to some sort of smelly green herb.

There was more than one reason that I didn't want Dev involved in my professional life. Beyond the fact that he was a complete novice and therefore a liability, there was the simple truth that I wanted him for myself. I wanted to explore what we'd started the night before. It was uncharted territory, and I really wanted to map it. He hadn't even kissed me yet, and I so wanted him to kiss me. I was the novice when it came to relationships, and I was more than willing to follow his lead.

But if he worked with me, then I had to change gears and view him as something else. I had to be professional. I had to be his boss.

I had to review the facts and be as honest with myself as possible. I'd never dated anyone but Daniel. I'd had one relationship, and it had been a deep and loving one. I didn't know how to do casual. The night before I felt a real connection with Dev. Maybe it had been one way. Maybe he hadn't felt that connection, or it hadn't been important to him. He was willing to throw it away to pursue some sort of revenge.

"I'm glad I'm not thyme right now," he said, watching me pulverize the herbs.

"Why don't you go and see if you can help Neil." I needed to think, and it would be so much easier if he was in another room. This close to me, I could feel his warmth and smell the soap he used, and it made me want to press myself into him. It had been so long since I'd had the solace of another body against mine that the loss of the possibility made me want to cry.

"No, I think I need to be right here doing some serious damage control." His voice was breathy. He reached out and laid his big hand across my arm, stopping my motion. "Zoey, please tell me why you're crying."

I hadn't realized I was, but now I felt the tears brush my cheeks as they journeyed down my face. "I…it's been a rough day."

"And I made it so much worse." He let his hand slide up my arm in a comforting fashion. There was nothing overtly sexual about his movement, but my skin was singing everywhere he touched.

I pulled back abruptly because I knew if I let it go, I wouldn't be able to pull back later. I needed that touch. I needed someone to want me, but now it couldn't be him. He was part of the crew, and there were good reasons to not get sexually involved with members of your crew. "Stop, Dev. If you wanted to date me, you should have stayed out of the business part of my life. We need to keep this professional."

His laugh was deep and rich and infectious. "Oh, Zoey, there is absolutely nothing professional about the way I feel about you. I want to be with you in every way possible and part of that is being in your world. Don't get me wrong. I have other reasons for wanting to do this particular job, and one day I promise I will explain, but don't doubt that I have every intention of being with you."

"That's a problem, Dev. I don't have romantic relationships with people I work with," I stated as flatly as possible.

He just stared at me.

"I'm not with Daniel. I haven't been with Daniel for many years. Our relationship was over years before I started to work with him."

"But you have feelings for him," Dev pointed out needlessly.

Feelings didn't begin to cover it. "Of course. We were going to get married. I loved him. I love him. I can't stop, but we're not together. There are…complications."

"He's a vampire with a chip on his shoulder, and you've been too stubborn to let go." Dev summed up the situation neatly. "Last night after the cleanup, I did some research. I know all about it, but I'm willing to take the chance. If I thought you could be happy with him, I wouldn't stand in the way, but I don't think he's going to change. It goes against the nature of vampires. You wouldn't be content in that world. I think I can provide you with a happy alternative. I don't know what's been wrong with the guys you've dated since Daniel left you, but you should know that I don't intend to follow the pattern, whatever it is."

I stared at the thyme lying there on the cutting board and hoped he would move on. He didn't.

"There have been other men?" Incredulity crept into his voice.

My silence was my answer.

"Zoey." Dev gently cupped my chin and turned me toward him. I felt so naked and naïve in that moment. I wished I could run, but my pride forced me to stay. "How many men have you been with, sweetheart?"

I was twenty-five years old. It was ridiculous, but I had only one answer, and it was a true one. There had been no high school fumblings behind the bleachers, no college experimentation. There had been only Daniel. I'd given myself in love and longing, and he was gone from me as surely as if he was dead. I couldn't stop the tears, and I wished in that moment that I could claim a hundred lovers. "One."

Dev smiled softly, but he was so serious that I knew he was handling me with care. He gently brushed away my tears and came close to me. "Know this, Zoey Wharton, I will take care of you. I have every intention of having you, and when I say have, I mean fuck, but in the sweetest way possible. I will fuck you and love you and after, I will hold you. You won't regret letting me have you, sweetheart. I will make sure you are satisfied in and out of our bed. I vow this."

It was as serious a promise as a Fae could make. "Are you always this way with your lovers?"

His chuckle was rich with amusement. "No, I don't normally pledge my devotion before I've even kissed a girl. You're different. Most of my lovers want my body. They want simple pleasure and kindness and maybe a gift or two. But you need more. You need commitment before pleasure, and if that's what you need, then I'll give it to you. I want you, Zoey. I don't think you understand how much."

I took a deep, steadying breath. I wasn't sure I could believe him, but I wanted to. He was close now, and I could feel the heat coming off his body. My heart started to pound with anticipation, and I wished I had been able to put on some makeup. I'd found a pair of jeans and a tank top I kept in my old room, but there was no makeup to be found, not even a tube of lip gloss.

"It's too soon." My voice was barely above a whisper as I let my eyes take him in. God, he was beautiful. It was a masculine beauty, but there was no other word for it. His eyes were sensual and greener than any mere human's. His dark hair was thick and slightly unruly. Last night it had been perfect, but this afternoon it looked lived in. I preferred the more casual Dev. And those lips…

I looked down to avoid staring at them. I was barefoot. I barely came to the middle of his chest without heels. He took my arms in his hands. I shivered slightly, but it had nothing to do with cold. He pulled me into the cradle of his body and held me there.

"I think you're wrong," he murmured. "I think it's the perfect time, Zoey."

It was the sigh that did it. Dev sort of sighed and let his head drop to mine. It was a sound of deep longing fulfilled, as though he wanted to be here with me and now he was content. My heart felt so full at that moment that I couldn't stop my arms from winding their way around his big, warm body and relaxing against it. It felt so good to fall into him. In that moment, I felt safe and loved and wanted.

Dev was smart enough to let me take the lead. He treated me like a shy deer he wanted to feed by hand. When I pulled back and looked up at him, he didn't pounce. He let me guide him down toward my lips and stood still while I haltingly explored his mouth. His lips were soft against mine. I pressed our mouths together in a chaste kiss. I'd always worried that Daniel would be the only man who could ever make me want him. This notion was now firmly put to rest as every nerve in my body came to life and sang a glorious chorus.

I tentatively let my tongue glide against the firmness of his mouth. Those lips were plump and I sucked the bottom one into my mouth, tasting him, feeling my power. The shudder that went through him satisfied me. He let me have my way with him, allowing my tongue an easy entry. He tasted like mint, and I knew he had hoped this would happen. Knowing he'd thought about this, planned for it, made it easier for me. I pressed my body against his and felt how happy he was to be here with me. His cock was already hard and rubbed against my belly, promising all manner of comfort and pleasure.

"Zoey." He groaned and pulled away slightly. "Sweetheart, you're really short."

I laughed. His neck was at an awkward angle due to our height differences. It must have been uncomfortable. "Sorry about that. I could stand on a chair."

I tried to find a solution to our problem because stopping our impromptu make-out session wasn't something I wanted to do. I felt alive around him. My worries melted away the minute he laid a hand on me. I wanted more of this feeling.

"I can handle it." He lifted me with one arm, and I suddenly found myself sitting on the kitchen counter, my legs dangling. Dev shoved himself between my legs, and we were finally at the perfect height. He pulled me close, his hands on my ass, nestling himself between my legs.

His hand slid up, tracing along my back and upwards. Dev gently cupped my face and looked into my eyes. "I don't want to push you."

His voice had a slight desperation to it. Every woman, even one with almost no experience, can translate that tone. It means *please, please, please let me...*

I smiled. "I think you can push me a little."

And then I wasn't thinking about demons or stolen money or lost loves. I was thinking about that long silent voice that was suddenly screaming at me to kiss and lick and let this man do whatever he wanted to with me. Dev let himself go now, and he was suddenly everywhere. His tongue seduced mine. His hands explored. His fingers ran up from my hips, skimming along my side until he found his way to my breasts. My nipples were hard points begging for his attention. I wanted his mouth on me, his hands roaming. The center of him pressed against me, seeking entry despite the barriers of our clothing. He was not a small man. His cock was large and blissfully erect. That glorious erection nudged insistently through the denim of my jeans. I let my legs wind around him and gave myself over to the moment.

"Please, Dev." It had been so long. I hadn't even touched myself. I'd been utterly alone.

He smiled, a slow curving of his lips. "You have no idea how much I want to please you. How much I can please you. I come from a long line of men whose goal in life is to please a woman. The right woman."

He tweaked my nipples, his fingers pinching lightly. I squirmed, the feeling going straight to my pussy. His lips kept up a slow grind against mine as his fingers made their way down my torso. I held on, pulling him close. I felt connected in a way I hadn't in forever. He delved under the waistband of my jeans. I sighed against his mouth as he found his way to my clit. With an expert touch, he started to rub.

"Hate to break up a tender moment." A bitter voice shattered the intimacy.

I didn't have to look out the window to know that night had

fallen, and Daniel was here.

It was only instinct that made me try to push Dev away, but he was having none of it. He helped me off the counter and turned to Daniel with absolutely none of the ridiculous shame I felt. I tried to get enough air into my lungs so that I could talk.

"Sorry," Dev said in a voice that didn't sound sorry at all. "I guess we got carried away." He put one arm around me. It was a casual thing, like he'd been my boyfriend for a while, but the truth was I needed his support to stand. He nestled our bodies together. "I didn't realize it had gotten so late."

"Obviously." Daniel's slight lisp let me know his fangs were out. He kept his lips tight so no one could see. "I need to talk to Zoey. Alone."

"I think that's up to Zoey." Dev tightened the arm around my waist slightly.

"It's fine." I didn't really want to talk to Daniel. It was going to go one of two ways. Either he was going to be horrible about it, or he was going to act like he couldn't care less. I wasn't sure which would be worse. But I couldn't avoid him, so I might as well get it over with. "Dev, could you go see if Neil needs help with the altar?"

He leaned down and planted a quick kiss on my lips. It was a promise of things to come. "Will do, boss." He nodded toward the counter. "Oh, I'm sorry about the herbs."

I looked over and was surprised to see the thyme I'd been chopping had apparently grown. It was green and lush and there was a lot more of it, as though every piece I had cut had grown a new sprig.

Dev grinned down at me. "I'm afraid that happens sometimes when I get excited. My grandfather was a Green Man, you see. I might not have gotten his immortality, but I'm good with plants and…fertility rites. I'm good at making things grow and reach their full potential, if you know what I mean."

I thought I knew what he meant, and I wished we'd had time to reach that full potential he'd been talking about. He walked out of the room, and I wished I had a tenth of his confident charm. I didn't, and I was suddenly left alone with Daniel.

I didn't owe him anything. He'd been with god knew how many

women since he left me. From what I heard, the Vampire Council wasn't exactly a monastery. The girls at the club were there for sex as well as blood, and Daniel had been seen with most of them. I didn't owe him fidelity or an explanation. So why did a thousand excuses pop to the tip of my tongue? If he'd shown the slightest bit of hurt, I would have dissolved into an apologetic puddle.

"Seriously, Zoey?" His tone held a bitter bite. "You've known him for five minutes, and you're already hopping into bed. I thought I knew you better. I didn't think you were a…"

He stopped as though finally realizing he was crossing a line. He looked surprised and closed his mouth.

Any thoughts of apologies were gone. I was across the room before I even realized what I was doing. My fist met his jaw with a satisfying crack. I even managed not to scream when pain exploded across my skin.

"Damn it, Zoey." Daniel grabbed my arm so I couldn't get in another one. "I didn't say it."

"You thought it," I snarled up at him. "That was enough."

"What did you expect? I walked in here and you were practically fucking him in your father's kitchen."

"I expected you to not give a damn, Danny. I expected you to cheer me on," I said. "Didn't you want me to find someone? And don't you dare say anyone but him. I get to choose who I sleep with, not you. I thought you would be happy I was moving on. Now you can go wherever it is you've been planning on going once your conscience was clear."

Daniel dropped my hand and seemed to deflate. He turned away. "I want you to be happy. I just wish you hadn't been happy here. It was a shock."

I took a deep breath and steadied myself. I knew what he was talking about. I felt it every time I walked into my dad's house. "Daniel, there isn't a room in this house we didn't make love in."

It was true. There wasn't a room in the house that didn't hold some memory of us. He first kissed me in my bedroom when we were barely fourteen. The first time he held my hand was on the stairs. We spent nights in the study doing homework and planning our future. Anywhere I went in this house there was a ghost. I was surprised he still felt it, too.

"I was happy here," he said as though he heard my thoughts. "It was the first time in my life I was truly happy. I always thought we would end up raising kids in this house."

"Damn you, Danny." My eyes filled with tears. "Why now? Years you spend pretending I mean nothing to you and now you say these things to me. Now you care about our past right when I'm starting to believe I could find happiness with someone else. You really are a bastard."

He turned to me, and I was so surprised at the sight. There were tears in his eyes, and he looked so confused. "I never pretended not to care. I can't anymore, Zoey. What I am, I can't love you like you deserve. I can't give you what you need so I had to stay away and make sure you were all right. You don't understand the truth of this world. I don't even want you to. I never stopped loving you. I just...I'm a monster. I would only hurt you. I'm sorry about...what I said. I never imagined it would hurt so much to see you...like that...with someone else."

I sighed, a deep, tired sound. "How do you think I felt about all those other women?"

"What other women?"

"The ones at your club." I wondered how many there had been. It was not in a vampire's nature to be celibate. Sex went along with the feeding. I knew it was just sex, but it still hurt.

Daniel grew still. "In all the years that I have been a vampire, I have never taken a lover. I have fed, but it went no further. I have no intentions of betraying you, Zoey."

I was confused. No vampire was celibate. The need for sex was hardwired into their systems. It was beyond longing. It was an actual physical need. It was part of the feed.

"How can that be true?" And then another question hit me. "You can't go an eternity without sex, Danny. What are you going to do when you've happily married me off?"

He smiled sadly, and I knew the answer. I bit back a cry at the thought. He was planning to walk into the light.

"Zoey, Daniel, it's time." Neil's far too subdued voice told me he'd heard enough.

I wiped the tears from my face. "We'll finish this later," I vowed.

I had a demon to call, but I walked out with the knowledge that my own personal demon was going to be so much harder to deal with.

Chapter Twelve

Neil had properly drawn the circle on the living room floor. It was a nice hardwood floor, which is so much better than carpet. Carpet consists of hundreds of separate fibers that have a habit of not always sticking together in the manner one wishes they would. When you're using the space for watching television and doing the occasional yoga session, it's a perfectly fine form of flooring.

When calling a demon, carpet sucks. It doesn't hold the circle firmly, and once the demon has the slightest centimeter of a crack, the carpet-loving demon caller tends to find himself in intimate contact with said demon. Those sessions never end well. Trust me, hard floors, wood or concrete, are best.

My father's house contained beautiful solid oak floors that now boasted a large, red spray-painted circle decorated with a bunch of arcane symbols meant to keep the demon inside. I was fairly sure my father would have a heart attack when he saw it, but he would probably be more pissed off that I called Halfer in the first place.

The doors to the room flew open and Sarah stormed in. "Zoey, I talked to my coven leader."

Christine walked in behind her carrying a sack. I was pretty sure the blonde was the reason for Sarah's annoyance. Looking at the pair, it was hard to imagine they were both witches. Sarah, I could see. She cultivated that cool Goth look pop culture associated with post-modern witches. She wore a black mini-skirt with fishnets and combat boots.

Christine had pageant hair and wore a cutesy business suit. She was wearing pumps, and no one who has to deal with the supernatural world on a regular basis would wear pumps to a demon calling. Christine looked like she should be heading home to make dinner for her hubby and two point five kids. She did not look like a chick who would be excited about calling her first demon.

"What did Emily have to say?" Emily was the head of Sarah's coven and the most powerful witch in the area. If anyone could give us advice about this calling, it would be Emily.

"What did she say beyond the fact that you're insane and we're all going to die?" Sarah flipped a lock of pink hair out of her eyes.

"Yes, beyond that." Emily apparently hadn't said anything I didn't already know.

Sarah frowned. "It isn't possible. Neither Christine nor I have enough magic to handle a demon as powerful as this one. You should have seen the look on Emily's face when I gave her the name Brixalnax. Man, I have never seen a black woman turn that white. He's old. He's royalty in Hell. This is dangerous, and we don't have the fire power."

"If we use the coven…" I began.

"Not a chance," Sarah said firmly. "There is no way Emily will put her people in danger. She tried to forbid me from having anything to do with this."

"She was very negative." Christine wrinkled her nose in distaste. "I would have expected a witch at her level to be more open to new experiences. It made me glad I'm a solitary. I don't think I'd like someone telling me who I can and can't call. I'm totally bringing up this experience at the next meeting of the Junior League witches."

I wanted to ignore her. I really did. I simply couldn't. "Junior League witches?"

"It's a small group but growing," Christine said. "Slowly."

Sarah rolled her eyes and got back to the point. "We need a

power source, and all we've got are two mid-level witches, a werewolf, a vampire, and a human who might actually have a negative magical center, no offense."

I shrugged because she was right. I was crap when it came to spells. They tended to do the exact opposite of my intentions. Note that I say intentions because I got all smart-alecky once and tried a reverse spell to give myself acne when I was trying to clear up my skin. Apparently magic was smarter than I gave it credit for and only Proactiv saved me.

As for Neil and Daniel, while they were supernatural creatures, they possessed no real magical power. Daniel's only magic was the ability to make his bite really pleasurable and to get humans to do his will, and I didn't think that would impress Brixalnax.

"So we're going to have to scrap this whole plan," Sarah said.

The doors opened again, and Dev walked into the room. Just watching him walk made my pulse increase, and then I felt guilty knowing Daniel was right there. It took me a moment to realize that Sarah was still speaking.

"We're going to have to figure something else out. Halfer left his number. We could call him and explain the situation…"

"Wow," Christine said, staring at Dev. Her eyes were round as she looked him up and down. I tried to feel some amount of jealousy as he was the guy I was dating, but I couldn't muster it. He was smoking hot, and it was ridiculous to think people wouldn't notice.

"You think he's hot now." Sarah's voice was bitter. "You should see this idiot when he tries a glamour."

"Yeah, sorry about that." Dev gave her a charming smile. "I would like you to know that my bouncers have been told to admit you to Ether anytime you like. First drink's on the house." She continued to frown, and Dev amended himself. "All your drinks are on the house?"

Christine shook her head and walked up to Dev, her eyes filled with a reverent wonder. "That wasn't what I meant. Though you are extremely attractive, I wasn't talking about your sex appeal. I was talking about the magic that's pouring off you."

Dev grimaced. "I'm sorry about that. I can't control it when I get…excited. It just kind of happens. I'll give you a demonstration."

Dev walked up to one of my father's houseplants. It was a small ivy plant that looked like it needed a bit of attention. He passed an open hand over the sad plant and it…well, it kind of exploded, but in a good way. The vines grew a good foot in any direction and the color was a lustrous, deep and shiny green. It reeked of life and health and, for a moment, I couldn't take my eyes off it. He hadn't been kidding when he said his grandfather was a Green Man.

"See, I meant to make it grow an inch or two." He frowned down at the plant. "I have a control problem."

"I can imagine that makes for disappointing encounters," Daniel said with a wry smirk. "If your timing is as bad…"

I shot him a "shut the fuck up" look. The last thing I needed was a boy fight. Just looking at Daniel made my heart ache, and I turned away.

Dev was nonplussed. "Oh, I find it makes me work all the harder. I haven't heard any complaints yet. Certainly none recently."

"Seriously? We're up against a lord of Hell and the two of you are comparing penises?" I didn't expect or want an answer, but I was hoping to shame them into compliance. I turned to Sarah. "Will he work?"

"Absolutely not," Sarah said.

"Absolutely," Christine answered at the same time.

I looked at the two and waited for a consensus.

Sarah folded her arms across her chest in a defensive gesture. "He's too much of a wild card. He said it himself. He can't control it. What happens if he loses control in the middle of everything? We can't trust his power. He's a complete loser when it comes to magic."

"Well, I didn't put it that way," Dev defended himself.

"Look, you said we didn't have enough power. You said we couldn't even try to do the spell because we needed an energy source." Christine put a hand on Dev's shoulder. "Well, here's the energizer bunny and he doesn't have to control himself. We simply pull the magic off him."

"No, I won't do it," Sarah said flatly.

I understood why Sarah was looking for any way out of working this magic. It was terrifying. We would be calling an old, powerful demon who was probably going to be pissed off at us. I understood her reluctance, but I didn't have time for it. "It's all right, Sarah. You don't have to say anything else."

She let out the breath she'd been holding, and I saw a wave of relief pass over her face. "Thank the goddess, Zoey. You'll see..."

But I was already moving on. I turned from Sarah and focused on the more amenable witch. "Can you do it?"

It seemed to take everything Christine had to not jump up and down at the prospect. She sort of vibrated as she stood there. "Oh, yes! I won't let you down, Zoey. I have been preparing for this all my life. I can't tell you how ready I am. As long as I have my battery here, it'll be a breeze."

"Hey—" Dev looked slightly offended at his relegation to nine volt status. "Nobody asked me if I wanted to be the power source for a demon calling."

I gave him my best "army sergeant" look. "Do you want to be a member of this crew or not?"

"Member of the crew?" Righteous indignation filled Daniel's voice. "Who the hell brought him into the crew?"

"Anything you say, boss." Dev gave me a little salute. He turned to Christine. "I'm at your service. Tell me what to do, and I'll make it happen."

"He is not a member of this crew," Daniel stated, as though stating a thing made it true.

"Zoey, you can't seriously be thinking about doing this without me." Sarah stared at me, her voice rising over all the other voices.

She looked shocked and hurt, but I couldn't consider her feelings. I hated the fact that I was hurting people I cared about and endangering everyone, but I had to steel myself and get this done. There would be time for guilt later. This was one of those times when it sucked to be a leader.

"I'm doing this, Sarah. You can't talk me out of it. I'll understand if you want to leave."

The boys continued their debate, seemingly oblivious to anything else.

"I'm going to be working with you, Dan." Dev had that face I was starting to understand he got when he realized he'd done something wrong and needed to make it right. "You should get used to it. Look, man, I'm sorry I've been kind of a dick tonight, but I got defensive when you walked in and looked at Zoey like you owned her." He put out his hand in a friendly gesture. "We got along well last night. I hope we can put tonight aside."

Sarah looked at Neil who was suspiciously quiet throughout the exchange. He sat on the couch, watching the drama unfold with rapt attention. "Neil, tell Zoey she can't do this."

"Oh, I wish I could, princess." Neil didn't take his eyes off the men. "But I'm far too busy waiting to see if Daniel is about to kill Dev. I'm thinking yes, but it could go a whole different way. Is there any popcorn?"

"Stop it!" I was sick of the arguing. I was ready to call the damn demon myself if it meant an end to the chatter. "Dev, stop baiting Daniel. Daniel, stop looking at Dev like he's a late-night snack. Christine, go and get ready. It's getting close to midnight, and we need to get a move on. Neil, make yourself useful. We still need that chair from the living room. Sarah, I'm sorry you're upset, but I have to do this with you or without you. I'm not exactly sure if your soul is on the line, but I know mine is. I need to do anything I can to give us the best shot at pulling off this job."

Sarah turned to Daniel. "You have to stop this. You have to tell her she can't do it."

Daniel laughed and it was a good sound, an almost human sound. "I know I might pretend like I have some control, but nobody tells Z what to do. She's going to do it, and I'm going to do what I always do—stand by and hope it doesn't all go to hell. Besides, I'm with her on this one. My soul, if I have one, is on the line, too."

Neil stood beside Daniel. He looked very young as he stood his ground, and I was reminded that he was barely twenty years old. "I'm sorry Sarah, but they're our friends. We have to help. I know I don't bring that much to the table, but if they're here fighting for their lives, I'm gonna be here, too. I'd do the same thing for you. You guys are my family."

I knew what I was doing was wrong even as I did it but a certain ruthless practicality had come over me. The boys stood behind me forming a sort of wall, and Sarah was on the wrong side of that wall.

I needed her with us even if it meant she did something she didn't believe in. Those of us who lead a particular type of life know that there are times to throw out your morals and beliefs in favor of saving the people you love. Someone tried to kill me last night. This morning they came after my father and Neil. It was only a matter of time before they got around to Daniel and Sarah and maybe even Dev. If I sat on my ass because I didn't want to do black magic and someone got killed, I wouldn't be able to live with myself.

"Look, Sarah," I said with all the empathy I could muster. "I realize that you don't want to do this, and that's all right. You don't do black magic. I get it. I understand we'll probably fail, but I don't want you to feel guilty if it goes wrong. You did everything you could. You tried your best to warn us."

There were angry tears in her eyes as she looked at me. She glanced back at Neil and Daniel, and I saw the minute she realized I had trapped her and there was no escape.

"You can be a bitch sometimes, Z," she said bitterly.

Yeah, I was definitely getting there. At the rate I was going, I might lose my soul all on my own.

Chapter Thirteen

Magic, when done properly, has something for every sense.

There's a certain smell that comes with each spell. I'm not sure if the experience is the same for each person, so I can only speak from my own encounters. Love spells end up leaving a faint smell of vanilla in the room. Prosperity spells smell like freshly mown grass.

There's also a feeling that washes across your skin. Usually it's a pleasant tingle, like someone brushed your arm gently with their nails. You shiver slightly with the pleasure. There's a light crackle or pop when a spell goes right and some people swear they can taste the air around them. You can also see the remnants of a spell, whether it's smoke or the faintest glow around an object.

Magic has an effect in the physical world that cannot be mistaken. The point is, you always know when magic has gone right.

I knew something was wrong when my every sense went crazy.

It started all right. Sarah placed Christine and Dev in their proper spaces around the circle. They formed a triangle protecting the circle within. She started burning the herbs and incense. Neil complained about the stench, but one threat about hexing his man parts and he decided to win the quiet game. Daniel managed to look disapproving while attempting to not spare me a glance. Everything seemed normal, or rather as normal as it could be when calling a lord of Hell. The ceremony began. After what seemed like an eternity of invocation, I began to wonder if it was going to fail. One minute Sarah and Christine were chanting in some language no one had spoken in a thousand years and the next…

Brimstone assailed me. It was so thick in the air, I gagged on it. It smelled like all the bad things in the world had gotten together and sunbathed on an August day in Texas. After the smell came the awful crack that threatened to burst my eardrums, and worse, the feeling of a thousand bugs crawling under my skin trying to find their way to the softer parts of me. I would have scratched through several layers of skin if I hadn't been blinded by the lightning that found its way into my father's living room.

"Son of a bitch," a low voice growled.

"Don't move, Dev." I could hear the tension in Sarah's voice. "I think we should stay in position. Consider it an added protection. Right now we have a magical connection, and that might help strengthen the circle."

I steadied myself and managed to open my eyes. Dev held his place as Sarah asked, but he looked ashen, as though being a magical battery had taken its toll. Sarah trembled, her normal grace seeming to desert her. Only Christine looked satisfied. There was a slight smile on her face that made me uneasy. It was easy to see her ambitions went way beyond learning a couple of spells under my dad's tutelage.

All thoughts fled because we were no longer alone. The demon, Brixalnax, alias Lucas Halfer, was in the circle. He was in full demon form, a massive display of bright red skin and muscle and he was…dear god…he was really not hiding anything.

"Whoa, dude, where are your clothes?" Neil asked the question. The rest of us simply stared.

"I was on a date," Halfer said through clenched fangs. "With twins, I might add. I didn't expect a bunch of morons to interrupt me."

"Sorry about that." I needed to keep him as calm as possible. I needed his help, and I needed him to not try to kill me the minute he got out of the circle. "I have to ask you a few questions. Oh, please, put some clothes on."

He stared at me with red eyes and settled his hands on his well-muscled hips which led inevitably to that part that his dates should have been really glad to be free of. What did a demon consider a date? Somewhere out there was there a set of twins still screaming in the night, trying to get away from an attacker they didn't realize was gone? I looked down and noticed his cloven feet.

They tapped against the hardwood. "I'm sorry I didn't dress properly before I was torn through time and space and imprisoned in a shitty circle. Listen, bitch, if you want the bull, you better get used to the horns."

"It's not the horns I'm worried about." That was a lie. The horns totally freaked me out, too. They were red like the rest of him and wound around his head like a goat. It looked like someone had carved shapes into them, but I didn't want to get close enough to be sure.

"Hey, don't you talk to her like that," Daniel threatened.

"Or you'll do what, night crawler?" The demon sneered, midnight black eyes narrowing. "You'll have to come in here if you wish to defend your bitch's honor. I'm afraid I find myself trapped."

"Stop." I forced a breath into my body. "I didn't call you here to fight."

"You didn't call me here at all, you puny human. Your witches called me, and trust me, I'm going to get well acquainted with them. Most witches on this pitiful plane know better than to call me." He looked at each as though memorizing their faces.

"Why did you try to have me killed?" I went straight to the point. I got the feeling that we had surprised him, and if he hadn't been distracted, we would never have caught him. We didn't have a lot of time.

He stopped, his eyes swinging toward me. "What are you talking about?"

Daniel stepped too close to the circle for my liking. "Last night you sent three men to track her down and take her. Neil and I made sure that didn't happen."

"I was there, too," Dev said.

"Yeah, you were there, getting your ass handed to you by a piddling snake. Zoey saved you," Daniel pointed out before turning back to Halfer. "But more to the point, why the hell did you think we would let that go?"

I'd placed a chair in the center of the circle, and Halfer now sank into it. He crossed his legs, and I breathed a sigh of relief. He seemed to think about what Daniel had said for a moment. As he thought, he took a deep breath and the skin on his body flowed around bone and sinew, changing shape and color right before my eyes. One moment he was a dark red that didn't seem to be a color one could find in nature, and then he was the same Lucas Halfer we'd met at the restaurant. He was still naked, but he seemed so much more in proportion now. Only his eyes betrayed him. They were black without a hint of white showing. There was nothing vaguely human about those eyes.

It was like someone turned the volume down and I could think again. "We're a bit confused. Do you want us to do the job or not? If there's something we should know, I'd like to know now."

Halfer sat back with a long sigh. "I'm not some chaos demon. Those idiots will lay out a plan and then fuck it up on their own because they can't help themselves. They have to push everything to the limit. They have to break everything around them. I'm an entirely different beast. I like an elegant plan. I prefer to get what I want with minimum effort, and I can keep my mouth shut. The question then becomes which one of you idiots blabbed and who did you talk to?"

"Blabbed about what? The job?" I asked, confused.

Halfer's lips thinned to a dismissive line. "Yes, the job. I know my people didn't open their mouths. I made sure I worked on this outside of the Hell plane. I had a powerful witch and her coven checking the signs and reading the cards for the last fifty years to discover when the box was being moved. I told no one and made sure the witches kept their mouths shut."

"How can you be absolutely sure?" Neil asked. "Just because they're afraid of you doesn't mean they didn't mention it to the wrong person."

"It's difficult to talk when your throat has been slit." Halfer sounded as though he were talking about the weather. Christine's sharp intake of breath was the first clue that she had a sense of self-preservation. "I killed all thirteen to ensure that something like this didn't happen. I don't want any competition. Now tell me exactly what happened in minute detail."

So I told him what happened. Every now and then Daniel or Neil would throw in some detail I forgot. Halfer sat listening to everything we said. He didn't move his gaze from me even when the others were talking, and I found myself trembling under the weight of his alien eyes. Even as I spoke, voices in my head told me this was all going to go wrong and it would be my fault. I wasn't good enough to even try this. I should stop and give up. I would be Halfer's soon, so why bother to try? It would be so much easier to give in.

I didn't realize I was crying. I was standing there reciting yesterday's events like an automaton when I felt a hand on my shoulder.

"Stop it." There was a command in Neil's voice I heard rarely.

"What's wrong, little dog?" Halfer smiled an evil half grin.

"You know what you're doing." Neil faced the demon.

I shook my head as though to free myself from a fog and looked around. Everyone seemed to have retreated inside themselves. Christine mumbled something I didn't understand. Sarah wept openly, asking someone for forgiveness. Dev's body trembled, and Daniel looked pissed. We all had retreated into our own worlds, ones Halfer had sent us to.

Only Neil seemed unaffected by whatever was happening.

"Yes, I know what I'm doing, but I'm surprised you do." Halfer focused all that darkness on Neil now, and I actually felt a weight lift from my soul. "I'm also surprised you would try to stop me. What are you afraid of, puppy? I know, of course. How common. You know you'll never find that man who wants a lover who turns into a dog once a month."

"Oh, you would be surprised what a guy will put up with to get at all this." Neil gestured up and down his well-formed body.

"But he won't love you."

"His loss," Neil said quietly but firmly.

"You're going to let her down, you know," Halfer said in a silky voice, and I realized it had been his voice I heard in my head all along. It had sounded like mine, but the smoothness was all Halfer. As he continued to focus his talents on Neil, the rest of us were coming out of our stupors.

Daniel looked my way. I wondered what the voice in his head had said.

"You'll let Zoey down and Sarah down and even that big, dumb vampire will be disappointed in you," Halfer was saying to Neil.

"Probably at some point," Neil conceded.

"You're the reason they are going to die."

Neil shook for the first time. His hand was still on my shoulder, and I felt the fine tremble in it. I let mine drift up to cover his and he took it, entwining our fingers. I felt him sigh against me as though our connection was a source of strength.

"If that's true then I'll go with them. I'll share whatever fate they meet."

Halfer laughed, an unpleasant sound. "I like you, wolf. You're a challenge."

Neil let out a long breath. "I grew up with someone a lot like you. You're not the first to try this shit on me. Hell, you're certainly not the best."

Halfer smiled, and I could have sworn his fangs were back. "Oh, but I haven't even tried yet, wolf. Please forgive my lackadaisical fumblings. I was only half trying. I can do better."

I felt the start of Halfer's second assault. The weight was back on my chest, and I felt an almost suffocating sense of sorrow.

"Bastard!" Dev reared his fist as he started toward the circle.

Daniel moved with preternatural speed. He caught Dev before the circle could be broken. In a blur of speed and strength, Daniel crossed the room and threw Dev back, slamming him against the wall. I heard the drywall crack as Dev slid to the floor. He slumped there against the wainscoting, unconscious. Through my stifling sorrow, I hoped Daniel hadn't killed him. I'd gotten Dev involved. I would be the reason he died. I should have been happy when his chest moved up and down, but the black cloud Halfer sent through us all held me in its grip. He was stronger than we could have imagined. Our crappy circle could hold his body, but his mind wasn't caged in the least. Halfer's wicked power surged.

Halfer stood again, and it was obvious the violence did something for him. "You liked that didn't you, night crawler? You enjoyed hurting the Fae creature."

"Yes," Daniel said. I knew in an instant he was still feeling the effects of Halfer because that yes came out with several extra esses as he struggled to speak around his fangs. Daniel was careful about those fangs, but now he seemed to not even notice they were there.

"He's gonna fuck her, you know," Halfer said with glee. "He's gonna ram his cock in her, and she's gonna love it."

"Daniel!" I yelled and tried to get between him and the circle.

Neil was at Daniel's back, and I was at his front. Neil was definitely more effective than I was as I seemed to be getting closer and closer to that damn circle, and Halfer kept running his mouth.

He clapped his hands with glee, like the ring leader of a sadistic circus. "She's going to howl when he does her. She won't even remember you once he's fucked her right and tight."

I forced myself to think. While I tried to push back the determined vampire, I shouted over my shoulder at the demon. "Do you want me to do this job or do you want a blood bath? If you kill Daniel, I won't be doing anything for you. I'll find whoever else wants that stupid box and I'll make sure they get it. If you think I'm bluffing then you didn't do your job right. If you know my deepest fears then you know I mean what I say. I won't have anything left but the deepest desire to screw you over."

And just like that the oppressive air in the room was gone, and we could all breathe again. Daniel stopped pushing me closer to our doom and let Neil drag him back. Sarah and Christine stopped crying, and I felt so much clearer without the demon's influence.

Halfer huffed and shook his head. "You're right, of course. I apologize for the discourtesy. Apparently I'm more like my chaotic brothers than I thought. It's really your own fault. You're all so full of delicious doubts. I could make a meal of you but business before pleasure. So, the money is gone. That is too bad. I guess that would have come in handy."

A nasty suspicion took hold. "Considering I was going to give it back, yes, it is unfortunate."

He chuckled at the thought. "I wondered if you would try that. Well, even if you could raise the money again, I think you would find I have a special attachment to those particular bills. I wouldn't be able to accept anything but the same money I gave you."

"You stole the money." And thereby put me in a neat corner with no way out.

"I admit nothing of the sort," he returned with a self-satisfied smile. "I will, of course, be happy to provide you with another payment. We can't expect you to work your magic on a limited budget. I'll have my assistant equip you with anything you need first thing in the morning."

"Zoey, he's getting you in deeper, can't you see that? He stole the money so that you couldn't give it back to him." I turned to see Dev holding his head as he tried to stand.

"Whether he stole it or not doesn't matter. We don't have it now. If she doesn't do the job, she fails to fulfill her part of the contract. What the hell else are we supposed to do?" Daniel asked.

"We'll figure something out," Dev said with a naïveté I was surprised he had.

I simply turned back to the demon. I wasn't going to have this discussion with Dev right now. Daniel was right. I was in a corner with only one way out. Halfer had made sure of it. "Fine. I'll have a list ready for him by morning."

Halfer nodded. "I'll try to find out who our competitors are. Although I suspect they don't have the information they need. You said they tried to take you. If they knew when and where the box was being delivered, they would have simply killed you and taken it themselves."

"Lucky me." There was one last thing I wanted to be clear on. "I want you to know that I forced the witches to call you. I wasn't sure you hadn't tried to kill me. I needed to know."

"Perfectly reasonable," Halfer replied in his business-like manner. "I would probably have done the same if I were a pathetic human in your predicament."

"So any repercussions should be on me." I heard the boys behind me start to argue.

"Agreed," Halfer said, and I was finally able to take a full breath. "We'll consider it one of the dangers of doing business. Get me the box, Zoey Wharton, and we'll be even. If not, I fully plan to devour that soul of yours. I'm going to eat it up and make sure you serve me well on the Hell plane."

I stopped breathing again since I figured without any real magical ability, my "service" would probably be hard physical labor of the grossest kind. "You'll get your box. Sarah, do whatever you need to do to get Mr. Halfer back where he came from."

The demon stopped me. "There is, of course, the matter of my payment."

"What are you talking about?" I asked.

"Silly girl, you don't call a demon without giving him a gift, unless, of course, you want to offend the demon greatly."

I looked at Sarah.

Sarah nodded, her whole body still trembling a bit. "He's right. I took a bottle of scotch from your dad's vault. It's old and expensive. If your lordship would look behind the chair, I think you'll find it to your liking."

"Normally I would, but I find I have different appetites tonight." He looked directly at me. "I'm afraid nothing will satisfy me but you, my dear."

I was revolted at the suggestion and couldn't hide my distaste. He laughed at the thought.

"Nothing like that, dearie." He walked dangerously close to the edge of the circle. "I have something different in mind."

He held his hand out, and I found myself in Hell.

Chapter Fourteen

In an instant, I was younger and older, the story of my life playing out in flashes of time. Hell, I discovered, wasn't fire and brimstone. Hell was a personal journey.

I run in the door to our house in Corpus Christi. I am six years old and so excited. I just made a new friend. Her name is Holly, and her dad runs a marina. He has a boat and everything. I run into the house giddy with excitement, bursting to tell my mother about what happened at school. She is my everything and nothing is really real until Momma knows about it. I love my dad, too, but it is in a vague, ill-defined way. I love my father because I'm supposed to. He's gone a lot, and I'm not allowed in his office where he spends the bulk of his time when he's home. So I want to see Momma. I run in and stop because Daddy is home, and he's yelling.

"For chrissake, woman, what do ya mean? What the hell are ya trying to say?"

I stop at the sound. My father rarely raises his voice. I listen closely, and Momma sounds so hard and cold.

"My plane leaves at 6:00, so I'll make this short and

sweet. I'm leaving. I hate this life. I hate these creatures you deal with. I hate having to worry about what happens to you. I've been having an affair with our accountant, and we're leaving tonight."

"Then good riddance to ya," my father says. "But don't think I'll be sending you a cent. I'll send money for the girl, but I better not find out yer spending a cent of it on yerself."

My mother laughs, but it is not the sound I am used to. "Don't bother, Harry. I'm so done with the mommy thing. That child clings and clings. It makes me sick. Let's see how you handle it."

I feel something inside me break. It is a real, physical pain.

"What the hell am I supposed to do with her?" Daddy asks.

I fall down on the linoleum floor when I realize no one wants me.

Then I'm standing in a colder place. I shiver because it's freezing here. I wish I had a sweater, but it's late spring and the days are starting to get hot. I didn't think I would be here. I thought I would be watching a little television and then studying for a biology test after dinner. I didn't think I would stand here in front of this utilitarian window with its gray curtain.

It isn't him. I would know if he was dead. I would know the second he was gone. I wouldn't sit in front of the fucking television while he bled out and died on the street. He's the other half of me. I wouldn't have sat there and complained that he was taking too long. I would have known.

"Are you ready, miss?" an attendant in blue scrubs asks.

My heart beats erratically, and I can barely breathe. Am I ready?

Then I'm running. I have the package. It's some old book, a grimoire, I think. I don't ask questions. I need the work too much. I need the work because I need to forget that he's gone. The client is a witch, so it's probably full of spells. It's only me and Morty tonight. I like him. He's not like the other contractors my father works with. He's kind and has grandchildren. He also turns into an old gray wolf. He likes being a wolf, and he's running behind me. We pass the gates of the house and hit the woods. The car is parked half a mile away, but it's a beautiful night, and I laugh as the wolf runs circles around me and then takes off.

He runs so much faster than me, but I pick up the pace. I hear the snap of metal, but it doesn't register that anything has gone wrong until I hear that howl.

I am standing beside Morty. He's in human form, his skin leathery and wrinkled and covered in blood. The trap is a shark's mouth with a firm hold on its prey.

"Go," he whispers.

I try to pull the trap off, but in the distance, I hear the sound of dogs. The alarm must have been silent.

"Go. Too much silver. Too old," he says.

I will try to save him.

I will fail.

The curtain opens, and I see the body.

You loved butterscotch pie, but I was always too tired to make one. It was too much trouble to make a damn pie. If you're just not on that fucking table...if it's someone else and you're at home wondering where the hell I am, then I promise to make a pie every day for the rest of my life...

He starts to pull the sheet back, and I realize I am not ready.

I watch them take Daniel from me. They pull him right out of our bed. They lock him in chains that leave welts wherever they touch and nothing I do can change it. I fight and plead and cry and they say nothing. Their will is implacable.

It is only when Daniel is gone that the last one turns his silver eyes on me.

"Pity," he says. "You are quite lovely but rules are rules."

I don't know what he means.

"There's no place in my life for a child," my father says.

"Are you ready?" the attendant asks.

"You killed my husband," an old woman cries, and her grandchildren huddle around her. They look at me with accusatory eyes. "He was all I had, and you let him die."

"I'll be right back," Daniel says, and he smiles and runs off to die.

"It was your idea to have a kid," my mother says as she takes a drag off her cigarette.

Daniel returns after three years with nothing in his eyes. I am his responsibility.

"Are you ready?"

Hell is a feeling. The rooms and landmarks are familiar, though there is not an ounce of comfort in them. There is only the certainty that I am nothing. The things I feel and do and the love I give means nothing. It is worthless. I am utterly alone.

This is the place for thieves.

I stand in that hallway at the bottom of the hospital, and I am ready because there is nothing else to be. This place is my home now.

The sheet is pulled back, and I understand.

* * * *

There was a terrible pressure on my chest, and I fought to breathe.

"She's back," Sarah said. She was on her knees beside me. When had I gotten to the floor?

Neil sat back on his heels, his face flushed. He ran a hand through his hair and tears pierced his blue eyes. "I thought we lost you."

Daniel was suddenly at my side, pressing Sarah out of the way. His hands moved across my body as though trying to find injuries.

And all I could think about was that place. It was deep inside me. I might have come back home, but Hell was inside me now. I would see it when I slept, know that it waited for me always. I shivered.

Daniel dragged me up and into his arms. "You're cold."

153

It was always cold in Hell. I had thought it would be hot, but I was shocked at how cold I'd been.

"The ambulance is on its way." Dev ran back into the room. He took a long breath as he realized I was alive. "Thank god. Oh, Zoey, that was horrible."

He couldn't know what horrible was. I groaned as Daniel held me too tight. "Why do my ribs feel like someone jumped on them?"

"Because Neil pressed too hard," Daniel accused.

Neil shook his head. "It's CPR. I had to press on her chest. And I had to do it because you were way too freaked out. The next time you want to control the compressions, keep it together, buddy."

Daniel cuddled me close. It was the most affection he'd shown me in years, but I simply wanted to breathe. "I'm just saying you could have been gentler."

Dev sank to his knees on the other side of me. "Are you all right, sweetheart?"

Daniel growled, a predatory sound.

Nope. I was so not all right. And I wasn't about to tell them about it. I wanted to be alone, to process what had happened. "I'm fine. I don't need an ambulance. Is Halfer gone?"

"He disappeared a couple of minutes ago," Sarah said.

"I was only gone for a minute?" It seemed so much longer. It seemed like forever.

"You weren't gone at all," Dev told me. "Halfer held a hand out and then he disappeared. You stopped breathing."

"You died," Daniel sounded hollow. "You died. He killed you."

"He didn't kill me. I just had a bad reaction to him playing in my brain." I pushed my way out of his arms. I had to be strong. I had a job to do. If I had learned one thing it was that I didn't want to go back to that place. I wasn't sure I could avoid it, but I was damn straight going to try. "I'm fine. I don't need an ambulance."

I needed to get to work. I allowed Dev to help me up.

I was ready. I was ready because I had to be.

* * * *

"Hey, are you coming?"

Sarah's voice pulled me out of myself for the fortieth time that day. I was slightly startled, and it took a moment to remember where I was. I was in the Greenley Hotel standing outside the Gilmore Suite. I was dressed in a maid's uniform, and I was pushing the cart that contained all of our cleaning supplies. I was lost, my mind back in that terrible place Halfer showed me that night almost two weeks before.

I shook off the previous moment and got doggedly to work, pushing the cart toward the now open door.

"Sorry. I'm tired. I can't sleep at Daniel's. It's too quiet. Even when I have the TV on, it still seems too quiet. I wish he'd let me go home."

"You know why he won't." I could hear the resignation in Sarah's voice. She was letting it go for now.

Daniel considered my apartment unsafe. Since the night we called Halfer, there had been no further attempts to kidnap me. Halfer sent a cryptic message telling us not to expect any more trouble, but Daniel chose not to believe him. I couldn't blame Daniel. I didn't trust Lucas Halfer either. So Daniel chose to hide me in the safest place he knew. That very night, over my father's vigorous protests, he took me to his building and introduced me to the concierge as his companion.

That single word worked some sort of magic on all the men in the underground portion of the complex. Michael was deferential, and even the dude Danny thought was a serial killer gave me a wide berth. It was like someone tattooed "property of Daniel Donovan" across my ass and no one bothered to tell me.

We had only been out of the house to buy groceries and order the supplies we would need for the job. Dev or Neil escorted me to work every day and Daniel was there to pick me up. We had dinner each night at my father's house to plan and discuss the heist, but other than that, Daniel kept me in his well-appointed prison. He'd even stopped going to his club for dinner, preferring to stay in with me to make sure I didn't get myself murdered. He was on blood from a blood bank. He kept it in the fridge and microwaved the bags. His new TV dinner diet had not made him pleasant to be around.

Even though it was driving me crazy, I knew better than to protest too much. It wouldn't do any good. And I didn't have the will to fight. I moved through the days like a zombie, willing myself to get through this job because the last thing I wanted was to go back to Halfer's tender care. It was sad that I looked forward to these shifts Sarah and I had taken to acquaint ourselves with the hotel we planned to rob tomorrow.

Neil had a job waiting tables and delivering room service. And Dev convinced the front desk girl to boot the people who were staying in the suite we needed. He was booked in a suite on the top floor right above the room where the Light was being moved to tomorrow.

We were set. The night before, Daniel drilled small, almost invisible holes in the ceiling and installed mini cameras to get surveillance on the room. Sarah and I would clean up any dust the drilling left behind and install a few bugs of our own before the party checked in to the room at four this afternoon.

I should have felt more anxious than I did. By the day after tomorrow, I would know my fate. I would either have the Light of Alhorra and turn it over to Halfer, or I would turn myself over to Halfer. Either way, at least the horrible waiting would be over. But I couldn't muster up a sense of anticipation the way I normally could when a job was coming to fruition.

All I could see when I closed my eyes was that place Halfer had taken me to.

"Well, hopefully you're back in your place soon." Sarah moved back, allowing me to enter.

The Gilmore suite was one of the best suites in the hotel. It consisted of two bedrooms, a large sitting area, a spectacular Roman bath, and a glorious view of the city. I walked over to the windows that spanned the entire living room. Light filled the room and I suddenly realized why they chose this particular suite. It hadn't been confirmed that we were dealing directly with the Fae, but now I was pretty sure.

The Light of Alhorra was a faery object. It made sense that a Fae would own it. I had, long ago, decided to discount the whole story about Halfer's friend losing the object. Halfer didn't have any friends. So if the Smith party was a faery group, then this was probably the perfect room for them. If you could pretend the glass wasn't there, the entire room became a well-appointed aviary. It looked over a large park. On the other side of the building, the views were of other downtown buildings. The lights would be spectacular, but to a faery the lights were simply one more manmade atrocity. The Regal suite that Dev had booked was larger, but the windows were much smaller.

"That's pretty." Sarah started the vacuum cleaner, making sure to pick up the tiny piles of dust that the camera holes had made.

"That's not the only thing that's pretty," a low husky voice said in my ear.

"Ear pieces are working." I mouthed to Sarah, pointing to my ear. She gave me a thumbs-up.

This was something like a dress rehearsal. During the heist, we would keep in contact through Bluetooth devices.

"You look mighty fine in that maid's uniform." I could hear the friendly leer in Dev's voice. "Though I have to admit I prefer the French version."

I wrinkled my nose at the extremely small camera. I knew where it was placed, but I had trouble seeing it. Daniel did an excellent job. Everything was set. Tomorrow night, Sarah and Dev would work the technical side of things from above while Daniel, Neil and I handled the actual heist.

"You know," Dev was saying in my ear, "in the movies, maids always wear sexy heels. What's up with the sneakers?"

I rolled my eyes at the camera. "That's porn, Dev," I said as articulately as I could.

"Is that what they call it?" His chuckle gave me warm chill bumps.

Dev's presence was a definite distraction and one I probably didn't need. I explained several times that as long as we were working together, I planned to keep my hands off him. He hadn't given up. I suppose if I was honest with myself, I knew that keeping Dev at arm's length had nothing to do with workplace ethics and everything to do with Daniel. The truth was I lit up when Dev walked in the room. It was simple to be around Dev and his easy, sexy smile.

When Daniel walked in a room, he brought the heavy burden of our past with him. Dev was like the first sunny morning after days of pounding rain. If Daniel hadn't been around, I would have leapt in with both feet. I would have jumped straight into Dev's bed.

Lately, the only time I felt like smiling at all was when I thought of Dev.

The vacuum stopped. Sarah looked at me with one hand on her hip. "You should do him and get it over with."

"What?" I pulled the comm link out of my ear and switched it off. This wasn't a conversation I wanted to share with Dev.

She laughed and pulled hers out as well. "Girl, it's all over your face. You have that 'gimme, gimme' look that women get when they want a guy who doesn't want them. The only thing wrong with that scenario is he wants you bad. I don't see the problem."

I stared at her.

She held her hands up in defeat. "Okay. I see the problem. I don't understand the problem. I realize that the two of you were engaged, but in the whole time I've known you, he's brought you nothing but heartache. Seriously, it's sad, Z. Daniel skulks in the room and you try to talk to him and he tries to avoid you, and then when you're not looking he watches you like a hawk watches a fluffy rabbit. I don't get the attraction."

"You didn't know him before."

"Well, I know him now, and I know he isn't making you happy."

"And you think Dev can make me happy?" I'd been wondering the same thing for days now.

"I think Dev can give you an orgasm, and that's what counts." Sarah gave me a practical smile. "Unfortunately, you're one of those girls who is madly in love with the first guy you had sex with."

"Why is that unfortunate?"

Sarah grinned wryly. "Because you haven't learned that sex can just be fun. You seem to think it has to be all passion and emotion and commitment. The truth is it can be nothing more than a good time. Last night I had a good time with Joe, and this morning I can't remember his name."

"You said his name was Joe."

"I call them all Joe. It's easier that way. The point is I had a good time. He had a good time. I didn't have to brood over his undead status, and he didn't care that he wouldn't ever see me in the daylight. I realize that you're never going to be so casual, but Dev could be a happy medium."

"Well, it's nice to see you finally forgave the poor man." It had taken a while for Sarah to forget her first meeting with our faery prince.

"He walked through my garden and, OMG, you would not believe the herbs I have now. Every witch in my coven is jealous. I hope my sister gets to see it." Sarah flushed a little, but pressed on. "I know you don't want to hurt Daniel, but you can't spend the rest of your life like this. There's a man upstairs whose grandpa was a fertility god. If you don't want him, please let me have a go."

I frowned at the thought, and Sarah pounced.

"Aha, jealousy rears its ugly head. If the thought of me sleeping with him puts that look on your face, then you better get busy yourself." She looked around the room and sighed. "I think we're done here. Where should we plant the bugs?"

I pulled out a handful of helpful listening devices, and Sarah and I played hide the bugs.

An hour later, we changed and clocked out. Sarah and I made our way up to the suite. Dev let us in, a smile on his face. It had been a long day and an even longer night before it, so I grabbed a bottle of water and headed straight for the big, fluffy bed in the master bedroom. I threw myself on the middle of the bed and sighed in contentment as I sank slightly into the mattress. Daniel was right about his bed, though it wasn't just undead backs it played hell on.

The red light of the digital clock read five minutes to four. The "Smith" party would be arriving soon, and I would spend the night on surveillance. Daniel and I would watch the marks and decide how to handle the job. We would argue and collaborate and compromise until we had the most efficient plan we could come up with. We would not discuss the fact that he wanted to kill himself rather than live the way he was living. We would not discuss anything but the job at hand.

I opened my eyes when I felt the bed shift. Dev sat on the edge looking down at me with a lazy half-smile that made my heart beat faster. His dark hair was mussed as though he'd run his hand through it to get it out of his face. For the first time since I met him, he wasn't clean shaven. It was terrifically sexy on him. I reached up and let my fingers play across that roughness.

"I can shave if you want." His eyes slid away from mine.

"No, I like it. It's sexy." I let my thumb rub against his cheek. I loved touching him. It made me feel connected, grounding me here.

Emerald green eyes fastened on mine, that slow, sexy smile crossing his face. "Then I'll grow a beard if you like. I usually shave twice a day. I forgot today. I was busy setting up the computers."

"Why do you shave twice a day?"

Dev looked at me seriously. "They don't have facial hair, the Fae that is. My family and their people, they don't have any body hair. When I hit puberty, it was the exclamation point that shouted I wasn't a full Fae."

"Well, I think it's incredibly sexy." I sat up. He looked so sad that I impulsively kissed his rough cheek.

His expression changed in an instant from melancholy to distinctly wolf-like. I found myself on my back with Dev pinning me down gently, his chest against mine. His weight was a delicious anchor. "That Sarah is a smart girl, but she got a few things wrong."

I felt myself flush. "You couldn't hear us! I unplugged the ear pieces. How did you listen in?"

"Did I fail to mention I can read lips? Well, I can, and she's right, you should definitely sleep with me." He laughed as he lowered his lips to mine in a sweet, quick kiss. Far too quick for my tastes. "But she's wrong about it merely being a good time. I'm serious about this relationship."

I wanted to believe him. I so wanted to believe him. "I don't think we've known each other long enough to have a relationship."

"Call it what you want. I'm not your good-time guy. I'm just your guy." He kissed me again, this time lingering over my mouth and making me tremble. His tongue foraged deeply in my mouth, rubbing against mine in a way that went straight to my pink parts.

His hand stroked my curves under the pants I was wearing. He came up for air and pressed his forehead against mine. "We need each other, Zoey. You'll see that. I'm not like that vampire. I won't try to keep you in a cage. I know the supernatural world. I can show you amazing things. I want to show you the world, not keep it from you."

"He's afraid I'll get hurt." I was uncomfortable talking about Daniel with Dev.

"He's afraid he'll lose control. Don't get me wrong, Zoey. As vampires go, Daniel is all right. But he is a vampire, and they're all the same. He wants to dominate everything around him. His instinct is to kill or control. He's protected you by telling the Council you're his companion. It's a good thing. No other vampires will bother you, but if I thought he was trying to make you a real companion, I would stake him myself."

I pushed away from him and scrambled to sit up. "How can you say that?"

Dev sat back, his eyes wary. "I can say it because I know more about that world than you do. I deal with a lot of vamps at my clubs. There's a reason he's kept you apart from that world. Some part of Daniel has managed to cling to his old life in a way I've never seen in a vampire. He remembers that he loved you once, and he wants to protect you."

"What's so bad about being a companion?" For so long I wanted nothing more than to be that for Daniel. It seemed like such a nice thing to be.

Dev looked at me like I was a naïve child. "Zoey, a companion isn't like the vampire's wife. She's the vampire's possession. She's required to obey her master. Legally a vampire can kill another vampire for even touching his companion in a sexual way. The Council would sanction the killing. They tend to kill anyone who tries to take their companions. Then there's the fact that the companion can legally be executed if she strays."

"Daniel would never do that." It seemed there was a lot I didn't know.

"Yes, he would," Dev said with a sympathetic surety. "He knows he would and that's why he's stayed away. The bond

161

between vampire and companion is twisted, and Daniel doesn't want that for you. He wants to see you safe. He knows how dangerous the Council can be to a woman like you."

"What does that mean?"

"You're special, Zoey. I don't completely understand it. Albert picked up on it." He frowned a little. "But Daniel is trying to be reasonable. I actually admire him for it. He knows something you don't. The Daniel you knew died long ago. Any affection and kindness from him is an echo, and before too long, it will be gone and all that will be left is vampire."

"He wants to meet the dawn." It was the first time I mentioned it to anyone, and the minute it was out of my mouth, I wished I hadn't said it. It felt like a betrayal to talk to Dev about this.

"They'll never let him."

"The Council? But the Council helps vampires who don't want to live."

Dev nodded and proceeded with caution. The way he was handling me made me wary that worse revelations were sure to come. "It's true that the Council helps old men meet the dawn, but I assure you they'll do whatever it takes to ensure that Daniel Donovan continues to walk the night. He hasn't told you anything, has he? Daniel is important to the Council. He's practically royalty."

I stared at him. It wasn't true. What he said went against everything I knew about the vampire world. Age was prized over youth. The young were merely tolerated. "Why is he important? He's so young that he doesn't have any power. Only very old vampires have real power."

I watched as Dev decided what he wanted to say next. "The day after I met you, I asked Albert to work up profiles on your whole team. Don't get pissed off. You would do the same thing if you had my resources."

I frowned but let him continue because he was right. I would totally have hired a PI to dig into his background if I had the time and the money. As it was, I had only the resources to Google him and take a look at his Facebook page. "What did you find out?"

"I found out a lot of things. I found out that Neil lived on the streets for five years before your father took an interest in him and introduced him to you. Sarah has some unsavory connections. Her mother was heavily into black magic before she died. You're a talented thief who secretly reads romance novels."

I threw a pillow at him. "How the hell did you find that out?"

"I didn't need a PI for that. I snooped. You leave them on the window sill in your bathroom because you read while you soak in that tiny tub of yours. I have a gorgeous antique claw foot tub at my place, by the way. There is more than enough room for two."

I ignored the invitation. "And Daniel?"

The flirtatious look on his face fled. "Daniel Donovan is the single most powerful vampire to rise in the last thousand years."

I was speechless for a moment. That was the most ridiculous thing I had ever heard. "Daniel isn't powerful. He can barely function as a vampire."

Dev shook his head. "You don't understand vampires, Zoey. The newly risen vampire always kills the first time he feeds. It's why the Council swoops down like vultures the second they locate a new vamp."

"Daniel didn't kill. Daniel has never killed," I stated.

Dev's green eyes widened. "Oh, he's killed all right, but not because he lost control. He had exquisite control from the moment he rose. A normal vampire takes hundreds of years to gain a single power. Some vampires have the power of persuasion. Some have incredible speed. They all have strength, but it is markedly more significant in some. Some can shape shift or call an animal. Some vampires even gain the power of flight after a thousand or so years."

"So if Daniel lives a long time, he might be able to fly?" I wondered exactly where he was going with this. I knew Daniel was fast and strong. I guessed he was a fast learner.

"Daniel could fly the night he rose," Dev said. "Vampires tend to have one or two powers after hundreds or thousands of years of living. Daniel had them from the moment he became a vampire."

Tears sprang to my eyes as he spoke. He was lying. He had to be. Daniel would never keep those things from me. If this was true, then Daniel was farther from me than I ever imagined. "Daniel can't do those things. He would have told me."

He looked at me and there was sympathy in his green eyes.

163

"Zoey, there was some discussion among the Council about executing him. There are some today who still believe it is the best course of action. Some members of the Council see him as a threat. It was only his ability to predict when a new vampire would rise that kept him alive. He's the first in thousands of years with the ability, and the vampires need it. With the way the news covers murders these days, the vampires need forewarning to stay secret. Daniel gives them that warning. Some vampires wanted to place him at the head of the Council. There was talk of a crown. The vampires haven't crowned a king in the last millennium."

My mind spun. Dev's words turned my whole world upside down. "That's insane. He's…he's Daniel. He likes science fiction and computers. He's not some vampire king. He's a nerd, for god's sake."

"I'll let you read the dossier. I'm sorry, Zoey. I knew you didn't know the whole story, but I never thought he'd kept you completely in the dark."

He put a hand on my shoulder, and I moved away.

"Zoey, don't blame me." Dev's green eyes were sad. I was sure he wanted to go back to the intimacy we'd been trying out earlier, but I couldn't. "I didn't lie to you."

But he'd been the messenger. "I know, but I need some space. I need to think."

"All right. I'm sorry. I didn't mean for any of this to hurt you," he explained with a deep sigh. "I actually came in to give you this."

He handed me a plastic packet. I looked at the bag in my hand. It contained dry herbs.

"Albert made it for you," he said. "It's for a dreamless sleep. I figured you needed it after whatever the demon did to you. You need rest, Zoey. You have to be at the top of your game if we're going to pull this off. I'm going to go back out and make sure the surveillance is working. Take this and get some rest. When this is over, I'm going to take you on a trip, and we'll get rid of those nightmares. We'll go anywhere you like, sweetheart."

He kissed me on the forehead, and I looked at the packet in my hand. I should have gone straight to the toilet and flushed it down. Who knew what was in those herbs? I'd known these people for so little time that there was no way I could trust them. So why did I walk to the bathroom and fill a glass with water? Why did I pour the packet into the water and watch it dissolve? Why did I swallow every last drop? Why did I trust that man so much?

I made my way back to the bed and didn't really care if I'd taken a sleeping potion or poison. Either way, I was going to sleep, and for a while, I wouldn't care about anything.

I sank into the sheets as blissful oblivion took me.

Long before I wanted to, I was jarred awake.

"Zoey," Neil was saying as consciousness slowly drifted back. "Something is wrong. We have to go now. If we're going to do this job, we have to do it tonight."

Chapter Fifteen

It took everything I had to ignore Daniel as I walked into the living area of the suite. A million questions ran through my mind, but now wasn't the time.

The whole living area was set up as a command center. There were three different computers throwing off low lights and humming quietly. The computer with the largest monitor showed the surveillance feed from the downstairs suite.

Neil talked to Daniel in hushed tones as I walked over to the monitor.

There they were. Our marks. Two men and one woman. Definitely Fae. They had long, elegant bodies and moved with sure grace. The men were dressed in khakis and polo shirts of varying color, but they tugged at the clothes as though the fabric bothered them. The female sported a brunette ponytail and wore a skirt and button down blouse.

A male with long, sandy blond hair and the female sat facing the open window. The bugs were obviously working as we could hear them plain as day. They spoke quietly in some language I couldn't understand. The last man paced in and out of the camera's range. He was the tallest, and if I had to bet, he was the blond one's brother.

"Do we have any idea what they're saying?" I kept my eyes on the screen, studying the marks.

Dev walked up behind me and pressed a mug of coffee into my hands. My mind was still foggy from sleep and the potion. The mug felt warm and solid.

He put a hand on my back as he leaned in and looked at the monitor. "I know what they're saying, most of it anyway. They're speaking Gaelic. It's not exactly what my mother's people speak, but it's close enough. Fun fact: the Gaelic language is a derivation of ancient Elvish."

"Thanks, professor." Daniel took up position on my other side, trapping me between him and Dev. "Could you cut the trivia and tell her what they said?"

Dev ignored the bait and slid into the seat in front of the monitor. He pointed to the female. "This one seems to be the leader. She's been telling the other two what to do. If I had to guess, the men are bodyguards. I think the word they used was escort, but I can't be sure."

"Did you get a shot of the box?" I asked.

"Yes." Daniel bit the word out.

I finally looked up at him. Usually, right before a job there was a sort of calm that settled over Daniel. It was the same way for me, rather like an actor about to go on stage. We were nervous right up until we were about to go on and then we realized that we knew our lines and it was all going to be all right. The night before a job there was tension, but there was also excitement, even for Daniel. He liked to pretend that he did this just to keep me out of trouble, but he liked the rush, too.

But I could tell from the way he held his body that he wasn't looking forward to the curtain going up on this particular performance.

"All right, is it in a safe or did they trap it?" I really hoped the answer was the safe. It was so much easier to deal with a nice, predictable safe than to have to figure out the Indiana Jones crap.

Dev pointed to the screen. "See, it's right there." He indicated a large box sitting on the coffee table.

I leaned forward to get a better look, and Dev obliged me by zooming in on the object. It was a large, rectangular box with ornate carvings. I couldn't see a place where the lid to the box would come off. It looked like a single block of wood. I supposed that was where the whole part about "only those with the purest of intentions could open it" came in. This was the box described in the files. It was sitting there, right out in the open. They weren't even looking at it.

"Awesome, huh?" Neil still wore his hotel uniform and the contacts that turned his normally blue eyes brown.

In our line of work, we took a few precautions. Our disguises weren't *Mission Impossible* good, but we did try to cover the major bases. The goal was to not be seen at all, but the reality was in a fight or flight situation, the only thing most people remembered was hair color, eye color, and size or shape. There wasn't a lot we could do about size or shape, but the rest could be fixed. Neil's hair was black tonight and tomorrow it would be a chestnut brown.

I looked around Neil and noticed Daniel was frowning at me. We shared the same concern. It wasn't right. They should protect the box. They should guard the box. It was sitting in the middle of the room like a big old cupcake with a note saying "please eat me."

Things were never that easy.

Dev tapped the screen. "They sat it down and haven't touched it since. There's a problem, though. I heard them talking about moving the box tomorrow morning at dawn."

"I thought the box was scheduled to be moved two days from now," Sarah said as she came in the room. She adjusted her short blonde wig and looked oddly normal in black tights and a black sweater.

"They talked about that, too," Dev said. "It was confusing but they were talking about the veil being its thinnest in two days, but the leader thinks he can get through it tomorrow morning in the in-between time."

"The veil between worlds?" I asked.

Dev turned the chair around. "Yes. There are Fae tribes who travel this way, or so I'm told. It's complex, but there are times when the dimensional walls are thin, and if you know when and where, you can move through one plane and into another. Apparently the veil will be thin somewhere close to here starting tomorrow morning."

It was how the Fae had left the Earth plane millennia ago. There were some who theorized that the supernatural beings on Earth were creatures from other planes that had gotten lost and adapted. If these faeries were trying to cross dimensions then it only made sense that they would try it during one of the in-between times. The story went that the veil between worlds was always thinnest at dawn and dusk, when night and day changed places and all things were, for that brief time, possible.

It explained why the Fae had moved up their timetable. It explained why Daniel decided we needed to move now. It didn't explain why that damn box was sitting in the open looking so ripe for the plucking.

I couldn't help but let my gaze go back to Daniel.

"Something's wrong," he said, reading my mind.

"Definitely."

Neil and Dev argued the merits of the easy job with Sarah while Daniel and I managed to meet in the middle of the room.

"It's too easy," he said quietly.

Nothing was that easy in our line of business. We weren't opportunistic thieves who broke into convenient houses and hoped that the owners left valuables lying around. We spent months planning jobs because the things we stole were the things an owner protects. Items of arcane value tend to be obsessively guarded. When we stole an amulet of protection a few years back, we had to go through three layers of wards, countless locks, a pit bull, and a safe. We made ten grand off that job, but here was a million dollars sitting in the open, waiting for the taking.

"Halfer is fucking with us, Z." Daniel ran a frustrated hand through his hair.

"I don't know. We have to have a legitimate shot at getting the job done or I might be able to wriggle my way out of the contract." After spending a little quality time with the demon, I doubted he was a wriggle-room kind of guy.

Daniel shook his head. "I don't trust this. It feels bad."

"I know, but what are we going to do? Are we going to watch them take that box into another dimension in the morning? We have no idea where the entry point will be. It could be a crowded street for all we know. This is a known quantity."

"Do the job, don't let the job do you," Daniel said with a reasonable impersonation of my dad's accent. It was my father's mantra.

"So we go in and do the job and be ready for it all to go to hell." It was our only option.

The phone on the table started to ring, and we all stopped. This was our chance.

Sarah made her way to the table and answered the phone with a crisp, professional voice. "Room service. How may we help you?"

I glanced at the monitor. The slightly smaller but still freakishly tall blond dude was speaking methodically into the phone. He seemed to be struggling with English. There was nothing in his manner that gave me the impression he knew anything was wrong. He seemed to be just another traveler ordering a meal from the hotel's in room dining service. On the surface, he had no idea Daniel had rerouted the calls to this suite.

"Of course, sir, would you like the house salad with those?" Sarah asked. There was a reply on the end, and Sarah responded. "Yes, sir, it will be about fifteen minutes. Thank you."

She hung up the phone. I watched the screen, looking for anything that could tell me this was a trap. In the background, the blond man was sitting in front of the television, switching through channels curiously, and his fellow travelers slowly joined him. They didn't even look at the box on the table.

"Dev, start the loop," Daniel said, checking his gun.

Dev pressed a few buttons so the security cameras on this floor would pick up nothing unusual, just empty, peaceful hallways. We'd cut into their security feed the day before and controlled the cameras. "Done."

I took a deep breath. I was so going to regret this. "Okay guys, it's show time."

* * * *

In the best of circumstances, a thief wants to pull a job when the mark is out. A house burglar always waits until the occupants of the house he wants to rob are out for the evening. A home invasion is a different animal. The home invader wants to hurt and humiliate. The burglar wants to steal. If given the choice, the burglar will always choose non confrontation over the alternative. I would rather deal with a minefield of lasers than have to confront one single person defending their goods. Lasers might hurt, but they didn't do stupid things like make you shoot them.

I didn't want to hurt anyone, so we switched to our backup plan and loaded a tranquilizer gun with enough ketamine to put down a rhino. Dev assured us it would work on the faeries. Daniel wanted to be sure by using it on Dev, but I nixed that experiment. I dearly hoped Dev was right because the last thing we needed was a violent fight. Still, I would put my vampire and werewolf up against faeries any day of the week.

Daniel and I pressed our backs against the wall as Neil approached the door to the Gilmore suite. I took a deep breath and flicked the safety off my modified gun. It was small and could be concealed but took several types of exotic rounds. It was one of Daniel's inventions, and it had served us well. That night it was loaded with the tranquilizer rounds, but it easily took silver, wood, or cold iron.

Neil pushed the cart to the door and knocked. "Room service."

Daniel's hand brushed mine. "Stay with me. Unless I go down, and then you run like hell, okay?"

I nodded because I wasn't exactly going to argue with him now. The door opened.

"Your order, sir." Neil pushed the cart inside the door.

And the man let him in. He didn't ask to check his credentials. He didn't ask Neil to stay in the hall while he checked the tray for weapons, which he would have found. He simply opened the door and let him in. My every instinct screamed that something was wrong with this scenario.

I heard the metal tray clink as Neil pulled it off the plate as though he were presenting the food.

There was no food, of course. There was only a gun, which Neil fired into the large faery as Daniel and I turned the corner and entered the room.

I shot the female, my tranquilizer dart finding her chest. It stuck there, squarely in the center of her lithe body, and I heard the slight hiss as the dart injected the drug into her system. She went down on one knee and then mercifully slid onto her back. Daniel shot the other male who was getting off the couch to find out what all the fuss was about.

It was all over in less than ten seconds, and no one made a sound. If I were more trusting, I would have said job well done. I'm not that girl, and the perfect silence in the room made me nervous.

"Neil, check the suite and make sure we didn't miss anyone." I held my gun over the female. Her eyes were still open, and I wasn't sure she wouldn't need another dose to send her to la la land. She seemed to have a stronger will than her male counterparts.

"We didn't miss anything, Zoey." Dev's voice came over my ear piece.

"Can't be too safe," I said into the mike.

"Why?" the faery managed to ask. She fought the drug with admirable effort. She finally looked toward the box, and I was surprised to see the look in her eyes wasn't covetous. She didn't appear to be angry. Sadness. Regret. Those were the emotions plain on her face.

Something took over. It was that rebellious streak that almost always got me in trouble, and it surely would now. I leaned over the fallen faery. "It's just a job. Nothing personal. If you want your box back, go see a demon named Lucas Halfer. His true name is Brixalnax. He's the one who wants the box."

She slumped back on the carpet.

Daniel laughed and the sound was rich. I looked over, and he was smiling at me.

"I thought you would be pissed."

He pulled out a card and laid it on the coffee table. "Great minds think alike. I was going to leave the asshole's business card."

"Zoey," Sarah's voice came over the ear piece. "Keep it down in there. We have guests coming off the elevator."

Daniel nodded and lowered his voice. "Get the box, Z. I'll watch the door."

Neil came out of the bedroom. "We're alone. Is that it?"

I slid the backpack off my shoulders and reached for the box. It was surprisingly heavy. I couldn't help but stare for a moment. What the cameras hadn't shown was how truly beautiful the box was. My hands caressed it as it went in the pack. It was so shiny and pretty. Someone had spent time on it. Some artist had poured himself into this box. It was made of love. For the faintest moment, I thought I heard it whisper…

"Ready?" Neil asked, abruptly breaking the moment.

I zipped the box into my backpack. It took every inch of space in the extra-large pack. I shimmied my arms into the straps and settled it on my back. "That's it."

"Guys! You have company." Sarah's voice was tense in my ear.

"What kind of company?" Daniel's gun was in his hand once more. He pulled a magazine out of his pocket and reloaded. This time the bullets were silver. It was a gamble but a safe one. Silver works on most supernaturals, and it goes without saying it works on humans.

"Five." Dev's calmness was reassuring. "As far as I can see, they're human. It might be a coincidence, but…"

The door suddenly opened, and I knew this was the trouble I had been expecting ever since I noticed the Light of Alhorra sitting out in the open. Whoever was coming through the door wasn't breaking in. They had a freaking keycard.

I stood there, rooted to the floor. I was pretty sure Dev and Sarah could hear my heart pounding through the ear pieces.

"Who the hell are you?" The first man to appear was large, his body built on muscular lines. His face was craggy as though the years between childhood and his current state had been rough enough to carve a perpetual expression of hate. His eyes shifted between me and Daniel.

Neil was nowhere to be seen. He'd disappeared, giving us the potential advantage of surprise if they thought Daniel and I were the only ones here.

Five men. Somehow they'd gotten through our wards and knew exactly where to find us. And they had come prepared. Each man carried two pistols and likely had more weapons hidden. But at that moment, I was mostly concerned with the ten guns pointed at us.

Daniel laid his gun on the coffee table, holding his hands up. "All right, everyone stay calm, and no one has to die."

One of the other men, a shorter fellow who looked like he could use hygiene tips, laughed. "Yeah, you'd like that. Why don't you give us that box and we'll see what happens."

"Box?" I took a deep breath and hoped they didn't notice the backpack. I couldn't lose the box now.

"My soul's on the line here, bitch." A short man with a plethora of tattoos stalked closer, stepping over the bodies of the faeries. "I want that box. Give it to me, and maybe I won't leave you for what was coming up behind us."

"You don't want that, girl," the unhygienic one spat. "You ever seen a demon?"

Fuck it all. It was my worst nightmare.

"Stop talking to the marks, Greg," the bald guy said.

I took great exception to that statement. I sure as hell wasn't a mark. I was the girl who took out marks. Except, of course, this time I had played straight into Halfer's hands or claws or whatever he had.

"Now, girlie, hand over that pack on your back," the leader was saying. "Thanks for taking out the faeries for us."

He looked at me, and for the slightest second I thought I could reason with him. "No. I can't do that. Let's talk for a minute."

I took a single step back, and then he smiled and fired his gun straight at my chest.

One minute I was waiting for the bullet to hit, and the next Daniel slammed me against the wall so hard I felt the breath knocked straight out of me. I hit the wall and bounced off it to the cold tile. Daniel's body covered mine, surrounding me completely. I couldn't move. I could barely breathe. Daniel rocked against me, his body jumping in odd, jerky motions. Every couple of seconds his back would spasm and press my body further into the hard tile.

Bullets. They shot Daniel over and over again.

The sounds cracked the air, threatening to split my ear drums. The box on my back pressed against my skin until I was almost certain it would cut through my clothes and stab into my flesh, but they were shooting Daniel. Pure panic assaulted me. How much could he take?

Daniel curled himself around me until I could barely breathe.

"Stop!" There was a chuckle. "I don't think we need to waste more bullets. Haul that corpse off her and get the box."

There was the comforting sound of a low, guttural canine growl and then the girlie-like sounds grown men can make when faced with a werewolf.

Bullets started to fly again, but Daniel wouldn't move. I couldn't see anything from my vantage point. There was a loud roar and then the sound Neil makes when he guts someone.

Then I felt a warm liquid hit my hands. I looked at the floor I was pressed against. Blood was everywhere, rivulets beginning to form rivers and pools. It was a rich, dark red, so red it had a purple cast to it. It was Daniel's blood, and it was everywhere.

"Daniel? Daniel, please talk to me." Was he already dead? Had he given his immortal life to protect my dumbass human one? I couldn't stand the thought.

"I'm okay, Z. Idiots used regular bullets." His voice shook, giving fine tremors to his words.

"Yeah, but they used a lot of them." I could hear the tremble in my voice and realized I was on the verge of tears. I couldn't afford to break down. I needed to stay calm and rational, so I took a deep breath and tried not to think about the fact that Daniel was losing his life's blood.

"I just need a little blood, and I'll be fine." There was a brief pause. I could hear the struggle continue, but the guns stopped firing. Daniel's hands tangled in my hair. "God, you smell good, Zoey. You have to stay away from me until I've fed, baby. That smell...it's been so freaking long..."

He growled, the sound skimming across my skin. He was dying and yet my skin lit at the sound of his hunger. I could feed him.

After what seemed like an eternity, he shifted his weight off me. Even through the obvious pain, he helped me up to a sitting position.

I winced as I realized I was sitting in Daniel's blood. It covered me.

"Dev," Daniel said, not looking up. His hands shook, and he

stared at me with a focus I found a bit frightening. And arousing. The world had exploded around us and I focused on Daniel and those alien eyes. I was staring at his fangs and wishing he would kiss me. "Nice of you to join us."

Dev's low gasp pulled me out of the moment. Dev stood in the living area. He held a gun in his hand, and his eyes widened at the sight of Daniel. "Holy shit, man, what the hell happened to you?"

"Flesh wound," Daniel said.

"You can't feed off her." Dev's hand clenched around his gun and, for the briefest moment, I thought he might raise it to Daniel. But it stayed at his side. "You know what it would mean."

It would mean he would live. "Danny, you have to."

He turned away from me. "Tell Neil to leave a couple of them alive, please. I need them alive."

Dev nodded, waiting a second before he turned and stalked off after Neil.

Daniel stood, his whole body shaking slightly. He stared into the room where Neil was playing with the men left over, treating them like chew toys. "Zoey, I need to help Neil and Dev. Promise me you'll stay down. And, baby, please keep your eyes closed. I have to…I can't do what I need to do with you watching. I can't."

"All right." I closed my eyes as he walked away. The sounds were terrible, but I kept my promise. Daniel needed to feed or he would die, and he hated it. I could handle it because it meant he would live, but if he didn't want me to watch, then I would keep my eyes closed. There were grunts and groans and then there was a sad moan and silence.

After what felt like an eternity, there was a tug on my arm, and Daniel hauled me up.

"It's all right now, Z." He looked no worse for the wear. In fact, he looked terrific. He practically glowed. His clothes were ruined, but he stared down at me with his alien eyes and his fangs extended, and, for a second, he was a dark god.

"I'm so sorry, Zoey." He shook his head and his eyes cleared. "I didn't want you to see me like that."

I ignored him because I didn't have time for his undead angst. I could have told him I didn't care what he did as long as he was alive. I would have gutted all five men myself if it would have spared him a moment's pain. I took silent satisfaction in the fact that he was alive and they were not.

I moved from my spot and surveyed the battleground. There had been five men and they looked to be fully human. Hardly a fair fight. Someone had sent them in without silver bullets. Cannon fodder. Whoever sent these men meant them to be the first wave, and I had no doubt there was more to come.

The previously lovely suite now looked like a battlefield littered with corpses. The man who had tried to shoot me lay at my feet, his throat sporting two prominent marks. His skin was an ashen gray. The blood that previously filled his body now ran through Daniel's veins and I thanked the universe for it.

Neil paced the floor of the room, his wolf body twitching and low growls coming from his throat. I rarely got to see him in his full wolf form. When we ran normal jobs, Neil usually just changed an arm or a hand. When he fully transformed, we were usually in deep shit, and I didn't get a chance to stare at him when we were running for our lives.

The wolf before me was a thing of beauty. He was huge but perfectly proportioned. His fur was arctic white and looked like it would be heaven to touch.

The wolf seemed agitated. He walked between the bodies, his snout coming down, scenting, and then he forced himself away. He whinnied a sad, pleading sound. Neil fought his base urge to feed. His tail swiped back and forth, his head coming up almost pleading my way. Except he wasn't looking to me. I was about to go to him when I realized he was calling for Daniel.

Daniel walked over to him and placed a hand on Neil's back. He stroked the white fur, and Neil calmed down. The wolf seemed more focused, and even his eyes seemed more human than before.

"Time for that after we save our asses, Neil," Daniel said quietly.

"You can call wolves," I whispered more to myself than anyone else.

It was a vampiric talent and one that should have taken Daniel hundreds of years to acquire. Dev had told me the truth. I didn't know the whole story where Daniel was concerned. He'd hidden so much from me.

Daniel was far beyond an ordinary vampire.

Daniel stared at me, his eyes betraying his guilt. "Later. I'll tell you everything later. We have to get you out of here now."

"No, we have to get Sarah." And we had to clean up. Bodies were messy. Bodies meant evidence.

Dev shook his head. "When I left her she was passing a magnet over the hard drives and getting ready to bolt."

"Good girl." Daniel nodded. It was standard procedure. It meant one less person for us to worry about. Daniel reached down and pulled the darts out of the faeries, pocketing the shells. "She'll be safer that way. Make sure we haven't left anything behind. What a cluster fuck."

After a quick search of the room, Daniel declared it was as clean as it could get. We hadn't fired a gun. The dead men had been taken apart by a wolf or exsanguinated by a vampire. "All right, let's get the hell out of here."

"That could be tricky," Dev replied, frowning. "The elevators are out. That's why it took me so long to get down here. I had to take the stairs. The wards are holding, though. We don't have civilians in the hallway."

Just before the heist, Sarah put up wards on the floor to keep the guests in their rooms. It was nothing harmful. They would have a sudden and complete desire to spend the evening in.

I looked down at the corpse Daniel had left. Sure enough, he was wearing a charm around his now defunct neck. They had been prepared for witchcraft. Someone had done their homework. If only they had been prepared for a hungry vampire and werewolf, maybe they would be alive.

Daniel grabbed my arm. "We'll take the stairs. You stay close."

I shivered as my entire body chilled. A cold wind swept through the room, like a wave lapping at my skin.

"Oh, that would be a great deal of trouble," a silky smooth voice said from the doorway. "Let me save you the trip."

I looked at our new guest. The demon the men had talked about had finally shown up.

Chapter Sixteen

"Vampires and faeries and werewolves, oh my!" the demon said with a smile of great pleasure spreading across his face.

He was in human form. He appeared to be a tall gentleman with lanky grace and a designer wardrobe. He wore an immaculately cut three-piece suit and the vibrant blue tie stood out.

"You run with interesting company, little human." The demon's accent was crisp and British. I wondered briefly if demons had nationalities. Halfer had a bland Midwestern accent.

"Did Halfer send you?" I tried to sound more blasé than I felt. I felt like screaming and running away, but I knew it wouldn't do me any good. The backpack I was carrying suddenly seemed heavier than before.

"Are you talking about Brix? He's going by Halfer? That's so obvious." The demon rolled his eyes. "Not at all. He would be perfectly perplexed to discover I showed up, which is, of course, the point. Did you enjoy the trio I sent to you at the club? Brix was pissed that I tried to take you. I wasn't going to hurt you. Much. I only wanted to ask a few questions. Luckily, he's easily led. He thinks he caught the culprit. For a doubt demon, he is really sure of himself. I like to think of it as his tragic flaw."

"Why would you fight another demon?" Dev asked. "Shouldn't you be on the same side?"

The demon laughed. "Oh, yes, the Hell plane is a magical place of demonic harmony where we all hold hands and shit rainbows. We're at war. Always. As for Brix and myself, you could say we're auditioning for the same part, and I've decided to play a little rough."

"What exactly are you looking for?" Don't say the box, don't say the box, was the mantra going through my head.

"Dear child, I'm looking for the box." He dashed my every hope. "Please call me...well, I'm certainly not going to give you my real name. I don't want to get summoned. Let's go with Stewart. It fits this meat I'm walking about in."

There was a moment of silence as my stomach churned at the thought.

"You're in a human being?" Dev's voice shook ever so slightly.

I looked at Daniel in the hopes that he would tell me this Stewart thing was lying. The only demon we'd dealt with up until now had been able to change form at will. Daniel frowned and nodded, indicating that everything he sensed was indeed human.

Stewart rolled someone else's brown eyes and sighed. "You don't have to sound so disappointed. Not all of us can do that thing Brix does. It's impressive, but do you understand the kind of will it takes to completely dominate a human? Even now I can hear this miserable piece of meat screaming in our head. It's distracting, but I persevere. And I can do things Brix can't even think about."

Neil growled at the demon.

"Now that's just rude." The demon gave him a coquettish frown. "And here I've tried to be so pleasant. Vampire, call off your dog if you want him to live. Don't think I won't do it because the truth of the matter is I'm really more of a cat person."

"Neil, you should change now," Daniel ordered.

There was that rush of power that always filled the room when Neil changed forms and then he was back to his human body and in all his glory. One minute he was a beautiful wolf, and the next he was a gorgeous man. Neil was utterly lovely. He was smaller than Daniel and Dev, but perfectly formed. His hair had changed back to his normal blond and it curled over his ears.

The demon stopped, his eyes widening, and I would have sworn there was a hint of drool. "Goodness, and by goodness I mean badness. I take back what I said about cats. You look scrumptious, puppy."

Neil shrugged but gave no obvious emotion. "I get that a lot." He picked up his clothes from the floor as I turned my head, trying not to blush. I was never going to get used to random nakedness.

"Please don't. Not on my account." The demon practically purred like the cats he purported to love.

Neil laughed, though it held no humor, and I turned again as he was pulling his white dress shirt on. He left it and the top button of his pants open for effect, showing off his perfectly cut chest. He smiled his best male model smile. "It's not on your account, Stewart. It's totally on hers."

The demon gave me a *tsk tsk* sound. "Humans and their odd morality. Here you are, little girl, stealing an important thing from these seemingly pleasant faery creatures, but god forbid you see a very lovely penis. I have no comprehension of your people."

"Right back at ya, buddy." I started to slowly shuffle my way backward as the demon seemed to be closing in on me.

Stewart stopped his stalking of me long enough to look at Daniel and Dev. "And the two of you are panting after her? Someone is going to have to explain that to me. At least I can somewhat understand the vampire. She has that special blood you crave. She can make you strong. But you, faery, explain the fascination the human girl holds. I can see she's vaguely attractive, but she's certainly not in your league. Yet you fear for her. Even now I can feel your anxiety for her. You hope that I don't break her. You and the vampire would exchange your lives for her pathetic human one. It doesn't seem like a fair trade to me." He looked between the men and then suddenly turned to Neil, frowning. "Not you, too, puppy. I thought better of you."

"In a heartbeat." Neil crossed his arms over his muscled chest. "She's my friend. I'll do what I need to do."

Stewart looked back at Dev as though waiting for an answer.

"I haven't slept with her yet," Dev said bluntly.

I shot Dev the dirtiest look I had in my repertoire. He shrugged and smiled sheepishly. I forgave him because I knew what he was doing. He was trying not to give the demon any emotion. It was already apparent this Stewart was an empath. He thrived on emotion, the nasty kind. We needed to stay as unemotional as possible, or he could use it against us. The menace was heavy in the air. All it would take was for one of us to panic and he would have us.

And my panic was only inches from the surface.

"And she's the vampire's whole world," the demon said quietly as though he truly pitied Daniel. He studied Daniel for a moment. "But she doesn't give you what you need, does she? You're Vampire. She is obviously a companion. I can barely look at her, she's so bright. It should be easy, but nothing is easy for you, is it? Everyone on the Hell plane is concerned with you, Mr. Donovan. You're different, and different in the vampire world is bad. You could say you're the talk of the town. So when I found out you happened to be involved with Brix, well, you understand I had to learn what was going on. And I had to find out why he wanted that box."

"Do you know what it does?" The longer I could keep him talking, the more time Daniel had to recover from being shot forty times. I glanced at him, waiting for some sign of what he wanted me to do. I planned the heists. Daniel got us out of hot water.

Stewart never took his eyes off Neil. "Not a clue. I only know that if he wants it, I have to keep it from him. That really won't do."

Dev raised his pistol and tried to fire. Stewart turned to him, and with a simple flick of his wrist, the pistol flew across the room. Dev looked down at his empty hand dumbly and then back to the demon. The demon smiled before flicking his wrist a second, more decisive time. This time it was Dev who flew across the room. He hit the far wall face first and slid down.

I tried to run. I tried to get to him. I needed to make sure he was all right, but Stewart was standing before me with one hand held out, and I found that movement was impossible. I couldn't get a single muscle to comply. My feet felt nailed to the floor, my hands at my sides. I had to concentrate in order to breathe.

"Oh, are you stuck, dear? How much farther should I go? I could stop your lungs or your heart." He turned to Daniel, a smug smile on his face. "You see, vampire. I am strong. I do what it takes to be strong. I don't let insignificant things like a conscience keep me weak. You should have taken her whether she wanted to be taken or not. You are Vampire. She is chattel."

I glanced at Daniel, who stood staring at the demon with no emotion at all in his eyes. He was relaxed and still in a way only a vampire can be. If I hadn't known better, I would have thought he was ignoring all that went on around him.

Neil helped Dev up. He stood on shaky limbs, a smear of blood on his face. I'd led everyone into this. They all depended on me, and I couldn't move my feet.

"Now, I will have that object on your back, bitch," the demon said with a snarl that went against his gentlemanly persona. "After that, I will kill you, and there is nothing your weak-ass vampire can do about it."

My heart seized, and I worried he'd decided to stop it. He started to come toward me when Daniel moved. I didn't so much see him move as felt the effect after he was done. One moment Stewart was coming toward me with a look of inexplicable evil on his face, and the next Daniel was behind him, turning his neck in a way the human neck doesn't turn. There was a horrific crack, and the demon slid to the tile, his borrowed body limp.

"Even weak ass, I'm still faster than you." Daniel looked at the slumping human form on the floor.

I could move again. I stumbled toward Daniel. He caught me, his arms encircling my body. Deep blue eyes stared down at me, lust plain in the alien orbs. The smell of blood still hung heavily though the room. There was an air of death and decay that was unmistakable, and it called to Daniel's beast as surely as it had called to Neil's. Now I was stuck, but for a different reason. Lust flowed between us. I would have sworn I could feel his heart beating, calling to mine.

"We should go." Dev broke through the moment. He wiped the blood on his face off with his sleeve. "You want to protect her, right? He's going to be back. It's your job to protect her."

For a moment, Daniel looked like he would argue. His fangs were out again, the violence of the moment bringing out his beast. His eyes were on my throat. I remembered how he'd handled Neil. Contact. He'd touched him. I placed my hand on his face. I heard Dev's shocked intake of breath but caressed that cheek anyway. I let both of my hands run across his face and down his neck, reveling in the contact. His eyes closed as though the touch brought him pleasure.

"Daniel, we have to go," I said as calmly as I could. He pulled at me, but my logical brain insisted we leave. "I need to go now. It's dangerous for me to stay here."

Daniel swallowed, and just like that, the menace in the air was gone. He shook his head as though ridding himself of bad thoughts. "Right, we have to get her out of here. Let's move. He'll be back any time now. If not in this form, he'll find another."

His eyes slid away from me, our moment, our connection, gone. I could breathe again, but there was a part of me that resented Dev for breaking it.

Neil went first, scenting the hallway to make sure Stewart hadn't brought along more friends. Dev followed him, then me. Daniel watched my back. An eerie quiet reigned as we made our way toward the stairs. I could hear my footsteps on the carpeted floor. The path to the stairs was illuminated by well-chosen lighting, each perfectly lit sconce another road sign to where we needed to go. We were utterly alone, the wards we'd placed on the floor now working against us. No one had taken notice of the struggle that had gone on in the room so close to them. We could fight and bleed and die and the world around us would sleep right on.

Neil opened the nondescript door that led to the stairs. We were fifteen floors up, but at least at the bottom there would be a certain amount of freedom. We had cars parked in various places to aid in our getaway. Neil gave the clear sign, and we started through. Neil and Dev were halfway down the first flight when I picked up the pace. The pack on my back felt heavier than before, but I needed to keep moving. My crew was only as strong as the puny human. I hit the first stair at a run, which is precisely why I fell so hard when I hit the ward protecting it.

I flew back, hitting Daniel in the chest, causing both of us to fall back. So much for hoping we could get through this without dealing with magic.

"Zoey!" Dev crossed the barrier with no trouble. Neil came fast behind him.

Dev put a hand out, hauling me up.

"It's the box," Neil said. "Leave the box, and we can get out of here."

Daniel pulled the box off me before I could protest. He threw it at the barrier, and sure enough, it bounced back, flying right at his face. Daniel caught it.

Daniel pushed me at Dev, securing the backpack to his own back. "Get her out of here. I'll meet up with you after I figure out how to get out of here with the package."

"Daniel, leave it." I had no intention of stranding Daniel. We could figure something else out. Dev took my hand to pull me down the stairs.

Daniel smiled, a sad expression. "Not on your life, baby. This is your soul. I'm not leaving it behind. I'll figure out a way around it. Neil, get her as far away as possible, and don't let her out of your sight. That's an order."

Neil nodded, and even as I struggled I felt myself being pulled toward the first step, and then Dev was on the step and I was face first on the floor.

The ward held without the package. Someone didn't want me to leave.

Dev grabbed my hand again and tried to pull me through, but there was no amount of physical strength that was going to get me through that barrier.

"Zoey, I can't leave you." Dev clutched my hand.

"Yes, you can." I moved back, twisting away from him, moving closer to Daniel. "Neil, get him out of here, and that's a freaking order."

I was pissed to see Neil look to Daniel for confirmation before dragging Dev down the stairs. If I made it out of this hotel alive, we were going to have a talk about the chain of command. What can I say? I have control issues.

185

Daniel and I looked at each other, tension thick in the air.

"Let's see if you can go up." Daniel took my hand, and sure enough, I could take the steps going up.

We were halfway up the first flight when the door flew open. Stewart was back. He'd managed to turn his head back around, though the bone jutted out at sickening angle. I gasped my horror when he started talking.

"Do you have any idea how much that hurt?" Stewart's voice was rougher than before, and his eyes were black with no hint of an iris. He seemed to have trouble controlling his legs, jerking awkwardly with every step. "Well, at least the screaming stopped. That's something. You like killing, don't you, vampire? Trust me, this arsehole is dead, and it's your fault. Add him to your victim list."

"Go, I'll meet you on the roof." Daniel shoved me upward.

Stewart was still talking, his inhuman voice echoing through the stairwell as I climbed as fast as I could. One flight at a time. One step at a time. I didn't stop though I thought my heart would burst. Every step brought a fresh burn to my pumping legs. If I lived through this, I was joining a gym.

"I don't want trouble with the Council." Stewart's voice echoed through the space. "I really don't, but you pissed me off. I can't let that go, no matter who you are."

I couldn't see what was happening, but there was no mistaking the gunshot that shook the walls. The close quarters made the shot crack in a way that caused my ears to ache. I stopped in my tracks as my hand touched the door to the roof. I shook as I turned, praying to see Daniel behind me. He had a gun. He had to be the one who shot Stewart, and he would be up in a minute, and we would get out of this.

We had to get out of this.

I nearly cried out in relief as Daniel stumbled up the stairs. He held a hand on his chest. Blood coated his pale flesh. His blood.

"That's silver, you bastard." Stewart's voice came ever closer. "Hope you like it."

A lock held the door to the roof shut, but Daniel placed a single kick and it flew off the hinges. We stumbled into the night. I took a deep breath of the early spring air. There was a chill hanging onto the evening. Before too long, every day here would be hot as hell, and looking down at Daniel, I wondered if he would see the summer. He tumbled to the ground. I fell to my knees and put my hands on his chest to try to stop the bleeding. Tears sprang to my eyes as I pressed close. It was coming too fast. There was too much.

"Danny, what do I do?" My voice broke with every word.

"Run, Zoey." His breath rattled in and out of his chest like a faulty radiator. "I can still hold him off. Run and hide and call Neil. He'll come back. He'll get you out of this. Sarah can get rid of the wards and you can get away from here. You can take the box and give it to Halfer."

"I can't leave you." I pressed harder against his chest. It might have been my imagination or wild hope, but I thought the bleeding was a little better.

"You have to, Z. He wasn't lying. The bullets were silver, and it hit too close to my heart. I can't survive it."

"Yes, you can," I spat back at him. My head spun. "You need blood. You can take it from that bastard, Stewart, when he finally crawls up here."

Daniel shook his head. I was horrified to see a tiny trickle of blood drip from his mouth. "Won't work. The body is dead. Dead blood is as bad as silver. There's no way out. He'll be here any minute." Daniel struggled, but managed to stand, and he pulled me close, his lips on my forehead. "I love you, Zoey. I have since the day I met you. You run and let me handle this. I can handle anything as long as you're all right."

And just like that a terrible idea occurred to me.

People sometimes get adrenaline rushes that allow them to do amazing things they normally wouldn't be able to do. Like the child who manages to lift a car off his father who got pinned underneath. We do amazing things when the one we love is in danger. Daniel was going to die if I didn't stop it. I didn't have the strength to handle a demon, even one in a damaged body. I didn't have the time to out think him. I was out of time and out of options, with only one way to go if I wanted off this roof.

"Daniel," I said quietly, "Dev says you can fly."

187

"Dev's an asshole with a big mouth." Daniel pushed me out so he could look in my eyes. He gave me a light shake. "No arguments, Zoey. I died a long time ago, and it's time to let me go. He's almost here. I can smell him. Get ready to run down the stairs when I pull him out here. Barricade yourself in the suite and call Neil and call the cops. Hell, call everyone. Promise me."

I stepped back and hated the fact that he faltered before gaining his balance. I looked at him and memorized everything about him, from his thick, sandy hair that was too short, to his too big feet. I loved every inch of that body. Our life together played through my mind. Every moment had been precious. Even the crappy ones had been worthwhile because they were ours. I wished things had been different. I wished Daniel hadn't died and we'd had that life we wanted. I wished we hadn't ended up on this shithole roof where we were probably going to die. I wished a million different endings, but I knew I'd settled on one because I wasn't going to leave him alone to die.

There was movement in the doorway as Stewart finally managed to make his way to us. He'd changed bodies, but there was no mistaking the glint in those eyes. He had a gun in his hands. "Nowhere to run, kiddos."

He was wrong.

I threw Daniel one last look. "I'm so sorry."

His face registered shock as he realized what I was going to do. "Don't you dare, Zoey!"

But I was already running, and he was slower than normal. I leapt across the wall that separated the roof from the ground eighteen floors below, and then I was free.

Chapter Seventeen

I would like to say that I fell soundlessly through the air. I was a graceful swan floating on the wind, letting fate take me wherever it wanted to go. I was free and flying with no thought but the joy of defying those who would kill me. I would love to be able say all those things.

The reality was more of a high-pitched, girlie scream that seemed to go on forever because falling is scary.

The speed took my breath away, threatening to stop my heart in my chest. The wind hit my eyes, forcing them to close, but not before I got a real hard look at how fast the earth below was rushing up to greet me. My arms and legs flailed almost of their own accord as though trying to find purchase and solidness in a world that had none.

It had been a spectacularly bad idea. I'd jumped off a perfectly good building in the hopes that the guy I was with could, maybe, if I'm really lucky, fly.

I closed my eyes for good, and prayed Daniel could forgive me.

Then I was jerked upward and my heart was in my throat as I flew even faster but in the opposite direction. I flew up, passing one and then two windows before I started to fall again.

I landed with a thud in Daniel's arms. He tried to nestle me like a groom carrying his bride over the threshold, but that was so not enough security for me. I threw my arms around his neck and wound my legs as tightly as I could around his waist. Daniel was warmth and security and everything damn good in the world in that moment.

His arms tightened around me and a warm chuckle brushed my ear. "What's wrong, Z? You were never afraid of heights before."

"I never jumped off a building before." My voice shook as I nestled my head between his neck and shoulders.

We floated there somewhere between the eleventh and twelfth floors. I held on for dear life, and Daniel, well, Daniel cupped my ass.

"Hey!" I said, surprised.

"You scare the crap out of me, I get to cop a feel," he said, proceeding to do just that. "It's a vampire rule."

"Fine." I couldn't keep the happiness out of my voice. "If it's a rule then I have to follow it." I rubbed my cheek against his, so relieved to feel him against my skin. I was alive. He was alive. We had the box. And holy crap, we were floating. "God, Danny, you can fly."

"Yeah," he said. "Call me Peter Pan."

I was thinking more along the lines of Superman, and I thought about asking why it bothered him. He could freaking fly! I didn't see how that could be a bad thing. I was about to open my mouth to argue when I realized he was shaking. He had to concentrate to keep us afloat, and I decided to save all questions for after the tour.

Daniel breathed, quelling his shakes, his body steadying again. He anchored me with one hand and the other sank into my hair as he began our descent.

I let myself look around from the safety of Daniel's arms. I was floating through the spring air with strong arms around me and the lights of downtown twinkling like enormous stars.

"Why isn't anyone looking at us?" I could see people walking on the street below, some even glancing up, but there was no pointing or shouting.

"I'm shielding us from sight, Z." His face rubbed against mine. "They can't see us. I do it every time I have to fly."

So many secrets. But for the first time in a long time, I started to hope that maybe this little episode would bring us close again.

We descended lightly to the ground, Daniel's feet hitting without a sound. He readjusted me in his arms, swinging my legs up and carrying me properly.

The people on the street continued to ignore us. They walked by, though many altered their paths as though they could sense us there. Daniel moved toward the parking garage. He stumbled as he reached his destination right inside the concrete walls.

"Sorry," he said, rolling off me. He got to his knees, his arms struggling to remove the pack from his back. His clothes were a ruined mess. Bullet holes riddled his jacket and there was a huge tear in the front where Stewart had gotten off his lucky shot. "I can't keep it up. They'll see us now. You have to run, Zoey. I'm done. I can't even walk."

He laid his head down on the concrete. He'd used all of his strength to fly and shield us from pedestrians. He was no longer capable of fighting or even getting away. The bleeding stopped as his body managed to heal the wound, but he was so weak there was no way he could get somewhere to feed. If Stewart found us, Daniel would be a sitting duck, ripe for the plucking.

"The Benz is on the third level, and the keys are in my pocket." Daniel's voice was beyond weary. He shoved the package into my hands. "Take it and go. No arguing."

I kissed his forehead and got up. He was right. Arguing was useless, and I would do what I wanted to anyway. I took the keys and found the stairs. My legs burned as I climbed, lungs straining, but I didn't stop. Couldn't stop. I needed to get back to Daniel before someone called the cops. The last thing I needed was a Good Samaritan calling an ambulance. I had no idea what a defibrillator would do to a vampire, but I figured it wouldn't be a good thing.

When I reached the third floor, I went to the middle of the level and punched the alarm button on the keys. There was a shrill beep, and I ran for Daniel's car.

"Miss!" I heard a voice call. Before I thought about it, I stopped and turned.

A tiny elderly lady stood in the middle lane. She was dressed in

191

a pale blue skirt and white shirt, a hat perched on her gray head as though she was ready for a Sunday sermon and fellowship gathering. She looked perfectly harmless. The enormous orange and black tiger twitching its tail as it paced back and forth behind her did not look harmless.

"Do you like this meat? It's the fourth one I've gone through tonight. They don't last anymore. Don't feel too bad for her, girlie," Stewart said through the old lady's mouth. "She poisoned two of her husbands, and she is terribly mean to her grandchildren. She was going to Hell soon anyway."

The car was behind me, and I pushed the button to unlock the doors. I had to take the chance that I could make it into the car before that freaking tiger ate me.

"Oh, does my friend here bother you?" Stewart petted the cat lightly with the old lady's white gloves. "I did mention I was a cat person."

Further conversation with Stewart gained me nothing. I pivoted and jumped for the car, my hands shaking as I tossed the pack inside and threw my body into the driver's seat. I slammed the door just as the tiger hit the roof. The car buckled and swayed, but the roof held. My hands shook as I shoved the key into the ignition, and the car came to life.

I slammed it into reverse as the weretiger shoved his paws through the roof. Razor sharp claws skimmed my cheek. He pulled a decent-sized chunk of the roof off as I floored it in reverse and slammed on the brakes, dislodging him. I watched in the rearview mirror as his huge body tumbled on the concrete.

I shifted the car into drive.

The only problem was that old lady standing right where I needed to go. Stewart smiled a sweet grandma smile with black-as-night eyes. If I went forward, I killed an old woman. If I went back…well, the tiger was already on his feet.

A familiar howl shook the air of the garage. I looked through the rearview mirror and saw a white wolf riding the tiger's back, his teeth firmly planted in the tiger's neck. Neil held on as the tiger tried to shake him off.

I turned back, ready to play a game of chicken with a possessed old lady. Neil could handle one tiger all on his own. Hell, he'd probably get upset if I interrupted his fun. Stewart snarled my way. His eyes were firmly on me. He didn't even notice that Dev moved behind him. I gave the now spectacularly angry demon the bird in order to keep those rheumy eyes focused my way. Dev held a nice tire iron in his hand. Stewart started walking my way as Dev brought it down on his head. Stewart's fourth body of the day crumpled and went limp. Dev hauled the now unconscious old lady out of harm's way.

Dev jogged up the lane and slapped his hand against the hood of the car. He had a reckless grin on that gorgeous face.

"Get in!" I yelled through the open window.

"Can't. I have to kill a tiger. Did I mention I love this job? Go!" He pulled his gun and ran back to help Neil.

And I went because I was no longer arguing with the men in my life.

I drove like a bat out of hell to get to Daniel, barely avoiding a Ford. The owner shook a fist at me as he drove by. He was headed to the third floor, so I was the least of his problems. I brought the car to a screeching halt at the entryway right in front of the unmanned security station.

He was so still, but I didn't hesitate. I threw open the back door. He couldn't be dead. He just couldn't.

I got to my knees and put a hand to his face.

"Zoey, I told you to go." He was weak, but I could still see the fire in his eyes. As long as he was pissed with me, there was still hope.

"Yes, you did." He was so freaking heavy. I pulled at his jacket, trying to force him into a position where I could gain some traction.

"Damn it, Zoey, I can't move."

He could certainly move his mouth. I put my arms under his shoulders and tried to push. I managed to get him to sitting, but he was all muscle, and muscle is heavy. "You have to get into the car."

"I can't." His jaw was a stubborn line, and his eyes drifted closed.

"Yes, you can." The whole flying thing worked out, so I decided to play the damsel in distress again. "You either get into the

193

car or a tiger is going to eat me."

His eyes flew open. "What? What tiger?"

There was a sudden roar, and Daniel's mouth dropped open. I took the opportunity to push harder against his broad back. "Yep, that's a weretiger. Stewart brought kitties to the party, so if you don't want to watch me become tiger food, you'll get your ass in that car."

"I hate you sometimes, Zoey," Daniel said sullenly as he struggled to his feet. "I'm tired. I want to die. I can see the light, but does Zoey Wharton let me walk into the light? Hell, no. She has to go and find a tiger to piss off."

"It's florescent, Danny." I draped his arm around my shoulder. It hung there limply as he started to shuffle. "I seriously doubt the light of the universe is florescent."

He didn't walk so much as fall into the car. I pushed his feet in and slammed the door. I got into the front seat and punched the gas.

"Hey," I heard from the backseat. "When the hell did I get a sunroof?"

I turned on to the street and was about to whip out some witty comeback when suddenly there was a body in the seat beside me. It was a big, hulking body dressed in an expensive suit, and I couldn't help the short scream that escaped my lips.

"Did I surprise you?" Lucas Halfer asked.

"Damn you," I said under my breath as I got it together and turned left. I needed to get to Daniel's club. They would be able to help him. I would take him home, but I couldn't be sure that Michael and Jack the Ripper would be both in residence and willing to help. The club was required to help.

"You're several millennia too late for that, dear," Halfer said smugly. "I see you have the Light of Alhorra. I congratulate you on a job well done."

"No thanks to you. You could have warned me I was getting into a freaking demon turf war."

"Them's the breaks, kid. When you steal for a living, you should count on coming in contact with all sorts of unsavory characters." Halfer gave me a smirk as he motioned to the back seat. "Your vampire is worse for the wear."

Daniel had gone utterly silent. His body didn't move.

"I don't have time to play these games with you. I have to take care of Daniel. Take the bag and go." I tried to shove the backpack at him as I took the ramp to the freeway. I say tried to, as the pack hit the passenger side door and fell uselessly to the floor. It went right through the demon's body, which flickered slightly as the object passed through.

"No can do." Halfer shrugged. "I'm afraid this is a call, not an in-person meeting. I have a few things I need to take care of at home before I can collect my package. Nem...well...let's just say the little prick you met earlier tonight, has been wreaking havoc down under as well. I can't leave yet, so I placed this intimate call. Protect the box. I'll take possession at one a.m. tomorrow. Don't worry about the location. I can find you wherever you are."

A horrible thought struck me. "Can Stewart find me?"

There would be no place to hide.

Halfer chuckled. "Not unless the two of you have a contract."

"All right." I glanced down at the clock. It was a few minutes after midnight, so all I had to do was play keep-away for twenty-four hours and some change. I took the exit I needed. I was close to the club. I hoped I could get them to come to the car because Daniel probably wasn't walking far.

"He's near death, and not the temporary kind." The demon looked into the back seat and shook his head. He looked almost concerned. "You don't have long at all. He needs blood."

"No shit. I'm trying to get him someplace where I can get some blood. I didn't think to keep a spare bag hanging around, though now that I hear myself saying it, I probably should have."

The demon ignored my panic-tinged rantings. "If you're thinking of taking him to the vampire club, you should know it's the first place the other one would have thought of, too. I know it's the first place I would look for you."

"You mean Stewart has men there?" The question came out of my mouth as a desperate plea. *Please don't let the club be compromised.* I pleaded silently with whoever would listen. I needed to get Daniel someplace filled with people who knew what the hell they were doing.

195

Halfer struck me down with a laugh. "If by Stewart you mean my demonic version of *Single White Female*, then, yes, Stewart has men there. You'll have to try again, and don't say your father's house because that would be location number two on his list. You'll find Daniel's place difficult as well. Stewart may be a prick, but he usually has all of his bases covered. He managed to hide his involvement in this enterprise from me until tonight. I tortured some close friends because of the false trail he laid out."

Dad's place had been my next brilliant idea, but what the demon said made sense. Stewart struck me as a guy who would have a plan. Cutting me off from resources was a logical step if he couldn't take me out at the hotel. Panic welled like bile in my belly. I had nowhere to go and no one I could trust to know what to do. Daniel was dying in the back seat. I was going to fail him. I was going to be driving around and around I-35 when Daniel expired because I couldn't come up with a way to save him. I was out of options.

"No, you're not, dear," Halfer said softly, his voice cajoling, the only bit of calm in my head. "You still have the best option of all. It's time to step up to the plate, companion. It's time to do what you were born to do."

"How did you know?" I was a little unnerved that he had read my mind.

His voice was silky smooth with a hint of sympathy. "I feed on doubt and indecision. I can read your doubts. They call to me. If you want me to go away, Zoey Wharton, then get off your ass and make a decision."

"What did you mean I was born to do this? I was born to do what?"

"Feed the vampire," Halfer said, his eyes darkening. "If you want him to live, you will feed him yourself. It's the only way he will survive this. He needs you. Only your blood will do."

I turned the car away from the club and back toward the freeway. I had to put some distance between us and Stewart and his zoo of hired killers. My mind raced, but the panic was gone, replaced with cool decision. Daniel needed blood. I had blood.

It was far more simple than I'd made it out to be.

I needed someplace quiet and out of the way. Someplace no one would think to look for. I started for the suburbs to the west.

When I looked again, Halfer was gone.

* * * *

I was shaking by the time I closed the door to the motel room I'd paid cash for. I forced myself to drive out of the city and past the first of the countless suburbs between Dallas and Fort Worth. I'd gotten off the freeway and found a highway and then a tiny motel. It was what I liked to call a murder motel because I couldn't imagine that people didn't die there on a regular basis. But it was off the beaten track and they didn't ask for ID or a credit card. The parking lot was hidden from the street. It was the perfect place for someone who didn't want to be found.

Getting Daniel through the door was the hard part though I found getting him out of the car so much easier than getting him in. I had to pull him out by shoving my arms under his shoulders and dragging him an inch at a time. At least I didn't have a weretiger practically breathing down my neck this time. He was dead weight, and there was a lot of him, but I was determined. He was well over six feet and he was somewhere around two-twenty, all of it muscle, but I got him inside.

There wasn't much to the room. There was just the king-sized bed, a TV that had to be a veteran of the eighties, a desk, and the bathroom. When I was certain nothing was hiding in the shadows, I forced myself to secure the package and pulled a sharpie out of the backpack. I always carried a couple. I drew a ward exactly as I'd been taught on the door. I proceeded to repeat the exercise on all four walls – north, south, east and west. The ward prevented witches from using locator spells to track us. It was a simple design, and I was hopeful it would hold.

When that was done, I finally let myself look at the man I'd loved most of my life. He was so still lying there on the floor. I turned on the light and couldn't stop a short, startled cry. He was ashen, as though I was too late and nothing could bring him back from the second, final death.

I fell to my knees beside him, tears streaking down my face. I hadn't told him. I hadn't told any of them that this was the place Halfer had taken me to. Not this cheap motel room, but a place where Daniel died again and again and there was nothing I could do to save him.

Then I saw it—the slightest movement of his chest. It was light. It was so shallow I would have missed it if I hadn't been close, but it was there all the same.

"Okay, buddy, come on." I put my wrist to his mouth. "Wake up. The dinner bell is ringing."

I got nothing. There wasn't even the slightest movement to let me know he was in there somewhere. I reached into the pocket of his leather duster jacket. Daniel was extremely handy and almost never went anywhere without his Swiss Army knife. He was forever pulling it out and using the screwdriver or the corkscrew or the file. I flipped through the tools, locating one that would work. The corkscrew was applicable. I was opening his favorite vintage.

Sharp pain bit at me as I forced the tip of the tool into my wrist. I didn't go far or drag it down. I cut just enough to bleed. If I could give Daniel a taste, he might be able to do the rest for himself.

I pressed the wound on my left arm against his lips and squeezed with my right hand to get the blood flowing. After a moment, I felt the beautiful press of his mouth on my wrist and then his tongue caressing my skin.

"Come back, Daniel," I implored him.

His eyes opened but they still had a sleepy look to them. He shoved my arm away and managed to push himself up to sitting. He slumped there with his back against the bed, an accusatory look in his eyes.

"What are you doing, Zoey?"

"Saving you." I tried to put my wrist back to his mouth, but he pushed it away. Anger bloomed inside me. "Do you want to die that badly? Or is it me? Do you not want me? Do you want me to get you some hooker, Danny? Would a prostitute be more acceptable?"

Daniel laughed, but it was a wretched sound. "Not want you? That's a laugh. I can't help but want you. Even if I hated you I would want you. I...Zoey, you don't know what you're doing. You don't know what you're asking for. Get my cell phone and call the club. It's where you should have gone in the first place."

"No." I wasn't about to argue with him. There wasn't time. Even now I could see the strength that one sip had given him was waning. "I'm the only one who can help you."

Daniel shook his head. "No. I won't take you. Not like this."

"We did this before and everything was fine." I didn't understand his stubbornness.

"I was an idiot. I could have killed you."

"But you didn't, and you won't kill me now." It was painfully obvious to me that my wrist wasn't going to be tempting enough for Daniel. We were going to have to do this the hard way. I pulled my T-shirt over my head.

"I can hurt you in other ways, Z." Daniel's eyes had closed. He leaned his head back against the bed as though even the act of talking sapped his strength. "When we did it before, we didn't know what it meant. If we did this now, it would mean something. It would bind us in ways you don't want."

"You have no idea what I want." I got out of my shoes and slipped my pants off. I wanted him to live, and I was willing to fight him to get my way. He had no idea how far I would go to not live in a world without him. Even if he went back to ignoring me tomorrow, I would be all right with it because he was alive.

"You don't want this."

I ignored him in favor of unclasping my bra and sliding out of my underwear. I wasn't the smartest girl in the world when it came to vampires, but I knew a few things. Vampires liked sex with their blood. It was an integral part of the feeding process, and Daniel had denied himself for a long time. Vampires fed off of sexual energy as readily as the blood. He needed both badly. I hoped the combination of the two would be too much to resist.

I straddled his half-dead body and sat on the part of him I hoped would come to life soon.

Daniel's eyes flew open, and for a moment, he simply looked at me and breathed. He shook his head even as his hands came up almost unwillingly to circle my waist. His fingers roamed over my skin in restless patterns, finally making their way up to cup my breasts. His thumbs flicked over my rigid nipples, sparking pure arousal across my skin.

"God, I can smell you." He breathed in, his fangs glinting in the low light. A single finger trailed down my torso to my pussy. He was right. I was already warm and soft. The intimacy of what we were about to do flared desire through my system.

"Touch me, Danny." It had been so damn long.

He pulled his hand away like he'd touched a hot stove. "Zoey, please walk away. Don't do this to us. Don't bring this out. Don't."

"I love you, Daniel." I leaned forward and kissed him. It was soft and sweet at first, and then I licked my tongue across that gorgeous, full mouth and felt his fangs. "Take me, Daniel. Call me by my title."

His hands shook as they caressed my breasts. He left one hand on my breast but the other sought my core and began to pinch and rub that place that got me moaning. He slipped his fingers into my pussy as his thumb rubbed against my clitoris. He sighed, and strength or no strength, he was coming to life against me. His cock swelled. "Companion." His voice turned dark and thick. "Mine. You are mine."

"Yours, Daniel." I pressed closer to him. Need suddenly filled the room. I needed to be with him. I needed to give the gift of my body.

I felt him change. I felt the instant he stopped being my Daniel and became all vampire. He pulled my head back, exposing my neck. His eyes bled to a dark blue and there was no white left. His fangs were longer than I remembered, and for the first time I felt trepidation.

"You will call me by my title, companion," he growled. "You will call me master."

The first orgasm hit as he plunged his fangs in. As I gave myself over to mindless pleasure, I had one overwhelming thought.

God, I prayed, let him remember. Let him remember that he loves me.

Chapter Eighteen

I woke up with a shriek, unsure of where I was. I'd had the dream again. I was back in Hell where nothing was meaningful and I was a useless thing. I tried to shake off the nightmare as my eyes adjusted to the dim light.

I was in a dingy motel room lying on a bed I probably wouldn't dream of sleeping on normally. Now it was heaven. I was under the covers, naked, and I was not alone.

"Hi," Daniel said quietly as though he was afraid of startling me. The gray color of his skin was gone, and he looked closer to normal than I had ever seen him. Even when he was healthy Daniel was pale, but now he was practically glowing.

I fell back onto the pillow. I was still weak, my head light as though I was slightly tipsy. Even weakened I felt a rush of relief that he was here and I was here with him. The only discomfort I felt was a slight pain in the muscles of my neck.

Daniel frowned as he leaned over and pushed back my hair. "I'm sorry, baby. I lost control. Your neck is pretty bad."

"Don't—" If I was thinking about how close I'd come to dying, then I was sure he'd already thought of it a thousand times. "Don't tell me how stupid I was."

The dream was still riding me, and I couldn't stand the thought of another lecture on my own idiocy. I wanted to curl up and cry. That feeling was so close to the surface it would overwhelm me if he said the wrong thing.

"Shhh, I promise I won't tell you how stupid that was. It can be our secret." He slid over to get closer to me. His smile was so warm and intimate, I began to relax. I could see the adorable dimples he got when he really lit up. "Thank you, Zoey. You were magnificent. Tonight, you were amazing, and I owe you my life. Now sit up." He lifted me up slightly, and there was a Styrofoam cup in his hand. "I took too much. You need to drink this. It will make you feel better."

I looked at the cup but couldn't quite make my hands reach out for it. "Do I want to know what it is?"

"No, you don't. Bottoms up."

He held the cup to my lips and I drank. It tasted better than I expected. It wasn't sweet. There was a solid feel to it. Even as it slipped down my throat, I started to feel better. When I had gulped it all down, Daniel tossed the cup away and pulled me into his arms.

"I thought you would be mad at me," I whispered into his chest. The drink was warm in my belly, and now I realized how cold I'd been without it. I nestled close to him, and I heard the reassuring beat of his heart. My blood was pumping in his veins. I had brought him back to life. I could keep him alive.

"I was scared for you. There's a difference." Daniel kissed the top of my head. "While you've been resting, I've been thinking, and I made a decision. I love you, Zoey. I'm not going to fight it anymore. I thought I was bad for you, and I probably am. I thought I would hurt you, but the truth is I could have done that when I was human. I did do that when I was human. I forgot how good it feels to be with you. I feel more like myself than I have in years. I can't believe I wasted so much time. I was wrong to deny us this. It's our right. It doesn't matter why I love you. It only matters that I do. I need you, and I'm not letting you go again. So you can tell that freaking faery who's been stalking you to go to hell."

Some of his words didn't make sense. Why he loved me? What did he mean by that? Why was it our right? But the feel of him holding me and saying the words I longed to hear crowded out all the doubts.

"I love you, too." And I did. He was the first thing I thought of in the morning and the last thought I had before falling asleep. For the first time in years I felt safe and loved, and I was going to hold on to that feeling for as long as possible. I felt strong enough to put my arms around him and was surprised he still had his pants on.

"You didn't..." The only other time I'd given him blood, it hadn't ended with him being dressed.

"Have sex with your unconscious body?" Daniel chuckled. "No, I was a gentleman. But I wanted to, Zoey. I really wanted to. I thought I should ask."

"What if I say no?" I wasn't going to say no, but it felt nice to joke with him again. I was already warming up in all the right places at the thought of being with Daniel again. I let my hand run across his chest. I loved his big, hard body and the way it felt when he was on top of me. My hands started to find the waistband of his pants and delve underneath.

"If you say no, then I'll ask again," he said in that low voice that told me he meant business. He pressed his pelvis forward and groaned when my hand swept across his straining cock. "I will wear you down. Please, Zoey. Please let me make love to you. It's been so long. I want to fuck you so bad I think I'll die if I can't."

All vestiges of the dream were pushed out of my mind. Hell had no place here. This was heaven and I was with Danny.

I pushed the covers off and brought one leg up around his waist. I looked into his eyes, and they didn't seem alien anymore. They were beautiful and filled with desire. It was a look he'd only ever given to me. "I worked hard to keep you alive, baby. I think I can make one more sacrifice."

Then he kissed me. He pressed his lips against mine so softly, so gently, I could feel them shaking. I wrapped my arms around him and realized his whole body was quivering slightly.

"Danny, what's wrong?" I asked, concerned he still wasn't strong enough. His body had taken a beating. I didn't want to push him.

He rested his head against mine. "I'm scared, Zoey. I don't want to fuck this up. I haven't...it's been a long time."

"Well, I haven't either." I tried hard not to laugh. The humor bubbling inside me was affectionate. He might not remember the first time we made love, but I did. He'd been worried that night, too. He'd shaken with anxiety at the thought I might not like it. We'd been dumb kids who hadn't understood the promise we were making. But it was a promise we'd kept.

"It wouldn't matter if you had," he said. "You could have slept with the offensive line of the Cowboys and I would still shake at the thought of being with you. My whole life my only real fear has been that I won't be good enough for you. I'm not a good man. I've done things in the last five years...horrible things, things I'm not proud of. I'm a monster, but if you'll let me, I will do everything I can to make you happy. You never have to be afraid of me."

"I could never be afraid you." I didn't care what he'd done to survive. It only mattered that he had. It only mattered that he was here.

His tongue surged in, playing against mine, tentative at first, but then he seemed to find his rhythm. He covered my body with his, his weight a welcome presence. He was so big. Danny made me feel delicate and feminine when he pressed me into the mattress, his muscular body holding me down. He kissed my mouth, his tongue sliding deep, but then he touched the tip of my nose with the lightest of caresses. His lips worked their way across my face, placing butterfly kisses on my eyes, a reverent kiss to my forehead. A low growl rumbled against my neck.

He worshipped me, not missing an inch as he kissed his way down my body.

Desire was a slow burn in my system. When he'd bitten me, he'd pulled me in, his magic taking me from zero to a hundred with a single look of those vampire eyes. But this was a long, slow, delicious ride. He lit me up, as though flipping a switch on pieces of me that had been dormant for years. Every inch of skin he caressed came to life for him.

I dragged a long breath in as his mouth hovered over my breast. My nipples strained, begging for his attention.

"You're beautiful, baby. So fucking beautiful. Precious." His tongue curled around my nipple, sending sparks through my whole system. He sucked and pulled, laving affection at one and then the other. My legs moved restlessly, my body overheating.

He kissed my navel, his hands cupping the curves of my hips.

"Please, Danny." I needed more than he was giving me. He was teasing me, and I wasn't sure how long I could take it. "Please fuck me, baby. I need you."

"I'll fuck you." The heat of his breath nuzzled against that most feminine part of me. My pussy. His. Always his. "I'm going to eat my fill first. God, you taste so fucking good."

He'd already fed off my blood, but there were other parts of me he liked to make a feast out of, too. Danny set his mouth on my pussy, his tongue spearing me. He sucked and kissed and rubbed until I couldn't take another minute.

"I missed that. God, I missed you, Z." He gave my clitoris a teasing peck and then climbed back up my body. He kissed me, the taste of my arousal on his tongue. He turned, flipping our positions. "Take me, Z. Welcome me home."

I straddled his hips and lowered myself on his cock with a sigh of pure pleasure.

He gripped my hips and guided me down. He was so beautiful as I joined us together. The fangs didn't bother me. They were just another part of Daniel, and I loved everything about him.

I worked my way down, taking him inch by inch until our hips met and he filled me. He filled my body, my heart, my world. I rocked back and forth against him. He pulled me down for a long, slow kiss, our bodies never once halting the rhythm we'd found. Over and over I moved until I hit that one spot and worked it, Danny's hands caressing my breasts, his face contorting beautifully as I came and he followed me over the edge.

I collapsed on top of him, his arms around me. The rest of the world was gone, and it was only us. I knew beyond any doubt that this was where I belonged. There was a certainty to this I never felt before, not even when Daniel was human. I would never leave him. He would never leave me again. Nothing and no one could come between us ever.

I should have been worried. I realized that later. We were on the run. We had to keep the package away from any number of nasty people until Halfer was ready to take it. My life was on the line. My soul was on the line. We should have moved the minute we were physically able, but we didn't. We made love on the bed and the floor and in the bathroom. I thought of nothing but Daniel and pleasure. The rest of the world, the rest of life, didn't matter.

Neither one of us noticed the box on the table. It was the whole reason we were here in this room reclaiming our relationship, but it sat there, ignored and forgotten.

We weren't watching when it began to pulsate and glow.

Chapter Nineteen

The digital clock beside the bed read 5:30 a.m. when I stretched and rolled over, my hands seeking Daniel. I'd only been asleep for an hour or so, but I felt fantastic.

"I'm over here, baby." He stood at the window that overlooked the not-so-scenic parking lot. His broad back was facing me, and I was disappointed to see his boxers were back on. It was odd to see Daniel naked as he was now. We'd only had the one night together before, and after that there had been no intimacy between us. Daniel had been no slouch in the looks department before, but becoming a vampire had taken him to a whole different level. Human Daniel had a great build, but he generally preferred playing around on his computer or reading a book to hitting the gym. Not so for the vampire version. He was all muscle, and watching the way he moved or even stood still made my mouth water.

"Whatcha doing?" I could hear the smile in my voice. I sat up and didn't think twice about the fact that I was naked. It seemed natural. I didn't need clothes when I was alone with Daniel. They would do nothing but get in the way.

Daniel didn't turn, simply stared out the window. "I couldn't sleep. I don't do that at night anymore, I'm afraid. So I was thinking.

I'm trying to figure out which member of our crew betrayed us."

"What?" I was surprised at the sudden turn of the conversation. I sat up and tried to focus on something other than his perfect backside.

"My money's on the faery."

"Dev wouldn't betray us." I needed to shut that line of thinking down fast before things went bad for Dev. Danny had been possessive before his turn, and vampires weren't known for their sharing ways. I didn't want to see Dev get hurt. Dev and I hadn't gotten past a heavy make-out session, and he shouldn't have to die because he'd made it to second base. "He doesn't have any reason to betray us. He doesn't need the money. As far as I know, I haven't done anything to him that would require revenge. I only went on one date with him."

I didn't mention the make-out session in the kitchen, and I certainly didn't point out that he had plans for me. Those plans didn't mean a damn thing now, so there was no reason to say anything.

"I'm actually kind of hoping it's the faery." Daniel turned from the window and walked toward me. He smiled despite the seriousness of the conversation. He put one knee on the bed, and I found myself on my back again. "I would really like to eviscerate him."

"Danny!" I protested as he started to kiss his way toward a nipple. "He hasn't done anything. You can't kill Dev."

He sighed as my nipple puckered under his thumb. "Watch me, Z. I find out he's working with either one of those demons and I will…is there a word for slicing someone open, draining them of all their blood and then, because I sure as hell wouldn't touch it, letting it run out into the street for the rats while I piss in it? I can't think of a word. I'll have to make one up."

I groaned, a mixture of pleasure and annoyance. I tried to sit up, but he was an immovable object. "Dev isn't working with demons."

"There are too many coincidences." Daniel kissed my breast in short, sweet assaults against my skin. "The first guys had a damn keycard, Z. They knew where we would be and when we would be there. They let us do the work, and then they came in to claim the prize. The only reason your soul isn't speeding away somewhere is Stewart decided to use some dumbasses. Someone is working with the enemy, and if it's not Dev then it's Sarah. God, I love your breasts. I missed your breasts. Hello, breasts."

I smacked him lightly on the head to get his attention. He looked up and pouted.

"Be serious for two seconds, Danny. It can't be Sarah, and before you bring it up, it's not Neil, either."

"I know it's not Neil and your two seconds are up." He settled himself between my legs. He'd already recovered from our earlier activities and was definitely ready to play again. "We can deal with this later, baby. Sun's going to be up in a couple of hours, and I'm feeling a little hungry."

I put out a hand to stop him. "Tempting. First, how can you know it's not Neil? I sincerely suggest you think before you lie."

He did. Daniel took a moment before he answered, and I found myself vaguely offended.

"Fine." He rolled off me, helping me sit up so I was facing him on the bed. "No more secrets, then. Neil can't betray me. He made a blood oath to me two years ago."

"What?" It came out louder than I actually intended.

"See," Daniel said, pointing my way. "I knew you were going to be pissed."

"What the hell is a blood oath?"

"It's an oath and there's blood and then he can't betray us," Daniel said as though he hoped that would satisfy me. I stared. It was my default move when he hesitated. I stared with arms crossed, and he knew I could keep it up for a long time. He caved. "Okay, fine, but you won't like this either. When I first came back, I knew I didn't want to bring you into my world. I thought it was too dangerous for you, but I needed to bring someone in. What you have to understand is…well…it's like this…how can I put this and not have you hit me? A vampire needs minions."

I frowned. "I am so not your minion."

"That's the point, Zoey. I didn't want to make you a minion but a vampire needs…people, a crew, call it what you want. Most vampires have a couple of people around them or they're considered weak, and a weak vampire is…"

"…an unsafe vampire," I finished for him, wondering for the first time how hard it was to be Daniel. There was obviously a whole political level I hadn't thought about before. "So you needed people. Why did you pick Neil?"

Daniel settled back, obviously satisfied I wasn't going to walk out. "Your dad found Neil. You know that, but what you don't know is he found Neil for me, not you. Your dad understood how dangerous it was for me to be completely alone, so he looked around. It was a happy coincidence that we needed muscle for the crew. Neil was a street kid and a weak-ass werewolf when we met. He had his ass handed to him almost nightly by the local pack. I've never gotten the entire story about his parents, but they were wolves, too, and I guess they were all right with what the pack did to him. They kicked him to the street a long time before. He was going to die, Zoey. They were going to chew him up and spit him out and laugh the whole time. He had one choice if he wanted to live. So he took a blood oath, and in case you hadn't noticed, those wolves don't bother him anymore. He's still an outcast. Now they turn their back on him because he 'betrayed' his kind. But they don't bother him."

"He takes your blood." I said it out loud so it was real to me. A blood oath required the taking of blood. Neil took Daniel's blood into his body and had for as long as I'd known him.

"At least once a week," Daniel confirmed. "It's mutually beneficial. Wolves normally hate vampires, so it enhances my reputation to have a wolf beside me. It looks like I'm strong enough to force him to do my bidding, but I don't even try. I can call Neil, but I certainly don't have a weird mind-control thing over him. God, I wish. He's a shitty minion. I think he memorized my credit card number because I apparently spend a lot of money at someplace called Aéropostale. I don't know what that is."

I laughed at the thought of Neil being anyone's minion, but the humor only lasted a minute before I was taken back to serious thought.

"What are you thinking?" Daniel's voice told me he wasn't sure he wanted an answer.

I took my time replying. "I'm thinking that the two people in the world I'm closest to have this whole relationship I didn't know about."

Daniel sighed. "It's not a relationship, Zoey. It's business. It's a way to keep other people from screwing with us. We're safer together than we are apart."

"It's more than that, Danny. You saved him."

"He saved me, too."

I shook my head. "I don't believe that. You're stronger than you let anybody know. Dev says you're the strongest vampire to rise in a long time."

"Dev has a big mouth." Daniel took a long breath, as though deciding how much to tell me. "All right, let me put it like this. Having Neil around helps keep out the vampires who would like to test that theory. He's kept me from having to do things I'd rather not do in order to survive. I didn't tell you because I was trying to keep you out of it."

"I'm not mad about it." And I wasn't. "I do think it's weird that all this time the two of you kept quiet about it. It seems intimate."

"There's nothing intimate about it," Daniel said, his head shaking in masculine denial. "I squeeze some blood into a cup, and he drinks it. It is so not intimate."

I started to say something and then sat there looking at him with my mouth hanging wide open as the truth poured over me. Strength. He'd given me a bit of his strength. That potion he'd given me after the feeding hadn't been full of herbs. It had been full of Daniel.

"Zoey…" Daniel said slowly, as though he could postpone the inevitable.

"That was blood. I drank blood. I drank your blood," I said in a zombie-like monotone as I tried to process that particular truth.

"You were weak and you needed it," Daniel reasoned. "Besides, you don't mind it when I drink yours."

"That's different." But it wasn't. I'd fed Daniel because he needed it. He'd given me his blood when I'd been weak. It was an intimacy shared by two people who loved each other. Was there anything wrong with it? "So if I ever need a short burst of strength, you just open a vein into a mug and instant bloody Starbucks?"

"It wouldn't be my preferred method, but if that's the way you want it, then, yes." He seemed to measure his words. "It's not a bad idea for you take it before you do a job. I know I would feel better if you had more protection. Consider it the supernatural equivalent of a Kevlar vest. I would prefer you took it straight from the tap, though. You know how good it feels when I feed from you?"

"Oh, yeah." My breath caught at the thought. It felt exquisite.

"Well, I wouldn't mind feeling that way, too."

I laughed, but there was no small amount of desire in it. I liked the thought of Daniel being the one who passed out from pleasure.

Daniel pulled me close again. "Do you have any idea how good you taste? Every day for the last five years I've dreamed of this. Being around you and not being able to have you has been hell. I could drain you dry, and I would still want more."

"Let's not try it." I let my head fall to the side. "But a late-night snack won't kill me."

He was gentler this time. I felt only the slightest sting as his fangs found the vein in my neck, and then the pleasure started to build with every tug of his mouth. When he'd had his fill, it was my turn.

"Baby, this is important." He held out his hand. "Don't be scared." He grimaced as his nails lengthened, growing into perfect claws.

I stared at them, in awe of the way he could change. "I'm not afraid, Danny."

He drew a single, sharp nail across his chest and blood welled. He put his hands on my face. "This is everything to me. This means we're together. No going back, Z."

I didn't want to go back. I leaned in and tentatively put my mouth on him.

"Oh, god, baby, suck me, please." Daniel's hand wound around the back of my neck and held me in place. "Suck hard. It feels so good."

I did as he asked, sucking his blood into my mouth, surprised at the hot velvety texture. Even as I whirled my tongue against his chest, he drew my hand down to his cock. It was hard, so damn hard. He pumped himself into my hand, and I tightened around him.

He groaned as I released my hold on his chest. My mouth had other places to go.

"Oh, yes," Daniel said approvingly as I moved lower and took him into my mouth.

I was pleased when he passed into sleep completely satisfied.

* * * *

When I woke up, I was cuddled against him. This time there was no pain or weakness. My neck felt fine, and when I ran my hand over it, I was surprised to find it smooth with no hint of the earlier wounds. It was his blood. It healed and made me stronger than I'd ever felt. I stretched, feeling every muscle move languorously. I let myself lie against him a moment longer before I sat up and looked at the clock. It was almost five in the evening. I slept all day, lying there next to Daniel who had no choice but to sleep.

I would have to get used to a nocturnal lifestyle because I didn't plan to spend my nights sleeping anymore. I would spend them with Daniel. My boyfriend was a vampire, so daylight wasn't going to be our special time. I smiled as I thought about it. There were things to be worked out and difficult conversations to be had, but I could get through that. I had everything I wanted. I was hours away from giving the package to Halfer, getting my contract back, and having a shitload of money to show for it. I already had the best thing of all.

I had Daniel back.

I glanced over at the package. It sat on the table where we left it. Everything was exactly as it should have been with one teeny, tiny difference.

The damn thing was glowing like a firefly.

I got out of bed and slipped into Daniel's T-shirt. I walked tentatively to the box. It glowed and started to pulse as I approached.

"Damn it."

This is where it all goes to hell. I will not touch that box, I continued my inner dialogue. *Pulse away, little box, I'm not playing Pandora. I am going to leave you right where you are, and Halfer is coming to get you and I'm gonna hand you over and fulfill my end of the contract. It's nothing personal, box, it's strictly business.*

And then I heard it.

The box, or whatever was in the box, cried.

All of my thoughts of self-protection flew away as I touched the box, and it opened without hesitation. The top slid open and there, sitting in the middle of the box that seemed much larger on the inside than it had from the outside, lay the one thing I could never hand over to a demon.

I picked up the soft, pink baby girl so perfect and human, with a ridiculously precious toothless grin, and held her close with a maternal instinct I hadn't known I had. She wriggled against me.

She made some soft sounds and settled against my shoulder, and I knew in that moment I was going straight to Hell.

Chapter Twenty

"OMG! This is the single porniest room I have ever seen!" Neil exclaimed two hours later as I let him through the door. His eyes went wide as he took in the sights. He stopped when he got to Daniel lying in the bed. It was obvious I'd occupied the other side of the bed. "Then there's the smell. Jeez, Zoey, change the sheets after you're done. It's quite overwhelming. Oh, look Sarah, Mommy and Daddy got back together. See, I told you dreams can come true."

"Porny?" I resettled the baby on my hip. I already felt better.

The last few hours I'd felt vulnerable. It had been just me, a sleeping vampire, and a baby who I had no idea how to care for. Though I figured Neil would be useless when it came to taking care of the baby, he did make me feel safer. Demons would have to think twice before dealing with Neil. It didn't hurt that I knew his strength was enhanced with Daniel's blood.

Neil smiled. "It's something new I came up with. Look, I made an adjective! I can't imagine what my inspiration was. So, I'll ask the question. Why are you holding a baby? You look cute—all Madonna and child. By the way, Dev is bringing in the stuff you asked for, and he'll be here any minute so you should...well, there's not a damn thing you can do to hide this, so be ready. He's been freaked out all day."

"We couldn't find you." Sarah looked at the wards I'd drawn on the walls. She ran her hands across the symbols as though she could feel the power behind them, and maybe she could. "We were up all night. I tried every locator spell I know but got nothing. This explains it."

"Thanks. I had a great teacher." I was the teeniest bit disappointed she didn't seem more excited. It was the first time I'd done something with magic that worked. We'd been safe here.

"I thought we should try your cell phone," Neil said. "But you know, Sarah, always with the witchy stuff."

"I tossed the cells." They were in itty bitty pieces all along 183. I couldn't take the chance that the demons knew about the whole GPS thing.

"And when would you have had time to answer?" Neil snarked. "What with all the porntastic fun going on? See, I made another one."

Dev chose that moment to walk in carrying a large bag from Target. I hoped it contained the list I dictated to Neil over the phone. I'd rattled off all the baby stuff I knew and hoped I hadn't forgotten anything. Up to this point, baby girl had been a perfect angel. If I'd thought about it at the time, I would have been suspicious, but the truth was, I didn't know what babies were like. I'd never had a baby sister or brother. I only had one real girlfriend, and Sarah was as far from procreating as she could get.

The baby hadn't cried or wanted food, which was good because all I had were a few Tic Tacs and a can of Red Bull. She'd smiled and gurgled and tried to put lots of things in her mouth but not a single tear yet. She even allowed me to take a shower after calling the troops. It had been cooler than I would have liked, but I was clean and she was clean, and that was what mattered.

Daniel would probably be pissed I'd given away our location, but I trusted these people, and I needed help. I couldn't believe that anyone on our crew had betrayed us. Lucas Halfer might have betrayed us but not Dev or Sarah. Daniel was going to have to understand why I'd called in the cavalry. He was dead to the world until eight thirty p.m., and I had a baby to deal with. I was so not cut out to be a single mom.

Dev smiled as he walked in, but the minute he surveyed the room, I watched a dark look fall across his face. His jaw clenched, and I realized that he was going to take this harder than I'd bargained for.

"Well, that was inevitable. I guess I should have gotten into the car after all." He let the bag drop to the floor. He glanced at the bed where Daniel lay, still as death, and I didn't like the look on his face. I remembered what he said to me earlier. He would stake him if he thought Daniel was seriously trying to make me a companion. I'd made myself a companion last night, but I doubted Dev would see it that way. "You were forced to feed him, I suppose."

"He was dying." I tried not to think about what happened. I'd been able to put it out of my mind the night before, but it would catch up to me eventually. I would see him again and again, so pale and close to dying.

"He died a long time ago, Zoey." Dev stared at Daniel for a moment and shook his head. "I've got another bag in the car. I'll be back."

Neil whistled. "He's going to be bitter, that one. Oh, well, he's the ex now, so who cares? You're back with Daniel where you belong, and Dev has to deal with it. Okay, so baby? Anybody gonna explain little Miss Sunshine here, or do I get the speech? You know the one where a mommy and her vampire love each other very much..."

"Neil, obviously she found a baby," Sarah said with a hint of annoyance. "The question is why hasn't she turned the baby over to the authorities yet?"

She looked down at Daniel and studied him for a moment. He wasn't like a human sleeping, as Daniel didn't move at all. There was no restless movement or squirming. He was just there.

"Was he really dying?" she asked quietly.

"Yes, he was," I replied. "That damn demon kept switching bodies. Daniel got shot full of silver and one of the bullets was close to his heart. He managed to hold on long enough to save us, but I had to haul him into the car. The bullets came out, but the silver was in his blood. It was terrifying. I did what I had to do to save him. He

217

needed blood, and I couldn't trust anyone else. And I didn't find the baby. She was in the box."

"What?" Sarah turned pale. It was odd to see Sarah scrubbed clean of all makeup. It made her look younger than her years and easier to read emotionally. She was tired and shocked at the prospect that the baby had been in the box we stole. I was with her on that one, but I'd had hours to get used to how screwed up the whole situation was.

"She was in the box. I know it sounds crazy, but that damn box is magic. It was bigger on the inside than the outside. It was kind of cool," I explained as I patted Baby Girl's backside.

It seemed to soothe her. Her bottom was covered in a pillow case I ripped up and tied off. The motel was going to need to rethink that whole "no credit card on file" allowance. I hunted through the first bag and pulled out a package of diapers.

"She's the Light of Alhorra?" Sarah asked, her voice sounding shaky.

"I guess." I settled her on the bed next to Daniel. She tried to turn around and climb on him. I pulled her gently back and wrestled with her to get her into the diaper. She kept twisting and turning and trying to look back at Daniel.

"That baby came out of the box?" Dev asked from the doorway. He set down the car seat he was holding. "The faery box?"

"Yep." I finally fit the diaper around her bottom and got the sides to close. Now random urine was one less problem I needed to worry about.

"You idiots." Dev walked over to the box and examined it. He looked at it for a moment, his eyes going over the inscriptions. They were in some form of Gaelic. Not being able to read Gaelic myself, I'd ignored them. Dev seemed to think they were important. "Let me guess the sequence of events. You fed him. You fucked him. Then the box pops open and suddenly there's a baby. Did you not notice when the box started to glow and move around on its own?"

I stood up and settled her on my hip again. She tried to wriggle toward Daniel. I was a little fed up with the attitude I was getting from Dev. It wasn't like we had a commitment. "Sorry, I wasn't really looking at the box. My mind was on other things."

"I bet it was." He walked up to me and touched my neck. He examined it for a moment, running his thumb up and down the skin. "Doesn't like it from the neck, does he? What part of you did he tear up, Zoey?"

"Not that it's any of your business, but he did bite my neck. He's gentle about it." I felt the need to defend Daniel. What we'd done together last night had been beautiful, and I wasn't going to feel bad about it.

Dev caught his breath and took a step back. He looked horrified, and I tried to think of what I said to put that look on his face. "Zoey, I need to talk to you in private."

"This isn't the time or place to have this conversation. I have things I need to get done."

Time was getting away from us. Halfer would be coming for the baby in a couple of hours, and I needed to do something about it. There was also the thought in the back of my head that if I pushed it far enough, I would never have to have this conversation with Dev. I would be in Hell, but at least I would avoid the awkward discussion about my sex life. There was an upside.

"Now, Zoey." Dev said firmly. His face was set. "Or I'll have it out with you in front of everyone, and this isn't a conversation you want made public."

"When will Daniel rise?" Sarah asked as though she hadn't been avidly listening to Dev and I argue.

Neil looked at her curiously. "Sunset, of course. I think it's eight-something tonight."

"So he's out of the picture for another hour or so." Sarah seemed to be talking to herself. I wondered if she'd seen more than she let on. The cameras had probably been active when Neil and Daniel dealt with our attackers. I wondered if the violence had affected her.

"It's all right, Sarah." Neil gave her a half hug, and I realized he was worried about her, too. "Everything will happen after the sun goes down. It always does. Daniel will be back in fighting shape, thanks to our girl. If we have to leave, I'll go get the body bag, and we'll shove his hot bod in the trunk and take him with us. We won't leave our badass vampire behind, I promise."

"Why don't you get him ready while Dev and I have this conversation he seems intent on having with me," I said through clenched teeth as I walked into the bathroom. "And don't forget to put the car seat in."

Dev followed me and shut the door behind him. The minute I turned to look at him, he sighed. "Did he force you?"

"Of course not." Baby Girl tried to pat my face, and I hugged her. There was something infinitely lovable about the child. She calmed me. "I love him, Dev. I've loved him since I was a girl. You don't understand what it's like between us. He would never force me."

Dev rolled his eyes. "I didn't mean the sex. Did he force you to take his blood? It's the only explanation for your neck being soft and smooth after an evening's romp with a dying vampire. Now that I really look at you, I can tell. You look healthier. It's from the damn blood you drank. Don't try to deny it."

I felt myself blush. Somehow the exchange of blood seemed more intimate than the sex. "He took too much, and I needed it."

"Oh, I bet that's what he told you, that bastard." Dev laughed, a bitter sound.

"It wasn't like that." I didn't owe him any explanations, but I seemed compelled to give them. Or maybe I felt the need to explain it to myself. Even as I spoke to Dev, some part of me said it was all too good to be true. "Being that close to death made Daniel realize how stupid it is to keep us apart. He loves me. He wants to be with me, and I want to be with him. I'm sorry if I hurt you, but I can't help how I feel. I never meant to…"

"Shut up, Zoey." There was a hint of maliciousness in his voice. "Everything you say right now is the rantings of an addict."

"What is that supposed to mean?" I asked, indignant.

Dev shook his head and looked at me with what I could only interpret as pity. "Was it good? His blood, I mean? Did it make you feel good? Was it just as good as the sex?"

"Yes, and I'm not ashamed of it. He's a vampire. There's always going to be blood involved."

Dev ignored me and went on with his point. "However good his blood felt to you, magnify that a thousand times and that's what you taste like to him. One taste is all it takes. I bet it took him years to detox from the first time he tasted you. He's stayed away from you because he was on the wagon. He's not in love with you, Zoey. He's addicted to you."

"He told me he loved me. He told me he was wrong to have left me," I said, but inside I was thinking different thoughts. He begged me not to do this to him. He fought so hard to not let me feed him, and at the time, I hadn't understood. He hadn't said it was wrong to leave me. He'd said he was wrong to deny us.

"He was high, Zoey," Dev said.

"That's not true." I tried to believe my own words. My hand caressed the baby's soft back, and I was the one taking comfort.

"You made love for hours and hours in this room without ever thinking to call your friends." Dev spoke more quietly now. "We thought you were dead. Your soul is on the line and you screwed for hours. You don't even remember when the box was primed. It wouldn't have been quiet. You were not yourself. You were drugged. His blood lets you feel a small piece of what he feels. You're an obsession to him, Zoey. In the end, that's what a companion is. I don't understand everything about it, but I know a true companion is very rare. I don't know who sold you the story about a companion being a vampire's pure love, but it's a lie. A companion is a vampire's addiction. I'm sorry to be the one who has to tell you this, but my god, Zoey, he has you so far in you made a baby. Do you know what that says about you?"

"How did I make a baby?" I was shocked at the suggestion.

Dev shoved his fingers through his hair. "I didn't recognize the name of the artifact, and maybe the name changes depending on the tribe, but I know that box. A faery tribe uses it as a gift to another tribe, probably a tribe on another plane. The faery tribe fills the box with pieces of their personal magics and sends it to another friendly tribe. The tribe receiving the gift then ruminates on what form the magic will take. Usually it's a tree or a domestic animal, and the magic brings luck and keeps the tribes together. When you made love to Daniel, you had to have wished for a baby with him. You had to have put your heart and soul into the wish. That desire had to be overwhelming to work on the box. He's pulled you in so far, all you want to do is have his baby."

I pulled that sweet baby in close and tried not to sob into her shoulder, so great was the emotion that swept over me. Dev, I'm sure, thought I was overwhelmed with disappointment at the thought that Daniel tricked me, but I knew something Dev didn't. I looked up at Dev through watery eyes. "Not once in all our time making love did I think of a baby. It never crossed my mind, Dev."

"Then what…" Dev closed his mouth when he hit on the answer.

Daniel wanted the baby. Daniel wanted a baby with me so much that his desire had filled the box and caused the change. We could have many of the things we dreamed of when he was alive. We could be together. We could love each other. But we could never have the babies we dreamed of. I knew that the baby I held in my arms was something magical and didn't belong to me, but in some small way she was mine and she was Daniel's, and I had to do right by her.

"I need to get her home." I wiped my eyes with my free hand. "Will you help me?"

"What do you mean?" For the first time since he'd walked into the room, he seemed unsure of himself. "Halfer wants that child. You have to give her to Halfer, or he'll take you. If you don't give her up, your contract is broken."

"I need to find the faeries," I said, smiling sadly. Those faeries were going to be pissed. I could only hope they would let me live long enough to explain who she was. "They can take her to where she belongs. They can take her where Halfer can't touch her."

Dev was silent for a moment. "Are you telling me you're willing to go to Hell for some faery child you don't even know? Please think seriously about this, Zoey. If you do this, you'll go to Hell, and there is no coming back."

"I don't have to think about it." I was going to give her back before I knew where she'd come from. Knowing she was a piece of Daniel's desire did nothing but make my will stronger.

Dev frowned as he studied the child. "Do you think Daniel is going to let you do this? He'll move heaven and earth to make sure his prize doesn't get taken away. You're saying you can make that decision for both of you?"

"I'm saying that I know Daniel Donovan, and I know what decision he would make."

Dev came close, and before I could do anything about it, he kissed me. Even having experienced what I had last night with Daniel, I have to admit Dev's kiss was sweet. He put his forehead to mine, and I felt a connection. "I wish we'd met some other time, some other place, because you're one hell of a woman, Zoey Wharton. While the thought of helping out faery kind goes against my nature, if you want this, I will help you. I'll do it because it pleases you."

He took a step back.

"She didn't make any mistakes." I looked into her big green eyes as she tried to eat my hair. I pulled it out of her mouth. "She was waiting to go somewhere and be something good. She didn't ask for me to steal her. The truth of the matter is I'm not a good person, Dev. I'm a thief. If I got the chance to do things differently, I probably wouldn't because it's all I know. So don't waste any tears on me. Let me do my good thing before I go out."

I didn't realize we weren't alone. I was caught up in the emotion. It was a mistake I'd been making over and over again since the day I met Lucas Halfer. When I saw Sarah come through the door, I knew I'd made the same mistake again. I should have listened to Daniel because he was right about one thing. Someone on our crew had betrayed us.

She stood in the doorway with her pink bob and sad eyes, and she held a gun which she pointed straight at my head.

"I'm so sorry, Zoey," she said. "But I'm not going to be able to let you do that."

Chapter Twenty-One

I remember vividly the day I met Sarah Tucker. I'd known Neil for a couple of months, and we'd run two small-time jobs together. They were what I like to think of as starter jobs, or auditions. They were little jobs for chump change that didn't involve much risk. I certainly didn't want to go into a big, dangerous job with someone I didn't know, but Neil had been a natural. I realize now that the strength and agility were a gift from Daniel, but the inherent knowledge of what to do and when had come from Neil himself. It was fine with me and Daniel and Neil for several months. We were comfortable and happy. Then we were offered thirty thousand dollars to steal an amulet for a witch. It was a good wage, and we needed the money. We found ourselves quickly out of our league as the amulet was protected magically.

It was then that Neil mentioned a girl he'd met at a club. Her name was Sarah, and she was a witch.

In my world, witches tend to come in two varieties – the "crazy bitch" kind and the "bunnies, kitties, duckies" kind. The first you don't want to mess with because they WILL cut you. The second tend to love nature and be concerned about their karma banks. While crazy bitch witch might not have any problem with stealing, she also probably doesn't play well with others. Someone on the crew will more than likely try to kill her. The white witch usually doesn't want to have anything to do with thievery as they expect it to come back on them threefold.

Sarah was different. I knew it the minute she walked into the restaurant with her electric blue hair and bright smile. There was nothing of the pretentious "I am one with the goddess crap" I'd come to expect from the witches I'd known. Witchcraft was just part of her world. She had grown up with it all around her.

Sarah was the first woman I ever spent hours shopping with for shoes and clothes. She was the first one I talked to about how I felt when Daniel died.

Sarah was my first real girlfriend, and that night she was my first real backstabbing bitch.

"Subsisto!" Sarah commanded as she looked at Dev, and I watched the way her eyes flared as she spit out the spell. Dev didn't have a chance. His body jerked, every muscle tensing.

"Zoey." Dev's face was a mask of frustration. He spoke through gritted teeth. He could blink, but otherwise not a muscle moved. "I can't move. You need to…"

"Silentium," Sarah said, and Dev went silent.

Sarah is a strong witch. Many witches are what I call technical witches. They know the craft. They study the spells and can do a serviceable job when it's required. It's the difference between book knowledge and street smarts. Sarah had street smarts in spades. She was born a witch, and there was no way to teach what her body knew instinctively. Another witch might say the proper words but get only half the effect. When Sarah started a spell, the room was filled with it and the air around her crackled with magic. She once described it to me as pulling energy she needed from the space around her.

Sarah smiled briefly and shook her head. "God, Christine was right. He really is a magical battery. Someone should teach him to shield. I could pull magic off him for hours, and I doubt he would even miss it. So much wasted potential."

The baby moved against me restlessly, and for the first time she seemed something other than perfectly happy. She understood we were in danger, and I found myself trying to soothe her. It would be all right. Any minute Neil would come in, and he would knock Sarah out until we could figure out what was going on. Something

225

was wrong. Someone had gotten to her because this was not the Sarah I knew. This was not my friend, and I needed to figure out how to get her back.

"I'm sorry, Zoey," Sarah said, quietly studying me and the baby. "Please understand I don't want to do this."

"Then don't." I wished Neil would show up. It occurred to me that lately I'd been relying on either Neil or Daniel to show up and save me. I was far too used to having real muscle around me, and I was getting weak. I'd worked jobs before Danny and Neil. I'd worked some alone and managed to get myself out of some tight situations.

"I didn't mean for things to go like this," she continued as Dev stood there frozen in place. He seemed to still be breathing, the rising motion of his chest the only way I knew he was alive.

"I know you didn't. It's going to be all right, Sarah," I said in my smoothest tone. I turned the baby away from the gun. "Why don't you ditch the gun, and we can talk about it."

Her face turned down, but that gun didn't waver. "I would love to do that, Zoey. You have no idea. I wish I never started this, but I can't get out now. I have to see it through."

"No, you don't." I kept looking at that open door. Where the hell was Neil?

Sarah must have seen my eyes dart toward the door. She shook her head. "He's not coming, Z. He's sleeping. I had to take him out, but I didn't hurt him. I won't hurt Daniel, either, even though I should. I need to get this done before he wakes up or I'll have to get rid of him, and I don't want to do that."

I didn't say what I was thinking. I was thinking she could try to take out Daniel, but she had no idea what she was up against. Maybe Daniel had been right to hide how strong he was. I just wished he hadn't hidden it from me. I stalled for time because it was what I did best. I asked the only question I could think of. "Why?"

Sarah rolled her eyes, but it wasn't sarcastic. She seemed to be angry with someone, but I didn't think it was me. "There are so many reasons, Zoey, and not a one of them good. It doesn't matter anyway."

"Of course it matters." It mattered to me.

She held her free hand out and the air around me ripened with magical intent.

"Tribuo mihi parvulus." Her voice sounded older and more forceful than I'd heard it before. I hoped Sarah hadn't been hiding her power the way Daniel had.

I winced and waited for something bad to happen. After a moment, I opened my eyes and Sarah was staring at me. "Yeah, I'm sorry. I don't know what that means."

Sarah took a deep breath and tried again. This time her voice was even deeper, her eyes darkening. *"Tribuo mihi parvulus iam."*

I shrugged, comfortable that whatever she was trying wasn't working. "Again, sorry, I don't speak Latin or whatever that is."

"Give me the child." The beginning of desperation was plain in her voice. "That should work. Why isn't it working?"

"I don't know, but maybe you should heed the warning." I tried to be as calm and reasonable as I could. Her magic wasn't working, but she still held that gun. "Maybe the universe is trying to tell you something. This is wrong, Sarah. This child isn't yours. She isn't mine. She's innocent, and she needs to go home. We can stop this right here and right now. Let Dev go, and Dev and I will take the baby where she needs to be and everything will be all right."

As she started to cry, I remembered that day we met. It had been sunny and bright, and I'd only planned on spending a couple of minutes seeing if she was the real thing. I was going to use her for one job. I was going to give her a cut and never see her again. My crew was a three-person crew, and that was all it needed to be. Until I sat with her for hours, and when I left, I wanted to see her again. It was a feeling not unlike a crush. It was the first time I wanted a girl to like me, and she had. She wanted to be my friend and listen to my crap about Daniel. She answered the phone at two in the morning when I couldn't sleep and needed to vent. She left her precious clubs to come to my place when I got drunk and called her crying.

She couldn't be the person who shot me and gave a baby to a demon. She was Sarah. She was my friend.

I held my hand out. "Give me the gun, and I promise you, we'll figure this out. We'll get through this."

And that was the moment my friend, my confidant, the one who had taken me for my first pedicure and introduced me to Cosmos, that was the moment she pulled the trigger and shot me.

I can't quite describe the way it feels to be shot. This particular time was the first time I hadn't managed to dodge the bullet, but it certainly wasn't to be my last.

First there was the sound, and while it only lasts a second, it blasts through the air. It felt like an eternity before I felt the burn of fire against my skin as my body bucked against the force. There's an awful lot of heat in a bullet. This particular round hit my right shoulder, and I felt the instant my shoulder blade cracked as the metal passed through it. I fell backward toward the shower, and I heard more than felt the shower door break as my body hit it. I remember thinking I had to hold on to the child. I shifted her against my chest as I went down. I pulled her close and tried to protect her little head and then my own head hit the tile and the world around me went black.

* * * *

"Zoey," I heard a sound but it was so far away I wasn't sure I needed to pay attention. The darkness was truly blissful, and there wasn't any pain here. If I listened to that voice calling me, I would have to go through a lot of pain to get to it.

"Zoey, wake up." The voice was awfully stern, and there was the lightest of slaps attached to it. I moaned as I shook myself awake.

I was lying on the bathroom floor, and there was broken glass all around me, except it wasn't glass. I shifted against it. It was some form of plastic, the kind that shattered into tiny, relatively safe pieces when you were unlucky enough to get shot by a crazy bitch.

"Zoey, are you all right? Can you talk?" Dev stared down at me. His green eyes were filled with concern and some form of warning. He was trying to tell me something without alerting Sarah.

I was disoriented for a moment. I was on the floor of the bathroom and the baby from the box was sitting on top of me while Dev cradled my head.

"It's okay, Zoey. She let me out to check on you." He leaned close to me and whispered in my ear. "The baby won't let her near you."

"Hey, no private conversation," Sarah hissed but stayed close to the door. "Is she all right or not?"

Dev looked me over. He passed a hand over the hole in my shirt. I was surprised to find my shoulder was sore, but it didn't hurt the way I thought it would. I grew very afraid that something was terribly wrong. I might not have been shot before, but I knew it was supposed to hurt. I learned a long time ago that if it was supposed to hurt and didn't, I was usually in serious trouble. There also wasn't anywhere near enough blood. It was there, but the blood on my shirt was already turning a dirty brown. There was none of the fresh, vibrant red one would expect when one was bleeding continuously.

Dev shook his head slightly, and I stopped my restless shaking. I actually didn't feel bad at all. The baby tried to climb to my shoulder, but she kept slipping. She finally allowed Dev to pull her into his arms so she could pat my face.

"Mmmmbwaw." She ran her hands over my nose and cheeks.

"Is she all right?" Sarah asked again, and I could have sworn there was concern in her voice. She'd been the one to shoot me, but now she seemed upset I was hurt.

I was going to respond when Dev stopped me. He put the slightest pressure on my head, a warning to stay silent. "Of course she's not all right. She's been shot. She has a bullet hole in her chest. Sarah, she's human. She's not full of vampire blood. You can't shoot her and expect her to heal up like a vampire."

Except that I was—full of vampire blood, as Dev was subtlety explaining to me. I was full of Daniel's blood, and that was why the bullet hole didn't hurt. The bullet hole didn't exist anymore. It healed before I hit the floor, but I stayed where I was because if Sarah realized I was fine, I was sure she would put Dev right back into mannequin mode, and I needed him limber.

"I am sorry," Sarah said. "I didn't want to hurt her. I...I like her. I just need the child and I'll leave."

"I'm sorry. I can't do that," Dev said.

"Pick up the baby or I'll shoot you," Sarah said. "I don't know why magic isn't working on the baby, but I doubt she can stop a bullet. Do you want to end up like Zoey? Don't think I will hesitate on you, Dev. I shot one of my best friends and put the other one in a sleep so deep I don't know if he'll come out of it. I don't even like you much. I won't hesitate to shoot you."

"Oh, I know you'll shoot, but I think you underestimate this baby." Dev turned toward Sarah, but he looked the baby in the eyes. I started to pull myself up because Dev was putting the baby in the direct path of the gun. "I think she'll hold her hand up and catch the freaking bullet because she's not a baby, Sarah. She's magic."

The baby stared at Dev with huge green eyes, and for a moment I wondered if she understood. He spoke to her intently, as though she could understand everything he said.

"I warned you," Sarah said before the room shook with the sound of gunfire.

And the baby in Dev's arms held her hand up and the bullet stopped in midair. It simply stopped and sat there until she giggled and pinched it with her delicate fingers and pulled it inevitably into her mouth.

"No." I was unable to stay down any longer. I pulled the bullet away. "Why do you put everything in your mouth? Bad. Nasty."

Sarah watched with her mouth slack-jawed with amazement. Dev was talking, not wasting a moment. He was the only one who understood what the baby was.

"You can protect us," he said quietly to the girl. "Think of a bubble. It's like a circle. Reach in my mind, and you can see it. That's right. Exactly like that."

And I felt the air shift. When Sarah tried to move toward us, she was stopped by some invisible wall. She was forced to step back. The baby giggled at her trick. She touched the wall she made and laughed.

"She's magic, Sarah. She's faery magic, and she'll learn quickly to protect what she loves." Dev stroked my hair. He seemed much happier behind our protective wall. "She's a part of Zoey. She won't let you hurt her."

"Fine," Sarah said with an ugly, angry shout. "Let's see if she will protect the things Zoey loves."

Sarah turned and walked out of the room. I had a horrible feeling in the pit of my stomach because Daniel and Neil were in the outer room, and they were completely helpless. Despite Dev's pulling hands, I broke out of the circle and ran for the room.

Sarah stood beside the bed where Daniel and Neil lay. Daniel was still as the death his sleep emulated, but Neil was curled up at the end of the bed like a puppy taking a nap. He snuffled in his sleep but didn't wake.

"You don't speak Latin, Zoey, so let me translate for you," Sarah said to me from across the king-sized bed. "*Exuro*. I'm going to hold my hand over the bed and put my will into it, and I'm going to say *exuro*. It means burn. This bed will go up in flames, and your vampire will go with it. Have you watched a vampire burn? It isn't pretty."

"Please don't," I begged. "Please, Sarah."

"Do you think I want to do this?" She practically shouted the question. "I just want the fucking kid. I don't want to hurt any of you." Tears streaked down her face. She took a breath and calmed herself momentarily. "Stay back," she said as Dev walked into the room.

"I'm sorry, but the baby wants to be with Zoey," he said. "She's quite insistent."

She bit back a cry, looking right at me. "It's all your fault. You're the one who had to sign a contract with a demon. You had to have that money. It's your downfall, that arrogant greed of yours."

Anger burned in my gut. "Oh, I disagree. My downfall is obviously my shitty choice in friends."

Sarah frowned. "I never wanted to betray you. I just want to save my sister. My mother contracted the both of us to Brixalnax before we were born. We have twenty-five years on this plane before we have to serve our master in Hell. I was told if I bring in the Light, he will let me and my sister go. She turns twenty-five next month. She isn't strong. She can't survive it. Please understand. I don't have a choice."

"So you're willing to give up Daniel and me for you and your sister." I finally understood the plot of the drama I found myself in.

"Zoey, Daniel doesn't have a soul. He'll be fine. This is all about you," Sarah said as though my naïveté was offensive. "I'm sorry, but she's my sister. And Daniel will figure something out to save you. He's the smartest person I've ever met. I'm counting on it. He won't let you go. He really does love you. No one is going to help me or Lily. No one gives a damn about us."

"I did. I would have helped you."

Sarah sniffled. "It doesn't matter anymore. I was put on this path before I was born. I just wish I hadn't...I liked being around you guys. I liked being your friend, and I am so sorry it has to end this way."

"But it doesn't." Tears streamed down my face. "You trust Daniel. He is a smart guy, and he can get us out of this." I tried to make it sound believable because I didn't see how Daniel could think or muscle us out of the contract, but I had to make sure she didn't torch that bed.

Tears streamed down Sarah's face and the gun fell out of her hand. "What am I doing?"

Just like that all the tension in the room fled. "Nothing. You haven't actually done anything yet."

"I shot you. Oh, god, I shot you. Zoey, you have to understand. He gave me a preview of what was going to happen."

I'd seen that preview myself. I could only imagine what Sarah's Hell had been like. And her sister would have to go first. What would I have done to save my father or one of my friends? "Calm down. No one died. We're going to be okay. So Halfer offered you a way out."

Sarah nodded, her face mottled and red. "Yes. He came to me a couple of weeks ago. He told me if I found the box for him he would cancel mine and Lily's contracts. I didn't know it would have anything to do with you. I was going to ask you to help me the night you met with him."

Dev kicked the gun away. "So Halfer wanted to cause some major chaos."

"I don't understand any of it. I don't. I only know that I don't even recognize myself anymore. Do you think there's any way out?" Sarah asked.

"I don't know, but I can't sacrifice this child for you." I could halfway forgive the crazy gun-toting act, but I was going to be immovable on this.

"I don't know how you healed that gunshot wound unless you and Daniel had a bunch of fun last night. And if you did, and what I heard about you is true, then I was right and he won't let some demon take you down. You're his companion. The Council won't let it happen." Her hands were shaking as she touched Neil. "He'll wake up in a while. I love him, too, you know."

I wasn't sure the Council would care about me one way or another, but I needed to think up a way to help Sarah. First, we needed to get the baby to the faeries. We had a few hours, but I wouldn't feel safe until she was home.

"Dev, will you drive us back to the hotel?"

He frowned, still holding the baby tight. "Us? You think I'm getting into a car with the crazy witch who recently tried to kill us all?"

Such a drama queen. "She only tried to kill me."

"Dev, I was desperate. I'm sorry. God, you have no idea how sorry I am. I didn't actually mean to hit her. I thought I would scare her. You don't know what he showed me."

I didn't have time for them to argue. "I'll get the baby's things. Dev, you go get her in the car seat. Sarah, follow him and try not to go insane on me again."

They walked out, Dev's suspicious eyes on Sarah. I gathered a few of the baby's things and kissed my sleeping Daniel. Hopefully it would all be over before he woke up.

When I walked into the fading light of early evening, the first thing I noticed was that we were not alone in the parking lot. There was Dev, and he was kneeling with his hands up. Sarah was flat on the pavement, her arms behind her back. The baby was crying, wiggling in another woman's arms. Two men stood guarding Dev. They all looked familiar, and I realized why. I knew in that moment that I wasn't going to have to find the faeries. They found us, and they were armed. One of them looked straight at me as he held his weapon up.

And that's the story of how I took my first arrow straight to the gut.

233

Chapter Twenty-Two

"Is she going to be all right?"

"You're going to have to explain to me why you give a shit, Sarah."

"I already explained this to you. I didn't want to hurt her."

"Then you shouldn't have shot her."

"I told you that was a huge mistake."

"You aimed and fired. It's not a mistake."

"I was aiming at the wall behind her."

This was what I woke up to. Arguing and the horrible feeling that someone had shoved a poker through my middle and left it there for me to writhe on. Even as I started to come back to myself, the pain sizzled through my system.

"The only reason she's still alive is Daniel's blood, and unless he gets here with a fresh supply, I don't think she's going to make it." Dev's voice was hushed but urgent, as if he didn't want someone to hear him.

"Daniel?" I managed to get the word out, but even moving my mouth hurt like hell. I opened my eyes and saw a ceiling and crown molding. It took me a few seconds, but I realized where we were. We were back in the Gilmore suite, but the last I remembered,

Daniel had been completely helpless in an entirely different place.

"Zoey?" Dev asked, and I wondered why he didn't come to me. I heard a shuffle and tried to move but stopped when my entire body lit up with agony.

"Don't move," Sarah said from across the room. "Stay as still as possible, Z."

Yeah, I was getting that. If I didn't move I could still sort of manage to make my lungs work. Any kind of motion and that whole part of me shut down, replaced with extreme agony. But there was one thing, one tiny motion I had to make. I probably shouldn't have. I should have lain there and let the image stay where it should have, in my mind's eye. Unfortunately, my face's eye just had to look.

"Oh, my god." There it was, sticking straight out of my gut. An arrow pierced through my torso. It wasn't even as long as it should have been, but that might have had something to do with how much of the sucker was inside me.

"Okay, so it's bad," Dev said, and I finally realized why it took him so long to get to me. He was on the floor beside me with his hands behind his back and his feet tied together. I could only guess that he was either tied up or they used handcuffs. Since there was a freaking arrow in my belly, I was betting on rope. My hands and feet were free. Either they'd only had enough for two prisoners or they'd figured the arrow in my belly was enough to keep me down.

"Did they stake Daniel?" I asked, wincing with every word.

"No, I don't think so," Dev replied quietly.

"You don't think so?" Even I could hear an edge of hysteria tinting my words.

"Well, I'm sorry, I was kind of knocked unconscious with the hilt of a crossbow," Dev replied irritably.

I didn't feel a lick of sympathy. "I got the other end, Dev, so lucky you. Please tell me Danny is alive."

"Like I said, I think so. I woke up in the van, and I heard them arguing. The big guy wanted to kill us all, but the female said something about the child and the child's will. She felt they should honor what the child wanted. I know the baby wanted to protect Daniel."

"Okay," I sighed. At least Daniel and Neil were probably safe.

"Just two more questions and then I think I'd like to die as peacefully as possible. One—is the baby all right? Are they treating her well, or are they pissed she's human and not a tree?"

Dev's eyes went soft. Damn, but he was a gorgeous man. "They wouldn't hurt the child, and you have got to get it through your stubborn head that the baby isn't human. She looks human, but she's something else entirely. I don't think they know what to do with her, but for now, they're honoring her wishes."

"Two—what are they planning to do with the three of us?"

Sarah piped up to answer this question. "We get to go to faery world and stand trial for crimes against magic or something. On the upside, I think Halfer will come for the two of us first."

"Yay." My sarcasm was as weak as my body. "So behind door number one, I get executed by a whole bunch of faeries, and behind door number two, I get raped by a demon and spend the rest of eternity on the Hell plane. Where's door number three?"

"Ummm, if you think about it, the most logical conclusion is you get executed by faeries. And from what I've seen, they don't have a problem with torture. Once you're dead, your contract kicks in and then you get raped by a demon on the Hell plane for eternity," Sarah pointed out. "I don't think there is a door number three."

"Thank you, Sarah," I said with a bitter laugh. "Great clarification."

"Well, I'm in the same boat, Z."

"Oh, not true. We are so not in the same boat," I shot back. I was feeling less magnanimous now that I had an arrow sticking out of my gut. In the heat of the moment, I'd been willing to forgive almost anything, but pain was making me a crabby bitch. "You're a witch. At least you get a job. I get to be his gimp. He'll probably lead me around on a freaking chain, and you know what, I blame you. If you had kept out of it, none of this would have happened."

"This is so not my fault," Sarah replied with righteous indignation.

"Did you or did you not steal the money? And the only answer is yes, Zoey, I stole the money because you're the only one who makes sense. You were alone with my dad, and you slipped him the hex bag, and then the next morning you slipped one into the coat I was wearing. You weren't trying to get Neil. You slipped it to me at breakfast. Your fault!"

"Yes, I made the hex bags. I slipped one to your dad so he would take the money and one to you so you would cause a ton of chaos and Daniel would take you away. If you had stayed out of it, I could have gotten the Light on my own. I'm not the one who decided it would be a good idea to work for a demon."

"No, you were just born into a family that serves one."

Sarah huffed. "That isn't fair."

"Ladies, as much as I love a good girl fight, I find myself sadly lacking the Jell-O that would make this worthwhile," Dev said quietly. "Keep it down or they're going to come in here, and I don't want to get kicked in the groin again. If I'm going to die when we get to the Faery plane, I'd like to go out with the boys intact."

Sarah and I frowned at each other, but we went back to our metaphorical corners.

"Fine. We'll drop it for now. Sarah, why don't you say some Latin stuff and get us out of here?" I wasn't sure why she hadn't done it before.

"Latin stuff? Like it's that easy. Besides, they hit me with some sort of dust when I walked out. I can't do anything. It must possess anti-magical properties. I'm sure it will wear off, but then I would have the problem of the wards they've placed all over. They aren't making the same mistakes this time."

Dev was trying to get himself in a seated position, contorting his lean body and twisting. I was the reason he was here. I knew damn well I should have found a way to keep him out of this, but my hormones had taken over my decision-making process, and now Dev was going to die. Even though I was back with Daniel, I still cared about Dev. I still felt a connection to him, one I didn't want snuffed out by death. If Sarah couldn't get us out, then it was up to me.

And then I had one of those awful ideas. I get them sometimes and they tend to be fueled by desperation, but I almost always follow through. I sighed and prepared myself for some painful moments because those awful, wretched ideas I have almost always cause me pain.

I braced myself. Clenched my teeth. Told myself to be ready for it. But even with the best of intentions, I couldn't stop the short, sharp cry that came out when I sat up. It was uncomfortable, to say the least.

"Zoey, get back down." Dev twisted around, his eyes widening.

"What are you doing?" Sarah sounded way more concerned than someone who recently shot me should.

"It's my fault you're here, Dev. I should never have let you come with me." I got on my knees and took several quick breaths because the next part was the hard part. "I'm not going to let you die, Dev."

And then I shoved the rest of the arrow through my torso. I was surprised to find it hadn't pierced my back yet since it felt like it had when I was lying down. I pushed it as far as I could and reached around and pulled it through and then I passed out again.

I knew immediately I hadn't been out for as long this time. Everything in the room seemed the same. Dev managed to get to a seated position and was trying to scoot to where I was. I forced myself to sit up, and it was only with the greatest will that I managed to not throw up.

"Zoey, please," Sarah begged. "Whatever you're thinking of doing, don't. It's almost dark. If they didn't kill Daniel, he'll come for you. Please lay back down."

My hands shook as I pushed my hair back. "So what, Sarah? Daniel comes for me and what? I get a few extra hours before Halfer drags our asses to Hell? I hope you're right and Danny can't be taken there, but Dev can be killed and the baby can be taken away, and I'm the only one who can stop it."

"How are you going to do that, Zoey?" Dev winced as I managed to stand.

I steadied myself and decided to go ahead and see how much worse I'd made the situation. I lifted the hem of my blood-soaked T-shirt and was surprised to see the wound was trying to heal itself. It wasn't doing a great job, but Daniel's blood was giving a valiant effort.

I took a deep breath, grateful everything seemed to be functioning. "I'm going to use reason, Dev. Sweet reason."

I walked toward the door that opened to the rest of the suite, and over the vigorous protests of my fellow prisoners, I shut it behind me. It was a short walk to the sitting area of the suite, but I needed to balance against the wall and kind of shuffle my way down the hall. Before turning the corner I called out, hoping to not surprise anyone who might have a nervous trigger finger.

"I'm coming out, and I'm not armed. I mean I still have arms, but…" I sighed and tried to collect my thoughts. I tend to go a little ADD when fighting for my life. "I don't have any weapons."

I took a step into the room and was confronted by the three faeries we robbed the day before. They had seemed so much less imposing when I had a gun, a werewolf, and a vampire with me. The baby was there as well, and she gurgled some nonsense words when she saw me.

They'd brought the box back as well. It sat on the table, exactly where it had been before. It was empty and no longer held much value. The faeries had also done a bang-up job on the body disposal. The suite was pristinely clean.

"Hello, my name is Zoey Wharton." I hadn't had a chance to introduce myself before the whole arrow thing. I pointed to the chair closest to me. "Do you mind? I'm having trouble, what with the blood loss and internal damage."

The female who was holding the child smiled wryly. "Please, I wouldn't miss this particular conversation for the world. Are your friends going to attempt to escape?"

I let go of a deep breath I hadn't realized I was holding in as I settled into the chair. The pain was starting to relent, and I thought perhaps it was because I'd pushed the arrow through. The vampire blood inside me was doing its best to heal my body, but it hadn't been able to work around the arrow.

I gestured back toward the room I'd come from. "Please, feel free to check on them. You'll find they are still tied up and completely unthreatening."

The female nodded shortly to the smaller of the men. He jogged down the hall. She returned to studying me. "Why would you not try to escape? You have to know that we intend to take you back to our home. We will bring charges against you, and you will be executed."

"Yeah, I got that." If there was one thing I was damn certain of, it was my death. One way or another, that would happen, and sooner than I'd imagined.

Her mouth turned down, a deeply regal look. "You stole something sacred to us."

There was no talking my way out of that one. "Yes, I did."

The man came back and whispered something into his mistress's ear. She nodded and turned her attention back to me. "Your friends are still there. It is going to be a very short trial if you simply admit to everything."

But that was kind of my plan. "I did it. It was me."

A light went on in her eyes. "Ahh, you seek to take the blame on yourself and save your friends."

"Except for the other girl. She was totally in on the plot. You should definitely torture her." She shot me, and I wouldn't mind having a cell mate. "As a matter of fact, you should force us to work for you for a prolonged period of time before our executions." I didn't know how much pull Halfer had on other planes, but if it bought me time not being raped, I would take it.

"You're an odd girl." She ran her hands soothingly across the baby's head. "She likes you."

"I like her, too." I hated the tears that sprang to my eyes. "You have to get her out of here. I know you won't believe me, but I didn't know what I was stealing. I was trying to bring her back when you found us."

"You shot us," the larger male said with a frown.

"Dude, I shot you with a tranquilizer dart. You put an arrow through me. The point goes to you. I think I can read a newspaper though my torso."

"I did not like being shot," he replied.

"Eh, I've had worse," the other male said. "I, personally, am impressed with any woman who can shove an arrow through her belly and still walk out here to negotiate."

"A good reason not to kill me," I pointed out. "Think of the party tricks I can come up with."

"I am impressed with any woman who can prime a transference

box." The female gestured to the box on the table. "My name is Haweigh of the Tuatha Dé Danann. I am a priestess of the realm. Had the Light of Alhorra made it to our tribe intact, it would have fallen to me to prepare our people to prime the box. Do you understand what I mean by a transference box?"

"Dev explained it to me. He knows about this stuff, but he didn't see the box until we took it." I was impressed with the fact that the Tuatha Dé Danann still existed. If I ever saw my father again, I would have to give him the news. "He said you usually turn the magic into a tree or something."

"Yes," the large man said sarcastically. "A tree is best because a tree has no learning curve. Sometimes we turn it into a cat or a dog because they reach maturity quickly. In six months to a year, the magical animal will have the emotional maturity to do things properly. Do you have any idea how hard her childhood will be?"

"What my husband is trying to say is we prefer that the magic be contained to something easily controllable," Haweigh explained. "The child will be somewhat unpredictable."

"Tell me you won't hurt her." I'd screwed up her whole life.

Haweigh chuckled a bit, pulling her hair from the baby's hand. "She belongs to us. We would never hurt her. She will bless our tribe with her unique magic, and we will be grateful to her. We are thankful you did not damage the box. It could have been much worse. Now, the truth of the matter is, I am inclined to allow the faery to live. He was not involved in the actual taking of our box. In truth, I am inclined to allow you to live. I find you unique, and I prefer to leave the unique things of the worlds whole. But you must return to our plane to face justice."

"I'm grateful." I figured that groveling was the best course of action. I decided to be brave. There was one thing I needed to know before I left this plane. "I have to ask you a question."

"I await it eagerly." Haweigh seemed amused by me. I could make that work to my advantage later, but for now I just had to know.

"Is he dead?" I meant for it to be a steady almost academic question, but I stumbled through it and gave away far too much.

She looked up at her husband. "I told you it was the vampire.

He is your lover?"

I nodded since there was no reason I could think of to cover it up.

"Lang believed you were involved with the faery, but I rather thought it was the vampire. I spent many years on this plane, and you have the look of a companion. As to your question, he continues to exist," she confirmed, watching me closely.

I nodded to let her know I'd heard, but I couldn't suppress the sob that escaped. I wiped the tears away and tried to contain my emotion. "Thank you."

I wouldn't see Daniel again. My heart ached. I didn't think about everything Dev had told me. None of it mattered in that moment. I only knew that I loved Daniel and he was lost again.

"Thank the child," Haweigh said. "I was inclined to kill him because of the danger he represents. Was he the one you were with when the box was primed?"

"Yes."

Haweigh contemplated this. "As you are an odd girl, he is not a normal vampire, is he? The box can only be primed through pure magic. We would have used a type of community magic, all of us working together for the good of our tribe. The two of you used sex magic, and while that is powerful, it requires an enormous amount of feeling between the two of you. The box would not have reacted to mere lust. I'm afraid vampires are more associated with obsession than genuine love."

"We have quite the history."

"Speaking of the vampire." The husband pointed to the window, which showed a spectacular sunset. "Shouldn't we be going? We've taken his mate. He will not let this go. We should pass through the veil now."

"Lang is right," the other male said. "I would rather wait until midnight, but I would also like to leave with my neck intact. Vampires are not known for their tolerance, which is why we should have killed it."

Haweigh looked at me. "Men. They believe violence is the answer to everything. We women know differently. Are you ready?"

I would never be ready, but Daniel was alive. Dev would live. I had to call this a win. "I'm ready, and so is Sarah. You can leave Dev here. Daniel will find him eventually. We won't cause any more trouble. Well, I won't. Sarah's a different story. You might want to gag her."

The priestess stood with the child in her arms. She was a beautiful woman and everything one would think a faery queen would be. She was tall with golden hair that brushed her waist and eyes that looked like jewels. She carried the child with no hesitation, and I was sure this was not the first baby she'd held. I guess you think a lot about all the crap you're never going to do when you know the world is changing. I wouldn't hold a baby again. I wouldn't see Daniel again. I wouldn't…well, I could go on forever about what I wouldn't do.

Lang pulled Sarah out, and I turned to look at her. She looked like I felt, sad and scared. I gave her a half-hearted smile. "I told them they should gag you."

Her face broke into a genuine grin, and she laughed. "Bitch."

I started to stand, but Haweigh held her hand up and I stopped. She looked at the child and arched an eyebrow. "Do what you think you must."

The child held her hand, and I felt something pass through me. I looked down, and the hole in my midsection closed while I watched. It closed as though it were sewing itself back together. Unfortunately, it also felt like someone was sewing me back together. I didn't even try to stop the scream.

I fell to the floor, shaking after the pain passed. Lang came in close and stared down at me. "See, if she'd been a cat, that wouldn't have hurt."

I held my stomach and vowed that the next time I made a magical creature, it would definitely be a cat.

Chapter Twenty-Three

I felt infinitely better by the time we reached the elevator. I was sore, but the hole in my middle was closed. That meant my day was looking up. Haweigh and her compatriots were definitely not used to the way things worked on this plane. I personally would have insisted my blood-soaked prisoner change clothes so as not to attract unwelcome attention.

I got several stares, but I smiled brightly and winked and no one said a word.

And I wondered if it was dark yet. I wondered if Daniel was awake and searching for me. I wondered if he would miss me.

Haweigh pushed the button for the parking garage, and the doors closed. Sarah and I were alone with our captors. The only bright spot was the baby and her toothless grin.

"I like her," the smaller faery said. When I describe him as smaller, I simply mean not as large as Lang. He still had a good six inches on me.

"What a surprise," Lang said sarcastically. "Craigen likes the pretty female."

"She's not just pretty," Craigen replied. "She's crazy. I like that in a female. The crazy ones are always the best."

I smiled at the attractive, funny Fae. I could use allies, and I was not above using my feminine wiles to acquire them. The longer I managed to stay alive, the more of a chance I had to see Daniel one last time. He would search for me. And Dev would tell him where they'd taken me. "What gave me away? Was it the arrowdectomy? That was nothing. I jumped off the roof of the hotel last night. Now that was crazy. Let's see, this month alone I've tried to kill my own father, fought off a big snake, destroyed a nightclub, and summoned a fully-functional demon. That was a mistake. I'd been hoping for the Ken-doll version."

Craigen laughed. "See, I have no idea what the girl is saying, but I like the way she says it. I think she can stay with me when we get home. She'll need an advocate."

Yeah, I could bet what that horny faery would be advocating for me. But the more I thought about it, the more I liked the "stay alive and hope Daniel made it to Faeryland" plan. Dev had connections. Daniel had pure willpower.

If they didn't kill each other, they might make a good team.

The doors to the lowest level of the garage opened, and I was escorted into the low light of the enormous space.

"Can you feel that, Z?" Sarah walked, following our captors, but her head swung around as though searching for something.

I felt scared because we were about to be taken to another plane, but I didn't feel anything supernatural. I prayed it wasn't Halfer. "What is it?"

"It's the veil." Sarah breathed in the air reverently. "It's here and it's going to open. Wow, that is some impressive magic. Do you do it?"

She pointed the question to Haweigh. "This I cannot take credit for. It is an Earth magic, but finding the veil and getting through it, that is our magic. We passed from this plane long ago, and we passed in just this way."

She led us down the long aisles and turned. There were few cars this far down. We were alone. I wondered what time it was. When the doors opened to the lobby, I'd noted it was close to full dark. There had been only a sliver of sunlight illuminating the lobby. Daniel would be awake soon. And I prayed Neil awakened as well.

"Why here?" Sarah asked as we stopped.

Lang shrugged. "It shifts all the time. We entered the plane in a place called St. Louis and made our way here to get back. The fact that the veil opens underground explains a lot to us. We wondered why the times between the opening of the veils varied so widely. Sometimes they open one after another, and other times it takes months to get back. Apparently the veil opens where it will. Before this structure was built, this place of passing would have been impossible to access."

"So what's it like?" I found myself curious. "Is it 'beam me up, Scotty'?"

All three looked at me blankly. Sarah rolled her eyes in an affectionate manner. My pop culture references were going to be so lost on the Faery plane.

"It is a door," Haweigh explained patiently. "But one you must be trained to see." She turned her attention to the child, who was suddenly staring at the ceiling, her fat baby arms pumping up and down. "No, child, it is this way. It is not here yet, but if you try, you can see it."

Baby Girl wasn't interested. Her head turned up, watching the ceiling, a big grin on her face. She suddenly let loose a squeal and clapped her hands.

There was a distant rumble humming through the air and accompanied by a shake of the pavement. It sounded like a car was moving through the garage above us. I didn't think much of it because it was only logical cars would be moving around a parking garage. Hopefully said car didn't barrel through at the wrong time and drive right through the door that was about to open.

The baby jumped up and down in Haweigh's arms almost as though the sounds made her dance. The car seemed to be getting closer, and the closer it got, the more it sounded less like a car than a big-ass truck. The rumble grew. The shaking continued until the ceiling above us began to quiver.

Halfer. It had to be Halfer. He was coming for me. He'd found out I couldn't make our late-night meeting and moved the timeline up. My stomach twisted. I locked eyes with Sarah.

"I'll try to protect you any way I can," she said, sniffling. "I'm so sorry, Z."

Craigen pulled me close to him, and at first I thought he was trying to protect me. Then he put a gun against my head. To clarify, he put Sarah's gun against my head. It was nice to know we helped them upgrade.

The ground beneath my feet seemed to vibrate. I gave up on the vehicular metaphors in favor of power tools. This was a jack hammer, and it was coming our way.

The faeries were speaking to each other in rapid-fire Elvish. I don't know precisely what they said, but I guessed the recriminations were flying around. Words weren't the only things flying. I ducked as chunks of concrete began to rain down, small at first and then larger as a hole began to form.

Lang pushed Sarah onto her knees and slightly behind him. It seemed a better protected position than what Craigen had me in. She looked up at me with wide eyes, and we were both waiting. Halfer was making his entrance, and we were all screwed. Who else could punch his way through six levels of concrete?

"So sorry," she said again.

I nodded because I was beyond being pissed at her. I tried to shift in Craigen's arms, but he held me fast.

"Can we go through?" I tried to gesture to the vague place where I thought the veil would be.

"No." He kept his eyes trained on the hole in the ceiling. It had started out tiny, but suddenly it was man-sized. His every muscle was tense and prepared for something bad to happen. "It's too early."

"You should let me and Sarah go. A demon is coming through that hole and I don't know that he'll let you live." I looked at Haweigh, desperate to make her understand. "He wants the child. Please. Please. Run. Hide her. I'll lie. I'll give you time."

If Halfer took the child, everything I had sacrificed would be wasted.

But it was too late. Too late to bargain. Too late to pray. Too late for everything because he was here.

A dark figure fell through the hole, though I shouldn't use the word fell. Fell implies some loss of control. This was intensely deliberate. He landed on one knee, catching himself on those hands that had finished clearing the way to his target. Me.

My whole spirit soared because it wasn't Halfer on the floor.

Daniel looked up, and I finally understood what he'd been trying to tell me for the last five years. He wasn't human. He was a monster, and he was capable of killing everyone in that room and never feeling a moment of regret. He would enjoy the ripping and tearing, and he would no doubt revel in the blood. He was Vampire, and there was no going back.

And I still loved him.

"All right, vampire," Craigen said, trying hard to keep his voice steady. "Stay back. I know you're fast, but this is right against her brain. I don't want to hurt her."

Daniel stood, turning toward me, those alien eyes fastening right on mine. He spoke to Craigen, but never took those eyes off me. His voice seemed to fill the room with his will. "You have my mate. Give her to me, and I'll kill you quickly."

Haweigh held her hand up, and the pressure left the room. Of all the faeries, she was the only who seemed calm. The men were tense and the baby practically jumped with glee, squirming to try to get to Daniel. But Haweigh was patient. "Impressive, vampire, but you are misreading the situation."

"My mate is covered in blood, and you say I'm misreading the situation," Daniel growled. "I may sleep during the day, but don't assume that I can't hear what goes on around me. I know what you did. Now, I'm going to give this warning once and only once. Give me my companion, or I'll kill you all. It will give me pleasure to rip you apart, and I will keep you alive as long as possible. You'll die knowing that I will find a way to your precious Faery plane, and I will kill your tribe and everything they love. When I'm done with it, your plane will make Hell look pleasant. It will be a dumping ground for the bodies of my victims. Now give me my mate."

Craigen swore in Gaelic, but that wasn't hard to translate. I also think he might have peed a bit.

"I believe the vampire is serious, Craigen," Haweigh said slowly. "Perhaps you should allow Miss Wharton to go."

"If I do, he'll kill us." Craigen's hands were shaking, and I prayed the trigger on that gun was steady.

"I think Miss Wharton might be able to sway him if you'll let her go," Haweigh reasoned. "If you keep her much longer, I believe the bloodlust will take over and not even her reason will be able to sway him then."

Then Craigen was pushing me forward, and I was in Daniel's arms. He ran his hands across my body, looking for the source of the blood he smelled. He pulled up my shirt, and I let him because he needed to see that I was alive and whole. The faeries couldn't conceive how lucky they'd been that the magic child had been able to heal me so completely that my skin was smooth. Had Daniel been able to get even a hint of the damage that had been done, I doubted I would have been able to stop him from killing the faeries.

I wrapped my arms around him, telling myself that everything Dev had said was bullshit. It didn't matter. Dev didn't understand. Daniel loved me. He wasn't addicted to me. After a moment, Daniel brought his arms around me and enfolded me. I felt him sigh against my hair. I looked up and gave him a smile. "What are you, too good for the elevator now?"

It took a moment, but he planted a quick kiss on my lips. "Too slow." He pushed me away gently. "Go back upstairs and wait for me, Zoey. I have some things I need to take care of."

Yeah, I was pretty sure the things he needed to take care of would end in a whole bunch of blood. We didn't have time for that. "I'm not going anywhere, and don't you even try that whole 'do my will' bit because it won't work."

"They shot you," he replied stubbornly.

"So did Sarah, and you're not going to kill her."

"Now that you mention it." Daniel turned his eyes toward Sarah.

"You're not killing anyone, Daniel Donovan," I said with as much finality as I could muster.

Lang laughed long and hard. He was still chuckling when everyone turned to him. "I am sorry, but it's good to know it's not only me. Give it up, vampire. She has you by the balls. Wives, they always have us by the balls."

Something about the word "wife" made Daniel stop. The tension seemed to leave the room, and he pulled me back into his arms, allowing his relief to finally overcome his rage.

"I couldn't help you." His hands sank into my hair. "I was

trapped, and I couldn't save you."

I kissed his cheek. "But you did. Your blood kept me alive."

"Miss Wharton," Haweigh said, clearly not wanting to interrupt the moment. "The veil is open, but the child is insistent. She wants to meet the vampire."

Daniel swallowed audibly, and he stared at the baby who was practically vibrating with excitement.

"Did you hear what Dev said?" It only made sense if he knew what had happened to me that he'd listened in on my conversation with Dev.

He nodded, not taking his eyes off the child. Haweigh walked forward and held the child out. Daniel hesitated.

"Don't be ridiculous," Haweigh said. "You won't hurt the child. You don't understand what you are, Daniel Donovan, but she does, and she has no fear of you."

He slowly held his arms out and took the baby against his chest. The child calmed and slowly explored his face with her tiny hands.

"She has things to say to you. You are not Fae, so you cannot hear her. I will translate," Haweigh explained. "She says you think you have but one path, and this is not the truth. Trust yourself and trust her. I believe she is talking about your companion. There is much going through her mind, and I can't possibly say all of it. She wants you to think about the fact that when your will, your need, and your soul were put in the box, she is what came out. She was born from your deepest desire. There is nothing evil about her. She wishes you to think on this."

Then Haweigh took the baby out of Daniel's arms. "We really must go now."

Daniel's hand found its way into mine, and I squeezed it tight as we watched the faeries pull open the veil. There was a tear in the air in front of us, and I glimpsed sunlight and green hills. I could smell a sweetness and hear the sound of a waterfall. Daniel moved away from that streak of light like it was a laser beam he needed to avoid.

Haweigh was the last to go. She turned before entering the veil. "The child wishes one last thing of you, Daniel Donovan. She would like a name from you."

Daniel pulled me close, and I knew what he was thinking. He

was back in my father's house, and we were eighteen and about to head off to college. We'd made love and sat up and argued about what we would name our babies. I knew what he was going to say.

"Summer. Her name is Summer."

And then she was gone, and that piece of daylight and magic closed behind her and Daniel, Sarah, and I were alone.

We didn't say anything for several moments, allowing the enormity of the day to wash over us. We clung to each other. Finally I looked up at him and asked the question I didn't want to know the answer to.

"How long do we have?"

"A couple of hours." He brushed back my hair.

"Ummm, I was hoping someone could, maybe, untie me," Sarah said haltingly.

Daniel turned to her, and she shrank back. "Sarah, the less I remember you exist, the more chance you have of making it to the Hell plane in one piece. I assure you that Halfer will have no problem dragging you there in two pieces, but you will find the experience unpleasant. Know that you live on her sufferance and her mercy because I have none."

Sarah's eyes went wide, and she nodded slowly.

I walked over to Sarah against Daniel's protests and untied her hands. "He's suddenly big into the overdrama. I think he watched too many Clint Eastwood films. Go, Sarah. Find some Joe and enjoy these last few hours."

She hugged me and then with a glance at Daniel, she began to walk toward the elevators. She never turned her back, and I knew what she was feeling. She was thinking she'd never really known him.

I took his hand and watched as the last of that volcanic rage left him, and he looked like my Daniel again. "So you can listen in while you sleep. Good to know. If you piss me off, I'll put on some Broadway CDs."

"Remind me not to piss you off. I don't usually listen in, you know. I can ignore most of it, but there are certain conversations that catch my interest."

There was a low growl and then a big white wolf fell from the hole in the ceiling. Unlike Daniel's graceful, deliberate descent, this was one big pratfall. When the wolf hit the ground, it only took him a moment to change back into human form, and when he came up, he was one righteous werewolf.

"Keys? Did you think about leaving the keys? The car doesn't work without the keys, and big surprise—I can't fly. But no, Superman here wakes me and then takes off like a superhot speeding bullet. I had to run twenty miles on an empty stomach. Twenty miles. Do you know what it was like trying to get across I-35? It was like playing Frogger, and I was the poor frog. And I think animal control is hunting for me." Neil paused briefly to take a breath and then started in again. "And then when my sad, starved body finally manages to make it to the place where my thoughtless boss has told me to go, I fall through a bunch of holes in the concrete. Who has sink holes in a parking garage? This hotel sucks. That said, I'm going upstairs to order room service. Did I mention I'm hungry?"

I was laughing as quietly as I could manage while Daniel slid out of his long, leather duster and handed it to Neil who was, once again, naked.

Neil looked at the coat and reluctantly slipped it on, sighing over the bullet holes in the back. "Great," he muttered. "Now I look like a flasher. I need a couple of steaks, and a lobster, and some carbs."

Neil walked toward the elevator.

Daniel took my hand and started to follow. "Come on. If I remember correctly, the faeries paid for the Gilmore suite until tomorrow afternoon. It's as good a place as any to wait this out."

Wait this out. Our meeting with Halfer. We had a few hours before I would have to go to Hell and all I could think to say was, "I don't have the keycard."

Daniel pointed toward the ceiling with the gaping holes in it. He could probably handle the door.

We made it upstairs without further incident. In the elevator, Daniel held me tightly, and I could feel the will he was using to have the people who got on the elevator ignore us. A couple looked our way but their eyes seemed to glide over or around us. I was grateful to reach the safety of the room.

Neil immediately got on the phone and started ordering two of everything. I began to make my way back to the secondary bedroom where Dev was still tied up. Daniel stopped me.

"Is he back there?"

I nodded. "Yes, I have to go untie him."

He'd been great. Even though I was with Daniel, I have to admit, there was something about Dev that called to me. It didn't matter because I had so few moments left and I meant to throw everything I had into Daniel, but I cared about Dev.

"I'll do it." Daniel held up his hands as though to say he had no weapons. The problem was Daniel didn't need weapons. "I have no intention of harming him. He isn't the one who betrayed you, so he's safe from me. I need to have a discussion with him, and I promise to keep it peaceful. I've done everything you've asked of me tonight. Let me have this."

He hadn't killed the faeries or Sarah and he'd really wanted to. I needed to give him this. He went off for what I expected to be a manly discussion about Dev keeping his hands off me. I wasn't sure why he felt the need. I had only a few hours of life left on the Earth plane. I intended to spend them with Daniel.

I was about to head to the master bedroom when I glanced at the table in the center of the room. The box. It sat in the middle of the table, forgotten in all the hurry to get home. Now it sat there, a sad reminder of what might have been. I ran my hands across it, feeling the detailed carving. What had Halle said to me? He'd said something about details being important, and on this box, the details were everything. They told a story.

The box practically whispered, but the moment was broken, my thoughts shattering as I was spun around by the elbow.

"Come with me, Zoey." Dev stood there, his eyes narrowed. "I'm going to try to get you out of this. I know people, important people. I may be able to work something out. I'm not going to allow this to happen."

Daniel walked up behind us but he simply folded his arms across his chest and shook his head. I suspected he'd told Dev that this wouldn't work.

I pulled my hand back. Of all the people I'd dragged into this awful situation, it was Dev I was most regretful about. I could feel for him. But my history with Daniel trumped everything. I loved him. I wanted these last moments with him. "Dev, I'm sorry, but there is no way out of this. You can't do anything. If you try, you'll probably get hurt."

He shook me a little. "You can't mean to just sit here and wait for Halfer to come for you."

"I'm so sorry I brought you into this. I never meant to hurt you. But I'm going to stay here and wait for him. The Light of Alhorra is gone. I'm not going to spend my last hours running like a rat trying to get off a sinking ship. If you had three hours left on Earth, how would you spend them?"

Dev shook his head in disbelief, his eyes sliding to Daniel. "I hope you're right about this. I'll do the first part, but I'll die before I let the second bit happen." He turned back to me. "You're making a huge mistake, Zoey. I care for you. When you wake up to what he is…to what this whole perverted thing with him is, you call me, but I won't stand here and watch him lead you into Hell."

Dev stormed out of the room, and I wished I could have called him back, but he would never understand. Daniel and I were different. I wasn't his property. He loved me long before his turn, and he loved me now. Whatever happened between other vampires and companions, it didn't touch us. It didn't define us. I was his partner. He would never treat me as less.

The door slammed behind Dev and Daniel lifted me into his arms and carried me into the big bedroom. We were in full agreement on how to spend our final hours together. I let the conversation with Dev go, and I let the day go, and I let whatever was going to happen tonight go, and lost myself in loving him.

He carried me to the bedroom, sinking on to me as we fell to the bed. We got out of our clothes, needing to be skin to skin. He stared at me, his eyes catching mine and holding them.

"I love you, Z." It had taken five years for me to hear "I love you" from Daniel again, but each word was sweet.

"I love you." I couldn't hold those words from him if I tried. My whole body lit up as Daniel pressed me down. We nestled together, chest to chest, legs tangling, mouths merging, feet tickling.

He promised he would take care of me, and I knew it was a lie. There wasn't anything he could do, but I also knew I would hold those words like a shield against the things that would happen. I had made my choice. I'd chosen that baby over both of us, but I needed to. She didn't belong to us, and I had to send her away. Summer. Our almost child.

Daniel kissed me, long and slow. His fangs grazed my neck, his hunger a palpable thing.

"Please." I wanted him to feed. I was already caught in his power. There was a part of me that hoped he would take it all. His fangs pierced, sweet pleasure coursing through my veins. He could take it all. I would float away as Daniel fed and fed. It would be a pleasant way to go. I would hold him and give to him and fade away.

"Stay with me." He pulled away all too soon, his words warm on my skin. "Stay with me until the end."

He opened a hole on his chest, right above his heart and cradled my head as I leaned over to drink. That blood took me to a different place, a better place. Maybe Dev was right, but in that moment, I didn't care about addictions or reason. I wanted to fade away, to ride that blood and never look back.

"My companion. My precious blood." Daniel kissed me after I'd had my fill. He laid me down and covered me again, his cock finding its home.

It was over too soon.

I didn't cry until he told me it was time. I didn't want to leave him. It was so fucking unfair. I just got him back, and now I would lose him again.

"Shh, Zoey," he whispered, strong hands stroking my hair. "It's going to be all right. I won't let anything happen to you. I'll take care of it. Trust me. This is the way it is between us now. I take care of you. It's my right, my duty."

But there was nothing he could do. And I still wasn't sure he wouldn't be forced to go with me. I intended to argue that I was the leader of the crew. I'd made the deal. I'd pay the price.

He dressed me in a clean shirt and jeans I suspected Neil had provided. We'd spent hours alone together, but Neil had been shopping. I was distinctly zombie like. I had one goal and that was to not let Halfer drag me kicking and screaming. If I did one last thing on this plane, it would be to get out with some shred of dignity. Daniel held my hand and led me out to the living area where Neil and Sarah sat on the couch. She looked like I felt.

"No Joe?" I asked.

She shook her head. "I wanted to be here." She looked up at Daniel, and I knew it took courage to face him. "I'm sorry, Daniel. I had my reasons, but I will do whatever I can to take care of her down there."

Daniel stared her down, but to her credit, she didn't flinch.

"Someone's coming." Neil sniffed the air as there was a knock at the door. "Not demons. Vampires. Is the cavalry here?"

"Don't expect help from them." Daniel shook his head as if he'd been expecting this.

"Help from who?" I looked at him for some explanation, but he simply opened the door.

"Hello, Marcus," Daniel said with a deferential nod to an impeccably dressed man who looked to be in his thirties. He was dark haired and impossibly attractive.

"*Buona sera*, Daniel," Marcus said with a frown, his eyes narrowing in obvious impatience. *"Che guaio sei tu in presente?"*

"È niente Sono incapace verso riuscire." Daniel responded. "Please, can we speak English? My Italian is rusty."

I didn't know his Italian existed.

"Of course, how rude of me," Marcus said politely. Daniel stepped back and allowed him to enter. He was followed by three more men, all of them dressed in suits and stunningly attractive. What I didn't find attractive was the coffin they carried between them. "Your Italian is rusty because you don't use it. I assume your French is even worse."

"So the Council sent you?" Daniel stared at the coffin. The vampires set it in the middle of the room.

"It could have been worse." Marcus shrugged, an elegant movement of strong, broad shoulders.

He wasn't as tall as Daniel, but he had a distinctly hawk-like presence. Of all the vampires in the room, even I could tell that he was the oldest. Power radiated off him. And he looked at Daniel like a father annoyed at his wayward son.

I didn't even know the name Marcus, but Daniel had a deep relationship with him. Daniel spoke Italian and French. Daniel was important.

Daniel was a mystery.

"I don't see how this gets much worse," Daniel grumbled.

"They could have sent someone else," the Italian vampire shot back. "They wanted to send someone else. I had to pull many strings to arrange this. We are only here to observe, Daniel. I am not even sure what it is I am supposed to observe. Would you care to fill me in?"

But Daniel was busy watching the other vampires. "Touch her and I'll have you in that coffin, Ivan."

It was then I realized all of the vampires were looking at me. I felt like I had in the elevator with Michael, except times three. Every eye was focused on me. I couldn't miss the fact that their fangs were out. Predators. I was in a group of hungry predators and I felt like prey. I walked over to Daniel and slipped my hand in his.

"Ragazzi, *dove sei tuo maniera?*" Marcus commanded, and the vampires stepped back, but they didn't take their eyes off me. "I apologize, Mrs. Donovan. They forget themselves around a lovely companion. Your light is extremely bright. I forget myself as well. I am Marcus Vorenus, Daniel's patron. I wish I were meeting you under better circumstances. Daniel should have had you properly presented to me in Venice, but he is not one to play by the rules."

Mrs. Donovan? And what rules? And why did people keep referring to how bright I was? I didn't feel bright. I felt as dumb as a post.

Then I was just scared. The air around me cracked, and the room filled with the smell of brimstone. The demon was right on time.

Halfer stood in the front of the window, immaculate in his suit and tie. His human form was perfect in every way except for the red cast to his eyes. He smiled broadly and clapped his hands together. "Excellent, we're all here. Let the negotiations begin."

Chapter Twenty-Four

It occurred to me as I stood there that I didn't understand what was going on. I looked around the room and everyone with the exception of Sarah seemed to be in the know. They might not know everything, but they were comfortable enough to not look confused.

Daniel placed himself in front of me, so I was forced to crane my neck around his body to be able to see what was going on. Neil made his way to Daniel's side, but I noted he didn't stand beside him exactly. The stance seemed practiced, as though where he stood mattered. There was some form of ritual going or protocol happening that I didn't understand.

Lucas Halfer was the only one in the room with a smile on his face. It was the self-satisfied smile of a man who knew he held every ace in the deck. I felt distinctly underdressed. All the vampires were as immaculate as Halfer. And why did I need a cadre of vamps to witness my descent?

"Danny, what's going on?" I asked, trying to get a good look at Halfer.

"Be quiet, Z. I told you I would handle it. All you have to do is be quiet." Daniel didn't turn to look at me, but his hand reached back and squeezed mine.

"We are here as you requested, Lucas," Marcus said shortly, ignoring mine and Daniel's domestic squabble. "Would you mind explaining why we are here?"

"Just to be clear, you're here representing the Council. You are not here as Daniel Donovan's patron," Halfer clarified.

Marcus nodded. "I represent the interests of the Council and am directed to speak for them."

I peeked around Daniel. Marcus approached Halfer and the two squared off like well-dressed boxers right before the bell rang.

"Excellent," Halfer said cheerily. "Then let me get down to business. Zoey Wharton, I see you there hiding behind your big, strong, dumb vampire. Do you have the Light of Alhorra for me?"

I tried to step forward, but Daniel held me back. "No. It's gone."

"Now that's too bad," he replied softly. "I seem to remember we had a contract."

Marcus stepped forward, his face flushing. "By the terms of our laws, you are not allowed to trick any of vampire kind into one of your contracts. It is an old law, and you do not want to break it. The Council will not stand for it."

"Marcus, I believe you will find it is not as simple as that." Daniel's voice was grave.

"The contract is with me, not Daniel." But they weren't listening. They were arguing with Halfer and doing it in multiple languages.

I breathed a long sigh of relief. If what Marcus said was true, then Daniel was safe. He wouldn't be dragged to Hell with me. It was enough. Daniel would live.

But I still had a whole bunch of questions. This was all about me, and I still had no idea why the Vampire Council was so concerned about it.

The way I understood it, demons and vampires at one point in the distant past had worked together. The demons, being demons, screwed everything up, and there was a war. It was costly on both sides because it was fought entirely on the Earth plane, where vampires had the advantage. To end the war and the bloodshed, they wrote several contracts that rule all interactions between the species.

The word "contract" was slung around enough that I realized I was in the middle of a legal battle.

"Silence!" Halfer commanded, and the room fell quiet. "What is the Council's objection to my contract with Miss Wharton?"

"You know what our objection is." Marcus stood closer to the demon than I would have been comfortable with. "You have no right to make a contract with Mrs. Donovan without a representative of the Council present."

Halfer smiled that shit-eating grin of his. "Oh, but Marcus, she wasn't Mrs. Donovan at the time."

Marcus was silent for a second and whirled on Daniel. "*Idiota!* You promised me you would perform the ceremony when I allowed you to return here. You were to perform the ceremony and make it legal, or you gave up all rights to her. She should have been brought before the Council and placed with another master if you chose not to bind her to you. I trusted you."

"I did perform the ceremony." Daniel's voice was low, and I strained to hear him. "Last night."

"Obviously, and from the way this room feels, you probably did it again tonight," Marcus said, shaking his head. "It was too late."

"What ceremony?" I was sick of being talked about like I wasn't here.

Marcus ran a hand through that pitch black hair of his, disturbing his perfect image. "The marriage of a companion to her master. He took your blood and you took his. You are married under our law and protected under our rules. Unfortunately, Daniel's stubbornness has cost you greatly. You were not married when your contract with the demon went into effect. You are on your own. There is nothing I can do for you."

My feet felt planted to the floor. A marriage? Daniel had said nothing to me. He'd taken my blood because he was dying. He'd given me his to make me strong. There had been no "I do's." No rings. He hadn't asked me. We weren't married. "I didn't marry Daniel. I didn't agree to anything."

"According to all vampire laws, you belong to Daniel. He is your master now. Your will is of no consequence," Marcus said, turning away from me and back to Daniel. "*Fottere.* Obviously you understand what the demon has done."

"I figured it out a couple of days ago." Daniel didn't turn around to look at me. He ignored me. But then it seemed my will was of no fucking consequence.

"But you didn't bother to clue me in. Just like you didn't give me a chance to decide if I wanted to be married." I stepped out from behind him. I didn't want to cower there. He'd kept so damn much from me. I needed to look him in the eyes.

"You forced me into that, Zoey," Daniel replied with every bit of the bile I'd thrown at him. "And this isn't the time to air our dirty laundry."

A clawed hand snaked around my shoulder and curled itself around my neck. It was cold, and though it held me gently, I could feel the potential in that hand. Halfer pulled me to him and let his other hand slip around my waist. Every inch of my skin crawled. If I struggled, he could easily pull me apart without any effort at all.

Two of the vampires stepped forward. A low growl pierced the air. Marcus snarled and the vamps stood down. Daniel's fangs were out, but he stood silently watching.

"It's time, companion." Halfer said it in my ear, but I knew everyone in the room could hear him with the possible exception of Sarah, with her sad human ears. "Would you like to know what I plan to do with you?"

"Nope." I tried to hold myself as still as possible. I didn't want to do anything that might arouse the demon. "Surprise me."

Halfer laughed. "I like your spirit. I think it will be extraordinarily fun to break it. Your master over there, he wants to know my plans. You glow for me, too. That light is going to be so nice on the Hell plane. Did you know your blood tastes as good to me as it does to him? The difference is, on the Hell plane, I can drain you dry and bring you back as often as I like. Of course, I won't use any magic to make it painless. I like to hear you scream."

"Halfer," Daniel commanded. "Stop playing with her."

"But she's mine to play with. Even your precious Council acknowledges that." Halfer laughed again, the sound crawling along my skin. "She's my pretty plaything. I can do anything I want to her. My penis is barbed, by the way. I'll have fun using it on her. She's mine, and she will stay mine unless you have something more interesting to offer me, Mr. Donovan."

And I finally caught up to the rest of them.

Lucas Halfer had never been interested in me. It was ridiculous to think that he had. I'd been naïve and fallen for every trap he'd set. I was nothing. I was a petty thief with no money and insignificant connections. I had nothing, except the most powerful vampire to rise in centuries happened to love me. Halfer set me up in order to pull Daniel in. He couldn't trick Daniel, but he could trick me.

"Daniel," I started to beg him to not do what I knew he was going to do.

The claw around my neck tightened ever so slightly, an elegant threat. "Hush, companion. This is between me and your master. You're nothing but a luscious pawn in our chess game."

"What do you want from me, Halfer?" Daniel stepped forward.

Marcus tried to stop him. "Do not do this, Daniel. Let her go, and we will find you another companion. They are rare, but I promise we will find you another. If you do this, I cannot save you. If you become his slave, his assassin, the Council will declare you an outlaw. We will be forced to hunt you and execute you."

Daniel smiled, but it was a hateful thing. "I'd like to see you try. Tell the Council to send their best, and I'll send them to Hell one by one. Or if you like, I can give them a group rate."

"Now see, that's why I want you, Donovan." Halfer sighed with appreciation. "You'll enjoy the work I have for you. If you're a very good boy, I'll let you have access to the girl. You'll like that."

"No, I've made arrangements for my companion," Daniel said, and I felt the tears start to run down my face as he discussed my dispensation. At least now I knew why he had to talk to Dev. "I sold her earlier tonight. It's my right as her master. As part of any agreement I make with you, she's to be taken to a man named Devinshea Quinn. The money has already been transferred by now. I won't do anything until I know he has taken possession of her. And Marcus, don't think you can swoop in and take her."

"She belongs to the Council. You can sell her, but it must be to another vampire. Companions belong to the Council." Marcus spoke in an academic tone. "She will be auctioned off, as she should have the moment she was found."

Daniel crossed him arms over his chest. "She'll be safe in a *sithein* before you can find her. I believe the faeries have forbidden vampire kind from the mounds."

"Do you understand what your husband is doing, Mrs. Donovan?" Marcus asked, finally glancing my way.

"Don't call me that." It was cruel. I'd wanted to be Daniel's wife, to have his name, and now it simply made me bitter.

"He is placing you in a faery mound from which he expects you to never return. He's paying another man to hide you," Marcus explained. "He's putting you in a cage because if he can't have you, then none of us can. What do you say to that?"

I shook my head. Now he wanted my opinion?

"My will is of no consequence." I repeated his earlier words because I finally understood what Dev had been trying to tell me. I was a commodity to be bought and sold. I didn't truly understand why. There was something about my blood, but I didn't care. I only cared that he'd lied to me. He'd sold me.

Somewhere in my rage, I also understood that this was what Daniel had been trying to protect me from. He'd stayed away from me. He'd begged me not to send us here. I played a hand in this as well, but in that moment, with a demon at my back and the love of my life treating me like property, I didn't feel like being fair.

Daniel was a gorgeous god, his face devoid of any emotion. "Let her go, Halfer. Let my servant take her to her new master, and we can discuss the terms of my service."

Halfer let me go, and I fell to my knees. Neil was suddenly at my side, helping me up. His eyes were filled with sympathy as he got me to my feet. All eyes were on me, some looking at me with pity, others with lust, and Daniel's with no emotion at all. I was nothing compared to those dark gods who could kill me without a thought. I was a tiny detail in their plots that could be brushed aside like a piece of lint.

"Zoey, I'm going to take you to Dev now," Neil said quietly. "He'll take care of you."

And that's when I got mad.

I pulled my arm away from Neil and walked straight up to

Daniel, who stood there so rigid and unmoving. He'd lied to me for years, hiding the truth of his existence even as I pined for him. I'd made mistake after mistake, but I was honest about them. My only real sin was being dumb, so damn dumb. But I was done playing the sad-sack piece of fluff. I was worth more.

I pulled back my hand and slapped him as hard as I could. "I have no intention of going into any *sithein*. I won't go quietly into a cage, Daniel. Consider that a divorce."

I turned to Marcus, whose dark eyes widened. "As for you, you piece of Eurotrash, I don't give a shit how old you are or what your rules are. I'm not your bitch. If you want to come for me, feel free to try, but you have to sleep, buddy, and I promise you I know how to use a stake." I included all the vampires in the room in my tirade. "That goes for every one of you. If you think you can master me, don't expect to see the sunset. I don't know what kind of women you've dealt with before, but you have no idea how to handle me. I'm not some detail you sweep under the..."

And just like that I knew how to save us all.

I stood in the middle of the room and went from screaming Harpy to hysterical laughter in the blink of an eye. Neil came up behind me, deep concern on his face. Even Daniel suddenly looked like he gave a shit.

"Daniel, she is unwell," Marcus said quietly, as though he didn't want to set me off again. "She does not need to be here. Your servant should take her now."

"Not on your very long life." I gave him my most brilliant smile. "I'm not going anywhere. I just found door number three."

Somewhere in the midst of my raging against fate, a simple voice came to me. I guess I'd been thinking about it for a while. It had been a thought in the back of my head, crowded out by terror and indecision. It was something Halle said to me when all of this began. I heard his voice as clearly as if he had been in the room.

Just remember that when dealing with the demon world, Halle had told me, *the devil is in the details.*

I was going to have to buy him a better bottle of wine the next time I saw him. A whole case!

It stood to reason that Halfer had to trick me. I wouldn't have gone into the trap willingly. But I wasn't an ordinary mark. I'd been around this world long enough to be naturally suspicious. If he'd pressed me with anything beyond a fairly simple plan and a gigantic wad of cash, I would have looked more closely before I agreed. The problem with Halfer's plans lay in the details.

I turned and faced the demon who had tried to trick me, and I gave him the same shit-eating grin he'd used on me.

"I invoke my right to a satan," I said triumphantly.

Chapter Twenty-Five

"How may I be of service?" the demon asked in a business-like voice.

He was small, almost cherubic, if it weren't for the cloven hooves and curved horns on his bald, red head. He was about as different from Lucas Halfer's masculine threat as you could get. He was, of course, still a demon spawn. It would be a mistake to underestimate him and give in to the almost overwhelming desire to pinch those cute cheeks.

In Hell, there is a small but important class of demons called satans. This should not be confused with the big guy. He goes by Lucifer, and you seriously don't want to summon him. I've heard he doesn't like to be bothered. A satan, however, can be summoned by anyone with a contract. Satans are the keepers and interpreters of contracts. If you have a contract with a demon and want clarification on anything from when the contract is fulfilled to how often your new demon master can perform a colonoscopy on you, you consult a satan. They are judge, jury, and executioner when it comes to contracts.

"Ah, Bri...," the demon started to use Halfer's name. "I apologize. You prefer Halfer on the Earth plane. Now, what exactly is the nature of the argument?"

Halfer's curved fangs made an appearance. "There is no argument. The girl is insignificant. My contract is now with the vampire."

The satan turned, frowning and making a disapproving clucking sound. "You are writing a contract on a vampire? Does the Council know? You're not allowed to contract with a vampire without counsel present."

"I have followed your rules, you paper pusher." Halfer snarled, a disdainful sound. "You'll find the contract will stand. Everything is on the table. The vampire is entering it willingly, and the Council will abjure him."

"Then why have I been called?" His cloven hoof tapped against the floor.

I stepped forward. "I called you because Daniel, the vampire, hasn't signed anything yet. Since he hasn't signed anything, my contract is still in play. I think I should have my argument settled before any other business is taken care of."

"Zoey, stop this." Daniel reached out for me, but I stepped away.

"Daniel, shut up," I told him with syrupy sweetness. "This is my contract, and your will is of no consequence."

Daniel started to pipe up, but his patron silenced him. "Let the girl try, Daniel. She is our only hope to keep you from killing yourself."

Marcus didn't sound like he had high hopes.

"The girl is correct," the satan said, his voice an unctuous whine. "All negotiations with the vampire must be suspended until her contract is sorted out and put to rights. Now, Miss Wharton, what is the nature of your argument?"

Halfer's long sigh filled the room. I ignored him.

"It's more of a clarification, really," I explained. "I would like to know exactly what I'm supposed to deliver to Mr. Halfer under the terms of our contract."

"You're prolonging the inevitable," Halfer complained under his breath.

"This was an oral contract," the satan said as his eyes rolled back and he seemed to be looking inward. "I don't like oral contracts. There are too many loopholes. It's a sloppy way to conduct business. Yes, there it is." His eyes rolled back into place. "You are contracted to deliver the Light of Alhorra to one Lucas Halfer."

"Big surprise." Halfer couldn't seem to stop interrupting.

Details. Details. "And, what, according to my contract, is the Light of Alhorra?"

I heard Daniel's surprised gasp as he figured out what I was doing.

"It is a medium-sized ornate box of faery origin," the satan recited.

"I was hoping you would say that." I walked straight back to the table where our kind faeries had left me a souvenir. I picked up the box and carried it back to Halfer.

"I believe you'll find I have fulfilled my end of the contract," I said politely to the satan. I turned to Halfer. "Got your box right here, buddy."

At first Halfer didn't even look mad. He seemed to not understand what was going on. It took a moment for him to realize what I'd done. The satan examined the box. He took it from me and turned it over in his hands. When he was satisfied, he handed it to Halfer, who took it without thinking.

"I pronounce this contract fulfilled, Miss Wharton."

"No," Halfer roared, finally coming to his senses. "This is not what we contracted for."

"Yes," the satan said, completely nonplussed by the demonic temper tantrum. "This is exactly what you contracted for. It was a sloppy contract, Halfer. I expected better of you. Perhaps you'll have a better contract with the vampire."

"That will be unnecessary," Marcus interjected, his smooth authority returning. "There will be no further negotiations today."

"Then my business here is finished." The satan gave us a polite bow. "Miss Wharton, my office will send you details on your funds in the morning. Will an offshore account be suitable?"

I had to think about that for a moment. It had been so long since I'd given the money a second thought. "Uh, yeah."

Neil was staring at the satan, dumbstruck. "We get the money, too?"

"Yes, of course," he replied. "It was in your contract."

"In your face, you demon asshole," Neil yelled at the pissed off demon.

I nudged him. "Don't make him any angrier."

"I thank you for your time and your wisdom," Marcus said formally to the satan. I realized this was not the first time he'd dealt with this class of demons. "I suggest you take Mr. Halfer with you. I believe you will find he has irritated the Council. Mr. Halfer, you should understand that Mrs. Donovan is now firmly under the protection of the Council. There will be no further dealings with her."

Halfer's horns flowed out of his human head as he assumed demon form once more. Gone was the business-like veneer, and what was left was pure evil.

"Come then, Halfer," the satan instructed.

"Not without my consolation prize," he sneered. "You won't find anything wrong with this contract."

He held out his hand, and Sarah flew across the room. She didn't even have time to scream before she was in the demon's grasp. I saw her start to bleed right before a crack and brimstone assailed the room and the demonic party left.

"He took Sarah," I said more to myself than anyone else. I stared at the place where she'd disappeared. That had almost been me. It was Sarah now and she was alone.

"There was nothing you could do," Daniel said, pulling me into his arms. He held me firmly, and I was so shocked by the look on my friend's face that I forgot how angry I was with him and let him comfort me. I felt numb, hollowed out.

There was movement all around me. The vampires talked among themselves, but I didn't listen to them.

"You were so amazing, Zoey," Daniel said as he stroked my hair. "If I live forever, and I might, I will never forget what you just did. I love you."

"Is that why you sold me?" I let a bit of my anger bleed through.

Daniel pulled away so he could look into my eyes. "Baby, I did that to protect you. If I had been declared an outlaw by the Council, you would have been considered fair game. Every vampire without a companion would have come running. They don't care whether you want them or not."

"Yeah, I get that." I tried to be reasonable. It wasn't easy. "Maybe if you had taken the time to explain any of this to me, I could have helped you. You haven't told me the truth about anything."

"I was trying to protect you," he insisted.

"Maybe I don't want to be protected." I finally got the strength to push away from him. I looked back at the vampires who were staring at me from a polite distance. Even though they weren't coming after me, I could feel their hunger. Every one of them. "They all want me."

"Yes, they do, and I have to protect you from them," Daniel said with the first hint of desperation in his voice.

"They want me the way you want me." It was what Dev had tried to tell me all along.

"No." Daniel pulled me toward him. "It isn't the same, Zoey. It's fundamentally different. I love you."

"I bet they would tell me they loved me, too." I looked at the strange, beautiful men who stared at me the way a cobra does before striking.

Marcus walked forward. "As interesting as this is, I am afraid we will have to move this discussion to Paris. Daniel, I am taking you into custody under the authority of the Council."

"Shit, Marcus, not now," Daniel swore. "Don't do this to me now, not in front of her."

Marcus shook his head. "I have indulged you far too much as it is. You have to answer for this incident, Daniel. You almost signed a demon contract without the approval of the Council. There must be a hearing, and I don't know what they will do. Please don't make this ugly."

"Do we have to go for the full Hannibal Lecter treatment?" Daniel asked.

"You know we have protocols in place when it comes to dealing with you," Marcus replied. "It is your own fault. You killed three vampires before we finally managed to get you to the Council chambers the first time. Now, please inform your animal and your companion to comply with procedure. They will fly on the jet, but they cannot share your quarters until we reach the catacombs. I will take care of her, Daniel."

Finally, I would get some answers. It was a long way to Paris, and I had a whole lot to learn from Marcus Vorenus.

Daniel stared at his mentor. "Neil can come, but Zoey stays here."

"What?" I practically yelled the question. He couldn't leave me behind after everything he'd put me through. "I am so going."

"No." Daniel's face once again turned into that stony, emotionless mask I was getting sick of seeing. "I forbid it."

My heart turned over in my chest. He couldn't do this to me again. He couldn't leave me here. "I'm going. I have a whole lot of things I want to say to that freaking Council."

Marcus looked seriously at Daniel. "Perhaps you are right. She should stay here." He flashed a look at the others, and they all pulled handguns. One of the vampires opened the coffin and pulled out what looked to be a mile of chains. There were gloves on his hands and he held the chains away from his body.

"Shit, I hate this," Daniel said under his breath.

"Don't you leave me like this." I watched as Daniel fell to his knees and placed his threaded fingers behind his head. "Let me go with you. Please don't do this to me again. I don't understand anything. You said we were married. That's for better or worse. Well, this is the 'worse' part."

"I love you, Zoey." He looked up at me, his eyes vacant. "They will not let you come."

As they started to wrap the chain around him, his flesh began to smoke where he wasn't covered by clothing. His mouth tightened, but that was the only indication that he felt the pain. I tried to pull it back off of him, but Marcus dragged me away and held me.

"That's silver, you bastard." I tried to kick him where it would hurt the most.

He held me too close for me to do any damage. "If it wasn't

silver, it wouldn't work. Your master has spoken, companion. Do not make this worse for him."

When his body was wrapped in silver, they picked him up and placed him not too gently in the coffin. I was allowed to see him before they placed the lid on.

"Don't do this to me, Daniel," I begged. Even after everything we'd gone through, I still wanted to go with him. "Let me come with you. Explain this to me. Don't shut me out. I still don't understand anything."

"I love you, Zoey," was all he said.

Marcus gave the order, and the lid was closed. Neil said something like good-bye, but I simply stood there. I watched him being carried away, knowing he didn't want me with him. No matter how much he claimed to love me, he would always shut me out. He would always keep his secrets.

I was left in that magnificent hotel room alone, mourning my friend and my lover.

Chapter Twenty-Six

A long, insistent knocking pulled me from my sleep. I shook myself awake, and it took me a moment to realize where I was. Light streamed into the room, and for a second, I thought it had all been a terrible dream. Then the knocking continued, and I was still alone.

I finally fell asleep on the couch sometime before dawn, but I wouldn't call it a restful sleep. Dark dreams plagued me all night.

I stumbled off the couch and toward the door. The clock read just before ten, and I wondered if the maid service was being especially polite or if the concierge had come to kick me out. I opened the door because an angry member of the hotel staff was the least of my concerns. It was worse. Marcus Vorenus stood in the doorway.

"Mrs. Donovan, I would like to talk to you."

"Don't call me that," I said, every bit the grouch. I left the door open and walked back to the couch. He didn't need an invitation. He hadn't needed to knock.

Marcus came in the room and held out a disposable cup of what smelled like coffee. "I brought it up from the dining room. I thought you could probably use it."

I stared at it suspiciously.

Those dark eyes softened and the barest hint of a smile curved his lips up. He looked like he was roughly thirty years old and had stepped off the cover of a male fashion magazine. "I am not your enemy, Mrs....shall I call you Zoey?"

"That's my name." I gave in and took a swallow of the coffee. If he wanted to kill me, he could have just ripped my throat out. And I wanted the coffee.

He stepped up to the big windows, looking out over the park, the sunlight on his face.

"Hey, shouldn't you be all crispy by now?" He was a vampire standing in direct sunlight. Not a sight I saw every day. He was dressed slightly more casually than he'd been last night, but everything was still designer. He was a hard-looking man, and I found myself wondering which era he'd been born into.

Marcus chuckled and turned back to me. I noticed things I hadn't the night before. Most vampires possessed almost alabaster skin, but Marcus had a nice tan. "I enjoy listening to you speak. It is refreshing. Too many people in my life are scared of me. To answer your question, I am a daywalker. It is the special gift of my class of vampires. All members of my class are born with the ability. There are other talents I have that took many centuries to acquire. You understand that after many years of living, a vampire often develops certain talents?"

"I know Daniel didn't need many years."

"Yes, well, our Daniel is a bit of a savant." Marcus sat down across from me. "He, however, cannot walk during the day. I have often wondered if he had a regular supply of rich blood, could he possibly do this as well? When he came back here, I thought no, but now I realize he has been lying about you."

He had my attention. I set the coffee down, ready for some explanations. If Daniel wouldn't give them to me, I would take them from Marcus. "So I have this rich blood, and that's why I'm attractive to vampires?"

"Attractive is a pathetic word to describe the way a vampire feels about a woman like you. I sincerely apologize for my charge. These are things that should have been explained to you. You should have been brought to Paris and presented with full honors to our society. You would have other companions to talk to. You would understand what you are."

"And what am I?" I asked casually, as though the question wasn't at the heart of my misery.

He sat down on the couch beside me, his voice becoming almost reverent. "You are strength and life to a vampire. A vampire with a companion is stronger, smarter, faster. There is no way to describe the feeling. Most vampires would do anything to possess one such as you. Our scientists have tried for hundreds of years to duplicate whatever is in your blood that calls to us, but it cannot be done. You should be glad it is the vampire's nature to follow our own laws or you would be passed around like a child's toy to whoever was the strongest to take you or the smartest to steal you."

"So my blood is different?" It didn't make a lot of sense. I wasn't a supernatural creature. I didn't have powers.

"Your blood is different. It's not the only thing. Has Daniel mentioned your glow?"

A whole bunch of people had said some things I didn't get. And Daniel left me ignorant. "What does it mean?"

He smiled, but this was a sexy thing. "You glow. It's how we find a companion. To a vampire's eye, your body practically pulses with life. Simply being close to you is soothing to me. I enjoy being in your light, *cara*."

Everything Dev said was true. I was a fucking drug, an addiction. "What am I?"

Marcus shrugged. "I have tried to discover this. I have theories, but I can prove nothing. It doesn't matter why you are a companion. Only that you are."

"Was it coincidence that Daniel and I were together before his turn?"

"Perhaps, but I think not." The vampire waved his hand negligently. "Daniel was a vampire even then, though he did not know it. You have always been a companion. Your blood called to his. It is sometimes this way. Occasionally when a vampire rises he was involved with a woman who turns out to be a companion. It is why you were left alone that night. He had a claim even though he had not taken the steps to make it legal. You're lucky the vampires who came for him that night did not simply kill him and take you for their own. By the time Daniel was brought before the Council, we knew what he was and that you were the only way to keep him under control."

"He doesn't love me. He's addicted to my blood." I finally said it out loud. He hadn't been attracted to me for my sparkling personality.

Marcus laughed. "I forget how foolish the truly young can be. What is this love you speak of? That is a child's game, Zoey. Daniel was offered the world by certain members of the Council. He was offered power and money and all the blood he could handle. He chose to come back here to this piss-poor part of the world and live a half life so he could be at your side. You have no idea what he could be. He could be king, but he refuses because that is not the life he wants for you. Take your childish idea of love. It is nothing compared to the devotion Daniel has shown you."

I turned from him and walked to the window. It was a gorgeous spring day. I looked down at the street so far below where people were going to work and kids were going to school. It was everyday and ordinary. Those people chose their paths, mundane though they may be. I'd never felt farther from that world. "Why are you here?"

"There are two reasons," he explained. "The first is a plea. I have been instructed not to force you to do anything you feel uncomfortable with, but you need to understand the situation. Daniel needs blood. He needs your blood."

Because he was addicted again. "What happens when he doesn't get it?"

Marcus frowned and, for a moment, I thought he might refuse to answer. "He will go through withdrawal. He will be in pain, weak and soul sick. It is terrible. He is going into a dangerous place, and I would feel better if he was as strong as possible. I would also feel better if I controlled his supply of blood. I would not like for it to be...tainted."

"Then he should have taken me with him." Even as I said it, I knew I would relent. I couldn't stand the thought of him having to rely on the people who discussed his execution. I couldn't leave him sick and vulnerable. "How do I get it to him?"

Marcus relaxed as though he'd expected a fight. "A nurse will come once a week for your donation. I thank you for being reasonable. There is something else. I felt the need to talk to you. I am here to press young Daniel's claim. I saw you last night, and I believe you are going to make a mistake. I am here to ask you to not give up on him."

"Why? You said last night that you could find him another companion. Just find him someone else, and let me alone."

"I was wrong," Marcus admitted. "I hate to admit it because I do not like to express anything so unsavory as having feelings, but I was frightened last night. You have no idea how close we came to disaster. If Halfer had taken possession of Daniel... Let me tell you a story about your Daniel. Perhaps that is the best way to make you understand. The Council is responsible for the training of new vampires. This training can be...you would consider it barbaric. It is meant to teach the vampire to follow the rules. One such exercise is called The Arena. A young vampire is placed in our training arena and told to fight for his life. He is not told that the enemies he faces will not actually kill him. The way the exercise is intended to go is the young vampire is beaten to within an inch of his life and then spared by the Council. He then feels some loyalty to the members who spared his life. The young vampire must face three experienced warriors. He has no chance against them. He is a lamb led to slaughter and then spared. Daniel killed twelve before the Council decided to save our numbers. Daniel is a Death Machine. He was born to kill. There is only one thing that ties him to humanity, and that is you."

"He likes Neil," I said absently as my mind tried to process what Marcus had told me.

"He has some affection for his wolf, but it is you who defines his morality. I watched you last night, and I think you are going to turn from him. I understand that Daniel has screwed this up, and you might feel the need to explore other options. I only ask that when he returns, you do not shut him out completely."

"Is he going to return?" This was the question that kept me up all night. He was going into that place wrapped in chains. If what I understood was true, then there were many vampires who might take advantage of his situation.

Marcus sat back and clasped his hands together. It reminded me of a scene from *The Godfather*. "I think there are members of the Council who will view this indiscretion as an opportunity to take out a threat, but they will find it difficult. Daniel can tell when a new vampire is going to rise."

"Yes, I know. It's important and rare. I heard there were only three or four vampires who can do it."

"Sadly those numbers have dwindled." Marcus sighed. "Only yesterday two of them were killed in terrible accidents. I believe the Council will find themselves in a corner. Daniel is too precious to execute."

"You killed them," I said under my breath.

Marcus had the audacity to look offended. "I have no idea what you are talking about, girl. I would never do such a thing. It would be a crime if anyone could prove it. But know this, I believe Daniel is important, and I believe he has two paths ahead of him. I wish to see him go down the path that saves Vampire, not the path that leads to war." Marcus looked at his watch and stood up. "My time here is done, *bellissimo compagno*. My jet leaves for Paris in an hour." Marcus walked over and took my hand. He brought it to his lips. I thought it was a courtly gesture, but at the last moment, he flipped my hand over and placed a lingering kiss on my wrist right where my pulse could be measured.

"If I did not believe in Daniel, know that I would have pressed my suit for you," he murmured. "I think you are the most intriguing thing I have seen in many years. I would be interested in you even if you were not a companion, Zoey."

He let my hand fall, and I watched him walk to the door. Just before leaving he turned around. "You will think on what I have said? Do not forsake him completely. It could be bad for your people."

"For my family?" I was confused. Daniel would never hurt me or my father.

Even in the light of day, Marcus's eyes were infinitely dark. "No, I wasn't speaking of your family. I was speaking of humanity." The door closed quietly, and I was alone again.

* * * *

It took me three weeks to make the mistake Marcus had been sure I was going to make. After Marcus left me, I went home to my apartment where a letter was waiting for me. It was a simple set of numbers and the name of a bank in the Cayman Islands. The money meant nothing. I'd tossed the letter on my desk and packed a suitcase with a change of clothes and other necessaries. After stopping by a liquor store and picking up a case of good wine, I went from bridge to bridge until I found Halle. I spent the days walking with him and the nights allowing Ingrid to brush my hair while I cried. The only time I went back to the real world was to make my weekly donation.

I woke up three weeks later and realized I had to know. I had to know if I could make my own choices. If a vampire was programmed to love a companion, it only made sense to me that it worked the other way, too. Had my love for Daniel been written into my blood? Did that make it love or something less? I missed him with every part of my soul, and I also was so angry with him. I felt the need to burn everything down around me.

So I bought new lingerie and a brand new red dress. I slipped on stiletto heels, and I made my way to Ether.

I hadn't spoken to Dev since he stormed off that night. I wasn't even sure he would let me in to talk to him. We hadn't left things in the best of places. I could still see his disappointed face as he walked off. I approached the entrance with a knot in the pit of my stomach, fully expecting to be told to get out of there.

"Good evening," Albert said in a grave, somewhat judgmental tone.

I smiled, happy to see a face I knew, but the half demon gave me nothing.

"How may I be of assistance tonight, Mrs. Donovan?" Albert asked politely.

279

I felt myself flush. "I'm not Mrs. Donovan."

"Whether you like it or not, Mrs. Donovan, you are wed by the laws that bind our world," Albert said, and finally some sympathy crept into his tone. "If you walk into that club and find my master, things will take a natural course, and he will suffer. He will be committing a crime against your master. It is serious and not to be taken lightly…"

Albert stopped, and his hand pressed against the communication device cradled in his ear. "Of course, sir. I'll send her right up." He returned his attention to me, and I knew he was obeying, not following his own wishes. "Please be welcome, Miss Wharton. My master will see you in his office."

I walked away from the half demon feeling low. I liked him, but now it would be hard to look at him knowing he thought I was leading his boss into sin. I didn't see it that way. I didn't see myself as married. I'd made no vows, and Daniel had proven he didn't trust me in his world. I was alone. Daniel left me. I had the right to walk up those stairs. I had the right to ask for what I wanted.

I was shown up to Dev's office, anxiety pulsing through me as the door opened. He was seated behind his desk and made no move to stand up as I entered. He looked up at me, but that gorgeous face of his showed no signs that he was happy to see me. His green eyes slid across my body, but I couldn't read them. I suddenly felt cheap in my seventy-dollar dress.

"Hello," I managed to say.

"Zoey." Dev looked every inch the businessman behind his desk. I hadn't thought of him that way before, but now I realized he had to be smart and quick to have built his businesses. "I was glad to hear you found a way out of your contract."

"Oh," I whispered, somewhat flustered. There went my first attempt at conversation. "Who told you?" Everyone I knew was either in France or Hell.

"A couple of Eurovamps came into the club late that night. You're quite the Daniel Webster, aren't you? I was surprised you didn't go to Paris with your husband."

"He's not…" I started, but decided to not argue any longer. The writing was on the wall with this one, and I needed to get out with my dignity intact. I wished I'd thought to put on a sweater or a light trench coat. It would have been hot, but at least I wouldn't look so ridiculous. I opened my purse and went with my backup plan. "Well, I just wanted to let you know I have your portion of the money. You did a good job. You deserve to get paid."

I laid the envelope on his desk.

He looked at it with disdain, sliding it back to me. "I don't want your money, Zoey."

I picked it back up and tucked the envelope in my purse. I took a deep breath, trying to stay calm. Daniel was gone, and Dev didn't want me anymore. I had what I deserved. I was alone.

"What was the second thing?" It couldn't hurt to ask. He would answer or he wouldn't. He raised one eyebrow. "Daniel was going to have you take me to the faery mounds. But you said you would do the first but not the second. What was the second thing?"

If anything his face became even blanker. "If I couldn't make it to the *sithein*, I was to give you to someone named Marcus Vorenus. I believe he's a vampire. Daniel was playing fast and loose with vampire laws. He was hoping that because he was still alive, his ownership of you could transfer at his will. I looked into it since then. Only a vampire can own a companion."

I tried not to show my surprise. I suspected Daniel thought Marcus would be better than some random vampire, but I had my doubts. Dev watched me but made no move to speak further.

I hated this feeling. I had no idea how to ask for what I wanted. I could face down a demon and fight off a giant snake, but I felt so vulnerable in that moment that my only option was retreat.

I smiled too brightly. "Well, all right, then. It was good to see you."

I wouldn't see him again.

Before I got to the door, he was pulling my hand, turning me to face him. His jaw was set, and his words came out in a harsh grind. "You didn't come here tonight to pay me off, Zoey. Why are you here?"

"I don't know," I lied.

"Yes, you do. You didn't put on those fuck-me heels to pay me off." Suddenly my back was against the door, and he was taking up all the available space. "Ask me, Zoey."

I didn't bother to pretend to misunderstand. I simply couldn't force the words from my mouth.

Dev came in close, so close I could smell the mint on his breath, and I suddenly knew that his casualness was an act. He'd prepared himself for me. He'd seen me on some monitor and talked to Albert and then rushed to make sure he was ready.

"I need to know." His mouth was so close to mine that all I had to do was lean forward. His green eyes stared down, catching me and pinning me there. "Do you still love him?"

"I don't know if it's love anymore," I admitted.

"So you want to experiment on me." He kissed my forehead. My every nerve ending went on red alert as he leaned in, pressing his body to mine. He was so beautiful and so close, I could almost taste him.

"I want to know if I can love someone else."

"Then ask me, Zoey." He breathed the words against my skin.

For a moment, I thought it was a trap. He was going to say no and walk away, and I would be left standing there looking like the idiot I was. It made some perverse sense. I'd done the same thing to him, though I hadn't been trying to hurt him. For a moment, I considered walking away before he could reject me. But I hadn't come this far to not take a chance.

"Dev, will you please make love to me?" I asked as simply and honestly as I could.

He smiled that bright, open smile that made my heart ache. He smiled, and then his hands cupped my rear and pulled me into his body where I felt his answer immediately.

"Zoey, you know this is a bad idea, right?" But he leaned forward and kissed me anyway, his lips soft against mine.

For the first time in weeks, some part of me felt alive. I let my hands drift to his waist, exploring the muscles there. I cuddled closer to him. "I have those from time to time."

But I needed this. It was a horrible idea, but I couldn't help myself. I wasn't trying to punish Daniel. I was trying to find myself.

"He's going to come back, Zoey." I loved the way he said my name, like a long slow cajoling. He could draw out those two syllables in a way that made my heart rate triple. "He has a claim on you that I can never have."

Yes. That was the problem. "I can't live like that."

He started to lift the bottom of my dress toward my waist, his fingers sliding against my skin, making me shiver. He kissed me again, his tongue sliding deep this time. My leg drifted up, tangling around his body. All of my problems seemed to drift away. I wasn't thinking about Daniel or the Council or the fact that I glowed. Dev couldn't see my glow. He didn't give a shit about my blood. He just wanted me.

He untied the back of my dress and let it slip to the floor. A sigh escaped his chest as he looked down at the tops of my breasts. Long fingers traced the curves of both mounds. "This won't be a one-night stand for me, Zoey. I want to be with you. If you're using me for a single night of sex, you should know it won't work. I intend to make you want to stay with me, to crave me, to never leave me."

"Dev, I want to try." I pulled at his shirt, wanting to feel his skin. "I don't want a one-night stand. I want to see if this can work."

His hands wrapped around and twisted the clasp of my bra in a single, easy movement. He slid it off and tossed it away. His hands slid up to my breasts, cupping them, flicking at my nipples. "That's a good thing, baby, because once I get inside, I don't think I'll want to leave."

He leaned over and kissed me softly before he picked me up. He walked to his desk and with one hand shoved everything off and down to the floor. He laid me out on the desktop, and before I knew what was happening, he had my panties off, sliding them down my legs.

I relaxed, every muscle softening for the first time in weeks. This was a good place to be. I wasn't worried. I was happy. And Dev proved what an amazingly dirty boy he was. He shoved my knees apart and sank to the floor.

"It's a crime, you know." He smiled, a ridiculously decadent grin on his face.

I held my head up. I was naked on his desk, and it felt right. I should have been self-conscious but I simply felt lovely. Dev and I didn't have a past. There was nothing between us but pure desire, and he could have anyone he wanted.

But he was here with me. It made my ego surge and someplace deep inside went calm and happy. Something in Dev called to me, but it was a simple thing. "Crime? What do you mean?"

He grinned just before he leaned down and ran that ridiculously talented tongue over my pussy. "You're married to a vampire. It's a serious thing in our world."

My eyes practically rolled back in my head. He sucked on my clit. Dear god, I could barely think. Every goddamn cell in my body was standing at attention. "I still don't understand the crime part."

Dev sucked my clit into his mouth. I nearly screamed. Every cell in my body lit up at the pleasure coursing through my system. His tongue dragged against me and there was a deep moan as though he thought I tasted like heaven.

His eyes were heavy as he looked up my body. "I assure you the Council will see it as a crime. And I don't care. I'll risk it to be with you. I'm crazy about you, Zoey. I've worked for years building these businesses but now all I want is to be inside you, baby."

He licked me again, causing me to shake and shiver. "What does it mean? The law thing?"

He rubbed his nose in my pussy. "It means Daniel has the right to kill me."

I nearly came off the desk. "What?"

He pushed me back down, flattening my body to the desk. His weight anchored me. "Stop. You're mine until the minute you tell me you're not. I'll handle the fallout. Baby, I want you so bad. I'll risk anything. I don't care what their rules are. We can make our own."

It was a mistake. I knew it. And I couldn't stop the words from coming out of my mouth.

"Yes, Dev." It was exactly what I needed to hear. That he would risk for me. That he would let me risk for him. Tears of pure joy pricked my eyes. No past weighed us down. But a possible future had opened up in front of me.

"I like the sound of that. You keep that up. Yes, Dev." He unbuckled his belt and slipped his pants off, kicking them to the side before reaching out to his desk drawer. He held a condom in his hand. "Touch me."

His cock stood out. It was huge. I looked at it, studied it, really. I totally believed that his grandfather had been a Green Man because that cock was superlative. It was thick and long and stood up against his belly, almost reaching his navel. I reached out and wrapped my hand around him, loving the way his eyes closed in pleasure the moment we came in contact. I pumped his cock in my hand, memorizing the feel of it. Soft skin covered a rigid hardness that made my heart pound.

He shook his head. "Stop, baby. I don't want to come in your hand."

I pulled my hand away, but not before brushing against him one last time.

He slipped the condom over his dick.

He was willing to fight. He was willing to go against the rules to get inside me, so I wrapped my legs around him and let him in. He thrust, forcing himself in inch by inch. He reached down and played with my breasts, pinching my nipples as he forced himself inside.

I let him, reveling in the close contact. I had only wanted— really wanted—two men in my whole life, and the second one pushed his cock inside and touched my womb. He let himself go, thrusting in and out and lighting up my flesh. My legs wound around his waist and held on for dear life. He was in control. He played my body like a fine instrument. In and out. In and out. Over and over again.

His hand came in between us and found my clit, rubbing insistently as he thrust his cock up, finding that special place that sent me soaring.

I called out his name when I came. *Dev. Dev. Dev.*

His gorgeous face contorted, and he held himself against me as his orgasm overtook him.

He fell down, covering my body with his. He was smiling as he kissed me, his cock still deep inside. I could already feel him getting hard again. "I'm crazy about you, Zoey."

I kissed him back, my whole soul satisfied. "Back at you."

"And don't think I'm done with you," he said. "I'm going to

take my time now."

I held on to him as he kissed me again, this time a long slow grind against my mouth. I relaxed and gave over to his unique magic.

It wasn't perfect, but it was safe and happy.

He picked me up and carried me to the bedroom, and I was ready to start a whole new life.

Chapter Twenty-Seven

"Hello, Z," Daniel said from my front porch. My heart fluttered at the sound of his voice.

He'd been gone almost four months when he showed up on my doorstep. I was told that whatever was happening with Daniel's trial would be over quickly. Unfortunately, quickly means different things when you're immortal. Four months passed and no news. The only way I knew Daniel was still alive was the fact that the Council-approved nurse came out once a week to collect my little bag of blood. She chatted throughout the process and tried to make it as quick as possible. She was my only link to the vampire world, and she was much more interested in talking about reality television than vampire politics.

I'd done a lot in the four months since Daniel had been carried away from me in chains and a coffin. I started a relationship with Dev, and I moved. I took my part of the money and bought a tiny house outside the city. It was quiet, and I was left alone for the most part. It sat on an acre of land and it was, to put it mildly, a fixer upper. That was what happened when you quartered a million dollars. I split the money into four parts because Dev wouldn't take his. Danny had his part, and Neil and Sarah had theirs. I held out hope that Sarah would need it one day. Thieves had a code, and I followed it.

I swallowed twice before I could answer. He looked so different. His hair was long and slightly unkempt. He was wearing jeans and a T-shirt with Captain America on the front. The expensive boots he'd worn were gone. He wore a new pair of Converse instead. He looked like my Daniel coming home from calculus class.

"Hello," I managed.

He smiled, slightly sad as he looked around the porch with its peeling paint. "It's a nice place."

"It's a dump," I admitted. "But I paid cash."

He ran his hands along the railing. "It has good bones. A little paint, a lot of sweat, and it'll be beautiful."

We stood there staring at each other, not quite knowing what to say. He'd lied to me and left me behind, not caring if I ever learned the truth. Dev was different. He didn't know everything, but he tried to find people who could answer my questions. He spent months traveling the country with me, asking questions, holding my hand.

"Zoey, I'm sorry. I did what I thought I had to," he said.

"I'm seeing someone," I blurted out at the same time.

He stopped for a moment and ran a hand through his thick hair. "Is it Dev?"

"Well, you did sell me to him," I pointed out. But I would have found my way back anyway. I had an odd connection to the faery. I was comfortable with him. I could breathe with Dev.

"I won't make that mistake again." Daniel looked down at his shoes. "I guess that means I can keep the two million, then."

"Two million?" I choked out. Dev hadn't mentioned that little number.

"He didn't tell you?"

"No, I guess it slipped his mind," I sputtered. "You are so giving that back to him."

"All right." Daniel smiled sadly. "Is he making you happy, Z?"

I nodded because Dev was trying. I don't know if I would call it happy, but I was certainly satisfied. What I had with Dev was simple. We enjoyed each other. We had fun. We had a lot of amazing sex. Content. I was peaceful with Dev. I didn't mention that last part to Daniel. Dev was what I needed right now. Being with Dev didn't consume my whole life.

Daniel nodded as though he'd come to a decision. "Then that's good. I want you to be happy. I know it doesn't matter now, but everything I did I did because I love you. I might have been wrong, but I thought I was doing the right thing."

We were quiet for a moment, all of our history hanging there between us, filling the night air with an oppressive sadness.

"Do you want me to go?" Daniel asked.

"Where would you go, Danny?" I needed to know.

"Probably back to Europe. There are a few loose ends I could take care of before I get down to business."

That was said in his badass-vampire voice, and it didn't make me feel secure. "What business is that?"

I thought for a moment he was going to ignore the question. He took his time, but he slowly turned toward the full moon and answered me. "I'm going to kill Halfer. I haven't figured out how to do it yet, but I will. I'm going to make him pay." He turned back to me and grinned. "Or I could stay here and hang out with you."

I remembered Marcus's words, and they suddenly made sense. Daniel would never allow what Halfer had done to pass. If there was a second war between vampires and demons, it would be fought on the Earth plane and humans would be collateral damage. I could stop that simply by allowing him to stay. Still, if he was going to hang around, we needed to set some ground rules.

"And how is that going to work, Danny? Are you and Dev going to share?" I knew the answer to that question.

Daniel's eyes heated at the thought, but I watched as he let it go. His voice was even as he pointed out the obvious. "You know, we were friends at one time, Z. You're the best friend I've ever had."

And he was mine, but I didn't say it. I didn't have to. "You think 'friends' is going to work?"

"I think I want to try," Daniel said. "I love you, Zoey. I don't have to sleep with you to love you. I only know I need to be around you."

"And you won't eviscerate my boyfriend?" That was one rule

we were definitely making clear.

"No matter how much I want to," he said as though the thought was extremely pleasant. "You'll be happy to know the Council is forcing me to see a psychiatrist. I apparently have anger issues. It's a part of my parole."

"Parole?"

"Yeah, almost signing away my life to a demon is some sort of crime," he said. "Who knew?"

"You sound so different." I shook my head and studied him. The change was astounding. He was more relaxed than I'd seen him in years. He was laughing and joking.

"It's your blood, Zoey," he admitted quietly. "I can think more clearly. I was trained to think a certain way and act a certain way. I was taught, rather forcefully, to believe certain things. When I started taking your blood on a regular basis, I stopped believing. I fully realize that I drank the vampire Kool-Aid. It's hard to explain, but I think your blood brings out the human side of me."

I pointed to the T-shirt. "I think it brings out the nerd side of you."

Daniel shrugged and smiled. It was a gesture I remembered from long ago, and it brought back so many memories. "Speaking of the nerd in me, I've been in a cell in underground Paris for four months. Can we watch some TV?"

I laughed, knowing that letting him in was probably a mistake. I also knew I would never be able to shut him out. I opened the door for him.

"Come on, Neil," he shouted at the darkness. "We're in."

"Thank god." Neil huffed as he carried a huge trunk up the steps. "I thought the two of you were going to leave me out there all night while you worked out your issues. Please tell me you TiVoed my shows. Oh, I got evicted while I was in Paris, but I bought you the sweetest Louis Vuitton bag. Which room is mine? Can we order pizza?"

"Take the last room on the left." I knew better than to argue. It would be nice to have a roommate. Besides, Neil was a pretty awesome cook.

"So." Daniel gave me a knowing grin. He looked so right

standing there in my rundown house. "When do we go?"

"Go where?"

"To get Sarah, of course."

My mouth hung open in surprise for a moment. I'd spent the last two of our months apart planning to do just that. I'd been putting out some feelers to people who could make things like this happen. It was tricky, but I managed to keep it from Dev. It wouldn't be easy to get into Hell and steal a person out from under a demon's nose, but hey, I like a challenge. And there was no way I was leaving her there.

"I'm in," Daniel said. "So's Neil. We talked about it on the plane trip back. Do you have a plan, yet?"

"Yes." It was an awful plan and would probably end badly. "We go to Hell, get Sarah, and kill everything that tries to stop us."

When he grinned this time, I got the sexiest hint of fangs. My breath caught, and I knew there was no way this "friends" thing was going to work for long.

"I like it," he said as he threw that gorgeous body onto my couch. "I always said I'd go to Hell and back for you, baby."

Daniel started fiddling with the remote, and Neil walked into the room chattering about the clothes he'd had some hot vamp buy him. Any minute now, Neil would realize Daniel was turning on some bad sci-fi movie, and they would fight over the TV. I was going to have to play referee.

The phone rang. I looked down and saw it was Dev. I was surrounded by the people I cared about. They would bring complete chaos to my life and I couldn't wait.

I stood in the middle of my formerly empty house and realized I was finally home.

* * * *

Zoey, Daniel, and Dev will return with *Steal the Day*, now available.

Sign up for Lexi Blake's newsletter
and be entered to win a $25 gift certificate
to the bookseller of your choice.

Join us for news, fun, and exclusive content
including the free short stories

You Will Call Me Master (Daniel's Story)
and
She Will Be My Goddess (Dev's Story)

There's a new contest every month!

Go to www.LexiBlake.net to subscribe.

Author's Note

I'm often asked by generous readers how they can help get the word out about a book they enjoyed. There are so many ways to help an author you like. Leave a review. If your e-reader allows you to lend a book to a friend, please share it. Go to Goodreads and connect with others. Recommend the books you love because stories are meant to be shared. Thank you so much for reading this book and for supporting all the authors you love!

Steal the Day
Thieves, Book 2
By Lexi Blake
Now Available

The world's most unusual thief faces her greatest challenge—stealing a soul from the depths of Hell...

When a member of her crew is dragged to Hell by a demon, Zoey plans the most dangerous heist of her career. With her team at her side, Zoey intends to sneak onto the Hell plane and steal Sarah back.

The job seems impossible until a new client makes them an offer too good to refuse. If she can find an ancient artifact called The Revelation, she can use it to locate an angel who holds Sarah's redemption in his hands.

Surrounded by warring angels and demons, the greatest threat may come from one of her own. Torn between her Fae lover and the vampire who has always held her heart, Zoey finds that she and Dev are trapped in Daniel's web of secrets, and it may be Zoey who has to pay the ultimate price.

* * * *

Chapter One

I stretched as I rolled out of bed, trying not to wake the man next to me. I caught sight of Devinshea Quinn and couldn't help but stare. His tan skin made a stark contrast to the white sheets. His dark hair was mussed from our activities, and though his face was relaxed, there was no way to soften that perfectly shaped jawline. The sheet was around his waist leaving most of his lean, muscular body on display. Everything about Dev Quinn was perfect, from his washboard abs to his cut chest, to those ridiculously sensual lips. I felt a smile cross my face as I sat there and just watched him sleep.

He shifted, rolling over in bed, and I decided it was time to go. As much as I liked to look at him, I really didn't want the argument that was sure to come when he realized where I was going.

I stood up and was finally able to get out of the Christian Louboutin's Dev had gifted me with earlier in the evening. I flexed my feet. The shoes were ridiculously gorgeous. My eyes had widened when I opened the box, and my heart had fluttered. It hadn't taken Dev long before he had me in the shoes and nothing else. Those shoes were exciting and sexy, and just the slightest bit uncomfortable. They were a bit like my relationship with Dev. The sex was incredible, and while I was in bed with Dev, I didn't think about anything but him. The minute I rolled out of bed, I wanted to get out of those shoes and put on a pair of Converse. That was our problem.

Well, that and my husband.

I walked through the grotto, collecting stray clothes along the way. Dev's apartment was at the top of a building he owned in the middle of downtown Dallas. The bottom of the building housed his club, Ether, the hottest club of its kind. But it wasn't the kind of club that showed up on the "Best of Dallas" lists since I'm one of the only humans to be permitted entrance.

Ether was the place where the supernaturals of the world went to mix and mingle and do a little business. It was an official place of peace, despite my last year's best effort to burn it down. I hadn't meant to, but then I never do. Trouble just follows me. That had been my first date with Dev. At the time, I wasn't married. It didn't take me long to remedy that.

I slowed, unable to rush through. Dev's "condo" took up the whole top floor of the building and was the most decadent space I'd ever seen. The first time Dev had taken me up the private elevator from his office in Ether to his penthouse, the doors had opened and I'd gasped. I called the whole place "the grotto." It was something like an indoor forest, complete with a brook that ran through the various rooms of the apartment. When the sun was out, the whole place was lit with soft, natural light. In the dead of night, moonbeams streamed through the overhead windows, shining down and making the room seem magical.

It's odd for a faery to live year round in the city. They don't like the feeling of being enclosed. It goes against their nature, but Dev was mortal. He was the only one of his mother's children who had not taken after her, and because of his mortality, he'd chosen to leave the *sithein* and cut off ties to his family. Since the day we'd met, I could remember two conversations we'd had about his family.

This place made me think he missed them.

I walked into the bathroom and turned on the shower. The bathroom was bigger than my entire living room. The splendor of Dev's home put in stark contrast our relative differences. Dev had money and a lot of it. I had recently finished a job that gave me enough money to buy a little fixer-upper in the country, but I was starting to hurt for cash. My account was down to the low four digits, and I didn't have more money coming in.

I would have given up all the money I had made on my last job if I could have changed the outcome of it. Some jobs aren't worth the payday.

I tossed my clothes on the sink and stepped under the rainfall of deliciously hot water. The water stroked over my skin, and I stretched again. Sex with Dev was inventive and exciting, and required a certain level of flexibility. I could see yoga classes in my future.

Suddenly two big hands came from behind and cupped my breasts. I sighed for two reasons—one because it felt so good, and two because there would be no getting out of a fight. I let my head fall back against his chest, his body nestling against mine. If we were going to fight, I might as well enjoy the first part.

"Zoey," Dev breathed in my ear, his voice the sweetest of seductions. "I sincerely apologize. I have treated you poorly."

I smiled because I knew what was coming next. "I disagree, Dev. I was treated incredibly well. At least three times."

One hand stayed at my breast, plucking at my nipple, pinching and lighting it up. Another clever hand made its way lower. His fingers slid over my clit, and that was all it took. I was warm and wet again. "If I had done my job properly, you would have passed out. The fact that you can move means I have more work to do. I didn't even get to the part where I tie you up and we play."

Dev liked to play. He liked to play with handcuffs and toys. He had a whole closet full of naughty little devices, like an FAO Schwarz for kink. With a low growl, he shifted, turning me toward him. His mouth took mine in a deep, luxurious kiss. This was what Dev and I did best.

He lifted me up, settling me on the ledge of the shower. I was sure the contractors who had built the place thought the wide shelf was to store shampoo and soap, but I knew better. Dev had designed it with sex in mind. He moved between my legs, the ledge placing my pussy at the perfect height for him.

"I can't get enough of you. I fucking crave you." He'd come prepared. He slipped a condom on and worked his way in. It wasn't long before my back was up against the natural rock of the shower and I was screaming out number four.

"Let's dry off and go back to bed," he whispered as he held me up because my legs weren't quite working yet. It wasn't easy keeping up with a man whose grandfather had been a fertility god. "I'll tell Albert to send up breakfast for two in the morning."

I hugged him close to me, hoping that my affection would make the next few minutes easier. "I can't. I have to go. I have a meeting with a client."

Dev stopped, his whole face lighting up. I suspected one of the reasons he liked me was my unusual job. I was a thief who specialized in procuring objects of an arcane nature. Stealing from supernaturals made my job one of the riskier fields. It was thrilling when the job ran well, and completely terrifying when anything went wrong. Dev had run one job with me and had been bugging me ever since to let him go again. He'd gotten off on the adrenaline rush.

He winked down at me. "That's great, sweetheart. I'll get dressed and go with you. I promise to keep my mouth shut and be good eye candy. Should I take the Ruger or the Glock?"

I pulled away from him because no amount of affection was going to fix this. "Sorry, but I have to go alone."

His deep green eyes formed suspicious slits. "Alone? You never go alone. That's your first rule." He took a step back, his mouth turning down. "So if you're not going alone, you're going with Daniel."

And there it was, the one word that could wreck our day. "He is my partner."

"He's your husband." Dev spat the word out as though it was poison. He stalked out of the shower, leaving me with an incredible view of his preternaturally glorious ass.

I picked up a bottle of something Dev liked the smell of and then put it back down in favor of plain old soap. I told myself it was because I needed to be professional. I didn't want to go into a client meeting smelling like a woman who had just had sex four times. If I was honest with myself, and I tried not to be, I didn't want to hurt Daniel.

I finished up in the shower and turned it off, wrapping a warm towel around my body. Dev was sitting on the sink when I went to retrieve my clothes. He'd slipped into silk boxers and looked at me with a sad smile.

"Sorry," he said. "I know I'm being an ass. I'm just jealous."

"You have nothing to be jealous of." It sounded like a reassuring lie even to my ears. "If I could get a divorce, I would."

I'd come to accept the marriage I had been tricked into. It wasn't like I had much of a choice. Tricked is a harsh word. Daniel had been trying to protect me at the time. It was his excuse for everything. I didn't resent the protection. I resented the fact that he'd left me ignorant. I had to find out from a demon that we were married. There'd been no vows of love and devotion, no white dress or fabulous reception. There had been blood and sex and a transfer of ownership between Daniel and myself.

And there was no divorce when you were married to a vampire.

About Lexi Blake

Lexi Blake lives in North Texas with her husband, three kids, and the laziest rescue dog in the world. She began writing at a young age, concentrating on plays and journalism. It wasn't until she started writing romance that she found success. She likes to find humor in the strangest places. Lexi believes in happy endings no matter how odd the couple, threesome or foursome may seem. She also writes contemporary western ménage as Sophie Oak.

Connect with Lexi online:

Facebook: Lexi Blake
Twitter: authorlexiblake
Website: www.LexiBlake.net

Made in the USA
Columbia, SC
20 April 2019